THE TROUBLE with ROOMMATES

a novel

Also by Marie K. Savage

The Oracles of Delphi

&

THE SEEDS TRILOGY

The Sowing
(K. Makansi co-author)

The Reaping
(K. Makansi co-author)

The Harvest
(K. Makansi co-author)

THE TROUBLE *with* ROOMMATES

a novel

MARIE K. SAVAGE

Layla Dog Press | Tucson, Arizona

CONTENT NOTICE

In this contemporary romance, characters express strong, politically charged opinions regarding responses to the Covid-19 pandemic and how the world was changing around them. It also includes subject matter related to online bullying, doxing, sexual assault, and suicide.

Layla Dog Press
Tucson, AZ 85719

For information, contact:
Layla Dog Press
an imprint of Blank Slate Communications
www.kristinamakansi.com

Manufactured in the United States of America
Cover design by Kristina Blank Makansi
Cover images: Shutterstock
Set in Adobe Caslon Pro, Gravesend Sans and Adorn Condénsed Sans

Library of Congress Control Number: 2024918280
Paperback ISBN: 9780998425979
Ebook ISBN: 9780998425986
Audio ISBN: 9798991272209

for my roomie

*Moments of joy, forgiveness,
and second chances exist even
in the darkest of times.*

ONE

MARCH 4, 2020

GABRIEL LANDON did not leave the stereo on when he'd headed to midtown that morning. In fact, he'd specifically not turned any music on. He'd needed the quiet. Space in which to think and prepare for the big day and to go over his presentation in his head. He'd always worked better with silence as his colleague, so why was music coming from inside his co-op? Why was the Rolling Stones' 'Gimme Shelter' playing loud enough to rattle windows?

Cautiously, he stepped inside and shut the door behind him just as his phone buzzed. He pulled it out of his jacket pocket. Callie again. He owed his sister a call or a text, but first he needed to figure out what was going on. He stepped forward to set the phone on the foyer table and take off his jacket when he tripped, his foot tangled in…something. His arms pinwheeled and his computer bag went flying, he grabbed for the marble-topped table, missed, dropped to his knees on the hardwood floor, and bashed his forehead on the corner of the table on his way down, all the while spewing a stream of expletives likely to stop Mrs. Feldstein's pacemaker mid beat. Luckily, his neighbor across the hall could never remember where she put her hearing aids.

Still cursing, he pulled himself to his feet, extracting his foot from whatever the hell he'd tripped on—a backpack? A fucking *pet carrier?*—and stalked toward the hallway where he turned the corner to discover a gargantuan blue and white polka dotted suitcase adorned with pink ribbons on its handle sitting right in front of the door to the master bedroom. A room that had been locked since he'd moved in two months earlier.

What the actual fuck? No one was supposed to be here. But someone *was* here. Someone who had the key to the front door and to the master bedroom. Someone who obviously thought they belonged here. It couldn't be the guy he'd subleased the place from. The famously reclusive J. Rodgers Caldwell, the literary lion who now lived in Vermont with his fourth wife—a woman well more than half his age—rarely left his farm anymore. Besides, Caldwell wouldn't show up at a place he knew had been rented because the man had approved the terms of the lease himself. It had to be Caldwell's daughter, the regular tenant who was supposed to be living in London for a year, hence the availability of the sublease.

He stalked back to the foyer, unwrapped his scarf and pulled off his jacket to hang on the wall-mounted coat rack. Cursing, under his breath this time, he opened his computer bag to make sure his computer didn't suffer any damage from being hurled across the floor. Then he blinked. Something tickled his eyelid. He reached up to wipe it away only to wince and, once again, let out a loud curse. Great. A knot had already erupted on his forehead, and his fingers came back covered in blood. Shit.

Stomping back to the hallway, he pushed the suitcase out of the way, raised his fist to pound on the closed door… and then lowered it. Fact was, the Morningside Heights co-op was everything he'd ever dreamed of, and he didn't want to risk losing it. Plus, if it was the owner's daughter, he didn't want to risk antagonizing her. As soon as Callie had sent him the notice for the sublease, he'd jumped at the chance to snag the place, paying the one-year lease in full to beat out any other would-be offers. He didn't want a roommate, but if Caldwell's daughter was back and he had to put up with her in order to stay, he supposed he would deal with it. Lord knew he'd dealt with shitty roommates before. Still, why hadn't he been informed that Caldwell's daughter was back in the city? He dabbed at his forehead again, grabbed his phone off the floor where he'd dropped it, scrolled to the saved number for the property management company, and hit the call button.

"You've reached Lillian Beauchamp at Coronet Property Management. I'm not available to take your call right now, so please leave a message after the beep. I'll get back to you as soon as possible. Thank you!"

"This is Gabriel Landon. Please call me back as soon as possible. You have my number." He ended the call and headed to the bathroom to check out the damage done to his forehead. Peering at his reflection in the mirror, he sucked in a breath. Damn. He was going to look like Frankenstein's ugly cousin. With a wad of dampened toilet paper, he wiped the blood away, dabbed at the cut in the center of what promised to be an impressive lump, and then searched the drawers under the sink for a bandage. There should be a box somewhere, he muttered, remembering buying a first aid kit when he first moved in. Where had he stashed it? Under different circumstances, he'd probably head over to the ER to get stitches, but he wasn't going anywhere near a hospital. Not with the threat of this damn Covid-19 virus blowing up like the Black Plague.

He found the kit in the bottom drawer, proceeded to wash and dry his face, then carefully placed a butterfly bandage over the gash at the center of what was rapidly turning into a Mt. Vesuvius-sized lump. Tomorrow, he'd have a helluva shiner. Sore kneecaps too.

Bandage in place and head starting to pound, he opened a bottle of ibuprofen, popped two, and leaned against the bathroom sink to check his gmail account. He hardly ever used that account anymore—except for online purchases and the resulting junk mail he didn't want cluttering up his main account—and hadn't checked it in what? Probably at least two weeks, even as he saw the number of emails in his inbox climbing on his iPhone app. If there was a message about Caldwell's daughter, he figured it'd be there.

And sure enough. Four emails from Lillian Beauchamp. Damn. He thumbed open the oldest one to read that the permanent tenant was returning home from London because of the Covid-19 pandemic. The permanent tenant, Lillian Beauchamp wrote, was amenable to a co-living situation, and if such a situation was amenable to Mr. Landon, arrangements would be made for his rent to be prorated through the term of the lease. If, however, he wanted to find another place to live, a check minus the security deposit and one month's rent would be issued to him upon receiving notice of the termination date of his lease, and Lillian assured him, she'd be happy to assist him in finding somewhere else to live. Yada Yada Yada… the email went on to say that in these uncertain times, Ms. Beauchamp trusted that a solution amenable to everyone's interests could be reached as soon as possible.

Shit. Shit. Shit. He sure hoped Caldwell's daughter was more pleasant than her father who, he'd read, was an irascible, womanizing, egotistical ass. Especially if New York went the way of cities in China, Italy, and Spain which were locking down due to the virus's spread. It might be okay to have someone around if everything shut down. Callie and Sylvie were just a short fifteen-minute walk away, but still. If this virus got too bad, that could seem like a world away.

Callie. He'd text her after he got a much-needed drink. He needed to think up a clever response to the *rah-rah* text she'd sent just before he'd walked into the first board meeting with his Series A investors since moving to New York: *Don't worry! You're either a) gonna WOW them or b) srsly fuck up…call me later to let me know.*

He *had* wowed them and had been in a grand mood right up until five minutes ago. Now, what had been a highly successful day was thoroughly screwed. He headed for the kitchen to pour himself a glass of wine and wait for his new roommate to emerge from her lair. Then, he was determined to be all smiles. He'd be on his best behavior. The perfect roommate.

TWO

S KIN FLAMING RED from the scalding water she loved, Aria Turner stepped out of the shower and reached for a towel. The Stones' 'Sympathy for the Devil' filled the room providing a much-needed, post-flight stress-reliever as she buffed herself dry and then ran the damp towel over her hair until it stood out in every direction. Like Medusa's writhing snakes adorned with fading pink rattles, she thought, surveying herself in the bathroom mirror. She'd worn it short the past few years, but if the city went into quarantine, maybe she'd grow it out again. If she was going to work completely remotely, there'd be no reason to worry about blow dryers or flat irons. She could let her curls go wild, quit dying her hair, and live in leggings and sweatshirts.

And maybe she could quit looking over her shoulder. She hadn't had a death threat in over a year. There were still a few crazies out there who left vile messages on her social media accounts, but she just blocked and reported them to the police and her attorney, hoped the police could identify the idiots to add their names to her stack of restraining orders, and moved on. It'd been three years since her disastrous run-in with Gabriel Landon and his 'Work Hard/Play Hard' Cro-Magnon crew of basement-dwelling incels, and her days as a focus for the ire of the not-all-men-are-misogynistic-assholes social media trolls appeared to be over. It was time to put the past behind her once and for all.

She wandered into the bedroom to pick up her phone. Still no word from Lillian Beauchamp, Caldwell's property manager. The woman hadn't even sent over the renter's name. Of course, Aria had made the decision to leave London practically overnight, so there hadn't been much time for figuring out the logistics of sharing the co-op with the guy who'd subleased it for the year. All Caldwell had told her was that he was some hot shot brainiac running some sort of big data start-up and that he'd been willing to pay the full lease in advance to snag the property. The man obviously wasn't hurting for cash, but how much of a brainiac was he really if he was blowing off the news that he was about to have a roommate. Or maybe he was 'too busy' to answer his emails. If the latter were true, odds were good he was an asshole.

Great. She hoped like hell he wasn't anything like Gabriel Landon.

Her stomach growled. God, she was glad she'd ordered groceries online and had them delivered. Especially since there hadn't been much in the fridge when she finally got home, and the kitchen looked like it hadn't been used since she left for London. Manuel—thank the stars for heroic doormen—had brought the groceries up and left them on the counter while she'd been trying to ignore her cabbie ranting about the Chinese virus all the way in from JFK.

She tossed her towel over the back of a chair and took a sip of the wine she'd poured earlier. Not bad. The bottle was one of the few items in the fridge when she'd arrived home. She probably shouldn't have opened it without asking her new roommate, but she had a wine fridge in her storage space in the basement and would replace it. She just didn't feel like going downstairs yet. She gave the glass a little swirl and held it up to the light. Nice color, she thought, taking another sip.

Looking up from where she'd curled up on a blanket folded over the foot of the bed, Frederica, Queen of All She Surveyed, flicked her tail, and gave Aria an expectant gaze as she rolled over to expose a speckled belly in dire need of petting. Aria gave her a quick rub and hoped this roommate situation wouldn't be too weird. And that the guy wouldn't be allergic to cats. Just because Fred was hairless didn't mean she didn't have dander.

Aria had tapped on the spare bedroom door when she'd gotten home from the airport, but no one answered. The co-op had been dark and quiet. Peaceful. *Home.*

She gave Fred a few playful scritches on her belly until the claws came out and the cat attacked her hand, ready to play. But Aria wasn't going to risk playing with the little beast until she put clothes on. Those claws were no joke.

Dreading the idea of unpacking her suitcase—a task she always delayed as long as possible—she rummaged through her dresser and came up with an old flannel shirt missing the top button and a pair of faded sweats with ARIZONA emblazoned on one leg. Since her roomie obviously wasn't home and she wasn't going anywhere, she went commando. No bra. No panties. Just soft comfort clothes. Good-to-be-home-clothes.

She grabbed her wineglass, opened the door, stepped around her giant suitcase still sitting in the hall, and headed toward the kitchen. The place was still quiet—except for her music. The second bedroom door was still closed. Maybe her roommate was out of town. Maybe he traveled for his job. Strangely, the idea was a bit disappointing.

The trouble with roommates was that they made her feel like she was intruding in her own space. She hadn't had one since freshman year of college and had always felt like she was in the way or bugging her. She was happier when she lived alone, probably because she'd grown up a single child with a mom who worked constantly. She'd never had to share a room and hadn't even had a pet since her mom was allergic to just about everything. But now, with the prospect of the pandemic shutting things down, at least for a while, she realized that the idea of having someone around sounded kind of nice. Someone with whom she could just hang out, share a meal, watch movies, or play chess or Scrabble. Maybe she'd finally learn how to play backgammon.

THREE

THE KITCHEN WAS empty except for an open bottle of red wine on the counter. Gabriel turned it around to see the label. A Bordeaux. The one he'd bought just yesterday in the hopes that his meeting would go well, and he'd be able to celebrate. Instead, his unexpected and unwanted roommate was drinking his celebration wine. He held the bottle up to the light to determine exactly how much was gone. Still nearly two-thirds left. Okay. That's at least something. He opened the cabinet, grabbed a wine glass, poured, gave the ruby red liquid a swirl and took a long, appreciative sip.

He closed his eyes as his head really started pounding. Then his stomach growled. His head swam. Reminders that he hadn't eaten since that apple he'd snarfed down for lunch and it was now, what? 7:00? He'd been too amped up and, frankly, too nervous, to eat much before his meeting, but it had gone well and now he was starving. And seeing black spots.

He set his wine down carefully, gripped the edge of the counter, and blinked several times to clear his vision. He needed food, but only had, what, half a package of cheddar cheese and a container of leftover rice from his Chinese takeout two nights ago? Some salsa? A jar of jalapeños? Maybe he'd just order in again. The best part of New York was restaurant delivery and if he wasn't hanging with Callie and Sylvie or going out to dinner, he'd ordered in almost every night since he'd moved in. He pulled the refrigerator door open out of sheer force of habit. *What the hell?* The fridge was full. Stocked to the brim. There was more food packed in there than he'd bought in the two months he'd been in New York.

It looked like his new roomie was either planning to ride out the whole pandemic on the food in the fridge or she was planning to feed everyone in the building. And then he thought, *she opened my wine, so why can't I have some of her food?*

But wait. Would helping himself to her groceries make her think he was an ass? He took a deep breath. He didn't want another antagonistic relationship in his life. He'd make this roommate thing work even if he had to bend over backward. He felt like he'd been in a shit mood for three years and was finally coming around, finally on solid ground again, pouring everything into work and into rebuilding his relationship with his sister. This co-op was perfect for that. It had a study lined with floor-to-ceiling bookshelves that he'd been using as a home office and a gourmet kitchen perfect for cooking and entertaining—not that he ever did that, but he could imagine doing it. But best of all it had a loggia—he'd had to look that term up—

with a breathtaking view of Morningside Park, Columbia's campus, Riverside Park, and the Hudson. Hell, with a telescope, he could probably peer into someone's window in New Jersey. The whole place was elegant, understated, and homey. Exactly the kind of place he always imagined living in someday, especially since he'd come to terms with living alone.

He gave his head a little shake and the movement sent the room spinning. His stomach lurched. He gripped the counter again. Surely, she wouldn't mind sharing some of her food if it kept him from hitting the floor like a felled tree.

He grabbed a container of chicken tenders, pried off the lid, and bit into a big piece. Damn that was good. Needed ketchup, but still. He snarfed down another piece, and opened the cabinet to look for ketchup, or something to dip the tenders in.

How long was this woman going to hide in her room? Maybe she hadn't heard him come in, even though he'd made a hellish racket. Maybe she was asleep. If she'd just come in from a long flight, she could have crashed for a while. But with music blaring at ear-splitting decibel levels? Maybe she'd taken a sleeping pill. Maybe he should check on her. No. That would be super creepy. He'd just have to wait her out. When she did emerge, he'd slap that smile on his face and charm the pants off her. Well, not literally. He didn't pull that kind of shit anymore.

FOUR

A FEW MORE STEPS down the hall, Aria noticed a computer bag on the foyer table and a leather jacket and scarf hanging on the coat peg. The roommate *must* be here. She probably hadn't heard him come in because she'd been in the shower with the Stones blasting. She continued down the hall toward the kitchen, turned the corner and *stopped at the sight of a man standing* at the kitchen island with a piece of her tofu tenders in his mouth. Her stomach dropped, her throat closed up, and she could've sworn someone bludgeoned her upside the head with a 2 x 4, she found her voice and choked out: "*What the hell?*"

The man choked too. He thumped a fist to his chest to swallow. Eyes watering, he gaped at her as if she had manifested as Medusa herself and he, without a mirror, had instantly turned to stone.

She blinked.

He blinked.

THIS. IS. NOT. HAPPENING.

Then she staggered backward and gripped the back of a dining room chair to steady herself. To make sure she didn't faint dead away in front of Gabriel Fucking Landon. "*What are you doing in my co-op?*" Her voice was about two octaves higher than normal, and she thought she might have just discovered what a banshee truly sounded like.

"*Your co-op?*" Gabriel's voice also registered in the *this-cannot-be-happening* range, and he waved his wine glass at her, the ruby red liquid swirling dangerously along the rim. "What the hell are *you* doing here?"

"I live here!"

"That's not possible."

"Not possible? What are you, omniscient now?"

"This place is owned by J. Rodgers Caldwell and *his* daughter, who is supposed to be in London, lives here."

"Exactly." Aria's voice was now something between a smug *I told you so* and a feral snarl.

Gabriel's eyes went wide. "Wait. You're Caldwell's daughter? But your last name—"

"*Illegitimate* daughter. *Only* daughter. It's in Wikipedia. I assumed you and your henchmen would have done your research. They were certainly able to find my address in Phoenix easily enough, so I—"

"Henchmen? For god's sake, I never had any goddamn henchmen. Who exactly do you think I am?"

"You're a misogynistic jerk who is going to pack his things and remove himself from my property. Now." She dug her fingernails into the palms of her hands and willed herself not to cry as a tidal wave of anger and incredulity washed over her and every horrible experience with men—

from Troy Jordan in the 8th grade to Gabriel Fucking Landon and his glorious fucking kiss—rose up in her throat like bile.

"I am not going anywhere. I have a signed lease."

Frederica, disturbed by the racket, skidded into the kitchen on a loud *yowl*. "Holy hell!" Gabriel yelped and jumped back. "What is that?"

Aria choked back her tears and gave him a dark glare. "What do you mean, what is that?"

"That demonic thing. It looks like it's from some Medieval painting of the Apocalypse."

"What the fuck? That's my cat!"

"Your cat? That's not a cat, that's a nightmare."

Aria let go of the dining room chair and squared off against him from the other side of the island. "I don't care whether you have a lease or not. You. Can. Not. Stay. Here."

Gabriel snorted and scowled down at the supposed cat—a creature with no hair, ridiculously large ears, eyes that bulged out of its skull, and a sinuous pink body that was now rubbing itself against his shins. Typical. Cats seemed to gravitate toward him. Not that he was one of those people who didn't like cats. He did like them. He and Callie had even had a kitten once, long ago. He'd been home from school one day, laid up with a sprained ankle, when he watched helplessly as a coyote streaked across the backyard, grabbed Mister Mittens by the scruff of the neck, shook his head a few times until the kitten went limp, and then trotted away with his dinner clamped in his jaws. Gabriel had been twelve and had cried the rest of the afternoon.

Shortly after that, Grandma Jack had brought home Boomer, the dog he and Callie had grown up with. Boomer was a Boxer/Mastiff mix and had lived to be sixteen and had died just one month after everything went to hell. He still got choked up thinking about the morning Callie texted to tell him she'd taken Boomer to the vet in Tucson, where she was doing her PhD, and that he was already gone. *Over the Rainbow Bridge,* she'd texted. Gabriel didn't even get a chance to say goodbye. Back then his sister was still so pissed about the whole Aria Turner shitshow that she wasn't speaking to him.

And now Aria Turner was standing in his kitchen scowling at him while her weird hairless cat was doing what cats tended to do around him, that is attaching itself to his body as if it was their personal scratching post. He must have a brain injury. He must have hit his head harder than he thought because it was impossible that this woman— the woman he'd dreamed of for three years, the woman who'd dragged his name through the muck and caused him to lose everything he'd worked so hard for—was standing not three feet from him. Close enough, almost, to reach out and touch.

He looked down as the cat rubbed itself against his jeans. "I have a lease signed by the person who actually owns this place, and that person is not you, so good luck complaining to the property management company which, by the way, is going to prorate my rent since it appears I now have an unwanted roommate. I assume I'll be getting a check in the mail as soon as I confirm I'm staying." He set his wine glass on the counter so hard Aria was surprised the stem didn't shatter. He looked down again to see the cat testing its claws on his pant leg and nudged it away with a gentle push.

"Don't kick my cat!"

"Jesus, I'm not kicking your cat. I'm trying to prevent it from adhering itself to my leg and shredding my jeans in the process."

"Look," she jabbed a finger at him, "my flight was delayed on the tarmac at Heathrow for two hours and it took me forty-five minutes to get a taxi when I finally got to JFK and the cabbie talked the whole way home about how this damn virus was cooked up in a Chinese lab as a 'Democrat' hoax designed to ruin Trump and I'm tired and hungry and…" She ran a hand through her wet tangle of curls and took a breath. "And now I'm going to eat *my* tenders and finish *my* wine and watch the news about how the world is falling apart on *my* TV in *my* co-op and then I'm going to go to bed. When I get up in the morning, I expect *you* to be gone."

"Since you're gonna claim *my* wine, I'm gonna claim *your* tenders and eat my dinner and watch the news about this damn virus that might shut down the city I just fucking moved to, and then *I'm* going to go to bed, and I will most definitely be here tomorrow and the day after and the day after that, so *you'd* better adjust your expectations."

"You can't stay here!" The prick of tears tickled at her nose as she fought the urge to scream and wail and hit something. Hard. Preferably Gabriel Landon's perfectly gorgeous nose.

"Maybe you should head up to Vermont and move in with dear old dad. I have a lease and I'm not going anywhere. Where's your signed lease? Or did daddy just hand the place over to you?"

Okay. That hit a nerve. Aria did not have a lease. All she had was Caldwell's word that she could stay in the place as long as she wanted since he'd grown tired of the city, and she'd eventually inherit it anyway. So, instead of punching Gabriel Landon in the face and risking an assault charge—because she wouldn't put it past him to call the police on her—she slapped a hand on the counter top and glowered at him. Besides, if that bump on his brow was any indication, it looked like someone had already beaten her to beating him up.

"One week." She drew in a long breath and exhaled slowly. "You have one week to find somewhere else to live." Then she reached over and grabbed the neck of the wine bottle and poured another glass. Slowly. Watching his reaction the whole time.

"You know that's my wine," he said, staring back at her.

"You know those are my tenders," she retorted, glancing at the half-eaten piece in his hand.

He counted to ten, fingers drumming on the counter top like a metronome. "We could share." His voice tight and flat with frustration. "For tonight only."

"Fine." She glared at him as she opened a drawer and grabbed two forks, opened the cabinet, and reached for two plates, then pulled out the deli container and dumped the rest of the tenders on the plates. Opening the refrigerator again, she grabbed a container of mashed potatoes and gravy and one of green beans and slopped the contents onto the plates. Then she grabbed two cloth napkins out of a drawer and threw one at him. "There," she said, pushing his plate across the counter top. "Look. We're sharing. Happy?"

"Delighted." He picked up his napkin, fork, plate, and wine glass and without another word limped into the living room where the television was mounted above the fireplace. After arranging himself at one end of the oversized milk chocolate-colored leather sofa, he grabbed the remote and turned on the news, not even acknowledging her following in his footsteps.

He looked up when she set her plate and wineglass on the coffee table and started to arrange herself in one of those mid-century modern armless side chairs Gabriel loved but never could remember the name of. He loved everything about the co-op, including the way it was furnished. But especially this room with its high windows and expansive views surrounding the old fireplace and the French doors that led out to the covered porch. Ever since he'd moved in, he'd loved the peace and quiet of it. "Do you mind?" He turned to look back down the hall toward the bedrooms.

"Mind what?"

"The music. I can barely hear the news over the music blaring from your bedroom."

"It's not that loud," she protested.

"I can't…I can't think, let alone pay attention to this"—he waved a hand toward the television—"if that's playing."

"And your point is…?" She could feel her chin automatically jut up in the air just like that first time she'd been aware of making the gesture. She'd been in the fifth grade and a cranky, ancient substitute teacher had asked everyone in the class to say what their fathers did for a living. Problem was, Aria didn't even know who her father was, so she'd stuck her chin out and said: *My mother's sex life is none of your business.*

As obdurate as an ox, her mother had teased her after picking her up from the principal's office, proud of her little firecracker and pleased that Aria had not let an authority figure intimidate her. When the emotion and embarrassment of being called out and sent to the principal's office finally washed over Aria, her mother had pulled her close, stroked her hair, and told her over and over again: *You should never allow anyone to make you feel ashamed of something you had nothing to do with. The best thing for you to do is for you to be you and never let anyone else define who you are. Even me.* Unfortunately, that hadn't always been as easy as it sounded, and self-confidence was always a struggle.

But that stubbornness erupted like magma from a volcano at the very idea of Gabriel Landon, let alone his opinions about her playlist. She liked her music loud and so what if he didn't. He'd just have to deal with it.

He stared down at his plate as she pulled her legs up in front of her and sat cross-legged. He ignored her and she ignored him. He didn't even look her way when Fred jumped up on the couch next to him and planted herself firmly against his hip—even though there was a ridiculously expensive cat tree tucked right next to a window in one corner of the living room. What was it about cats, Aria wondered, that made them focus on people who didn't like them? Then Fred stuck one leg in the air like a feline ballerina and began to lick her asshole.

Aria hid a smile at that move. Then, out of the corner of her eye, she saw his brow furrow. He winced. Rubbed his temple. Touched a fingertip to the corner of his rapidly purpling eye.

"Fine." She threw her napkin on the coffee table and got up to stomp her way down to her bedroom to turn off the music.

"Thanks," he grumbled when she stomped back in.

So, there they sat in silence—the man who had almost ruined her life and the woman who had nearly destroyed his career—together and apart, watching as news of the presidential primaries and the worsening Covid-19 virus played out on the television before them.

FIVE

"**O**KAY. I'LL BITE."

Aria had held her tongue as long as she could until the questions threatened to burst out on their own. She hadn't said anything as they each ate their dinner—in silence—and watched the alarming news of Covid-19's death march around the globe. On that front, she knew that no matter what kind of spin officials were taking, it was all going to get much worse before it got better. She'd cast one or two surreptitious glances at Gabriel Landon and more than once had felt him slide a glance her way. Did he have family he was worried about? Parents? Grandparents? Loved ones who were immunocompromised and vulnerable, like Caldwell? Where would he go when he moved out? Did he have friends in the city? What was he doing here anyway?

Whatever. She truly did not care. She especially did not care that he was even more attractive than she remembered, but somehow put together in a more mature, settled, self-assured way. Same broad shoulders under his white button down. Same impressive chest that evoked both solace and sensuality. Same dark reddish gold hair with a bit of a curl at the nape that she knew would feel like silk under her fingertips. Same bright green eyes that made her want to bask in their glow—except for the one that was rapidly turning black around the perimeter. And, of course, that alarming bump growing on his forehead.

The whole situation was beyond infuriatingly ridiculous and awkward and so improbable as to be laughable. It was as ludicrous as one of those ridiculous romance novels her mom stocked in her bookstore. She'd devoured them all through high school. And college. And grad school. Never in her wildest dreams would she have envisioned being in the same room with this man again, let alone living in the same co-op. She could almost feel the steam building between her ears and wondered how many pounds per square inch it would take for the pressure to blow the top of her head clean off.

So, she'd watched the news and eaten in silence until— feeling just a teensy bit bad that despite being one of the most gorgeous men she'd ever laid eyes on, he looked like utter shit—she'd set aside her anger long enough to carry both plates to the kitchen and return with the bottle of wine. He didn't even look at her as he topped off his glass, set the bottle on the coffee table, and went back to typing on his phone's messaging app.

"What the hell are you doing in New York and why does your face look like utter shit?"

Gabriel pretended to ignore her to concentrate on his text to Callie.

"Were you in a fight?" she prodded, studying his profile and the angry lump that had the brow over his right eye swelling at a remarkable rate. "Accosted in the subway? Walloped by an ex-girlfriend who finally came to her senses and realized you're an unmitigated ass?"

Gabriel to Callie: *Thnx for your words of encouragement. Ha. Sorry to disappoint but did not srsly fuck up.*

"You've been rubbing your temple like you have a headache."

Selfishly gratified that Aria was paying enough attention to notice he was in pain, he glanced over at her.

"You playing the quiet brooding role now?" she asked. "I seem to remember you being quite the conversationalist."

"Why do you care?"

"Ah, he speaks!"

He rolled his eyes, grunted, and kept texting: *Board gave the go ahead to start hiring, so it was a good day. How was the first day of closure? Did Sylvie have to teach via zoom?*

Aria shrugged. "Call it professional curiosity. Who, what, when, where, why? I can't flip a switch and turn off my journalistic need-to-report impulse."

"I'm here because I'm working in New York now and," Gabriel said, waving a hand toward his face, "I look like this because I was attacked by your cat carrier backpack thingy." He cast a baleful glance at the naked cat now curled beside him, purring loudly. He closed his eyes for a moment. He was pretty sure he had a concussion. He felt better after eating but was still a bit woozy. Last time he'd had a headache like this, he'd taken a header over his bike handlebars and cracked his helmet on a trail in Cave Creek.

Callie: *It was an adjustment. Yes. She can tell you about it. Everything is just…strange*

Gabriel: *Speaking of strange…*

Callie: *Go on…*

Gabriel: *As my beloved elder sister, you'll probably say it's only what I deserve…*

"My cat carrier? What's that supposed to mean?"

Callie: *You being drawn and quartered in the public square?*

Gabriel: *haha funny*

He slid a quick glance over to see Aria's brows drawn together in a look that appeared part skeptical scowl and part concerned frown and something in his chest squeezed tight just like the first time she'd smiled at him before he'd ruined everything and she'd piled on and things had really gone to shit. He looked away and concentrated on his phone.

Gabriel: *I've got a new roommate*

Aria refused to let him off the hook. "I mean, when you say my cat carrier backpack thingy attacked you, do you mean it came to life, scampered about your ankles, and then sprang up to attack your face à la *Alien* or what?"

Callie: *I thought you were philosophically opposed to roommates now*

Gabriel *was* philosophically opposed to roommates. The trouble with roommates was that the last time he'd had any, he'd ended up almost ruining his life. He'd shared a house in Phoenix with three rowdy "dudebros," as Callie called them, and for a while, it had been amazing. But then it had all blown up in his face. And yes, like not paying attention and sticking his foot in a stupid pet backpack and nearly knocking himself senseless, everything he'd gone through had been his fault. His entitled, egotistical whining was the inciting incident for everything that happened after. Everything that happened to the woman sitting across from him with a darkly amused look on her face. The trouble with this roommate was that he…well, he hadn't expected to ever see her again but now here she was and his stupid heart didn't have any idea what to do about it.

He glanced up at her. "You left it in the middle of the floor in the foyer. I wasn't expecting luggage because I wasn't expecting anyone to be here, and so I wasn't looking where I was going and caught my foot in it, tripped, fell forward, hit my head on the corner of that marble table, and nearly knocked myself unconscious. That's what that's supposed to mean."

Her eyes went wide as she coughed out a laugh. "Oh, jeez, I'm sorry."

The woman had the audacity to lean toward him as if to examine his face from across the room. As if she cared that he'd nearly split his skull wide open. Probably messed up his knees as well. If they were swollen in the morning, he'd have to go get a heating pad and ice pack. Last time he'd injured a knee it'd been playing four-on-four in grad school, and he'd torn his meniscus and moved like a 90-year-old for weeks.

"You could have a concussion and not even know it. Plus your eye is going to be all sorts of shades of ugly tomorrow."

"In case you're wondering, it hurts like hell." He couldn't help but try to wring a little sympathy out of her. It was her fault, after all. Sure, he should have been paying attention, but it's not like he was expecting luggage lying about from a roommate that wasn't supposed to exist.

Gabriel went back to texting. *The permanent tenant came back from London bc of covid. Left shit in the foyer. I tripped, fell, and now I've got a lump and a shiner. Probably need stitches. And my knees are banged up bc I went down on the hardwood*

Callie: *Damn. Want me to send Dr. Sylvie over to check you out? She said she's stitched up her brothers a few times when they were camping…brothers are such a bother you know…*

Gabriel: *So I've been told. Repeatedly. So thanks, but I'll live. Probably have a battle scar tho*

Callie: *So what's the roomie like?*

Gabriel: *Reminds me of Aria Turner*

Callie: *Ha! That DOES serve you right. Poor woman*

Gabriel: *Reminds me of Aria Turner bc it FUCKING IS ARIA TURNER!*

Callie: *OMG. NO WAY! ARE YOU SHITTING ME???*

Gabriel: *How could I possibly make something this horrific up?*

Callie: *I'm coming over. Can I come over and watch the fireworks? Sylvie wants to come too.*

Gabriel: *No.*

Callie: *But how is this possible? Where's Caldwell's daughter?*

Gabriel: *She IS Caldwell's daughter. Different last name*

Callie: *OMG*

Gabriel: *And she has a demon spawn familiar that has attached itself to my hip*

Gabriel thumbed over to his photo app, reversed the lens, and took a pic of Frederica—or whatever the cat's name was—and sent it to his sister.

Callie: *Awww...sweet baby. Looks like a sphinx cat. Supposed to be super smart and maybe okay for people with allergies. Like Sylvie*

Gabriel: *It appears to have decided I'm its new favorite thing*

Callie: *And what about Aria?*

Gabriel: *Still not her favorite thing*

"Having fun over there?"

He looked up to see Aria watching him. "My sister." He held up his phone as if that explained everything.

He didn't elaborate, so Aria prompted, "Your sister and…"

"And what? I'm texting her."

Aria refrained from rolling her eyes and groaning loudly. He'd definitely been a much better conversationalist when they'd first met. Charming, down-to-earth, yet somehow self-assured and sophisticated in an approachable and very sexy kind of way. The chemistry…wow. Just thinking about it—which was why she absolutely never thought about it—was doing funny things to her insides. They hadn't talked much about family, but she did remember that he'd mentioned an older sister in their initial interview. She was doing a postdoc or something. Down in Tucson.

"She's an assistant professor at Columbia."

So, obviously not in Tucson anymore.

"That's why I moved here. To be close to her."

Holy shit on a shingle. Aria did not want to know that Gabriel the Asshole had a sister he actually cared about. She didn't want to think of him as anything but a major dick. And she definitely did not want to think about his *actual* dick. She didn't want to remember that she'd liked him—a lot—when she'd first met him. She didn't want to remember how his crooked smile and green/gold eyes sent little sparks up and down her spine. Or that when he'd kissed her after that second interview that had turned into dinner and a very nice bottle of wine, she'd looped her arms around his neck as he'd leaned her back against her car and that she'd pulled him closer, wanting more and—

Nope. Nope. And nope.

What she needed to remember was that he was personally responsible for months of pure hell caused by his misogynistic Work Hard/Play Hard fanboy followers. What she needed to remember was that he was Gabriel Landon and she was Aria Turner and they were sworn enemies. At least she had sworn they were enemies. And that was that. She shifted in her seat to get up and leave before she could learn anything else that might make him seem remotely human, but he'd already started talking again.

"Dendrochronology. That's her field." He held out his phone for Aria to see the screen open to Dr. Callista Landon's profile page on the university website. He'd navigated to that page so quickly she suspected he kept the tab open on his phone's browser. "She's an expert in paleoclimatology and historic climate modeling." He huffed out a little laugh, thumbed over to his photo app, and held his phone out again for Aria to see. "She really is a tree hugger."

Aria couldn't stop herself from leaning closer to see the photo of an attractive woman dressed like a lumberjack in hiking boots and a flap hat and with her arms spread wide around the trunk of a majestic Ponderosa pine, her lips puckered up pressing a kiss to the bark and damn if she didn't look like someone Aria would've hung out with. A vision of hiking and camping with Gabriel's sister flashed through her mind before she could put the brakes on her imagination.

"This one's actually taken in your neck of the woods, in the Coconino National Forest, near Sedona," he went on.

Okay. She needed to remove herself from his presence, go lock herself in her bedroom or something before she forgot why she loathed him with the intensity of a thousand exploding stars. "Impressive," she said, her voice dry as tree bark in high summer.

His lips curled up in a smile that sent little crow's feet raying out from the corners of his eyes. "She's brilliant. Lives with her partner over on Claremont in faculty housing. I'm sure you'll meet her."

She absolutely was not going to meet his sister. "Before the week's up and you move out? I doubt we'll have time for that."

A muscle in his jaw flexed. Carefully, he reached forward and set his phone, screen down, on the coffee table. "Oh, I think you'll have plenty of time to get to know her before I move out."

Fuck you, you arrogant a-hole was what she thought. What she said was, "After everything you put me through, why the hell would I want to get to know anything about you or anyone connected to you?"

He chuffed out a sarcastic laugh. "After everything I put you through. Wow. You were the one who went to the press. You were the one who turned the whole thing into a media circus."

She jumped to her feet and looked down at him. "I *was* the press! I *am* a journalist. Online misogyny and bullying is a serious story and millions of women backed me up because of what you did. You never even made an effort to address what happened!"

Now he was on his feet, looming over her. "Never made an effort? What the hell? How many fucking apologies do you need?"

She would not allow his size to intimidate her. She took a step forward and poked him in the chest. "How about one? How about one single solitary genuine apology from you. From Gabriel Landon the man, not Gabriel Landon, CEO of Seven Wonders Gaming."

His gaze flicked down to her finger pressed against his breastbone and then back up to hold her gaze.

"I did apologize. You were the one who announced to the world that it wasn't good enough. What else do you want from me? You want me down on my knees begging?" Well, shit, that image was immediately seared into his brain—his hands on her plump ass, holding her to him as he tasted her.

At that, she decided she absolutely could not engage with the ignorant cretin one more minute. She absolutely was not going to think of him down on his knees in front of her. She was too stunned, too furious, too tired, and now, half a bottle of wine into feeling like she was teetering on the edge of a chasm, she was at serious risk of throwing her last swallow right in his bruised-and-swollen-but-still-aggravatingly-gorgeous face and probably spilling wine on Caldwell's antique Persian rug in the process. "Nothing," she spit out. "I want absolutely nothing from you."

She drained her glass and turned toward the kitchen. "I rinsed the plates. The least you can do is put them in the dishwasher."

He sat back down on the couch with what could only be called a frustrated growl, and before she could say anything else that she might regret in the morning, she hustled herself out of the room. Frederica looked up at her, but stayed right where she was, curled up in the radiant heat emanating from the body of Aria's worst enemy. Traitor.

SIX

MARCH 12

THEY'D BEEN ROOMMATES for a full week, a period during which they had neither seen nor spoken to each other. He got up early every day and disappeared before Aria stepped out of her room, and at night, he came home late, showered, and went to bed, closing his door with a solid, resounding, *don't-bother-me thunk.*

Avoidance was fine in the short term, but getting rid of him was still Aria's priority because, frankly, the mere idea of him was driving her to distraction. Just because she didn't see or talk to him didn't mean she didn't think about him. She couldn't stop herself from wondering where he went and how he spent his days. God, he hadn't only taken up residence in her co-op, but he was occupying her mind space too. He needed to be evicted from both ASAP.

To add insult to injury, this morning, Aria had woken up to find that Frederica, who usually slept on her pillow, was not in her bedroom. Usually, she kept her door cracked so the cat could get to the litter box in the utility room, but Fred rarely moved in the night. So, where was she?

Aria rolled out of bed to head out toward the kitchen only to see Gabriel's keys on the foyer table and his coat and scarf on a peg. Usually, he was long gone by this time. So, if he was still in the co-op at 7:30, did that mean he was going to be there all day? Like he lived there? Which he did, apparently. It was still difficult to wrap her mind around such an outrageous idea. But what really made her angry—stupidly pissed off, honestly—was the possibility that her cat had chosen to sleep with Gabriel Landon instead of with her.

She strode into the kitchen to see Gabriel sitting on one of the black leather and chrome kitchen stools with his head in his hands, sections of *The New York Times* scattered around him on the island, his phone face down next to his half-empty cup of coffee. Frederica, who knew better than to get on the counter, was stretched out on the business section.

She put her hands on her hips. "Did Frederica sleep in your room?"

Gabriel glanced up, shrugged, and reached out to run a hand down the cat's hairless back. "I guess I didn't shut my door all the way when I got up to go to the bathroom because she was on my pillow when I woke up. It's always like that with cats. I don't get why they take to me."

Aria got it. Apparently, Frederica was a feline of easy virtue and abominably low standards. Let one handsome ne'er-do-well into her space, and suddenly Aria was yesterday's news. What a way to start Week Two of the second season of *Misadventures with Gabriel Landon*. Hopefully, it would be short. Better yet, it'd get canceled.

She turned and opened the cabinet to retrieve her favorite coffee cup only to realize he was using it. She turned to complain but held her tongue. He looked terrible. Since she hadn't seen more than a glimpse of him since he'd done that faceplant in the foyer, she was shocked at the black eye, already fading to gruesome green, and the bruised remnants of a lump with a disgusting scab where the corner of the table had pierced the skin. He'd probably have a scar. Plus, he hadn't shaved in a couple of days, and he looked like he hadn't slept in a week.

He held up his cup as if making a toast. "I made coffee. Borrowed some of your half and half too." He grimaced. "Mine had turned to cottage cheese—or something infinitely worse. So, I tossed it."

She almost laughed as he shuddered and made a face like a five-year-old forced to eat a pile of peas. "How surprising. Besides a few beers, a jar of jalapeños, and your disgusting half and half, the fridge was nearly empty when I first got home from the airport. Made me wonder if my new roommate had already decamped."

"You seemed to like my wine." Gabriel gave a little snort. "I don't like to cook for one, so I usually eat out. Or order delivery."

Ugh. That sounded suspiciously like something some lonely person would say, and she *loathed* the little sliver of sad that threatened to worm its way in the direction of her heart.

He tipped his chin toward the paper. "Did you see the news?"

"No, what?"

"The mayor's gonna declare a state of emergency, and the governor barred gatherings of more than 500. So say goodbye to Broadway. Case numbers are going up. From ten at the beginning of the month, to 328 and rising. That's in New York State alone. Now they're saying there are 95 confirmed cases in the city." He ran a hand back and forth over his unshaven jaw. "The math doesn't look good."

Shit. Well, that's why she'd come home, wasn't it? As a freelance journalist finishing a book project and pitching a few new stories, she could work anywhere and, although she'd wanted to be in London for a change of scenery, it wasn't necessary. Now, because she knew the virus was taking an especially terrible toll on the elderly, she wanted to be within driving distance if something happened to Caldwell. He may have been a terrible father, but she loved the arrogant, self-absorbed, narcissistic bastard despite herself. She figured that's why kids made such easy targets for abuse—they wanted to love and be loved by their parents no matter how shitty they were.

As for her mom, she'd been sewing homemade masks with elastic earpieces and putting them out for free in a little bin on the sidewalk outside her Sedona bookstore since February. She'd taught Aria to sew when she was little, but it was a hobby that didn't seem to stick past college, so Vi packed up a dozen masks and sent them to New York before Aria left for London. As for the store, she'd already closed it to foot traffic and was only taking online orders via pick-up and touchless payment. Like everything else in her life, Vi Turner was taking the virus seriously and being responsible in her no-nonsense, competent way.

But Caldwell was a different story. After a lifetime of hard drinking, hard living, and chain smoking, he suffered from emphysema and severe gout, and his current wife, Heather, was a strong believer in aromatherapy, juice smoothies, and a good dose of turmeric for whatever ailed you. They'd met at a book signing somewhere—that seemed to be Caldwell's go-to gig for getting laid—and she'd fawned all over him. At least that's what Aria pictured. She hadn't been there. But four months later, the old goat had married his young filly and had bought a farm in Vermont on which she could raise her show jumpers while waiting for her husband to die.

She poured some half and half in her coffee, leaned back against the counter, and watched as the little cyclone of white and brown swirled in her cup. "So, what does the state of emergency mean? In practical terms?"

"I think it's all about freeing up money to purchase supplies and hire workers. Apparently, there are hundreds of people self-isolating because they think they have symptoms or that, at least, they've been exposed." He drew in a harsh breath and let his fingers linger on the rim of his mug. "Depending on how it's transmitted, the virus could spread exponentially and that means we could all be fucked." He swallowed hard and looked up at her. "Did you wear a mask on your flight from London?"

"Yeah. But not the whole time. Not while I was eating or drinking anything. As a freelancer, my office is here at home," she continued. "What about you? You mentioned investors. Do you have an office? What is it you do these days anyway?"

"I started a new company. Did I already mention that? I can't remember."

"You said you work here now, but that was it."

"Yeah, I started a new company. I've got investors but no employees. And no office. One of the members of the board is on the faculty at Columbia, involved with the Data Science Institute. Got us a contract so we can use their computing resources and arranged it so I can use an office in the computer science department if I need it. It's more like a closet. In the basement. No windows. I prefer working from home."

From home. Aria gritted her teeth. Working from *her* home, in other words.

"I've been spending quite a bit of time in Midtown," he went on. "Diamondback Ventures has an office at Rockefeller Center, and I've been using it for interviews and meetings. That's where I've been all week." He rubbed his temples.

He winced and something clutched at her gut. "You feeling okay?"

"We're gearing up to interview our first employees, so I guess I'm a little stressed. I've still got a low-level headache, and I haven't been sleeping well, but I think it's because of this—" he waved a hand over his face "—not because of any Covid-19 symptoms."

He also couldn't sleep because he'd been acutely aware that Aria Turner—the woman he'd done his damnedest not to fantasize about for the last three years—was between the sheets just down the hall from his bedroom. For the past couple of days, he'd cried uncle and, when the lights were out, he'd let the fantasies run wild, imagining all the ways he would take her, beginning with pressing into her as she stood against that hot car in a public parking lot. Just as he'd very nearly done three years earlier. At this very moment, he was doing his damnedest not to fantasize about her supple body spread out beneath him on her bed—or his. Or on the couch. Or the floor. It wasn't working. Mentioning that kind of thing would be like the old Gabriel, not the new reformed one who had learned his lesson but good.

Aria couldn't stop herself from staring at him. He really did seem like he was in bad shape. Her brain headed straight to *poor baby*, but she slammed on the brakes before it could actually arrive at the station, before she could reach out and run a finger over his face to smooth his troubled brow. Troubled brow? What an idiot, she scolded herself six ways to Sunday and schooled her expression into one of mild interest. Just in case he cracked open a lid and looked at her.

He drew in a long breath and straightened back up. "All of Italy is on lockdown. If the city shuts down like that, we'll all need to work remotely. Which shouldn't be a problem for people like us, but for everyone else…"

For everyone else…? She wanted him to finish the thought but didn't want to ask him to finish it and so she waited. But he didn't go on. Internally, she took a deep calming breath and let it out slowly like her therapist had instructed over and over again. It didn't matter what he was going to say. She didn't care.

But no. That wasn't technically true. She did care if he thought he'd be sharing *her* home office. If he'd been using her study, would he expect to keep using it until he moved out? Was the co-op big enough for the two of them to co-exist without killing each other? She nodded thoughtfully and said, "Your old company was all about using artificial intelligence to create more realistic gaming graphics and faster response times, right? I heard you sold your shares."

He rubbed at his temples and looked up at her. So, she'd followed his exit from the company he'd founded. Seven Wonders Gaming. His baby. The one he'd walked away from because of her. What else had she followed? Did she know what his life had been like after he'd slunk back to Flagstaff, tail between his legs? Obviously not. No one did. Except Callie. And now Sylvie. He held Aria's gaze. "After everything, I decided to go a different direction."

After everything. Aria supposed he meant after his stupid social media post unleashed a couple hundred thousand misogynistic gamers on her and nearly sent her into hiding. "So, a new company…?"

A dull pain still pushed at the remnants of the tender bump on his forehead, radiating down to behind his eye where it throbbed like it was part of a drum circle. He winced and nodded. "With the proceeds from the buyout. But I kept two percent just because." He shrugged. "It was my baby. I started it in my apartment in Berkeley and I couldn't let the whole thing go."

She'd been fascinated by this man ever since she'd first seen him featured on the cover of the *Phoenix Biz Magazine* as founder of start-up Seven Wonders Gaming and one of the '30 Under 30' to watch. There was something about him that snagged her attention—besides the breadth of his shoulders, his artfully mussed hair, the color of wet sand in sunlight, and his bright green eyes. He'd looked so… open, honest. Not smug or arrogant. Just flat-out thrilled to be doing what he was doing and sort of wonderstruck at the fact he could make money at it. He was handsome and smart and buff as all hell, and after she'd read his 30 Under 30 profile about a hundred times, she'd pitched a story to the magazine she freelanced for about a deeper look at how four Type-A extroverts could live together, work together, and party together so successfully that they'd transformed their friendship into the *Work Hard/Play Hard* brand complete with a VC-backed gaming business, a lifestyle Instagram account boasting half a million followers addicted to photos of these buff, half-naked men hanging out with beautiful women by the pool and at the beach and on the slopes, as well as a podcast all about Iron Man competitions and mountain biking and rock climbing etc., etc., etc. On top of all that, they'd managed to leverage their brand into a book deal. She'd dreamed for years about getting a book deal and a bunch of muscled gamer boys had snagged one just like that. She wondered if any of them could even write. Probably nothing more than scratchings on a cave wall.

The day before the first interview, she'd been so keyed up over the prospect of interviewing Gabriel Landon that she'd even gone to get a mani-pedi. A rare splurge, but nails gnawed to the nub didn't look professional, and she wanted Gabriel Landon to see her as a professional. A journalist. An equal. And, because she always *tried* to be honest with herself, she had to admit, she wanted him to see her as a woman too. That was monumental. Her experience with men in her life ranged from mortifying to disappointing with a healthy dollop of inadequacy on top.

A stab of something vaguely like longing lanced through her when she thought about how he'd made her feel when she'd walked in the room for that first interview. He'd been sitting at the conference room table typing busily on his laptop and when he looked up, the world stopped. He stood, slowly, and just gazed at her. Like a fool, she'd patted her hair as if something had sprouted out of the top of her head, but then he smiled, walked around the table, and pulled out a chair for her. As if he was so stunned by her mere presence, her natural beauty and professional poise, that he couldn't speak. But he'd had plenty to say after that second interview. After that kiss. Well, she'd rather not think about that.

But here he was. Her roommate. In her kitchen, still looking like a mule had kicked him in the face and she couldn't stop—what? Wanting to kiss his boo boo and make it all better? Or slap him silly because it would make her feel better. God, this situation was ridiculous. Still, a conversation was happening, and she ought to pay attention to it and quit dwelling on whatever it was she was dwelling on.

"So, if it's not gaming," she heard herself ask, "what's the focus of your new company? What's it called?"

"Q.BC."

"Q. Is that like a cue ball or a waiting in line queue? And what's the 'bee cee? Like Before Christ B.C.?"

He snorted. "Hardly. It's the letter Q then a period then the letters BC. All caps."

"What does it mean?"

He rubbed his temple, had an almost sheepish look on his face. "I watched a lot of *Next Generation* growing up. *Star Trek?* There was a character named Q. Part of the Q Continuum. He—or she—is sort of an extra-dimensional being. Omniscient. Is a bit of a smart ass, but basically a fun character. As for the BC, it stands for blockchain."

"Blockchain?"

He set his coffee cup down and looked at her across the shiny black surface of the kitchen island. "I have a thing about personal identity and security. I don't like things being done in my name."

Oh. Aria blinked then looked away. *Oh.* "Doesn't blockchain have to do with cryptocurrency and porn? Are you into that?"

He snorted. "Cryptocurrency is just one small piece of it and that's not what we're into. And we're not into porn either." He let out a dark laugh. "I mean, the company's not into porn."

Men. She wanted to smack him. "So, what *are you* into?"

He opened one eye and cut her a hard look, but answered her question. "We specialize in permissioned blockchain networks for financial institutions and other organizations that need airtight security, a way to validate transactions, and immutable record keeping."

"How does blockchain do that?"

Hi sighed. "Look, is this an interrogation because if so, maybe I should have my attorney present. As I recall, you seemed to enjoy interacting with my legal representative more than with me."

And just like that—*snip snip*—he'd cut through all the little tendrils of good feeling that had taken root in her belly. She turned her back to him and very calmly and deliberately opened the refrigerator. Food. She needed something to distract her from the fact that no matter how she sliced it, Gabriel Landon was an ass.

"I'm sorry," he said with a voice heavy as lead. "I know that was a dick thing to say, but I really do feel like shit this morning, and I know that's not an excuse, but—"

"No." Her voice was tight. "It's not an excuse." Behind her she heard the scrape of the kitchen stool on the tile floor.

"Let me make breakfast. I can cook when I need to."

"You don't *need* to cook for me."

"How about, I can cook when I *want* to. And I *want* to make you breakfast. Do you like omelets? I think you've got at least two dozen eggs in there."

"I can make my own breakfast."

"I'm sure you are perfectly capable of doing whatever you set your mind to but let me do this. I'll feel better if I eat and I won't be so grumpy. Please."

He stood behind her, put his hand on the door handle, and opened the fridge a little wider. He was wearing a white crew-neck T-shirt and gray sweatpants that sat low on his hips. He was barefoot, standing so close she could feel the heat from his body. It wasn't fair for him to use his body like that, to make her want to lean back against him. She wanted to feel his body against hers.

No. Absolutely not.

She didn't want any of that. She wanted to stomp on his bare foot. Or plant an elbow in his gut and force him to step away from her. Asshole probably wouldn't even feel it. Unfortunately, she remembered what his arms felt like wrapped around her. What his abs looked like on those pool-side posts. She couldn't get those Instagram photos out of her mind. Another reason social media should be outlawed.

One by one, he peeled her fingers off the door handle, then picked up and put her coffee cup in her hand. "You're the journalist. Why don't you sit and read the paper while I cook. Then we can talk about work arrangements. You can have your study back, and I can set up here in the kitchen. Or in the dining room. We'll make it work."

Now, she really wanted to scream: *Do not play nice with me!* Instead, she said, "Okay, if you're up for it. How about a western omelet with salsa and jalapeños."

"My favorite." He pulled out the other kitchen stool for her and re-opened the fridge.

"You like jalapeños for breakfast?" She climbed up on the stool. "A lot of people turn up their noses at the mere thought."

"Love 'em. Especially with spicy chorizo." He shrugged. "I guess us Arizonans have stomachs of steel. Or maybe copper. Copper's one of Arizona's five C's, right?"

"What are you talking about?"

"Didn't you have to learn the five C's in middle school? Copper, cotton, cattle, citrus, and climate. Or something like that."

She shook her head at him, wondering how his brain worked that he could come up with such ridiculous drivel.

He paused and then, with a crooked smile and a slow gaze raking her head to toe, said, "Or maybe we just like to start the day with something spicy."

Her whole body went hot. Nope. Nope. Nope. Not reading anything into that. No sir. No way.

SEVEN

AFTER BREAKFAST, during which neither had spoken another word, Aria volunteered to clean up since he'd cooked, and then she'd gone into the foyer to finally deal with her luggage while he finished reading the paper. When he was done, he chucked the paper in the recycling bin and headed toward the study to gather his things from where he'd set up a workspace on the desk since he wasn't going to be going back down to Diamondback's offices every day. He'd reconciled himself to letting her have her study back, but no way was he allowing her to push him into moving out. Maybe he'd buy a desk and put it in his bedroom. One of those Ikea things he could have delivered and assemble himself. As soon as he got set up at the dining room table, he'd do some online shopping.

On his way to the study, he paused in the hallway to watch Aria sort through the ginormous suitcase that had been sitting in the hallway for a week.

"I can't believe you're just now unpacking. You've been back a week."

She gave him a one-shouldered shrug. "I always put it off as long as possible. Drives everyone crazy."

"I unpack before I do anything else. Otherwise, what would I have to wear?"

"I already put away everything I wear regularly." She pulled a purple lace bra and panty set out and put it on the floor beside suitcase. "This is all just special occasion stuff."

He could imagine a hundred special occasion scenarios for which he'd pay good money to see her wear that purple lace bra. "So, where do you store that gigantic bag?" he said, trying his damndest not to fixate on the shimmery see-through something—dress, nightgown, whatever the hell it was, he could almost feel it slipping through his fingers—that she was now shaking out.

"I keep it in the basement."

"I didn't bring much to New York and didn't even know we had basement storage available until a couple weeks ago when I asked Manuel where I could store a bike if I got one." For some reason that Gabriel didn't want to investigate, the idea that they could be a "we" sent a little frisson of warmth straight to his solar plexus.

"*We* don't have basement storage. *I* have basement storage."

So much for his solar plexus. His dick didn't take that comment well, either. He tried to ignore her snark and went on. "That thing's almost as big as you are. Wasn't it awkward maneuvering something that ginormous around a busy airport. Especially with a messenger bag and a squalling cat in a backpack."

"First of all, Fred doesn't squall. I give her anti-anxiety meds when we travel. And second," Aria didn't look up, "this isn't *that* big. Are you insinuating I'm not capable of pulling a damn roller bag?"

"Of course not. It's just looks unwieldy."

"I may be just an average girl, but it doesn't take a brawny bruiser to pull a suitcase on rollers."

Average? There was not a solitary thing about Aria Turner that could remotely be classified as average—from her pink-tipped dark curls that shone red or copper or gold depending on the light to her gold-flecked brown eyes that seemed like fathoms-deep wells of mystery sheltered by lashes like little feathers and her full lips that begged to be kissed and her very *very* voluptuous curves that he remembered running his hands over... He cleared his throat.

"Besides," she turned and cast a skeptical glower his way, "I was planning on staying for the year, remember. It's not like I could just throw a few things in a backpack and go."

He folded his arms across his chest, leaned against the wall, and watched until she turned again and raised her brows at him.

"Am I keeping you?" She said this as she shook out a little slip of a low-cut, sequined dress and folded it on the floor. Fire engine red. Next, she pulled out a pair of matching open-toed stilettos. God bless America. From sea to shining sea. He thought he might need to call 911 to put out the fire that had spontaneously ignited in his groin. If he wasn't going to lay her down in the hallway and show her what he'd been fantasizing about—which he most certainly was not going to do—he'd need to head to the bathroom for a quick right-handed release or take a cold shower. Maybe both. He swallowed and shifted so she wouldn't notice the bulge in his pants. "Are red sequins standard attire for a journalist these days?"

She shrugged and said nothing. Then she pulled out an even shorter black slinky dress with a dainty ruffle of blood-red lace along the hem and he almost choked. She held it up and slipped a hanger through the neckline. The dress appeared to be missing its back. What the hell was she writing about in London anyway?

"Looks like you went prepared to party or get laid, not to work."

She laughed at that. "Work hard, play hard. Isn't that your mantra?"

Was his mantra. When was the last time he'd gone clubbing? The work-hard part of the mantra definitely still applied, but the play hard part had been, well…He was still running, still lifting weights, still…what? Playing? Hardly. More like *paying*. For his sins. Rehabilitating himself with every mile and every bench press. Damn. If his new gym shut down, he'd have to change his routine.

"What kind of story are you working on anyway?"

"I'm working on a book, actually, and since I can write from anywhere, I decided to go stay with a friend from journalism school who grew up in London. He got an internship at the British Museum and stayed. He's doing PR now, helping to navigate calls for returning half the collection to the countries the pieces were 'expropriated' from—i.e., stolen. Anyway, he loves to dance and goes to all the artsy-fartsy 'see and be seen' events around London, so

I thought I should be prepared. I wasn't there long, but I did go to an event that William and Kate attended. I would've rather seen Harry and Meghan, though." She set a pair of shiny black pumps beside the dress.

Gabriel's mouth went dry. He knew he didn't have a right to feel this way, but he didn't want to imagine her dancing with some other guy, let alone living with him. He decided to change the subject. "So, what's your book about?"

"It's a subject you might be interested in, as a matter of fact. Maybe you have some thoughts on the title." She paused and looked up at him. "*Piling On: How Online Bullying Can Wreck Careers, Destroy Relationships, and Ruin Lives.*"

Holy. Fucking. Hell. Gabriel's throat closed up. He couldn't breathe. His heart skipped a couple of beats and then went clanging about like a bullet ricocheting around his rib cage. The room spun, his brain fuzzed, and his ears seemed to stop working. He was having a panic attack. First one in two years. Logically, he knew what to do. Breathe in through his nose. Breathe out through his mouth. Sit down. Close his eyes. Put his head between his knees and count his breaths until the anxiety passed. *Confront your fear*, his therapist had told him. Well, he was confronting it all right. It was smirking right up at him like the cat that ate the canary, the cream, the cheese, and a whole other goddamned cat.

Aria Turner was going to dredge everything back up again just when he thought his life was getting back to normal, getting back under control. Until last week, he'd figured she was still in Arizona doing freelance reporting for magazines and newspapers in Phoenix and making hay off his mistakes without even giving him a chance to tell his side of the story. *Or to apologize.* She'd blocked his calls. And his texts. And his emails. And when he'd tried showing up at the magazine's offices in the hopes of talking to her, she'd called security. Then, when he told his lawyer that he'd gone to her office, the poor man's eyes nearly shot out of his skull. In no uncertain terms, he'd made it clear that Gabriel had to cease and desist immediately and to stop being a fucking idiot or risk a restraining order.

So, even though he'd never been a quitter, he'd quit. He decided that it was better for him to walk away and not look back than for her to think he was some sort of stalker creep. Jesus. A restraining order? The fact that she already thought the worst of him had made him want to kick something. Yes, he'd been an unthinking idiot, and he'd been arrogant as all hell, but he'd never meant to insult or hurt her. Hell, he'd been half way to head over heels as soon as he set eyes on her. Last thing he'd wanted was to expose her to ridicule.

But now, just as he thought he'd put all that behind him, here she was, about to ruin his life again by dissecting his mistakes in the pages of her book. Maybe he really should give up the lease and try to find another place. He didn't think he could live with a woman intent on making him relive all that shit. What kind of masochistic idiot would put himself through that all over again? Even though he'd shielded himself from the worst of it. Even though he'd shut down his social media accounts and hid out at Grandma Jack's place where television was verboten and the only wifi came from his phone's hot spot, he'd still been well aware that his name was routinely being dragged through the mud on national radio and television. He'd never forget dozing to the dulcet tones of NPR's Terry Gross while sitting beside his grandmother as she went through another chemo treatment. "Up next is journalist Aria Turner talking about her recent piece in *The New Yorker* on the risks of being a woman in an online world. Stay tuned."

He'd ripped his AirPods out of his ears so fast one flew across the room and landed in a fake potted plant.

And now…now it was all going to start up again. He was suddenly tired. Completely *cosmically* exhausted. And sad. Sad all over again. Still, he'd tucked tail and run away once. He didn't relish the idea of doing it twice. So, he did his best to pull on his big boy pants, school his features, and take the news of the book in with the merest hint of a nod.

"I'll check it out when it lands on *The New York Times* bestsellers list," he managed to say. "After all, as Caldwell's daughter, you're sure to have a leg up in getting good reviews."

Then he pushed off the wall, albeit a bit unsteadily, and headed for the study.

EIGHT

GABRIEL LOOKED UP when Aria went into the kitchen. It was her fifth trip—not that he'd been counting—and it wasn't even three o'clock yet. They'd barely spoken yesterday after their confrontation in the hall, after he'd watched her unpack the sexiest clothes he'd been even remotely close to in ages and then she'd dropped the bomb about her book. He would have gone back down to Diamondback Ventures offices in Midtown after that, but they had meetings with another start-up group, and he didn't want to be in the way. So, he'd set up shop on the dining room table, worked until she'd appeared out of her study, and then had zapped a frozen burrito, grabbed a beer, and retreated to his bedroom to read some space opera he couldn't remember the name of. When that distraction didn't work, he opened his laptop to play the latest Seven Wonders video game.

Now, from his position at the end of the dining room table, he could see directly into the kitchen and watch her every move. Just like the other four times, she ignored him as she busied herself—first making a cup of hot tea, second, getting a glass of ice water, then grabbing an apple for lunch, then back for a bunch of grapes, and now, she was apparently back for more tea.

He watched as she refilled the electric kettle and studied the selection of teas in the cupboard. She acted like he wasn't there. He acted like she wasn't there. But from the tension in the air, they both knew better. Or worse, depending on one's point of view.

She finished fixing her tea and started to head back to her office, stopping just long enough to dig her knife in a little deeper. Give it a little twist. "If you haven't contacted a realtor about finding another place yet, I'm sure Lillian Beauchamp would love to help."

He looked up and held her gaze. He wasn't about to admit he'd spent much of the last week looking at apartment listings in his spare time. He certainly wasn't going to admit he'd thought about crashing on Callie and Sylvie's couch for a while. But the smug look on her face pissed him off just enough to supplant his anxiety and panic with plain-old, white-hot rage. "Oh, I'm contacting Lillian Beauchamp, alright. To get my pro-rated rent reimbursement check processed. Since I have an unwanted roommate."

She let out an exasperated sigh. "You know as well as I do that we can't both live here."

One corner of his mouth tipped up in forced amusement. "So go stay with Caldwell. I bet spring in Vermont is lovely and the farm-fresh air and *eau de horse manure* will do you good." He leaned back in his chair, surveying her between the two large monitors set up on either side of his laptop.

"And just think of all the writing you could get done with a Pulitzer Prize-winning papa helping you out." Just thinking about her damned book made him want to shut himself up in a dark closet and cry or put a fist through a wall and scream. Ignore it all and pretend it wasn't happening or break a few knuckles just to feel like he was doing something. Neither were legit choices.

"We'll make each other miserable," she said, waving her cup around and ignoring the jab about her father. "There's just too much bad blood."

"Who knows? Maybe having me around will inspire you."

She snorted. "As if I need more inspiration."

"Look, this place is plenty big enough for two," he said, unable to stop himself from purposely provoking her. "From what I can tell, it's huge for New York, so I don't see the problem." She shook her head in disbelief as he went on. "You're a mature adult. I'm a mature adult. We should be able to be mature about being roommates. I'm perfectly capable of putting the past behind us and being civil, why aren't you?"

"Are you being deliberately obtuse to piss me off or are you truly insane?"

"Why is it so hard for you to be mature and professional about being roommates?" he asked. "You were the one who was all about the importance of professionalism. What was it you said? Something to the effect that I 'insulted your professionalism' and treated you like some 'Instagram fan girl trying to get laid by the hot gamer guy.' That sound familiar, Aria?"

As soon as her name was out of his mouth, Gabriel realized it was the first time he'd said it aloud in over two years and that hearing it was as painful as ripping off a bandage, opening an old wound and watching blood and pus ooze all over his carefully reconstructed life. And that made him even angrier.

He'd done exactly what she'd demanded: 1) issue a suitably groveling formal apology and 2) stay the hell away from her. And he'd done as his attorney instructed—he'd cut ties to everyone who'd gone all in and embraced the righteous, entitled, misogynistic attitude that he'd been the one wronged and she'd been the judgmental bitch who'd tarred and feathered him.

He'd never seen it that way, but it didn't matter because after his formal apology—issued through the company lawyers—he'd slammed the door shut on the whole episode. He'd never spoken about it since. To anyone. Anyone except Callie and Grandma Jack. Callie had read him the riot act at concert-level decibels and then refused to speak to him for nearly a year while Grandma Jack had baked him a strawberry rhubarb pie, patted his cheek, and told him he was a good man and that it would all work out in the end. His grandmother had most likely been high that day. She was high a lot. And not just because it helped with the chemo side effects.

"Jesus, you're impossible," Aria fumed now.

"At least you called me 'hot.' I heard Tucker Carlson really loved that part." Gabriel hated everything Tucker Carlson stood for, but he couldn't help but throw that bit of hypocrisy in her face.

Mouth gaping, Aria stared at him for a solid five seconds. "You really are an insufferable ass." She shook her head and headed back toward her office.

"A *hot* insufferable ass though, right?" Gabriel called after her. He raked both hands through his hair and leaned back in his chair. He really was a fucking jerk sometimes.

NINE

AN HOUR LATER and he still hadn't done any productive work. He'd scrolled through images of a hundred shitty apartments and a hundred more he couldn't afford. Or didn't want to afford. His job in grad school had paid the bills, but that was it. When he'd deposited the first check from his first angel investor, he'd sworn he was going to do his level best to make the man proud. So, he'd counted every penny and agonized over every decision and every hire. But most of all, he'd wanted to make Grandma Jack proud. And, although he didn't believe in heaven or hell, he imagined his mom and dad out there somewhere, part of the cosmos, and he'd wanted to make them proud too. So, he'd forsworn the new car and the fancy apartment, instead keeping his old truck, and moving in with his partners. He should've sprung for the fancy apartment.

Maybe he should cut his losses and spring for a different apartment now too.

Problem was, he didn't want to. He'd analyzed his thought processes until he'd made a muddle of them and couldn't tell up from down. On the one hand, he suspected he was digging in his heels and declaring his determination to stay just because his roommate was Aria Turner and, like a petulant child, he wanted to make her as miserable as she'd made him. On the other hand, he suspected he was digging in his heels just because his roommate was Aria Turner and he wanted to wake up in the mornings and watch her fumble all sleepy-eyed around the kitchen or watch her fingers hold lightly to the stem of her wine glass as she twirled it back and forth or watch the gold rim around her chocolate brown eyes gleam like firelight when she glared at him.

He chuffed out a laugh and closed his laptop. He needed to go for a run. He checked his watch. Almost five. Aria still hadn't emerged from her study. He crept down the hall and pressed an ear to the closed door. Sounded like she was on the phone or in a Zoom meeting or something. Whatever. She was preoccupied. So, he popped a few ibuprofen for his low-level headache, changed clothes, laced up his running shoes, grabbed his AirPods, phone, and keys and headed out. He had more than an hour before sunset and could easily get ten miles in. Maybe then, he could get his thoughts sorted, figure out how he really felt about his troublesome roommate, and make a decision about the co-op.

It wasn't every day that Aria went to the trouble to cook an actual meal, from scratch. Gabriel had made breakfast for her as some sort of peace offering for being an ass that morning, and so she—in some foolhardy attempt at her own peace offering, because she felt just a tiny bit like an ass for how she'd talked to him earlier when he still looked so battered and bruised—had decided to return the favor. Veggie lasagna and a side salad. Garlic bread. A favorite Italian Barolo from her basement wine stash. They both had to eat, after all. Might as well use food as an excuse to try to make things a little less tense, especially since she knew she had to come to terms with the fact that he wasn't moving out, at least not immediately.

After their earlier conversation, she'd spent the afternoon not working on her book. Instead, she'd replayed the events of three years ago over and over in her head and brooded on how even though the co-op was over twice as big as her apartment in Phoenix, it still felt as cramped as a prison cell with Gabriel's 6-foot, broad-shouldered, green-eyed presence in it. A presence she still felt drawn to even though once she was too close she felt like she couldn't breathe. How many times had she made a trip to the kitchen that day? Too many. She'd consumed enough tea for her own Boston tea party.

When she'd finally finished for the day and left the study, she figured Gabriel was working in his bedroom. He wasn't at the dining room table, so where else would he be? Maybe he was one of those people who took afternoon naps. Maybe he had such a bad headache that he'd had to lay down. His coat was still on the peg in the entryway, so he hadn't gone anywhere. His bedroom door was closed. When she'd leaned in close to listen at his door, everything was quiet, but he had to emerge sometime, right? Eventually.

Even if just to go to the bathroom. Her room had a private bath, but his didn't. When Caldwell broached the idea of subletting the place while she was in London, she agreed with the understanding that the master bedroom suite was hers and would be locked for the duration. Gabriel had to cross the hall to use his bathroom, the guest bathroom, and she'd hear him when he did.

When the lasagna was done, she'd headed down the hall to knock on his door. No one answered. So, she went to set the table. After that task was done, she poured herself a glass of wine and waited. And waited. She finally got up to go knock on his door again and that's when she noticed his keys were missing from the little bowl on the foyer table. Then, she realized he must have gone out when she'd been on a conference call with her editor, otherwise she would have heard him leave. When had Jessica called? Around 5? Had Gabriel been gone since then? Why hadn't he left a note?

For god's sake. She wanted to slap herself upside the head. Why would he leave a note? We're just short-term roommates. Very short term. Nothing more. I've made that clear, she told herself. He doesn't owe me anything. Still, wasn't it plain-old common courtesy to let a roommate know you were going out? Maybe guys were different. She'd never lived with a man, but it figured they'd be inconsiderate louts.

At any rate, she expected he'd be home soon. He'd certainly devoured enough of her tofu tenders the night before to know he had a healthy appetite.

After their earlier conversation, she'd been infuriated at his obliviousness, but over the course of the day, she'd calmed down. Managed to tell herself that she had no idea what his life had been like after everything had blown up, so why should he know what hers had been like. Forget that he'd retreated and gone dark while her plight had been all over the local and regional news. Ignore the fact that she'd caught the attention of the morning show hosts and had been flown to New York to do multiple interviews for numerous programs. Disregard that she'd been on CNN and MSNBC countless times and that she'd made a name for herself as an advocate for women claiming their space, claiming their right to exist without being bothered, badgered, belittled—or threatened with bodily harm—online, in their workplaces, and in their own homes.

Arrrrghhh. Just thinking about it made her livid all over again.

Of course, he'd claimed he hadn't written the Twitter or Instagram posts, that it was the company's social media intern, but so what? He must have said something over-the-top nasty to make the idiot think it was okay to talk about her the way his team did. And then to fucking dox her when she protested. As founder and CEO of Seven Wonders Gaming and the most prominent member of the Work Hard/Play Hard Instagram brand, Gabriel was responsible for what his employee did, and he just couldn't seem to accept that.

Yeah, she wasn't proud of her part in escalating the whole fiasco or in threatening to get a restraining order against him, but his apologies were for shit and she'd been so *disappointed*—and not a little heartbroken—that he'd turned out to be just another jerk that she'd maybe overreacted. Probably overreacted. But damn. The whole thing still pissed her off. *He* still pissed her off.

So, she waited. She didn't have his phone number to text him and even if she did, she'd never ever stoop so low. What would she even say? Come home, honey. Dinner's ready.

TEN

T HE RUN HELPED. Okay, it wasn't a run. The throbbing from the bump over his eye was still bad enough on its own, but his feet pounding the pavement made it exponentially worse. So, it was a walk. Still, it did help him sort a few things out. And he'd made a decision—not about the apartment, but about not wanting to know what had happened to Aria after he'd gone dark.

Callie had never believed him when he'd sworn he hadn't followed the news after he'd moved back to Flagstaff, but it was true. Mostly. Well, not 100 percent true. But still. He hadn't trusted himself. Not just to see Aria's face, but he hadn't wanted to see his own name dragged through the mud by the #metoo crowd or held up as an exemplar by friends defending him for the #notallmen crowd by claiming Aria she'd caught the spotlight and was capitalizing on the whole situation. That she was monetizing Gabriel's mistake to build a career as a TV talking head and headline-seeking harpy. It was a cop out, but he'd preferred to wallow in ignorance.

Once, he'd followed a couple of subreddit threads on the future of AI only to find himself the subject of fevered imaginations fantasizing about whether he and Aria had actually had sex or not and wondering if there were any photos or videos they could hack from the cloud. He'd had to get a new screen for his phone and patch and paint the hole in his bedroom wall after that.

So yes, before he'd packed up and headed to Grandma Jack's in Flagstaff, he'd known that shit was going down on online, but he'd done his damnedest to tune it out and to shut down every emotion—the rage, the remorse, the absolute and nearly unbearable mortification. He paid just enough attention to know what statements his partners and their lawyers and investors were putting out and what the gamers they courted were saying. He still had to pay attention to his business, even though he'd been forced to sell most of his shares. Beyond that, he'd had no desire to be in the middle of a cultural moment, and if he was in the news, he didn't want to know about it. Besides, he'd had Grandma Jack's cancer to worry about.

Now, after three miles through Morningside Park, Gabriel sat on a bench, pulled out his phone, and opened a new tab on his browser. He took a deep breath and he typed: Aria Turner Gabriel Landon. And holy shit...

Arizona Republic:
Seven Wonders Founder Doxxes Local Journalist

ABC15 – Phoenix
Apology Not Accepted in Online Harassment Incident

Arizona Daily Star:
Gamers Pile On After Turner Criticizes Landon's Apology

AZFamily news website:
Uproar Over He Said / She Said Controversy

Fox 10 Phoenix News:
The Dangers of Doxxing: Online Harassment
Leads to Home Invasion

Wired:
The #MeToo Movement VS #NotAllMen in
New Gamergate Match-up

Los Angeles Times:
Interviews Gone Wrong: Gaming Wunderkind v.
Up-and-Coming Journalist Leads to Death Threats

MSNBC:
Online Harassment Leads to New Gamergate

Good Morning America:
Meet Aria Turner, the Journalist
Fighting Back Against Online Harassment

Arizona Republic:
Local Journalist Featured on Rachel Maddow

The headlines went on and on. Gabriel scrolled through them, not breathing. The cells in his body had stopped respirating. Quarks and muons and electrons and whatever else simply stopped moving. His vision blurred and a high-pitched buzzing started up in his ears. He wondered if this was what a heart attack felt like. Maybe his brain was on fire. How could he not have known? Why didn't anyone tell him? How? Why? *What the hell had he done?*

Without thinking, he reached for his phone and texted Callie. *You home?*

Callie: *Where else would I be? Lab is closed till we get covid protocols in place*

Gabriel: *Can I come over? I need to talk*

Callie: *Sure. What's up?*

Gabriel: *Talk soon…I don't have a mask.*

Callie: **sigh* I hate this damn virus. We've got extra masks but the chances of any of us being exposed are still really low. Come on over*

Cutting across campus from Amsterdam to Claremont, it wasn't even a fifteen-minute walk to Callie's apartment. She lived with her girlfriend, Sylvie Batista, also an assistant professor, in a pre-war building reserved for faculty, staff, and postdocs. The two had met in their first year at Columbia and had been together ever since. The way they told the story of their 'meet cute,' as they called it, they'd both been hurrying across campus, neither one looking where they were going, when they each walked around a hedge from opposite directions and slammed into each other. After all the apologies and the gathering up of books and papers and cellphones and laughing at the awkwardness of it all, they'd decided to meet later for coffee and the rest was history.

Callie was tall and like Gabriel, muscular, a natural athlete. Like their mother and grandmother before them. Pioneers. Built like they could drive the wagon train west, plow a field, and wrangle a herd of recalcitrant cattle all before breakfast. And then there was Sylvie. She had the face and physique of a Dominican cherub, huggable, sweet, wide-eyed and innocent-looking with a mouth that could out-swear a boat full of Barbary Coast pirates and a penchant for wearing colors so bright they could damage the retina.

Gabriel had liked Sylvie from the start, but he'd had to work to win her over because, of course, she'd heard of him. She'd been a big online supporter of Aria Turner and her fight against online harassment and even though he and Callie had declared a wary détente when Grandma Jack had finally passed, Sylvie was skeptical. He'd taken both women out apartment hunting with him when he'd come out in October and had done his best to charm them both, including taking them both out to dinner on his new expense account every night he'd been in town. It didn't work. You're too handsome for your own damn good, pretty boy, she told him. Don't go adding charm to the package. You're barking up the wrong tree on that score. But eventually she'd come around, and now Gabriel hoped she was home too. He needed her perspective.

He pushed the buzzer and waited. Pushed it again.

"Impatient much?" Callie's voice sounded tinny through the speaker. "Come on up." The lock clicked open, and Gabriel marched up to the third-floor apartment like a man who'd already pled guilty and was eager to get on to the sentencing.

Once inside, he typed in his phone's passcode and held it for Callie to see the Google search results.

She drew in a breath and pulled out a chair. "That's brutal. Reality is a bitch, as they say."

"You know what else they say? Ignorance is bliss."

"Did you do the search just now?" She looked him up and down. "On your run?"

"Yeah, but I couldn't run." He gestured at his face. "Turns out pounding the pavement still gives me a headache, so I took a long walk." He sank into another chair at their small kitchen table. "Shit, Callie, why didn't you tell me?"

She coughed out a laugh and shook her head at him. "Are you serious? I did try to tell you. In fact, I wasted a considerable amount of lung capacity yelling at you to listen to me. All to no avail, I might add. You kind of shut down, went all turtle-like. Withdraw into your shell and ignore the world, that's always been your way of dealing with stress. You were too angry, too embarrassed and, if I could venture a guess, too heartbroken to listen."

The bedroom door swung open, and Sylvie appeared in faded jeans, an NYU T-shirt, and a flowered towel wrapped around her head like the colorful turban of a Caribbean calypso queen. A short, very curvaceous queen with a spray of freckles and light hazel eyes that stood out against brown skin and seemed to change colors with what she was wearing. "Wow," Sylvie said, taking in the fading bruise of Gabriel's shiner. "Callie showed me the pic you sent of your face, but in real life you still look like certifiable shit."

"Yeah, I know." He touched his lump." It's been a week, and it still hurts like the devil. But I'll live."

"You've been taking it easy, right? Odds are you had a mild concussion," Sylvie said, pulling out a chair and joining them at the small kitchen table. "So, who are we talking about? Who's too heartbroken to listen to what?"

"Me, apparently." Gabriel said with a scowl. "Or at least I was. Also, I was a heartless idiot."

Sylvie wasn't shy about anything. And now, she looked at Gabriel with a mixture of sympathy, pity, and understanding. "Not surprising. Most men are. But what are you not listening to?" Gabriel slid his phone toward her. "Ouch." Sylvie looked up at him. "Honestly, I didn't believe Callie when she insisted that you didn't follow the controversy and that you hadn't been Internet stalking Aria Turner all this time. I won't lie. I would've stalked. Well, maybe not stalked, but at least peeked now and again. Like at least once a day."

"I guess my attorney scaring the bejeezus out of me with talk of restraining orders and my investors telling me to walk away or lose any chance at future funding kept me from peeking. And besides—" He leaned back and stared at the ceiling.

"Besides what?" Callie asked, her voice soft as if she knew what was coming.

"Jesus. I don't know. I really liked her, and it all went south so fast, and I was just so fucking humiliated that I wanted to crawl under a rock and never come out again. Then there was Grandma Jack's cancer, and the business of managing her treatments and hospice and her memorial service and selling the property and then just trying to salvage something of my dignity and get to work again. I told myself not to think about her, so I didn't."

Sylvie raised a skeptical brow at him and drummed her lacquered nails on the tabletop.

"Okay, okay. I thought about her all the time, but I didn't bother her. I didn't online stalk her. I didn't set up a Google alert for her name—or mine."

"But you thought about it?" Callie said.

"Of course, I thought about it." For Christ's sake, he'd thought about it half a dozen times every damn day. "I wanted to make sure she was okay, but she'd made it crystal clear what she thought of me, that she never wanted to hear from me again, and I may be a lot of things, but I am not a masochist or a glutton for punishment. And after I shut down all my social media accounts…" He shrugged.

"So, you truly never knew what happened to Aria?" Sylvie asked, still skeptical.

He shook his head. "Callie must have told you Grandma Jack never owned a television. Of course, I had my computer and phone, but I was, I don't know, so goddamn fucking embarrassed. I mean, how many people want strangers analyzing and dissecting their failed love life?"

"So your fragile ego stood in the way of you following the news about the asshole who broke into Aria's apartment and left a giant turd on her dining room table?"

"What the fuck? No. Seriously? Was he arrested? Charged? What?"

"Not arrested. Not charged. He wore a ski mask. I don't even think he was ever identified."

Gabriel pinched the bridge of his nose. "Holy hell."

Callie leaned back in her chair. "And you didn't know that someone let the air out of her tires, repeatedly. Spray painted some really lovely poetry on her car. And someone broke into her place and stole her cat."

Gabriel shot to his feet. "Frederica?"

Callie cast a quick glance at Sylvie and they both watched Gabriel pace back and forth in the tiny kitchen. "I don't know what the cat's name was," she said, "but she was found all the way out in Gilbert. Apparently the catnapper took her home and then just dumped her on the side of the highway."

"The damn thing is hairless! How could she survive? What kind of person does that?" Gabriel's hands clutched at his head as if trying to keep it from spinning off his shoulders and bouncing off the kitchen cabinets like a loose basketball.

"It was summer, remember?" Callie said. "And someone found her right away and took her to the ASPCA. She was chipped so Aria was able to retrieve her the next day. It was all covered on the news."

"Jesus."

Sylvie pursed her lips and gave him a skeptical look. "You seriously never knew any of this?"

"I knew she was out there talking about what was going on. I even heard her announced as a guest on NPR, but I didn't listen to the interview. I actively avoided knowing anything specific about Aria Turner."

"Whether or not you were tuned in, everyone else was paying attention," Callie said. "For a while you even had a few of your own Twitter hashtags. #GabrielsNoAngel. #ArchangelActsLikeDevil. #ArchasshatGabriel were particularly creative."

"The story was everywhere." Sylvie added. "We talked about it at length in one of my graduate seminars at NYU. Your crew managed to rile up the #MeToo movement and the #CatsArePeopleToo activists."

"It wasn't my crew. Not after I left."

"It was your crew right up until shit hit the fan," Callie said. "You loved the attention until it stopped being flattering."

"No one wants that kind of attention."

Sylvie smirked. "I imagine that's one thing you and Aria Turner can agree on."

"With my reputation as a first-class, misogynistic ass following me everywhere, it's a miracle I was able to get any backers at all for Q.BC."

Sylvie waved that comment away with a dismissive snort. "Capitalists like your buddies at Diamondback Ventures would take you on no matter what. They're a bunch of arrogant white men who made their millions off mining and ranching and stealing land and mineral rights from Indigenous People. They were probably more concerned with you keeping a low profile for a while than with anything you actually did or didn't do. Besides, they're not idiots. They're ruthless about making money and know a good bet when they see one. Despite the fact that you can be a clueless manchild, you are something of a brainiac."

"I don't feel like a brainiac, that's for sure. And I would counter with #NotAllMen, but I guess that'd be the wrong thing to say about now."

"See? Brainiac." His sister waved a hand at him as if his physical presence proved her point.

Gabriel rubbed the back of his neck. "This is a nightmare."

"It was a nightmare," Sylvie pointed out. "For Aria."

"Look," Callie said, "I know you're having a bit of a 'come to Jesus' moment, but let's keep this in perspective. I know the whole incident wasn't a walk in the park for you, but you were able to step away while Aria had to face it. It was brutal. Yes, she was able to leverage the disaster into a good thing for her career, but being on *Good Morning America* or *Rachel Maddow* doesn't translate into feeling safe in your own home. Or being able to walk out the door without fear. Your Work Hard/Play Hard crew and your hundreds of thousands of juvenile cavemen followers made it their business to make her life miserable because they thought they were defending your honor and standing up for men everywhere by attacking a woman who'd done nothing more than call you out on an ill-conceived come-on. Once you'd demeaned her professionalism by talking about how she had her legs around your waist and was practically humping you in a public parking lot only to turn down your offer of a one-night stand, she was toast. Your team of troglodytes crawled out of the subreddit muck, jumped into action, and the whole thing took on a life of its own."

"I swear I didn't say all those things. Or at least not in the way it was characterized. And I apologized, dammit!"

"Your apology was for shit, and you know it."

He sucked in a breath and let it out slowly. "My attorney wrote it. Wouldn't let me change a word."

Callie shook her head at her brother. "The only good thing your attorney did was tell you to shut up and stay away from her. It probably saved your career. But, Gabriel, think about it. He wasn't your attorney. He was the company's attorney and everything he did was for the company, to save—or enhance—the brand. Not to save you. And certainly not to protect Aria. Hell, I've told Sylvie a thousand times that I think Seven Wonders Gaming profited from the whole mess. Whether you wanted to or not, you became the smart, sexy poster boy for incel assholes everywhere thinking that if Gabriel Landon can get shot down by a woman, how can they expect to get any action? If a man who looked like you look was sexually frustrated, they could sit in the dark in their mama's basements and beat off knowing they weren't alone. You were one of them."

"Fuck."

"Let me ask you this," Sylvie cut in. "What prompted you to do the Google search today?"

Gabriel sunk back into his chair. "She called me insane, obtuse, and clueless. She thinks I know what happened, but that I don't care. That it doesn't mean anything to me. That I have 'no idea' what she went through. And she's right." He rubbed his hands down his face and turned to his sister. "Jesus, no wonder you wouldn't speak to me."

Callie studied her brother for a moment. "There's no question you were arrogant and entitled." She turned to Sylvia, "I can't believe I'm about to say this out loud, but—" she turned back to Gabriel— "you didn't do any of the shit your fan boys did. You didn't post her address online. You didn't stalk her or break into her house or steal her cat or let the air out of her tires or pile on to all her social media accounts to send her death threats or go down to Sedona and harass women shopping at her mother's bookstore."

Gabriel groaned and dug his knuckles into his temples as if trying to drill holes in his skull.

"You met a woman you were attracted to," Callie went on. "By your account—and hers—she was attracted to you too. And then you took it too far. Came on too strong. And when she told you no, you whined to your houseful of dudebro idiots like a toddler who'd had his favorite toy snatched away."

"It's classic misogynistic manchild behavior," Sylvie cut in, "to expect a woman to put out just because you buy her dinner."

"That's not how—" Gabriel started to cut in, but Callie put a hand up to stop him.

"Doesn't matter if she was into you one minute and then changed her mind the next because it's the 'no' that counts. And it's not an excuse for what happened next because no matter what everyone told you, you probably could have done more to stop it."

"But I was told—" Again, Callie held up her hand.

"I know what your lawyers told you. We're just trying to get you to understand how the rest of the world saw it all unfold. The bottom line is that other than whining like a baby about getting rejected by a beautiful woman, you weren't the one who turned her into a cause célèbre. You weren't the one who went online and dragged Aria Turner over the coals, but you also weren't the one who stepped up to stop the pile on. No one stepped up except Aria."

"And a virtual army of women who took to social media to back her up," Sylvie added.

"Your idiot intern took all the credit for doxing Aria and for egging on the fan boys, with your partners' encouragement. The little shit was proud of it, and he made the podcast and subreddit rounds bragging about it. You may be interested to know he works for FOX News now."

"I didn't want to hire him in the first place," Gabriel groused. "He wasn't the most qualified, but he'd been an avid gamer and was a senior at ASU who was basically willing to work for booze and access to the pool and the parties."

Callie rolled her eyes. "Point is the damage was done but most of it was done by others. Not you. You just didn't do anything to stop it."

"The whole world agrees you fucked up," Sylvie added. "And neutrality may be a legal defense, but it's not an ethical one. But all that was in the past. The question is what do you want to do now? What do you want from Aria Turner? What do you want to do about this implausible serendipitous situation the universe has given you? Do you want to try to make the situation work as platonic roommates? Do you want a second chance with her? Are you still attracted to her?"

He placed both hands on his face and then looked at the two women through his fingers, like a little boy hiding his eyes while watching a scary scene in a movie. "What do you think?" He dropped his hands to the table. "Of course, I'm still attracted to her. It's like…it's like…I don't know. I don't want to sound trite, but it's almost—" he shrugged and turned a deep red from the collar of his shirt to his hairline—"incendiary. I feel like my skin's on fire when she walks into the room."

Sylvie smiled and glanced at Callie. "You've got it bad."

Gabriel groaned and put his head down on the table.

Sylvie slapped a palm on the table and made him jump. "I know what you need!"

"What?" His voice was very nearly plaintive.

"A grand gesture. Something that turns a hollow apology from mere words into something real in the world. Something that proves you're not who she thinks you are."

He opened one eye and peered at her. "What kind of grand gesture?"

"I don't know. How about a big donation to a foundation that studies online bullying? Or start supporting a halfway house for abused women? You've got plenty of money right now and you're a clever guy, think of something truly impressive that will make a difference in the world. A difference for women like Aria."

He sat up and rubbed his temples, nodding. "Hmm…a grand gesture. Wouldn't that be like me trying to buy her affection? Let me think. Surely there's something. I don't want to have to bunk on your couch if she kicks me out."

"Yeah, that's not gonna happen," Callie said with a laugh. "One thing's for sure, though, it is a sweet co-op and you're going to be hard pressed to find something that nice now. Especially with the virus and shutdowns looming."

Gabriel ran a hand through his hair. He needed to marshal his thoughts. It was obvious that what had happened to Aria was way more serious than he'd known, but what was happening right now was serious too. He needed to be thinking of how Covid-19 was going to affect his business—both Q.BC and Seven Wonders Gaming, even though his ownership share was tiny now—instead of pining away for a woman who, justifiably, hated him.

"I need to keep everything in perspective," he said. "This is a bizarre situation with Aria, but this virus is next level. I can't stop thinking about all those kids having to go back home to live when they should be having the time of their lives on campus. And what about those kids who have no place to go? What about foreign students?" He didn't want to contemplate moving again, but at least he would have a choice.

"There'll be a limited amount of housing available for foreign students and those with nowhere to go," Sylvie said. "The university isn't going to toss them out in the street."

Gabriel looked at the two women, the two most important people in his life, and knew with certainty that they would not toss him out on the street—even if they joked about it. They were his only family. He trusted them. Could be honest with them. But he didn't know how to answer Sylvie's question about Aria. What did he want? When it came to Aria Turner, sorting out what he wanted and how he felt seemed overwhelmingly complicated. "You asked what I wanted to do about Aria, and the answer is I don't know. I mean I know I don't want to move again, but…"

Callie and Sylvie glanced at each other, and a pang hit Gabriel in the ribs, somewhere in the vicinity of his heart. How could two such different people love each other so deeply. What did it even mean, love? Was it something you fell into? Something that hit you over the head or that you slammed into when you weren't looking where you were going? Was it something you could deny? Ignore? Fall out of? What had he felt the moment Aria Turner had walked into that conference room three years ago? Simple attraction? Animal lust? Something deeper? Something more? He and Aria were different. But so were Callie and Sylvie. Could there be a reconciliation? A second chance? Did he want to expend the energy to find out? What would it take to even try? What would he have to do to convince Aria to start all over? As if they'd never met? Or, as if he'd never gone home and whined to his buddies about how she'd rejected him?

"I don't know what I want." He said again, as if to convince himself.

"You sure?" Sylvie said, her voice calm, soothing. "I think you know exactly what you want."

The damn woman had him cornered. And now, she had trotted out her counseling voice. He couldn't go up against that and win. Not right now. So, he swerved. "Got any beer?"

Callie stood, but he stopped her. He went to the fridge, pulled out three cold ones, popped the tops, and set them on the table.

"I think I'm doing a helluva job avoiding answering Sylvie's question, don't you? But If you two smarty pants know the answer, why do you need me to say it out loud?"

"Because you need to own it," Sylvie said. "If you want a second chance, you need to at least admit it to yourself."

He gave her a crooked smile and raised an eyebrow at her. "And to my nosy counselor?"

"If you were my client, you'd be paying me instead of me feeding you."

"You feeding me? What're we having?"

Sylvie snorted. "Your sister and I were planning on ordering Thai."

"Perfect. I'll buy as long as you let me hang out here a while." He pulled his phone back toward him, the list of headlines still staring at him. "I think I need to catch up on my reading. And do some grand gesture brainstorming."

ELEVEN

I T WAS AFTER NINE when Aria heard the key in the lock and the door swing open. It was after nine and she'd been furious for a full three hours. She knew perfectly well she didn't have any right to be angry and he didn't owe her an explanation for where he'd been. Besides, she'd be happy if she never set eyes on him again, anyway.

After admitting to herself that he wasn't coming home to eat, she'd left his serving on his plate and plopped down in front of the television to eat and watch the news by herself. It was beyond sad, both the news and the fact that she felt so alone. And disappointed. And, stupidly, a little heartbroken all over again. Just like she'd felt three years ago when she thought she'd found someone special only to discover he was just like every other idiot she'd gotten messed up with.

Actually, it all was worse than that. The personal stuff was pathetic enough, but then there was the global disaster piled on top of petty grievance. More cases of Covid-19 recorded around the world. Things going from bad to worse in Europe and who the hell knew what was happening in China. Lockdowns multiplying. Death rates skyrocketing. She felt almost claustrophobic, like the world was closing in on her and she couldn't breathe.

She reached for her phone and called her mom in Sedona. All was well, so far, and the Covid precautions she was making hadn't taken a toll on bookstore sales—yet. Then she called Izzy, her best friend from high school, now married with three little ones, a rugged fire jumper for a husband, and a job as a nurse in a hospital in Albuquerque. As usual, they gossiped about friends and reminisced about sleepovers, sewing clothes for their Barbies on Vi's sewing machine, painting each other's nails, and hanging out together in her expansive backyard with the red rocks of Sedona watching over them. When the conversation turned to Covid, Izzy admitted she was scared. So far, it wasn't too bad at the hospital, she said, but they were preparing for the worst.

Next Aria texted with a couple of journalist friends from Columbia to see if they were covering Covid-19. And she called Miles, her buddy in London, and they'd talked about his on-again-off-again relationship with a gorgeous guy who happened to be an expert on the Elgin Marbles and who had invited Miles to go to Athens with him to see the Parthenon. But the virus canceled their plans. "Covid's fucking everything up," Miles had lamented, "but at least George and I are still fucking."

Leave it to Miles to put a positive spin on disaster. Unfortunately, as a glass-half-empty kind of girl, Aria was not one to put a positive spin on anything and the longer

Gabriel fucking Landon's lasagna sat on his plate—salad wilting and garlic bread hardening—the angrier she got.

She suddenly realized she hadn't mentioned Gabriel to Miles, Izzy, or her mother. Why? Did she think it would dredge up too much of the past? That her mother would go crazy worrying that she'd be in danger if she was alone with him? That Izzy would hop on a flight to New York just to punch the asshole in the nose? That Miles would…? Well, Miles would want pictures. He thought Gabriel was hot. H. O. T. Hot! That was how he'd put it when she'd shown him the "30 Under 30" magazine cover.

She heard the door close. She tensed up. She should get up, march down the hall right past Gabriel, and slam her bedroom door in his face. No. Bad idea. She was not a child and behavior like that was beneath her. It might make her feel good in the moment, but it would prove nothing. *Why did she feel like she needed to prove anything, anyway?* Besides if Gabriel was as clueless as he appeared to be, the gesture would go right over his head. He'd been hailed as a tech genius, but that didn't mean he wasn't a human idiot. So, with her back to the dining room table, she remained in place on the sofa and focused on the television even as she heard him—or rather felt him—walk in the room.

"Hey, I…*oh*."

Gabriel stopped and looked down at the dining room table. He didn't know what to think. He saw a glass of wine on the coffee table in front of where Aria sat on the couch, so the wine glass on the table was not hers. Which meant that the food on the table was not hers. And since there was no one else in the room, it must mean that Aria had shared her food with him. She had prepared a plate of lasagna and salad and there was a napkin and silverware and a piece of bread on a small plate and a glass of water and a glass of wine and…*what the hell?*

"I…uh…I was at my sister's place." He swallowed, bit his lip, and went on. "We had dinner, but wow. Is this for me?"

"I made it for my dinner. Figured I'd share. Pay you back for breakfast."

Her answer was clipped. She was angry. Question was, was it you're-late frustration or I-want-to-shove-that-food-down-your-throat-until-you-choke-on-it fury.

"Okay. Wow. It looks amazing. Really. I love lasagna. Who doesn't? Thank you for sharing." Aria still had her back to him, like she didn't even hear him rambling on. "We ate earlier, around six-thirty, so I could eat again. Especially since you went to all this trouble."

Sure, he, Callie, and Sylvie had eaten about twenty pounds of Thai takeout, and he'd had two beers—no make that three—and was stuffed to the gills, but he'd eat this food and drink this wine if he had to cram it down his throat.

He pulled out the chair and sat, picked up the silverware, folded the napkin across his lap, and took a bite of the garlic bread. *Cronch.* It was dry and hard from sitting out for however long, but he swallowed and made the best of it, washing it down with a long drink of now tepid water. The fork clinked against the plate and finally Aria slowly and deliberately picked up her wine glass and turned to face him.

"It's vegetarian. The ground beef is fake meat."

"I didn't know you were vegetarian," he said. "You had chicken that first night."

She gave him a strange look. "Those were tofu tenders."

He stared at her and then laughed. "Seriously? Damn, they were good!"

"You honestly couldn't tell the difference between tofu and chicken? Do you have the palate of a caveman?"

"I was starving and, honestly, a little nauseous. Anything would have tasted delicious. My sister Callie has been vegan, vegetarian, pescatarian, paleo, gluten-free and is now settled on locally-sourced omnivore—unless it's takeout." He took another bite. "All bets are off with takeout. Thai's her go-to. There's a really great Thai place on 111th." He sipped his wine. "This is really good. Seriously. Thank you for cooking. I'm sorry I wasn't here to eat with you earlier." *Why was he babbling?*

"You should microwave the lasagna."

"No, it's good cold." He tried the limp salad. "I should've left a note," he said between bites. "Common roommate courtesy." He took another sip of wine and it dawned on him that he was nervous. "Guess I'm out of practice."

"You don't have to account for where you were," she said, but Gabriel could still hear the edge in her voice. She'd gone out of her way to be nice, and he'd disappeared. Didn't matter that he'd spent the evening trying to wrap his mind around what she'd gone through and getting Callie and Sylvie's perspectives so he could try to come to terms with what he'd done—and not done. What to feel guilty for and what was out of his hands. And what, if anything, he could do about it now. He could only imagine what was going through Aria's mind at this moment. Probably running through a litany of complaints: *Gabriel Landon is a thoughtless bastard. Oblivious. Uncaring. Heartless boor. Selfish oaf. Fucking asshole.*

Aria brought a knee up beneath her, propped an arm on the back of the sofa, and watched him eat. How could such an unmitigated ass look so good eating leftover lasagna at almost nine-thirty when he'd been up since six? Why did she have the urge to run her fingers through that gold and copper hair of his and why was she wondering what it would feel like to smooth her fingers over it and lick that little drop of wine off his lips?

"You don't have to eat it right now, you know," she said. "If you like cold pasta, you could save it for tomorrow. Lunch or something."

"I know, but you went to all this trouble." He smiled and offered a one-shouldered shrug. "And I can always eat."

"Growing boy and all that?"

"Exactly," he said. Seeing her lounge on the couch—wineglass dangling between her fingers, wild curls with those pink tips grazing her shoulders, oversized vee-neck T-shirt exposing an enticing amount of cleavage and a tiny peek of a pink bra—ensured that at least one part of him was growing. At an alarming rate. He shifted in his seat, trying to rearrange his erection without grabbing his crotch. An impossible maneuver.

"So how is your sister?"

"Good." Yes, think about Callie, not Aria. "She and her partner—Sylvie—were talking about the university closure. Sylvie teaches a full load, so all her classes will now be on Zoom. Callie works in a lab, so she probably won't be as affected. But she can't go in until they get safety protocols in place—plastic shields around workspaces, hand sanitizer dispensers, and masking notices. Figure out schedules and how many people can be in the lab at the same time. All that social distancing stuff."

"You said Callie's a dendrochronologist, right?"

"Yeah. She uses tree rings for climate modeling. She's also fascinated by the research this guy out of Arizona is doing on some kind of deep sea mollusk."

"What do deep-sea mollusks have to do with tree rings?"

"Apparently this one kind of mollusk lives for a really long time, and it accumulates ridges on its shell just like trees accumulate rings. The ridges can tell researchers about water temperature, salination, and I don't know, nitrogen saturation maybe? I'm not sure of all the details, but it sounds cool, and she's jumping in with two feet. Working on getting her scuba certification. Well, she was. I hope this virus doesn't screw everything up for her."

"And what about her partner. Sylvie?"

"She's an expert in gender studies and human sexuality." He glanced at her before getting up and carrying his plate, water glass, and silverware into the kitchen. He rinsed everything, stuck it in the dishwasher, and returned for his wine glass. He took it to the kitchen and dumped the last bit into the sink. The last thing he needed was more alcohol. He went back to the living room where he took the spot on the other end of the couch, picking up the conversation. "Sylvie's not shy about sex and relationships, so don't be surprised. Sometimes she just says whatever pops into her mind—or pushes the conversation to be provocative."

"You think I'm a prude? That I can't talk about sex like an adult?"

Oh, God, was he already screwing up this chance at a normal conversation? He shook his head. "No, not at all. It's just a head's up."

"And just when do you suppose I'll meet them if you're moving out soon?" Aria said it almost reflexively. She still meant it, was still convinced he needed to find somewhere else to live.

Gabriel ignored the question. "We were talking about Covid pods."

"Covid pods? What's that?"

"A group of people who agree to see each other exclusively if the city shuts down. So, like we'd be in a little pod of people who could get together without masks and hang out. But whenever any of us had to be around anyone else, we'd have to mask up, be really careful about social distancing, and—" he grinned at her "—scrub ourselves raw with hand sanitizer."

The image of Gabriel Landon naked, slathering every inch of his golden skin with gel almost blinded her. She glanced at the television for a moment, re-gathering her thoughts.

Covid pods. Who would she pick to hang out with during a global pandemic? Certainly not Gabriel Landon. But who? Most of her friends from journalism school had spread out across the globe, taking jobs at major news outlets and television stations. A few, like Miles, had parlayed their Columbia credentials into prominent public relations gigs or had gone to DC to work as press secretaries for their favorite politicians. There was the one guy—Baldridge? Baldur? Balrog?—who'd gone straight to the Wall Street Journal and the perfectly sculpted, bottle-blonde Phoebe

Pilgrim—a.k.a. Phoebe Pablum—who was now at FOX news, a weekend wannabe hoping to replace the morning show bimbos.

What would a shut-down look like? Would they be restricted as to where they could go? Could she still run in the park? How would they get groceries in? Would everything have to be delivered? How would it all work? If it got to the point where interactions with other people were restricted, would it be so terrible if she weren't all alone at home? Would it be horrible meeting Callie and Sylvie and having them in her pod? They sounded like women she'd like to hang out with. She'd even Googled Callie and read about her work in Central America studying the health of trees up in the mountains and how rising temperatures could affect coffee growers. She and Sylvie sounded like very cool people. Which begged the question: Why on earth did they put up with Gabriel?

"Any more news worth knowing before lights out?" Gabriel asked.

His voice was rough. He sounded exhausted and looked even worse than he had that morning. His eye and forehead were still swollen, the skin around the injury now purple and blue and red. She got a headache just looking at him.

"Major League Baseball canceled spring training, and they're postponing the start of the season. Nationwide, cases are up over 1,500 and a bunch of states are closing public schools. Not New York yet, but probably within the next few days. Several districts in Connecticut are closing. A bunch of universities too. Ohio State, University of Hawaii. Alabama. Auburn. Everything will be online."

"Just like Callie and Sylvie said." Gabriel scooted down to lounge on the cushions, toed off his shoes, put his feet on the coffee table and let his head fall back against the couch, his eyes drifting toward the windows and beyond, where city lights glowed against the night sky. "How's that even going to work, though? I mean, remote works for people like you and me, but I keep hearing talk about essential and non-essential workers. Who decides who those people are? They're the ones who're gonna be most at risk."

He paused, shook his head, and Aria spoke up. "Government and corporate emergency management teams have plans and protocols in place for just about everything under the sun. Even pandemics."

He croaked out a hoarse laugh. "That's what they say, sure. But like I said before, the math doesn't look good, so I gotta wonder how extensive these plans are. How much money is involved? And who decides how it's allocated? Just think about it; until there's a vaccine, there's no braking system on this runaway train."

Aria studied his profile. "How bad do you think it can get?"

"1918 Influenza bad? I looked it up yesterday. World-wide, best guess was between 25 and 50 million dead."

"I looked it up too," Aria said with a long sigh. "Five hundred million cases. Surely, we've learned from that, though. We know about social distancing. We know about masking. I've got half a dozen masks that my mom made and sent me. She's been sewing them at home and setting them in a box outside her bookstore since the beginning of February. She operates in a 'just-in-case' mode."

"I got mine from Sylvie. She got a pile of them from a friend at Columbia Presbyterian. Surgical masks and N95s or KN95s. Something like that."

"Mine are cotton. Polka dots, kittens, burros, saguaros. Little elastic bands for your ears."

He smiled and tilted his head to look her way. "Sounds adorable, but Sylvie says the N95s are better. I'll give you some."

"Thanks."

They sat in silence for a long while. His head back against the couch, her wine glass resting loosely in her fingers. It was almost okay, Aria thought. Comfortable. Almost *nice*. Then he spoke again, his voice soft, low. His words slurring slightly.

"I get it's gonna be doctors and nurses. Hospital orderlies and janitors. Folks who keep the subways from flooding. But if all us non-essential people stay home, what about everyone who keeps the whole damn place running? Delivery people? Stocking clerks in grocery stores? Cooks in restaurants offering takeout? I keep thinking about the kids whose parents are essential workers and can't stay home with them when the schools close. Or the people who live paycheck to paycheck and don't have paid time off for sick days or families without high-speed Internet at home. How can parents pay the bills with no income and how can kids keep up with online instruction if they don't have home computers and their broadband is sketchy? And the college students who can't afford to move back home or foreign students who can't fly home to countries with high infection rates? " He heaved out a long sigh. "I close my eyes and all I see is disaster."

Aria held her body still. Dumbfounded. How was it be that Gabriel Landon, the very epitome of egotistical asshole, could articulate or even think things like this? He was the crass, insensitive bastard who had betrayed her, but now he had to go and be all...*sensitive? Thoughtful? Caring?* Damn.

She started to say something and then heard a noise. A soft inhalation. A ruffled breath like a barely-there snore. He was asleep. One hand lay open on his thigh and one rested on the couch cushion, just a foot or so from her knee. Lips barely parted, head tilted slightly. The picture of relaxation. She felt a sharp pain ricochet around her ribcage as she watched him. Afraid to move. Afraid to disturb him. But not afraid to take this opportunity to study him.

How could it be that the man sleeping on her couch tonight was the same man that had unexpectedly captured her heart three years ago and then abandoned it in that Phoenix parking lot to burn and wither in the blazing sun. *Had he changed?* Or had he always been the kind of man who thought about hospital orderlies and janitors, stocking clerks and cashiers, children home alone without good Internet to help them study?

When she'd first met him, she would have said yes, of course he was that kind of man. But after what happened later, she'd doubted he had a single molecule of decency in his entire, admittedly gorgeous, body. What did she think now? Honestly, she had no idea.

Slooowly she stood and picked up the old, crocheted throw folded on the arm of the couch, the one she and her mother had worked on together when she was in middle school and had tried her hand at every sort of craft and sport and club. Carefully, she draped it over his midsection and shoulders. Then she stood back and looked at him. Just looked. As the sharp pain developed into a dull ache and settled like a hot brick just behind her breastbone, she turned away, flicked off the light, and went to bed.

TWELVE

MARCH 14-15

T HE NEXT TWO days passed without incident. Gabriel was up before Aria. Up and gone. Her favorite cup was in the sink, rinsed clean. There was always still plenty of coffee in the pot.

On the 14th, he'd left her a package of black masks and a folded piece of paper sitting beneath the cup she'd been using since he'd commandeered hers. He'd noticed what cup she'd used. He'd taken it out of the dishwasher and put it by the coffee maker for her.

Drawing in a breath, she'd picked it up, set it aside, and unfolded the paper.

Aria-

This note is my attempt at new & improved roommate etiquette. Thank you for loaning me your throw/cover/thingy when I so rudely fell asleep mid-sentence last night. I'm pretty positive I don't snore, but just in case I'm deluded and sounded like a freight train barreling through the building, I apologize.

And I wanted to tell you thanks again for sharing your dinner. And for sharing your cat. Frederica has apparently decided I'm to be her personal heating device. I finally crawled in bed around 1:30 and when I woke at 5, she was wrapped around my head. She is a pillow hog. Evil cat.

I made coffee and used your half and half again. Sorry. I would stop by the store and get more, but you apparently buy it by the gallon, so I'm saving that goodwill gesture for when we're running low. Also, if you go out, wear one of the masks I left you. According to Sylvie, these are better than the fabric ones.

Anyway, I'm going downtown for couple of interviews. Maybe I'll snag my first employee today. We're meeting early to avoid as many people as possible. And we've all agreed to mask up. Don't know when I'll be back. If no one else goes into the office, I may work there today. Lots to do when you're a tech tycoon! Haha.

- GL

p.s. Also, my number is 928.363.4002. Text me if you want me to pick anything up from the store—even more half and half.

She set the note down carefully and poured herself a cup of coffee. Then she opened the fridge and pulled out the half and half. He was right. It was a giant carton. She stirred a good dose into her mug and then put the carton away. Carefully. Deliberately. After drinking three quarters of a bottle of a Willamette Valley Pinot Noir last night, Aria was still processing how to perform tasks in an upright position while Gabriel had apparently dressed, had coffee, written her a note with several whole sentences in it. Sentences that made sense and were contrite and that made that pang behind her ribcage wake up and make itself known. And then he had left. After having folded said note and positioned it so she'd see it first thing. And he'd given her his phone number.

Then, that night he'd come in after eight, saying he'd already had dinner. He'd stood in the kitchen guzzling a glass of water and then had said good night and gone back to his room and closed the door while she spent the evening watching the news, worrying about Covid-19 taking over the world, and wondering what he was doing. She didn't know how to process it. So, she didn't.

And this morning, he'd left her another note beside the coffeemaker. Again, slipped under the coffee cup she'd used on the first morning in the co-op together.

Aria,

I'm headed back downtown again today. We're conducting a couple of follow-up interviews and a Q.BC strategy session. Trying to get some face-to-face (masked) work done before everything shuts down... since it looks like that might be inevitable and sooner rather than later. And since it's Saturday, the office should be empty.

p.s. If you don't have dinner plans, maybe I could bring home takeout. Or pay you back and cook.

p.s.s. Remember, you have my number if you need me to pick anything up on the way home.

—GL

Home. The way he bandied that word about made her crazy. She took her coffee out to the front room and stared out the window. Gabriel Landon is out there right now and I'm here and I don't know how I feel about anything. And, in a few hours, he'll return and what will I do then?

What did it mean? *Why should it mean anything?* For the time being, they were temporary roommates. Notes were what roommates did. That was all. Nothing more. She had no interest in more of anything with him.

She squared her shoulders and marched herself into the study to get right to work reviewing the page proofs of her book. First, she Googled *Q.BC*. She found a story in *Forbes* and another in *Fast Company* about Diamondback Ventures going all in on private blockchain technologies and that Q.BC, a start-up out of Flagstaff, was a new part of their portfolio. But neither story mentioned Gabriel. Had he only come on board recently? No, he said he was the founder. It didn't make sense that he wasn't referenced. Instead, the story was all about one of the Diamondback partners, Brian Johannsen, and the direction he was taking the investment fund. Strange.

Gabriel. What was he up to right now? She wasn't going to text him to find out. And he didn't have her number, so he couldn't text her. Besides, he was probably busy. Hiring staff and making plans. Sitting in an office in some of the most expensive real estate in Manhattan. He was a tech tycoon, after all. Ha.

Well, she was busy too.

Reviewing page proofs of her book. A book that she had an actual agent for and an editor and a contract with a publication date. A date which was now only seven months away. October 6. Soon her book would be out of her hands and to the printer. She still had time, but it didn't matter, the deadline for getting the markup back to her editor made her nervous. Somedays it felt like it was looooming over her.

She'd always wanted to be a writer, a journalist. When she was little, she'd walk around her mom's bookstore with a notebook and a pencil and interview customers. Of course, everyone indulged her, and she met people from all over the world. Sedona was a magnet for idiosyncratic people. Then she'd write up little stories about how they ended up in Sedona and sometimes those stories spun into wild tales that had nothing whatsoever to do with the who, what, when, where, why of journalism. Her mother would read each story, hug her tight, and tell her she had stories and books in her blood.

After reading the *Diary of Anne Frank* in middle school, she'd become obsessed with World War II and had devoured everything she could get her hands on. Several years later, after staying up night after night, eyes red from crying, to finish the epic Pulitzer Prize-winning novel titled, simply, *The Choice*, her mother finally sat her down and told her that the author, a man named J. Rogers Caldwell, was her father.

She'd been fifteen.

She had a father.

He wasn't dead.

He was very much alive, and he was a famous writer. A literary lion. It hadn't been a fun evening. Or week. Or month.

Her mother had lied to her and her only excuse had been that she didn't want Caldwell to have the chance to mess her up, to reject or hurt her, until she was old enough to deal with it. Her father, in contrast, had never lied to her, but that was only because he had never bothered to reach out to her even though her mother gave him regular updates on her life. He'd simply neglected her. Rejected her.

She felt the betrayal of both parents on a cellular level, and that betrayal had become the lens through which she saw the world. Through which she saw her role as a journalist. No more flights of fancy involving tourists who'd traveled from Timbuktu to Sedona on dirigibles or who were famous jewel thieves on the lam, hiding from Interpol.

Now she wanted to understand why people did what they did, told the lies they told, betrayed the people they betrayed, and she wanted to back up those stories with as many cold hard facts as she could dig up. Her relationship with her parents was filtered through this lens. And the disaster with Gabriel Landon—piled on top of her previous experiences with men, especially that one time she'd been made a fool of in eighth grade, the incident she'd never told a single, solitary soul about, except her therapist and she didn't count—had just reinforced all her worst fears. *Don't take anyone at their word. Don't trust anyone. Even people you think are good friends can have secret agendas.*

What was Gabriel's secret agenda? And why did her thoughts always seem to slither back to him? Damn thoughts.

She refused to spend her day focused on her soon-to-be-gone roommate. Instead, she turned back to her book. She'd interviewed over fifty women and had spent the last three years accumulating transcripts of emails,

Reddit posts, and Twitter death threats, rape threats, and run-of-the-mill sexual harassment posts. The narrative she'd woven laid bare the risks women took in just being online and the dangerous and often blatantly criminal things men got away with saying or posting with few or no repercussions. And, although the book wasn't a chronicle of her own experience in the eighth level of social media hell, the Gabriel Landon experience was the foundation upon which everything else was layered.

Now she was living with him. Or, rather, imprisoned with him. And every time she caught a glimpse of him—in the hallway, coming out of his bathroom, in the kitchen, over coffee, watching the news together—she was both angrier at him and…more confused by him. So now, she was thinking about him again.

Shit.

A news alert popped up on her phone. More Covid-19 cases. Cities locking down. Closing schools. Sending university students home. She was a journalist and should get out of her own head and back into the real world. She cleared her throat and closed her browser.

Focused.

Time to get back to her book.

THIRTEEN

OUT OF ALL THE RESUMES Gabriel combed through, and all the preliminary phone interviews they'd completed, they'd picked three candidates to bring in to talk to face-to-face. All three had been more than qualified, and all three understood what Gabriel and Diamondback were trying to create.

To start, they needed a chief technology officer, a chief marketing officer, and a business development officer. The chief financial officer, a partner in Diamondback Ventures, was already on board, and Gabriel had already completed the basics of the programming. He'd been working on that part since he'd spent time sitting in the hospital with Grandma Jack while dangerous chemo cocktails coursed through her veins to try to keep her alive. Of course, they'd have to hire more programmers as they grew, but for now, they needed the corporate structure in place.

They had a product. They had the financial backing needed to make a splash in the marketplace. Now, they needed to look like a company. Luckily, they'd found candidates who would help do exactly that. But unlike his first company, these weren't college buddies out to grab onto a good thing. These were grown-up professionals who would not post juvenile shit about his love life on social media.

He felt good. Ready to celebrate. If it weren't for Covid, he'd invite Callie and Sylvie out to dinner. He'd include Aria in the invitation too. Just to see what she'd say.

But since that wasn't a possibility, it was either delivery or cooking. Maybe since he'd made breakfast and then Aria had made dinner, and he'd eaten with the Diamondback team last night, some good old-fashioned delivery would be a good option. He let himself into the co-op, hung his coat on the peg, dropped his keys in the wooden bowl on the damned marble table that had brained and maimed him, and went to tap on the door to Aria's study.

"Hold on a sec," Aria called out. A moment later, "Okay, it's open."

Gabriel pushed the door open but didn't step inside. He crossed his arms and leaned against the door frame, looking around the room at the over-stuffed bookshelves that seemed to sag in the middle like a swayback horse and the cushy little leather couch and chair set, and the thick oriental rug that looked like it could hang on the wall of a museum. It felt as if he hadn't seen the room in ages. It'd been two days. Aria sat behind the desk looking like a vision. Well, a vision in a hoodie sweatshirt and a bandanna headband, with her curls spilling out to frame her face.

"So, I had a very productive day," he said, "and thought I'd celebrate by getting delivery for dinner. My treat. Does that sound okay to you?"

Her brows drew together. "How do you know I don't have other plans?"

A muscle in his jaw clenched. "Do you?"

"No. But don't think you owe me dinner just because I shared my food with you the other night."

Stubborn. She wasn't going to give him an inch. But that was okay. As he'd been in interviews and meetings all day about building his second company—about getting a second chance to pursue his dreams—he'd also been thinking about Sylvie's questions: *What do you want from Aria Turner? What do you want to do about this serendipitous situation the universe has given you?* And he'd decided he knew the answer. He wanted a second chance with Aria Turner too.

He wanted to show this woman, who had knocked him sideways when he'd first laid eyes on her, that he was not an unmitigated asshole. Not just because his ego had been bruised (make that demolished) because she'd rejected his advances or because he'd been embarrassed on a national stage (with his name and reputation dragged through the mud), but because he really liked her. He wanted to know her. And he wanted her to know him. The real Gabriel Landon. Today's Gabriel Landon. Exactly how much he wanted that worried him a bit, but he wasn't going to examine that right now. He just wanted to spend some time with her on neutral territory. No finger pointing or playing the blame game—which he knew with absolute certainty he would lose anyway. Just dinner. Just conversation.

"It's not payback," he said. "It's a celebration. I just hired my first employees. If it weren't for this virus, I'd take Callie and Sylvie out on the town." He flashed her a crooked grin. "I'd even invite you. But…" He shrugged. "How about delivery instead?" He checked his watch. It's almost five, and I'm already starving. What'd ya say?"

Aria closed her laptop and considered him. He could almost hear the warning klaxon going off in her head: Attention! Do not be fooled by the charming but egotistical jerk standing in your doorway. She pushed back her chair and stood. "Since my calendar happens to be open for the evening, delivery is fine. You said you had Thai the other night at your sister's place. How about Ethiopian?"

He couldn't help letting go and unleashing a full on, face-splitting smile at that. "Excellent! I love Ethiopian!" Grandma Jack, as open to new experiences as anyone he'd ever met, thought the bread felt a bit too much like a damp washcloth, but she'd always relented when he and Callie begged. "Do you have a favorite place?"

He looked up when she didn't say anything. Honestly, she looked a bit sick. Or stunned. Maybe he was trying too hard. She gave her head a little shake and then said, "Let's try the Red Sea. I haven't been there in a while, but it was great the last time I went."

Gabriel already had his phone out, searching Yelp. "Here it is. Oh, God, this looks good." He smiled up at her again. She hadn't moved out from behind her desk. He crossed the room to hand her his phone. "Why don't you pick? Make sure I don't mess up and order something you don't like. Besides, I'll eat anything."

She put her hands up, refusing to take his phone. "I'll look up the menu on my phone. I'll order and you can pay. Deal?"

"Perfect. Here…" He dug in his wallet, pulled out a credit card, and handed it to her. "Use this when you call it in." He retraced his steps back to the hall and slipped into his bedroom, shutting the door behind him. Once inside, he ran both hands through his hair and down over his face. He felt like he'd scored a critical goal in the rematch of Aria Turner v. Gabriel Landon. God, it felt good. Supremely satisfied with himself, he flopped back on his bed and smiled up at the ceiling like a little leaguer who'd just managed to hit the ball over the fence.

FOURTEEN

AS GABRIEL UNLOADED the food containers and arranged the feast on the dining room table, Aria pulled out a corkscrew.

"I hope red's okay." She held up a bottle and turned it so he could see the label. "It's Spanish. A Tempranillo."

"I'm sure it'll be amazing. I don't know that much about wine, but I have had a Tempranillo before. It'll probably go great with Ethiopian food."

She poured two glasses and scooted one toward him.

"Thanks." He held it up in a mock toast. "Now, I have a question. Can we go without having the news on during dinner? Maybe we could even have some music."

"You sure it won't distract you from eating?" Aria quipped. "Or thinking?"

"You're hilarious. As long as it's not so loud it makes my teeth rattle. Maybe some jazz or something."

She cocked her head and looked at him. "Ah. You're looking for background music. Mood music."

She stretched out the double-o so it sounded more like *moooooood* music. So, it sounded, to Gabriel's ears, at least a tiny bit suggestive. Or maybe he was reading into it. Probably reading into it. Still. It made his insides tingle.

"Yeah. We can catch up on all the terrible news later. For now, let's just enjoy dinner."

Aria pulled her phone out of her sweatshirt's front pocket and played with it for a moment. Then, Gabriel looked up, eyes wide, as soft jazz filled the room.

"There are speakers in here?"

"Bluetooth. You didn't know?"

"Obviously not. Very cool." He couldn't help but smile and mentally add *hidden Bluetooth speakers* to his list of reasons why he was not moving out.

Aria took her seat and started in on the food, tearing off a piece of injera and scooping up a helping of chickpeas in red curry sauce. She popped it in her mouth and moaned. "*Mmmm.* So good." She went to wash the curry down with a sip of wine and looked up see Gabriel staring at her, a piece of injera hanging from his fingers.

"You have a problem?" she asked. "Don't you like it?"

He blinked. Cleared his throat "Like it? Yeah. I love it."

"You haven't even tried it yet."

"What?" He looked down at his hand. "Right. Digging in now," he said and went for a serving of tofu, onions, and potatoes in a dark sauce. "Oh, man," he said in between chews. "You're right. This is delicious."

They spent a few moments silently tearing pieces of injera, scooping from various piles—beets and potatoes, collard greens and onions, cabbage and carrots, red lentils, tofu curry, spinach, and more potatoes—and sipping their wine. Music played in the background and the twinkling lights of the city were visible through the tall windows in the living room. It was perfect. He didn't want it to end. Ever.

Gabriel had decided to tell Aria about the night he'd spent at his sister's reading about what happened to her, what she'd gone through after the Gabriel/Aria blowup and to apologize for not knowing before. To *really* apologize for everything that he'd set in motion. But he hadn't figured out how to broach the subject and, truthfully, he didn't want to do it tonight.

They hadn't even had two full weeks under the same roof and already they were able to have a conversation that wasn't laced with acrimony and four-letter words, so tonight was for trying to peacefully co-exist. Like roommates. Friends, even. A slow, careful start in the Gabriel-Aria second-chance re-match. Hopefully start all over in getting to know each other. Pick up where that magical dinner they'd shared three years ago had ended. They could start with things like favorite bands. Favorite colors. Favorite teacher. Books. Movies.

And then she broke the silence. "Where did you go after Phoenix? You sort of fell off the map."

Damn. There went his plan. His first reaction—the asshole reaction—was to say, *I didn't fall. I was pushed. You pushed me off the map.* But he didn't say that. Instead, he said, "I went home. To my grandmother's place. Where Callie and I grew up just outside of Flagstaff."

"You closed all your social media accounts and—"

He snorted out a soft laugh. "On advice of counsel."

"—and never answered your phone. I know a lot of reporters tried to contact you."

I was told to stay out of sight and to make no comments to the press. Attorneys and investors at Seven Wonders Gaming wanted it that way, so I did what I was told."

She frowned. "To protect your company."

"Well, that, yes. And there was that one time I showed up at your editor's office when I knew you were there because I sort of staked out the office parking lot and saw you go in and then security told me to 'remove my person' from the premises and that if I didn't, they would call the police and you and the magazine would get a restraining order." He shrugged. "So, I removed my person. From Phoenix."

Aria drew in a long breath and held it. Then she let it out slowly. "And did what? I was all over the place and no one had any idea what was going on with you. People really couldn't find you."

"Plenty of people knew where I was. My partners and our investors. Our lawyers. My sister. I didn't disappear completely, but the thing is, my grandma, Grandma Jack, was a free spirit. A true old school hippie. Her place wasn't completely off the grid, but it was...grid adjacent. No television. No Internet. Grew her own. Veggies, yes, but"—he mimed taking a hit off a joint.

Aria's eyebrows went up. "Your grandmother?"

He smiled at that. "She wasn't a Norman Rockwell kind of grandmother. She was an artist. A potter and sculptor. Built her own kiln, had her own forge. Sold her stuff at fancy shops all over the Southwest but lived like she'd never left the free love artist commune she'd been part of in the Sixties." Gabriel reached over to pour them both more wine.

"You said you grew up at her place. How did you end up living with her? Or is that too personal?"

He scooped up a serving of spinach and chewed thoughtfully. "Mom was pregnant with me and Callie was three when my dad died. He was a private pilot. Had been a navy pilot and when he got out, he started his own company flying for surveying companies, logging interests, mining groups, and all sorts of other stuff. There was an accident. She taught first grade. Then she got sick. Ovarian cancer. She passed when I was nine. Callie was eleven. So, we went to live with Grandma Jack."

Aria froze, a bite of injera and eggplant halfway to her mouth. "Good God, Gabriel. I had no idea. You never told me this in the interviews."

"It's not something I lead with, you know? Honestly, it's all still a bit raw, even after all these years."

"I'm so sorry. Really." She paused to finish the bite and swallow as Gabriel twirled the wine in his glass. "What was it like living with your grandmother?"

His gaze went inward for a long moment, and then with a tiny shake of his head, he said, "It was okay. Grandma Jack's property, about twenty acres or so on the edge of town, backed up on national forest land. It was beautiful. And she had no rules. No curfew or anything like that. Well, except we had to make the honor roll each marking period or else."

It hadn't been okay at all. It had been devastating and heartbreaking and terrible and frightening. After his mother's funeral, he'd thrown up before school every day for weeks, thinking that he would go home and find Grandma Jack dead of some freak accident—and his imagination conjured up a million scenarios, including the especially gruesome grizzly attack and the exploding kiln—leaving him and Callie orphans. He never told anyone how many times he'd imagined having to drag Grandma Jack's body up into the woods behind her place to bury her so no one would find out she was dead. So, he and Callie could go on pretending to live their weird lives. Grandma Jack hardly ever went into town, and he figured he and Callie could go on catching the bus every morning to school. Callie could figure out how to drive the old truck so they could get groceries, or they'd learn how to order groceries and have them delivered. He figured maybe the school librarian would help since everyone knew that Grandma Jack was eccentric, and the librarian was sweet and kinda pretty and Gabriel had a little bit of a crush on her. Anyway, they'd make it work. They had to. Otherwise, it was the foster care system. There was a kid in his English class in foster care and the guy always looked so sad, beaten down. He wasn't going to allow that to happen to them. And no way, he'd ever allow anyone to separate him from his big sister. He wouldn't survive without her. Back then, he would've rather confronted a grizzly in the woods than go into foster care.

"Or else what?"

"What?"

"What happened when you didn't make the honor roll."

"I don't know. We never found out."

"You made honor roll each marking period?"

"We spent a lot of time in the school library. Always attended an after-school program and took the late bus home. When Callie finally got her license, she drove because I played sports and there was always some sort of practice after school. Callie spent that time in the library or in some club." He shrugged and gave her a half smile, remembering. "Grandma Jack was a complete scatterbrain when it came to anything other than her art. When we first went to live with her, she'd often forget to pick us up and since she hardly ever answered her phone, some teacher or school secretary would have to drive us out to her place. She was hyper focused when she was at her pottery wheel, though. You could strip naked and dance a jig beside her and she'd never even look up."

"Dance a jig. That sounds like something a grandmother would say," Aria said with a smile. "But you're talking about your grandmother in the past tense."

He nodded slowly, wiped his mouth and hands on his napkin. "Turns out that right before…you know"—he gestured between the two of them—"her cancer came back. Both my mom and grandma had the BRCA gene mutation that put them at risk for ovarian and breast cancer. Grandma Jack first had ovarian cancer way back before I was even born. She was in remission for, well, a long time. And then it came roaring back. At first, she didn't tell Callie or me. That really pissed me off. Then, when I called to tell her that, well, that things had taken a turn with my business and I might want to come stay for a while, she said, "Good. I need someone to drive me to chemo.""

Aria choked on her cabbage and potatoes. "That's how she told you?"

"It was a double whammy. All this…and then that." He drew in a long breath. "She didn't even last five months. She tried chemo for a few weeks and then quit. I took care of her in hospice. Then, I took care of her place and all her stuff.

Spent a lot of time at the library working out the idea for Q.BC. Then I sold the place and traveled."

"Where'd you go?"

"Scotland. I backpacked all over. Walked Hadrian's Wall. Orkney. Skye. It's where Grandma Jack's folks were from, and she always said she'd like to see it someday. But she never went, so, I went for her."

Truth was, he'd gone for himself too. To reboot his life. After Grandma Jack died, he'd spent most of his time at the county library reading journal articles on blockchain, writing code, working on his new business plan, and binging on science fiction and fantasy novels. Once he felt like he had a good handle on the business concept—good enough, at least, to go back to his original funders at Diamondback Ventures with the idea—he'd needed a break.

He put Grandma Jack's property on the market and spent six months walking Scotland, trying to imagine the Scots, Vikings, and Picts Grandma Jack claimed she'd descended from. Imagining the Romans making their way north only to be held fast by her people, the barbarians. It was easy to imagine her as a Wild Woman of the North traversing the rolling hills of the lowlands, the jagged mountains of the highlands, or at the prow of a Viking ship. Especially when he slept rough and woke under the same skies that countless other wanderers and adventurers had lived and died under, from time immemorial.

The time out allowed him to think about the path he had traversed too, the rolling hills of academia—which he'd left when his first angel investor wrote him a check—and the jagged mountains of one, Aria Turner. He kept trying to forget her, but no matter who he flirted with or kissed or fucked, he couldn't get her out of his mind. The one-night stands he'd allowed himself provided momentary physical release, but nothing more. The ache he tried to ignore returned as soon as he pulled his pants back on.

Setting the fantasy of a future with Aria aside, he thought about what sort of a life he might make for himself. To prove to himself that one mistake—albeit a big, messy one—didn't define him and didn't have to ruin the rest of his life. And then he'd come home, worked on making peace with Callie, and moved to New York.

"Jesus, Gabriel. I had no idea."

"Why would you. As you said, I went dark. I needed to, I dunno, recalibrate."

"And did you? Recalibrate?"

"I like to think I did," he said with a contemplative nod. "Callie's speaking to me now, so that's some sort of proof of concept."

"She didn't speak to you for a while?"

He barked out a bitter laugh. "Are you kidding? She was on Team Aria all the way. She wouldn't even take my calls at first. Didn't even call me when she put Boomer to sleep. Our old dog. She texted me from the vet in Tucson where she was in grad school. That was cold. To say I was angry is putting it mildly. And we spoke when Grandma Jack passed. And then when I finally settled the estate. But other than that? It was pretty much radio silence for almost two years."

"What about contact with your partners from Seven Wonders?"

"Very little. The board bought me out, all except for two percent."

"And that's why you decided to move to New York to start your new company? To be close to your sister?"

"I needed to make things right with her." He turned toward the living room, as if looking out the windows, across the dark expanse of Morningside Park and Columbia's campus all the way to Callie's place. "She's all I have."

FIFTEEN

MARCH 16

I T WAS AFTER EIGHT when Aria finally dragged herself out of bed the next morning. The sun shone in through her window warming the room. She checked her weather app: partly cloudy with a high of 54. Perfect for a walk to wake up her brain. After coffee.

She'd finally fallen asleep about the time the sun was coming up and she was still groggy. All night, the same words kept going round and round on the little hamster wheel of doom: *She's all I have. She's all I have. She's all I have.* The wheel would not stop spinning, would not stop replaying their dinner conversation. Gabriel's revelations. Father, dead. Mother, dead. Grandmother who didn't provide any structure for the children in her care. Also dead. Who knew if there'd ever been a grandfather in the mix. Free spirits are one thing. Her own mother was a sort of independent free spirit. But she also had rules. Lived by them. Ran her business by them. Raised her daughter by them.

And what had Gabriel and his sister had? A grandmother who built her own kiln, grew her own pot, and who didn't care what her grandchildren did as long as they made the grades.

She brushed her teeth and stared at her reflection in the bathroom mirror, thinking of the first line of Anna Karenina: *Happy families are all alike; every unhappy family is unhappy in its own way.* And what did that mean for fractured families? Injured families. Families with secrets? Nothing good, that was for sure.

She thought of her half-brother. Jeremy. The one she would never know. He probably never knew he had a sister. Maybe she could've helped him. Meant something to him. Loved him. She'd never know because her father—*their* father—was a narcissistic ass and her mother was too busy keeping secrets to 'protect her from disappointment' to even let her know she had a father and a brother out there in the world.

She spit her toothpaste out, rinsed, wished she could rid herself of the taste of disillusionment in the human race.

She pulled on some leggings, an old camisole, and an oversized cardigan and headed to the kitchen for coffee, wondering what Gabriel was doing. After dinner last night, they'd turned on the television to catch the latest news. They were still reporting on the city's first death from the virus, an 82-year-old woman with emphysema in Brooklyn. She'd had a pre-existing condition but still. Hospitalizations were rising all over the country. How many were infected was anyone's guess. There was a debate about whether masks were effective. Could you get the virus from surfaces? Just from breathing it in? How effective was social distancing? And the catalog of potential symptoms kept growing. The scenes from Europe were harrowing. News from closer to home was getting scarier by the day. It was sobering. They were both a bit dazed from dinner to say much.

Eventually, Gabriel said he was going to go take a shower before bed. He disappeared down the hall. She listened for the sound of the shower but couldn't hear anything over the news. Eventually, she'd given up and had gone to bed to stare at her ceiling all night.

Now, she wondered if he'd gone to Diamondback's midtown offices again even though he said he usually worked at home.

She paused at the half open door to his room. He was obviously here. Cursing.

"Motherfucker, did I lose a screw?"

She knocked softly. "Gabriel?"

"Yeah?"

Aria pushed the door open wide to see Gabriel on his knees, patting his pockets.

"Ah, here it is."

He was kneeling beside what looked to be an upside-down desk in the process of being assembled. "What are you doing?"

"People in New York just leave shit on the street for anyone to take. I found this on my run this morning. Apparently, some Columbia student bought a new desk and then abandoned it when they had to go home. I came home, borrowed a screwdriver and a wrench from Manuel and went back for it. And get this; there was a note taped to it. He fished around in his pants pocket, pulled out a folded piece of paper. He handed it to Aria then went back to work on one of the desk legs.

Aria unfolded the note and read aloud.

"Roses are red

violets are blue

I bought this desk new

but Covid-19 sucks

so now it's yours."

Her lips quirked up in a smile. "Obviously not a poetry major."

"Maybe they were a freshman. Not well-versed in iambic pentameter yet." Gabriel smiled up at her and her lungs suddenly seemed to be deprived of air. She was thankful when his attention returned to the desk, and she could avail herself of a good long inhale. But then she realized his room smelled like him. Like his cologne. Or soap. Or maybe he was into candles. She had no idea what it was. Sort of like a pine forest after a rain. Maybe a bit of creosote. A high desert scent. An Arizona scent.

"I'll need to rearrange things a bit in here," he was saying, "but I can get out of the shared space. I don't like having my stuff spread out all over the dining room table and bothering you if you need to be in there."

Even though she knew deep down that he was not moving out, she still surface-level pretended he needed to go. Pretended she wanted him to go. "I seem to remember saying you couldn't stay here and yet you're setting up a workspace like you're planning on sticking around for a while."

"I told you I'm not going anywhere." He looked up at her just long enough for her to feel the intention in his gaze. We're going into on our third week, and we haven't murdered each other yet."

"There's still time."

"You're absolutely right. I have a year's lease."

She let out a long sigh. "Did you make coffee?"

"Not sure how much is left, and it's probably cold. You slept late."

She didn't say she hardly slept at all for thinking about him. "I can heat it up." And she turned and headed for the kitchen thinking that as she stepped into the hallway, she heard him whisper, *In that barely-there top, you can heat up the whole damn place.* She stopped at the threshold and turned around, but he was hard at work tightening a screw, the tiniest smile tugging at the edge of his mouth.

The paper was folded neatly on the island counter. Aria figured Gabriel had already read it, but maybe not. He usually left it in disarray, sections out of order. She heated her coffee in the microwave, added a generous amount of half and half, and sat down to read the front section. After skimming the front page, she let out a long breath and swore softly.

According to the CDC, between 160 million and 214 million people in the U.S. alone could eventually be infected and up to 21 million people could be hospitalized from Covid-19. Over a million people could die. How is that even possible? How could this be happening in the twenty-first century? Weren't plagues for the history books? She reached for her phone and pushed the saved number for Mom.

"Good morning, honey," her mom answered immediately. "How are you?"

"I'm good," she said, then corrected herself. "No. Not good. I'm worried. Just reading the paper this morning about this virus and the numbers are scary as hell. I want to make sure you're okay."

"I'm fine. Wearing my mask every day, everywhere I go. No one is allowed in the store but me, Marilee, and Kathy and they're masking too. We're still doing a good business, but it's all phone or online orders and pick up in the doorway, on the sidewalk. It's not ideal, but I think we'll survive."

"What if it gets so bad that you have to shut your doors? Like in Italy? Can the bookstore weather that kind of hit?"

Her mother coughed. "Sorry. I was eating a scone, and it is dry as a bone." Aria heard her take a drink. She imagined her mother sipping from her favorite *Sedona. Red Rocks are the Best Rocks* mug. Vi had always been a tea drinker with a favorite blend for every time of day and every occasion. "I've got savings, you know," her mother said. "A little nest egg that I've been tending in case I want to take a trip around the world someday. If I need to dip into that, I will. But we'll be fine. Arizona isn't like New York. You're the one I worry about. Especially you being there alone. If the city shuts down, you'll be so isolated. You work alone. You live alone. I worry about you being lonely."

"About that…"

Of course, Gabriel chose that moment to saunter into the kitchen. "I'm going to set up my workstation in my room, and then I've got to go back downtown. Probably be there till late."

Aria turned toward him, phone clamped to her ear.

"Oh!" He put a finger to his lips as if to shush himself. "Sorry," he whispered. "Didn't realize you were on the phone."

"And who is that?" Vi Turner's voice betrayed her eager interest.

"Yeah, I was going tell you. Turns out Caldwell subleased the place while I was supposed to be in London. So, now I have a roommate."

"And…?"

"And he's getting ready to go to work, so I've got to go. I just wanted to check in on you. Okay?"

"Aria."

"Talk to you soon, Mom. Love you." And Aria cut the call.

"So, you're not going to tell your mother who your roommate is?"

"At least I told her I have one. Have you told your sister about this…situation?"

He laughed at that. "Remember our first night? Me texting my sister while we watched the news?"

Aria's eyes widened. "You told her then?"

"She and her partner, Sylvie, wanted to come over and watch the fireworks."

Aria dropped her head in her hands. "Oh, jeez."

"And I've been over to their place since then, remember? That night you made lasagna? I'd been over there all evening. But no need to worry," Gabriel said, heading back to his room. "I told you Callie's #TeamAria all the way and so is Sylvie. I think they're taking bets on how long it will take for you to kick me to the curb."

SIXTEEN

MARCH 17

FREDERICA JUMPED UP on the kitchen island, arranged herself carefully on the morning newspaper, and peered at Gabriel, as immobile as a statute of Bastet, the Egyptian goddess of protection—and pleasure.

"You're not supposed to be up there," Gabriel admonished. In response, she narrowed her cat eyes at him as if to say, *First one up feeds Fred. Don't you know that yet, minion?* Gabriel ignored her and scooped beans into the coffee grinder.

"Get down, Fred," a sleepy voice said. Aria shuffled into the kitchen, rubbing her eyes. You know better."

"You're up early." Gabriel turned to look at her, heart stuttering in his chest as he got a good look at what she was wearing. "It's not yet six," he managed to choke out.

"I went to bed early." Aria smoothed a hand over her hair, still not quite awake. She'd gone to bed before 9:30, because she didn't want Gabriel to think she was waiting up for him. But she'd ended up spending another night tossing and turning, wondering what he was doing. She might as well have stayed up until he got home so she could ask him. Or maybe if she'd been up, he would have volunteered the information. After all, they were having actual conversations these days. "What time did you get in last night?"

"Not long after that. A little after ten."

"You worked at Diamondback's offices all day?"

"The place was as quiet as a sepulcher, so I was able to get a lot done."

Aria scowled. "It's too early for fancy words like that."

Gabriel raised an eyebrow. "And you, a writer."

"Spare me the sarcasm. What's a sepulcher? Is it like a church?"

"It's a tomb. A mausoleum. That kind of thing. In other words, the office was quiet as the grave. No distractions. No one blaring music at airport runway-level decibels."

"That's what noise-canceling headphones are for. But do go on. You were saying how you absolutely live for crypt-like conditions."

His mouth twisted in a smile that said, *Really? Nice try.* "Are you sure English is your first language?"

"You are an absolute delight in the morning."

"One thing Grandma Jack was big on, besides pot and pottery, was reading, and she loved her scary ghost stories, myths, Gothic tales of sinister betrayal and brutal murder. Lots of bodies turning up in spooky sepulchers which totally creeped me out. Anyway, whenever Callie or I didn't know a word, she'd make us look it up in the ginormous Oxford English Dictionary that sat open on a pedestal podium in a corner of the living room. And then she'd make us spell the word and use it in a sentence. Such as: I prefer quiet when I work, but crypt-like conditions are not conducive to productivity because *Tales from the Crypt* scared the bejeezus out of me, and I still haven't recovered."

Aria laughed out loud at that. "Well, that's something we have in common. I was traumatized by the one scene I ever saw of that show, I hate vampires and mummies, and I probably needed therapy after watching *Mars Attacks!*"

"Oh, God, I know. Those brains and big eyes? Yeah. No."

He shuddered and turned back to the coffee grinder, secured the lid, pressed the button, and the kitchen was filled with the *whirr* of blades cutting through beans. He felt good about the rapport they seemed to have this morning. No weird silences. No awkward pauses. No waves of antipathy rolling off her and slamming into him.

He dumped the ground coffee into the filter and filled the water reservoir as Aria fed Frederica and pulled the container of half and half from the fridge, setting it down with a heavy thump on the counter. Gabriel pressed the on switch for the coffee maker and turned to look at Aria.

"So…there's something I've been meaning to talk to you about, but I'm not sure if this is a good time." He looked her up and down then, from her floppy fuzzy slippers and the wine-red velour robe hanging open, belt dragging on the floor behind her like a tail, to barely-there flannel pajama shorts and matching top, an ensemble that looked as if she'd been wearing it since middle school—or at least one or two bra sizes ago. He imagined slipping that robe off her shoulders and pulling her to him, feeling her breasts against his chest…and then mentally shook himself free of the fantasy and said, "Looks like you may not be awake enough for efficient brain function."

"Never too early to learn you're moving out." Aria shot back as she unfolded *The New York Times* on the counter.

He gave her a pitying look followed by a *tsk tsk* of the tongue and a full-wattage smile that made her want to shade her eyes from the intensity.

Instead, she shrugged. "A girl's gotta try."

"Shall I go get you a copy of my lease?"

"Maybe you should attach it to the refrigerator with a magnet, so I don't forget. Or tattoo the signature page on your forehead so I see it every time I look at you."

"And mar my flawless complexion?"

"Ah, beautiful men," Aria said, shaking her head. "Always worried about their looks."

Gabriel's eyes went wide. "You think I'm beautiful?"

"Let me amend that. Vain, arrogant men."

He laughed. "Too late, Aria."

She gave an exasperated sigh, took a seat on one of the kitchen stools, and ran her hand across the fold of the newspaper to smooth it. "Whatever. If it's going to be a serious conversation, at least wait until the coffee is done. Maybe until I've had my first cup."

She watched him fiddle with one of the frayed cuffs of the faded long-sleeved T-shirt he was wearing, a shirt that fit him just right across the chest, across the shoulders, around his biceps. He pushed the sleeves up to his elbows, revealing muscled forearms covered in red-gold hair. Unlike her best friend Izzy, who was as blonde and delicate as a fairy princess and who burned to an angry lobster red when exposed to sunlight, she could tell Gabriel would be one of those people whose golden complexion tanned like a sun-kissed god. Like Apollo. What the hell? Who knew arms were so distracting this early in the morning? And late at night. And in her dreams. And when she touched herself and imagined his arms around her, his fingers inside her, his mouth on her breasts. She sighed.

"Okay. This is as good a time as any. It's not like I'm rushing off to some important appointment." She gestured to her pajamas.

"You sure?"

She caught and held his gaze. "Yeah. This does sound serious."

Gabriel drew in a long breath. "There are things I need to say to you. Things that are long overdue."

"Is the coffee done yet?"

He frowned and turned to look at the coffeemaker. "Not yet."

"I was kidding. Using my need for caffeine as a delaying tactic." Aria folded her hands together on top of the paper. "I'm ready now. I'm listening."

"The other day, you asked me if I was deliberately obtuse or totally insane." He cleared his throat. "After you asked me that, I did what I'd never done before."

She tensed, fingers going white. "And what was that?"

"I read about what happened. To you. After I left. I swear to you, Aria, I really didn't know. I mean I knew that shit was going down on social media, but I had no idea how bad it was. I deliberately ignored it. Guess I figured it would all blow over soon enough."

She stared at him, studying his face, trying to decide whether he was being truthful or not. She gave a short, almost imperceptible, nod and he went on.

"Look, I know it sounds unbelievable, but the other night when I was at Callie's, that was the first night I really understood what happened after I left Phoenix for Flagstaff. I spent much of that evening reading contemporaneous news stories and, Jesus, I swear I didn't know about the break-ins or the death threats or the rando men following you. I didn't know you were doxed. That someone put your address and phone number on Twitter. Or that someone let the air out of your tires and stole Frederica and took a shit on your dining room table. I didn't know any of it and I'm appalled by all of it and sorrier than I can ever express for my part in it."

She wrapped her arms around herself, as if trying to contain her body, her emotions. Her reaction. As if keeping herself small would keep her safe from whatever was coming next.

"I told you about what was going on in Flagstaff, and I don't know whether or not I could've done something to help or to make it stop or—" he licked his lips to wet them—"or whether me doing something would've just added fuel to the fire and made it worse. But I feel like I should have done something. Or at least I should have known. I was…okay, my *ego* was wrecked after you shut me down. I know that now. And it's not an excuse but I was so in my head about fucking up what could have been something really special, in losing the company I'd built, in Grandma Jack's cancer, in self-loathing and self-pity. I was just so *fucking angry*. At everything, but mostly at myself that it was probably best I stayed away from you. Still. I want to give you a real apology now. *My* apology. Not one written by company attorneys."

She wanted to clap her hands over her ears. She didn't want to hear this. Not if it was just more excuses. "You don't need—"

"Yes, I do need. Please. You don't have to accept it, but I need to do it."

She shook her head. "You can't assuage your conscience now with an apology for what happened then and expect everything to be fine. It's not enough to have words come out of your mouth and then go on as if nothing happened."

"I realize that. I do. Callie and Sylvie have made my culpability abundantly clear. I fucked up, but I want to give you this one thing. From me." He looked out toward the living room and the tall windows and the city beyond them. "Especially since, through some bizarre circumstances neither of us could've conjured in a million years, we ended up in this place together at the beginning of what could be a very difficult time for everyone. I need to say these words if just to get them out in the open. I've been thinking about it since I came home that night and you had that plate of lasagna on the table, waiting for me. I wanted to say the words then, but it was all still new and jumbled up in my head and I was surprised and…I don't know, touched that you made dinner for me."

"Clarification: I *shared* my dinner."

He smiled at that. "Shared, yes." He swallowed and looked down at his hands. He didn't know what to do with them. "Listen, what I'm gonna say is for you, and you can do whatever you want with the words." He stuck his hands in his pants pockets. Then he pulled them out and rested his palms on the counter behind him, elbows out like wings. He bit his bottom lip. Then licked it.

"Aria Turner, I am sorry for being a first-class jerk. I am sorry for demeaning you professionally when truly I had—*have*—the utmost respect for you and for your work. The first time I saw you, I was…you were—" he let go of the counter and ran both hands through his hair then resumed his position, gripping the counter behind him until his fingers were white "—it was like I couldn't breathe. And sometimes when I see you now"— his eyes flicked down to that snug pajama top and those skimpy shorts—"it still feels like that. Like something inside of me is ready to unfurl—or maybe combust. And maybe back then I didn't feel worthy of that. Maybe I tried too hard because I figured I didn't deserve someone like you if you knew what I was really like. Everything happened so fast with Seven Wonders, the VC money came in fast, the company grew fast, the notoriety came fast, and…maybe I had a bad case of impostor syndrome.

"Anyway, what I'm trying to say is that I am sorry I fucked it up. I'm sorry for pushing you too fast after what was the best dinner date of my life. I am sorry for reading the situation all wrong and not understanding or respecting your boundaries. I am *not* sorry for kissing you, and I will never forget what it felt like when you wrapped your arms around me, the feel of your fingers in my hair, on the back of my neck. I'm not sorry for any of that. But I am sorry that I pushed. That, at first, I didn't want to believe you could say no and actually mean it. Not after what I thought you felt, what we *both* felt, was rushing toward us like some sort of tsunami. To me, it felt like an inevitability that we would end the night together, and I was…bruised that you pushed me away. Bruised and confused. So much for the confident, young 30 Under 30 CEO. That man didn't exist. Never existed. If there's one thing, I'm not an impostor at, it's suffering from severe impostor syndrome. My self-confidence was as substantial as a fucking mirage. So, I second guessed everything. Why you wanted to interview me in the first place. Was it me or the company or some agenda of your own. I tied myself into knots reading all sorts of dark and twisted things into it. And then I acted like a child. I lashed out at you. And then went home, tail between my legs, and complained to my roommates—my partners—that you'd shut me down but only after practically climbing me like a tree and wrapping yourself around me in a goddamned public parking lot. I did say that. I admit it. But it was Bryson, that fucking intern, who first called you a cock tease out fishing for a good #metoo story to make yourself famous. And then, well, they all let loose. And I was stupid and frustrated and I have no idea how many drinks I had that night, but when I woke up the next day, the damage was already done. And I'm sorry for all of it."

SEVENTEEN

GABRIEL WAITED, every muscle and tendon poised as if in fight or flight mode, hoping and wishing for an *apology accepted, let's take this opportunity to start all over* but prepared for a *fuck you, it's too little too late and I never want to see you again*. But she didn't say anything. Didn't even meet his eyes. So, he turned back to the counter and poured coffee into both their cups, added a healthy dollop of half and half to each one, and then set her cup in front of her. She wrapped her hands around it and stared into it as if she'd find her words in there. After a long moment, he picked up his cup, and said, "Anyway, I know it's a lot. But it's yours." And he left the kitchen.

He had to come up with that fucking grand gesture. He felt like a donation would be lame. Anyone with money can give money and so what? It might do some good, but it wasn't grand enough. Not for Aria.

He sat on the edge of his bed and surveyed his workspace. To get his bedroom to work as a home office, he had to move his bed and the upholstered armchair with the ottoman so there'd be room to work at the desk and not block the door to the closet. Once that was done, he carefully set up his two large screens and his laptop, turned them on, made sure everything worked and that he had access to the WIFI, and then he sat on the bed staring at the desk. A chair. He needed a desk chair. Nothing fancy.

He pulled out his phone and looked for an office supply store nearby. In Arizona, the big box stores would have office furniture. Then he stopped. He didn't want to have to assemble anything else today. He wasn't in the mood. Wasn't sure he could keep his hands steady enough to hold a screwdriver. Wasn't sure he could stop himself from throwing a wrench through the wall. So, he searched for thrift stores. He'd find something used. Didn't care how beat-up it was. As long as he could haul it home in one piece.

What the hell had he been thinking saying all that to Aria? What a goddamned fool. He scrubbed his hands down over his face. He might as well have admitted flat out he'd fallen for her the first time she'd walked into that conference room in Phoenix. Might as well have told her he still had it bad. And she hadn't said a word. Hadn't even been able to look at him. Served him right thinking an apology could work any kind of magic. Not after what she'd been through. What a blithering idiot.

Still, he wasn't about to give up. He'd told himself he was going to take advantage of this gift, this strange, serendipitous situation that they'd found themselves in and make the most of it. And he was still determined to give it a go. So, maybe it wasn't bad that he'd put himself out there.

He'd told her his apology—his words—were for her to do with what she wanted. Maybe it was for the best that she knew where he stood, how he saw her, what he felt. Then it would be up to her.

Last time, he'd pushed too hard. He hadn't respected her boundaries and she'd had to practically push him away from her. Not practically. He'd been so lost in that amazing first kiss. The kiss that sent shock waves racing through every nerve in his body, that seemed to be a affirmation of all that was good and hopeful and possible in the world. The kiss that made him feel like he'd found a safe haven, found salvation. The kiss that she'd returned with equal fervor. She'd arched her body into his and wrapped her arms around his neck as his hands roamed over her curves. He'd pressed himself up against her as she leaned back against the warm metal of her car—God, they'd been in a public parking lot!—and then, then she'd said *Wait. No. Stop.* And she'd had to slip her hands up between them, place them firmly against his chest, and push him away with a little shove. His face went flame red, remembering.

"I said no. This is going too fast," Aria had kept her hands up in front of her. "Tonight was amazing, but—"

"But you know you want this as much as I do," he'd whispered in his most sultry voice, cajoling even as he placed his hands on her car, caging her body between his arms. She couldn't be stopping. Couldn't be rejecting him. Not after what he knew they both felt.

"You're wrong. I *don't* know that I want this. I know I really like you and it's obvious I'm attracted to you, but I don't do one-night stands and I don't sleep with men I just met."

"We didn't just meet," Gabriel had protested in frustration. "You've spent two hours interviewing me and we just had another two hours of getting to know each other over dinner."

"All that's true, but I'm just not ready for this."

His chest felt like it'd gotten a good kick from an angry mule. "This is not a one-night stand, Aria. That's not how I see this."

"Gabriel. You're not listening to me, so I'm going to make it very clear. I am not going home with you, and you are not coming home with me. This is not happening."

He'd felt like he'd been shoved headfirst in front of an oncoming car. Everything slowed. His movements were heavy, as if he were struggling against the enveloping pull and drag of quicksand. His heart knocked against his ribs, he broke out in a sweat, and his vision swam. He'd stepped away from her, arms up as if in surrender as she opened her car door and placed it between them as if she were afraid of him. *Afraid of him!* And it dawned on him that while he'd been ready to hand over his heart on a silver platter, she'd had a different agenda. Probably been using him from the beginning. She was a talented journalist, making a name for herself. He was just another story for her portfolio. He thought they'd connected, but it was probably just artifice. Subtle interviewing techniques to get him to open up.

His mind spun a web of scenarios. She'd agreed to dinner, just the two of them, as a ruse to get him to tell her more about Seven Wonders Gaming, his partners, and their Work Hard/Play Hard brand. Her interest in interviewing him wasn't because he was the newest CEO on the block, but because of the admittedly hedonistic lifestyle brand that a hard-nosed journalist like her, a journalist working in the wake of the #metoo movement, could latch on to and use to launch a career exposing the toxic masculinity of a bunch of college roommates who refused to grow up, who all still lived together in one of their parents' houses, and who aimed to make their millions by playing games.

Hell, he'd known even then it was past time they all grew up. A good journalist could make a name for herself exposing the uglier side of their partnership. The booze. The drugs. The parties. The women. Even if he'd tried to keep himself apart from most of it, even if he was the one working eighteen-hour days to make Seven Wonders a success, he wasn't immune. He'd indulged plenty of times. There were pictures on Instagram to prove it.

The thought made him nauseous. He felt exposed. Cornered. Hollowed out. And it made him want to lash out. So, he'd narrowed his eyes and looked down at her. "Did you get what you wanted from our cozy dinner, then? An inside scoop you can turn into a clickbait headline?"

He remembered the shock on her face. "What I wanted? What are you insinuating?" she'd said. "You asked me to dinner, and I said yes. That's it. No ulterior motives. Besides, I told you I already sent you the article so you can fact check for inaccuracies. It should be in your inbox. My editor's already reviewed it."

He felt disembodied, like a version of himself was standing next to him, listening, and watching, telling him to shut the fuck up even as he couldn't stop himself from talking. "You going to tell your editor about this?" He'd gestured between them. "About dinner and the kiss? About me wanting to take you to bed?"

Her expression went dark, eyes narrowed, mouth turned down in a frown. "Not unless it becomes an issue. Is it going to become an issue, Gabriel? Me not sleeping with you?"

And then he'd given her a slow smile. "Of course not. Just because you said no tonight, doesn't mean you'll say no next time."

God, how could he have been so stupid? It'd been three years since that night in the parking lot and he felt it like a punch in the gut every time he thought about it. As if it had happened just now. No wonder she hated him.

He ran his sweaty palms up and down his thighs. *I need to get out of here. A chair. I need a chair. I need air. And then I need a chair. And then I need a grand gesture.* He stood and stepped out into the hall, headed to the kitchen. It was empty. He went back to his room and stared at the door next to his. The study. Aria's workspace. The door was closed. Should he knock? Tell her he was going out? No. He couldn't face her yet. Maybe didn't ever want to face her again. Okay, that was a lie, but God. He was a mess.

He went back to his room, found a pen, and tore a sheet of paper off his notepad. He wrote furiously, then grabbed his mask, keys, and wallet, left the note on the kitchen island, and headed out.

EIGHTEEN

ARIA DIDN'T EMERGE from her study until after three. She'd intended to start the day with a walk and somehow that idea got away from her. It was the apology. That was the problem. It had screwed up her entire day. She hadn't been able to think of anything but what Gabriel said that morning and what he looked like—and sounded like—when he said it. *And how she felt hearing it— furious, stunned, moved. Confused.*

At one point, the distraction had gotten so bad, she'd closed her laptop, pulled the decorative blanket off the back of the little couch in the study, and curled up to try to escape her thoughts with a nap. She never took naps, but since she'd hardly slept the night before or the night before that, she crashed within minutes. Turns out napping didn't help, though, because she dreamed of that damned apology. And of that magical, infuriating evening three years ago, when she'd had the best date of her life, followed by the most erotic, hair-curling kiss of her life, followed by the weirdest exchange of her life, followed by utter and complete disaster.

But, *oh*, that kiss. Leaning against the sun-heated warmth of her car in the middle of a public parking lot, she'd slipped her hands up over Gabriel's shoulders, let her fingers play in the hair at the nape of his neck, and had gone all in. It started as a warm brush of lips against lips. Tender. Lush. Then a bit more pressure as he leaned into her, fitting his mouth to hers and sending a shower of sparks shooting into her bloodstream along with a surge of lust that went straight to her core. And then the plundering began. The want and need driving them both until she was nearly climbing him. Once her brain regained control, she was mortified. She was on tiptoes and had one leg wrapped around his hips and *they were in a public parking lot!*

Jeez. It was still mortifying. She couldn't think of it without embarrassment flooding through her. Didn't matter. She had to stop thinking of it. At all. She needed fresh air and she needed to put distance between her and Gabriel. A walk would help. But before she took off for her walk, she needed to fill her water bottle, and that's when she saw the note on the kitchen counter.

11:10 a.m.

Dear Aria,

It's another roommate note! I've gone out in search of a chair for my new 'Roses are red' desk. Be back when my quest is completed. You have my number. If there's something you need while I'm out and about, text me. (I don't have your number.) I'm happy to make extra stops.

p.s. Sorry about the awkward apology this morning. I didn't mean to make you uncomfortable.
—GL

p.s.s. I'm not sorry about the apology. I meant every word of that. I am sorry about the other stuff… the awkward stuff about how, you know, I feel sometimes like I might spontaneously combust when you walk into the room. Since we're roomies, I thought you should know I could be considered a fire hazard.

p.s.s.s. But you should also know that I understand about boundaries now and it dawned on me afterward that maybe telling you all this is putting a burden on you. I'm sorry—another apology!—if that's the case. If you want, we can pretend I never said any of that. It's your call. (I hope this is not making it worse. Awkward confessions[3].)

p.s.s.s.s. Either way, I recommend keeping a fire extinguisher handy.

It definitely made it worse. Every time he opened his mouth, or picked up a pen, apparently, he made it worse. Aria didn't know what to think. She was heavily invested in hating Gabriel Landon. She'd had three years to stew on what had happened and had a lucrative book deal writing about men just like him and how they ruined the lives of women just like her. He couldn't be a good guy. It wasn't possible.

She filled her water bottle, checked Fred's water bowl—the cat was stretched out luxuriously in a splash of sun in the front room—and then took the note back to her room where she tucked it in her journal, next to Gabriel's other notes. Then she laced up her walking shoes, grabbed her jacket, keys, and mask, and headed out.

NINETEEN

S HE DIDN'T GET FAR.
"Miss Turner! Come see." Manuel, wearing a pale blue, pleated hospital mask, waved and called to Aria as soon as she stepped off the elevator. No taller than 5'7, with a broad smiling face, a shiny bald head, and longshoreman's shoulders, Manuel Espinosa had been the doorman for almost twenty years. The man got along with everyone and had even developed a friendship with her father when he'd lived in the building. The two favored a particular type of cigar and could talk boxing and horse racing until all hours. Caldwell may have reached the pinnacle of success as an American writer, but he'd grown up on a farm in rural Illinois and was, he readily admitted, more comfortable with 'working class' people than literary snobs. He often boasted that he could out-snob the snobs and out-work the working man. Depending on the situation. And his mood. Everything, of course, depended on his mood.

"What's up?" Aria said, slipping her mask on and looping the elastic bands over her ears.

"You know Professor Radcliffe on the fourth floor?"

"Yes, of course. How is she?"

"Her ridiculous daughter—her words, not mine—decided she needed a puppy for her eightieth birthday, to keep her company since both kids had moved out of the city.

"Oh, no. That doesn't sound well thought out."

"I know." Manuel rolled his eyes. "Her daughter thought a puppy would keep her mom young. But Professor Radcliffe is legally blind and has lately started needing a cane and cannot take care of the poor thing. And she's afraid she's going to trip over him and break a hip. So, she asked me if I would see if anyone else in the building would want him. She's become attached to the little guy and doesn't want to send him to a shelter. Plus, she'd like 'visiting rights.'" Manuel put that in air quotes.

Aria's stomach dropped. She knew exactly where this was going. As the youngest resident in the building, she knew in her gut that everyone would turn to her to take on a task like this. And she figured that's why Manuel had cornered her as soon as she stepped off the elevator.

"Along with the pup," Manuel went on, "her daughter gave her a bed and food bowls and leashes and fancy little sweaters and all the things a city pup would need, including a year's contract with a dog walking service. And a snug little crate for the poor guy."

"What kind of pup is he?"

"A dachshund. Apparently, she thought a short dog would be a placid dog. But," he said with a laugh, gesturing at his own physique, "it doesn't work that way."

"No, I don't imagine it does." Aria smiled and shook her head, thinking the worst thing about masks is no one can see you smile. "Ridiculous children, indeed. Aren't dachshunds bred to hunt, dig for badgers or something?"

"I believe you're right. They are hounds, after all." Manual looked at Aria now and noted her attire. "You going for a walk?"

"I need some air."

"Want to see the pup before you go?"

She sighed at the inevitability of it all. "Might as well." She genuinely liked Professor Radcliffe. A retired history professor at Barnard with a specialty in the Renaissance, she was always fun to chat with and came up with the most fascinating historical tidbits about food or sex or travel or clothes. She even played the harpsichord. Aria didn't like the idea of Dr. Radcliff or any of her neighbors being alone or lonely. It was a relatively small building, only ten floors and four units to a floor. She'd met most everyone, but she only knew a few of her neighbors well. Still, everyone had been nice to her since she'd first visited her father, and then welcoming her when her father moved out and she moved in when she started journalism school. Most of them had lived in the building for decades, some since before Caldwell had even bought his place.

"He's in my office." Manuel led Aria around the concierge desk and through the mail room into a small office where Gabriel Landon sat on the floor, leaning against the wall, a black mask hanging from one ear. With his long legs stretched out in front of him, he gazed down at the most adorable puppy sprawled out against his chest, belly up, head lolling sideways. The pup was crème colored.

Or maybe the color of butter. Or beige. And what a bland word that was. He was certainly not brown or black like most dachshunds Aria had seen. And he was sound asleep, making the most adorable little *snuffling* noises.

Gabriel looked up at Aria and the first thing she noticed was that his eyes were red rimmed and glistening, like he'd been trying not to cry. And then she remembered what he'd said about his sister Callie. How she'd been Team Aria all the way and hadn't spoken to him for a long time, even to the point that she'd only texted him when she'd put the dog they'd grown up with to sleep. And now...*shit*.

Gabriel Landon was in love. It was written all over his face.

She didn't think Frederica had ever even been face-to-face with a dog except on walks. And why had her brain automatically gone to Frederica's non-existent relationship to dogs? *Was she seriously considering this?* Dr. Radcliffe would owe her big time. Manuel would owe her big time. Gabriel...well...

Gabriel hadn't said a word so far. He didn't have to.

Manuel was standing in the doorway, beaming. Aria could tell even though the man wore a mask. "Professor Radcliffe says he's a Longhair English Cream Miniature," he said. "Three months old. And quite a handsome critter, isn't he?" The sneaky man knew Gabriel had already given his heart to this dog. And he'd certainly heard Aria *ooh* and *ahh* over cute dogs plenty of times. But, dammit, she'd always been a cat person precisely because cats were low maintenance. She certainly wasn't going to get up and walk a puppy in the middle of the night. Or clean up puppy messes on the rug.

Damn. Damn. Damn.

Manuel went on. "Her daughter claimed the pup was house-trained, but Professor Radcliffe says he's not quite there yet. So, there may be a few accidents. It's another reason she felt she couldn't handle him."

While Manuel was talking, Gabriel pushed himself to his feet, keeping the sprawled pup tucked against his chest. He walked straight to Aria, looked down at her with those big green eyes swimming with emotion, and raised a brow in a *You want to hold him?* gesture.

She reached out to put a fingertip to one of the pup's tiny, almost translucent nails, and whispered—*whispered!*—"I don't want to disturb him." Then she looked around the office. There was a ratty office chair on wheels with part of the faux leather seat cover missing, revealing its foam padding. And next to it, a couple of *The New Yorker* canvas tote bags that appeared to be stuffed with dog food, puppy pee pads, and, she figured, the food and water bowls, chew toys, leashes, and sweaters Manuel mentioned. There was also a cushy bed with a padded rim and a depression in the middle that looked a bit like a fuzzy donut and a metal crate with a pad and a plaid blanket. Everything a new puppy would need.

She looked back at Gabriel, who was still gazing down at the puppy, and all she could think of was: *She's all I have.*

Shit. Was she really doing this? Were *they* really doing this?

"Listen," she whispered. "If we're doing this, we have to have some rules."

He nodded.

"Number one, the dog is your responsibility."

He nodded again.

"Number two, you clean up his messes and you take him out whenever he needs it."

He nodded yet again, lips pressed together, brows drawn down, a *very serious* look on his face.

"And number three, when you move out, the dog goes with you. He's yours. You understand? You'll have to figure out visiting hours with Dr. Radcliffe on your own." She looked him up and down. "Though I imagine you'll charm the socks off her with that besotted smile you're trying so hard to hide."

And there it was. A full-blown Gabriel Landon smile that made his green eyes look like freshly mown grass dressed up in morning dew and little lines raying out from the corners like sunshine, warming Aria right down to her DNA.

Oh, God. She was in trouble. With both man and dog. So, yes. Apparently, they were doing this. And yes, a sucker was born every minute, and she was obviously a card-carrying member of the *Look at Me! I'm a Member of the Sucker Society*.

But, she rationalized, maybe a puppy for the pandemic would be a good distraction to keep them from murdering each other. Maybe a puppy would keep Gabriel occupied, and he wouldn't bother her with any more apologies and dangerous talk of spontaneous combustion. Maybe it would be good to acclimate Fred to another pet. When she was in high school, hadn't she wanted a dog? Well, now she had a chance to have one without doing any of the work.

She looked at the little guy, floppy ears with a bit of fringe on the edges, fat Buddha belly dotted with butterscotch speckles, long tail curled up between his dangling hind legs, a little tuft of *floof* at the tip. He'd given himself over to Gabriel with complete trust. As if Gabriel was a guy you could depend on.

She let out a long, elaborate I'm-so-very-put-upon sigh, and whispered, "What's his name?"

The puppy wiggled, made a little *groany growlie* sound, and settled back in for his snooze as Gabriel slid a finger around his collar to pull out his tag, shaped like a bone and engraved on one side with Mrs. Radcliffe's phone number—he'd have to fix that—and on the other, the dog's name. LYMOND.

TWENTY

ANUEL PILED the doggie bed and the two canvas totes onto the seat of the ratty office chair—which, to Aria's dismay, appeared to be Gabriel's new desk chair—and then shooed the new dog owners toward the elevator, promising to let Professor Radcliffe know Lymond was safe and sound and to follow with the crate. Aria pushed the disgusting chair while Gabriel hugged Lymond to his chest, emitting a soothing *shhh* as he used a fingertip to smooth the pup's brow whenever he happened to let out a sigh or a little wiggle. On the ride up to the tenth floor, Aria stared at the elevator doors, conscious only of Gabriel's presence in her peripheral vision. That and the pain that blossomed in her chest with every *shhh* and soothing touch.

They didn't speak in the elevator, the air between them taut as a held breath. Once they were inside the co-op, though, they couldn't avoid each other. Luckily, Manuel soon arrived with the crate and set it up in the living room, and he and Aria both watched as Gabriel gently tucked the pup in, covered him with the plaid blanket, and then oh-so-quietly closed and latched the door. Then Manuel took his leave and Aria and Gabriel were alone.

Gabriel cleared his throat. "Thank you for—"

"I'm doing it for Dr. Radcliffe," Aria interrupted before Gabriel could go on with an emotional outpouring she wasn't prepared to handle.

He gave her a slow nod. "Well, she is a very lucky woman to have such a generous and caring friend."

"So, I guess we need to see exactly what we've got here," Aria said, ignoring the comment while digging into one of the canvas totes.

And then they got to work unpacking the puppy paraphernalia. Together.

There was a doggie brush and hard chew toys and soft plush toys—some with squeakers and some without—and ridiculous doggie sweaters, little snow booties, and even a little raincoat with a hood that made them both laugh. By the time they'd sorted through all the doggie accouterments and Gabriel had placed a few pee pads in the foyer by the front door, Lymond was awake and raring to go. Tail wagging furiously, he stuck a paw through the bars of his crate and let out another little growly sound.

"Should I take him out?" Gabriel asked. "He probably has to pee after that nap. Then, I guess, we should tackle the first task."

The first task was to introduce the new pup to Frederica, Queen of All She Surveyed. Fred was not content to wait. She'd smelled the intruder as soon as they hit the foyer and had been weaving her way through Gabriel's legs, since he smelled like the pup, ever since. For a while, she'd even staked out a spot next to the crate, wanting a look at the newcomer, which they supposed was a good sign. At least she wasn't arching and hissing and swatting at the little guy. Fred had traveled and gone on walks with Aria and although she might not have had direct experience with a dog, she'd certainly seen and smelled plenty of them. And Fred was smart and curious. She'd taken to Gabriel immediately, so maybe she'd take to Lymond too.

"That's a good idea," Aria said. "Let's not start this experience with a piddle on the floor." She reached for one of the leashes and handed it to Gabriel. Then she tore off a little poo bag from a green roll with doggie prints on it. "You'll want to take this too."

"Thanks." Gabriel stuffed the bag into his pocket and took the leash to the crate. "We can see how Fred reacts to Lymond when I let him out." He carefully unlatched the crate door and reached in for the pup, picking him up slowly so Fred could get a good sniff. Then he clipped the leash on Lymond's collar and turned to Aria. "Do you think he needs one of those sweaters?"

Her lips quirked in a smile. What a doting doggie dad. Then she thumbed open her phone and checked her weather app. "It's still in the fifties. He should be fine."

"But he's so little."

Aria rolled her eyes and plucked up a little blue cable knit sweater that looked appropriate for an exclusive canine country club. She bunched it up to go over the pup's head. "You need to unhook the leash first. See," she poked a finger through a hole in the neck of the sweater, "there's a little slit for the clip to go through."

Gabriel unhooked the leash and held Lymond out while Aria slipped the sweater over the pup's head, gently pulled first one then the other leg through the little armholes, and then pulled the metal ring for Lymond's tag through the slit. Gabriel re-hooked the leash and looked up at Aria with a sheepish smile.

"I would never have figured that out. Boomer weighed about 170 pounds, and I guarantee you he never wore a sweater." He headed for the door, Lymond still in his arms, leash dangling.

"Don't forget to wear your mask," Aria called after him.

Twenty minutes later, Gabriel was back, hugging Lymond to his chest and telling him he was the best boy ever and that he'd pooped and peed in the exact right spots. Aria rolled her eyes and wondered what he'd be like as a real father—and then, aghast that her brain had gone there—she shut that thought down immediately.

"Dr. Radcliffe called while you were out," she said. "She is, of course, thrilled we took Lymond in. She insists on paying to have him neutered when the time comes. And she said he is chipped and has had all his shots. She gave me the name of his vet. It's on the counter. It's not the same vet I go to for Fred."

"Did she schedule a visit to come see him?"

Aria laughed. "She asked to come by tomorrow, as a matter of fact. She wanted to give him some time to get acclimated, and said she's overdue for a visit to Mrs. Feldstein, across the hall."

"Great. I know Sophia has been lonely since Mr. Feldstein died, so I'm sure she'll appreciate the visit."

Sophia? Aria blinked. Had Gabriel made friends with all the old ladies in the building?

Gabriel was still talking. "So what's the best way to get Lymond acclimated?"

"First, we need to deal with introducing Fred and Lymond. This says we need to introduce them in a neutral spot." She held up her phone to show him a website about integrating a new puppy to a household with a cat. "One thing they suggest is to keep the cat in a separate room for a while, to allow it to get used to the idea and the smells of an active puppy." She looked up. "But that's not going to happen. I'm not locking Fred up."

"Fred was sitting right there by the crate while Lymond was in it," Gabriel said, "and she just seemed curious. No complaining so far."

Aria picked up the doggie donut bed and put it next to the crate. "This is really soft, and it smells like Lymond. Let's see what Fred does with it before you put Lymond down. And maybe you should keep his leash on him. Just in case you need to make a grab for him. Dr. Radcliffe said he is apt to get a good case of the *zoomies* after a long nap. I shut the doors to the bedrooms and the study, but left your bathroom door open. He can't do much damage in there."

Gabriel lowered himself to the floor, sitting cross legged by the crate and the doggie bed. Lymond wiggled in his arms, but he kept him in place as Fred sauntered over and gave him a curious sniff. Then she climbed into the doggie bed, turned in circles a few times, sat down and promptly stuck a leg in the air to groom herself.

"What do you think?" Aria asked. "Keep him on his leash, but maybe put him on the floor? Let him explore?"

Gabriel looked up suddenly, his face dark with worry. "What about the loggia? Do you think he could fit through the posts? Maybe I should get some chicken wire and wrap it around the bottom."

"With that belly?" Aria laughed. "I don't think he can fit, but you should measure it just to make sure."

"Here, hold the leash." He handed it up to Aria who took it without question as he got back to his feet. "Do you have a measuring tape?"

"In my tool kit. It's on the little shelf beside the washer-dryer."

He headed down the hall to his bathroom, the guest bathroom, where the stackable washer and dryer unit was fitted into a little alcove next to the shower. Moments later, he returned with a lime green construction grade measuring tape and held it up. "Voila. You keep hold of the leash and I'll measure." He opened the door to the loggia and stepped outside into the chilly air of an early spring evening.

Aria watched as Gabriel lowered himself to his knees and drew out the measuring tape to bridge the gap between two of the posts making up the loggia railing.

"Three and a half inches," he said, resting back on his haunches. "He could get his little snout through there, but not his whole head. And you're right, that belly will keep him safe." He looked over at Lymond, now peeking through Aria's legs at the new, unexplored space. "And I imagine he'll be growing like a weed."

"He is a miniature, remember."

"Yeah, but I looked it up. The average male gets to be between six and eight inches tall at the shoulder and weighs around fifteen or sixteen pounds." He laughed. "Boomer could've eaten him in one bite." He pulled the tape out again and measured the height of the posts. "Forty-two inches. No way those little legs will be able to jump that."

He got to his feet. "Aren't you worried about Fred out here? That she'll get up on the railing?"

"I never let her out here without a leash."

He laughed. "You put your cat on a leash?"

"Well, yes. I mean, when I travel with her, I need to take her to the little pet potty areas in airports. So, she has a little harness. And just like Mr. Lymond here, she has a whole wardrobe of sweaters for when I take her out when it's cold. She is hairless, remember."

"You take her for walks?"

"I've been known to. When she's in the mood, she'll trot right beside me like a dog."

Gabriel's face lit up. "Let's take them for a walk together! One of the websites says that's a good way to acclimate a new pet to an old one."

Aria shook her head. Gabriel Landon looked like a little boy who'd just opened his most wished for Christmas present. "How about tomorrow? For now," Aria said, looking over at her cat who had moved from the doggie bed to the highest platform of her scratching tree, "Fred looks completely uninterested in Lymond. Why don't you take this opportunity to give him a tour of his new home."

TWENTY-ONE

MARCH 18

AFTER GABRIEL TOOK Lymond on a sniffing tour of the co-op, they'd ordered pizza—surprisingly agreeing on a large pie with extra cheese, pineapple, and jalapeños—and settled in for the evening's regularly scheduled activity of watching the world fall apart with rising Covid-19 infections, increasingly crazy election news, and all manner of conflicts around the globe. They decided to keep Lymond on his leash in case they needed to pull him away from a potential Fred attack, but they did let him explore the living room on his own. Gabriel only had to leap up once to catch him just as he started to do a puppy squat. He scooped him up and ran to the front door to the pee pads. Then he slipped on his shoes and took Lymond outside, calling *We're going out. Don't eat all the pizza!*

Later, they'd decided to put the crate in Gabriel's room and to keep it in there while he was working but then to move it out to the living room in the evenings. The websites said to put the crate where people would be so it would be a safe space for curling up in but not isolated away from the owner's activity. The first night in his new surroundings, Lymond whined a bit, but eventually fell asleep and slept through the night. By 5:30 in the morning, Gabriel was up, dressing Lymond in his cable knit sweater, and carrying him downstairs for his walk.

Aria had left her door cracked open for Fred and could hear Gabriel whispering to the pup as they left. "We have to be quiet, so we don't wake Aria or Fred," Gabriel said. "So, no whining or barking. Hey, I haven't even heard your bark yet. Do you have a fearsome bark, Mr. Lymond? Are you going to grow up to be a big scary guard dog? Wait, no wiggling and no peeing on my shirt." Aria had listened to the one-sided banter with a smile on her face and a stabbing pain smack in the middle of her chest.

And now Lymond, sans leash, explored the kitchen as Fred watched from her perch on her tower by the window, and Gabriel and Aria sipped their morning coffee and looked over the paper.

"Look at this," Aria said, "schools and restaurants are closed, but there are over 2,000 confirmed cases in the city."

Gabriel shook his head. "In a high population density city like this, it's going to go from bad to worse fast. Exponentially fast."

"Still only one death reported so far, but…I worry about Caldwell. He has emphysema too. Like the woman who died. And they're the same age."

"When was the last time you talked to him?"

Aria fiddled with her coffee cup. "I called him when I got back from London. We don't…we don't talk much."

She thought back to the day she found out she actually had a living, breathing father and that he was famous as all hell. She hadn't thought about it in a long time. Remembering served no purpose. It just made her angry at her mother for keeping the secret. Angry at her father for not trying harder. Angry at herself for being angry. For acting like such a baby about the idea of missing her daddy when all the while he'd been out there, larger than life. A man to look up to. To emulate. Admire. Until she found out about all the womanizing and multiple wives and the tragic death of his one legitimate child, her unknown half-brother. Jeremy. An estranged son who hadn't spoken to his father in years and who'd died of a drug overdose. She'd poured over the few articles she could find about his death. On one of her rare visits with Caldwell, she'd asked him about Jeremy. But Caldwell had been evasive. "He was a darling boy, but then he grew up," he'd said without a scintilla of empathy.

"What do you mean by that?" Aria had pressed.

Caldwell had sighed deeply, as if the entire conversation, which so far had been two sentences long, had worn him down to the nub.

"I never knew I had any siblings," Aria said. "I'd just like to know what he was like."

Caldwell waved the question away and Aria didn't think he was going to answer. But he did. "Jeremy was a perfectionist," Caldwell said finally. "Always trying too hard to measure up. Always wanting too much from me. Never satisfied. Said everything was my fault."

"What did you say?"

"I told him to grow a pair."

Aria had just stared at the man. Chilled at his callousness. How had he ever managed to write such beautiful, emotionally raw prose? God Almighty, her father was a first-class bastard.

"Don't look at me like that." He'd pinned her with an intense glare. "My father—your grandfather—joined the navy when he was seventeen. Wanted to go fight the Nazis and the Japs. Died when his ship hit a mine in the South China Sea. Before I was born. I served in Vietnam even though I didn't believe in the war. But I wanted to go to college and the G.I. Bill was my only way in. We were willing to make sacrifices to get what we wanted. But even the word 'sacrifice' was anathema to Jeremy. He wanted everything handed to him. Private school. Study abroad. New cars. And he pissed it all away."

He'd paused and looked at Aria thoughtfully. "I think watching Jeremy's struggles from afar was one of the reasons your mother kept you away from me until you were older. Smart woman." While Aria took that in, he'd gone on. "Anyway, I put Jeremy in rehab. Tried to visit, but ..." Caldwell shrugged, "he refused to see me. A month later, I got the call."

Caldwell was definitely a dick, but the look on his face when he'd said that—He refused to see me—had broken Aria's heart. Ever since then, she'd given him the benefit of the doubt. After years of therapy, she'd achieved a sort of peace with her parents. More like an accommodation than actual peace, really. Still, with this damned virus, she worried about them both. Especially Caldwell and his idiotic fourth wife. The one who spent money on yoni eggs and coffee enemas. The one who believed measles, mumps, and rubella vaccines caused autism. If there was a vaccine for Covid—and there would be sooner or later—would Heather even take Caldwell to get it? Since her father had been diagnosed with Parkinson's, he'd given up his driver's license and was dependent on Heather. But would Heather get it? Or would she just double down on her turmeric, crystals, and vagina cleanses? Gabriel would get the vaccine. Aria was sure of it.

She blinked and realized Gabriel had said her name. "What?"

"I said a call to your father probably wouldn't go amiss. Just to check in."

Go amiss? Who talked like that? Someone raised by their grandmother, probably. She shrugged and said, "Yeah," in a half-hearted tone of voice.

"So...," Gabriel said after a few moments of silence, shaking out a section of the paper and refolding it. "I get that K-12 schools are closed to arrest the spread of the virus, but what are parents who have to show up to work supposed to do? Just leave their kids at home by themselves? High school kids, fine. But what about middle school and elementary school? Those kids can't just do school by themselves. They need resources. School nurses. Lunch. The library. God, Callie and I wouldn't have survived without the library. And remote learning? How does that work if you don't have your own computer and high-speed Internet?"

"I was thinking about Italian Village last night and our pizza delivery guy," Aria said. "Small businesses like that..."

"Yeah, family businesses that can't afford to lose customers and can't afford to pay a lot or provide benefits to employees. And can't afford to have people out sick. Think about it. If the city goes into quarantine, there will be eight and a half million people holed up at home wanting pizza delivery…I mean what the hell? And think about everything we import from China, which is basically shut down. And global shipping and supply chains. I saw online that people are buying toilet paper and hand sanitizer like we're facing the apocalypse." He shook his head and ran a hand down over his face. "Fact is, we are facing systemic collapse if we don't see serious and coordinated government support."

"Good thing I stocked up on groceries and supplies like that when I got back." Aria refilled her coffee cup and held the carafe up to Gabriel. He nodded and slid his cup toward her. "Sometimes I can't wrap my head around the fact that this is even happening," she said. "I mean global pandemics seem like something you only see in zombie movies."

"Yeah, it's like a bad sci-fi movie. No known treatments. No vaccines. No cure. A population at the mercy of an un-known virus. Jesus, and just think about how many workers don't have paid sick leave," he went on. "This country…"

"Our healthcare system sucks. As a freelance journalist, I don't get health insurance through my job; I have to buy it through the ACA. Having your workplace involved in your healthcare always seemed screwy to me anyway. I mean, it seems so *company town, company store, company health care.* Like they own you. It's creepy. It's just a way to lock people into their jobs."

"I get it. I mean, we're setting all that up for Q.BC now that we're going to have employees, but after I left Seven Wonders as an employee, I lost my company health insurance. Medicare for all makes sense to me. Research shows it'd be cheaper and more efficient anyway. Especially for entrepreneurs. And I hate having to worry about that part of the business."

Aria poured more half and half in her cup and swirled it around with a spoon. She didn't even know what his business was, really. Blockchain? How do you make money with that? She thought it was all open source and used on the dark web to somehow facilitate cryptocurrency and porn. And last time she'd asked him about it, he'd gotten all testy. *Maybe I should have my attorney present.*

Of course, a lot had changed between the two of them since that first night. The shock of seeing each other in the flesh after three years had worn off, for one thing. Replaced by, unfortunately, at least in Aria's case, an obsessive curiosity about what seeing each other in the flesh and nothing but the flesh might be like. Yes, a lot had changed but there was a lot more that they were ignoring. A lot that was... *combustible.* More and more, Aria found her eyes drifting toward Gabriel's mouth, remembering the plush warmth of his lips on hers. Remembering running her hands up over those broad shoulders. Remembering how his body felt pressed up against hers. God, she could feel her skin warming even now.

"I wonder how long this is going to last," she said. "How long it'll take to get good vaccines and effective treatments and what the final toll will be when this pandemic is all over. In terms of dollars and lives."

"If it's as bad as the doomsayers predict, it'll be in the hundreds of trillions of dollars and millions of lives," Gabriel said in a matter-of-fact tone.

"Holy shit."

"That's globally. Who knows what it'll be here, in the state and nationally. I guess it all depends on the mayor, the governor, and the Administration and how they handle it."

"We're fucked then. I mean *this* Administration?"

Gabriel snorted. "And it depends on people being careful. Masks. Social distancing. Vaccines, once they're developed."

"Speaking of," Aria said, "you mentioned something about a pandemic pod."

Gabriel straightened up, his face brightening. "Like with Callie and Sylvie? You'd consider that?"

She let out a sigh. "Yeah, I'd consider that," she ran a finger around the rim of her coffee cup. She'd been thinking about it a lot. She'd been thinking about him a lot. And the fact that he'd moved to New York to start his company just so he could re-establish his relationship with his sister and that if this damn pandemic shut everything down, it would make that process more difficult. Callie had taken Aria's side and now, for some absolutely insane reason, Aria would like to be a part of healing the brother-sister rift. "My editor is doing it with her partner and two other couples," she said. "They're only going to meet every other week in case someone is exposed."

"To take the incubation period into consideration?"

"Yeah, so if one person is exposed the whole group doesn't have to isolate."

"I'll talk to Callie and Sylvie," Gabriel said. "They may have already decided to do this with some of their neighbors, but I'll ask. We'd all have to agree to seriously limit exposure to other people, but I guess we need to do that anyway." He looked down at the pup at his feet, now diligently trying to bite one of the wings off a little plush dragon. "Should we include Dr. Radcliffe? Since she's already claimed Lymond visiting rights?"

"We can ask her. She's going to stop by around noon."

"Does she need help," Gabriel asked. "I mean, getting around?"

"She's legally blind from macular degeneration. It causes blind spots in her vision, but she can see well enough. And she's lived in the building for like fifty years, so she knows her way around."

"As long as a puppy isn't darting around at her feet, I guess." Gabriel pushed away from the counter and stood. "Let's ask her about the pod when she gets here. And I'll talk to Callie and Sylvie. Can we invite them over tonight?"

She bit her lip, trying not to allow herself to smile at how happy, how *eager*, he looked.

"Wait, no." He turned to look at Fred on her perch in the living room. "How about tomorrow night. We should give Lymond and Fred more time to get acclimated without introducing more people."

"Oh, good idea," she said. "And let's make this first pod gathering a very casual 'get acquainted' potluck."

"Perfect. I'll talk to Callie and Sylvie. See if they're up for it. Can we say 6:30 tomorrow night?"

"Works for me." And she allowed herself a smile as Gabriel strode down the hall to his room with Lymond pouncing after him, the little dragon clamped firmly in his teeth. She looked across the room at Frederica, still perched on her tower. "What are we getting ourselves into?"

If Fred had an opinion, she did not share it.

TWENTY-TWO

GABRIEL SAT ON HIS RATTY desk chair, gently turning back and forth as he thumbed through the photos he'd already taken of Lymond. He selected two, no three, of the cutest ones. And then looked down to see the little guy gnawing on a chew toy at his feet. "Hey, Lymond," he whispered and when the pup looked up, he snapped yet another. Then he sent them to Callie.

Gabriel: *Got another new roommate.*

Callie: *WHAT?? Who is that sweet thing? Look at that nose!*

Gabriel: *His name is Lymond. An elderly woman in the building couldn't take care of him and didn't want him to go to the shelter, so… long story short, I got a dog.*

Callie: *And Aria Turner agreed to this???*

Gabriel: *Yeah*

Callie: *What about her cat?*

Gabriel: *So far, so good. Hey. Remember when you told me about pandemic pods? You still want to do that or are you already doing that with some of your neighbors? We'd like to do one*

Callie: *Sure! We're game. We're not doing it with anyone else. But again…did Aria agree to this?*

Gabriel: *She brought it up.*

Callie: *What's going on over there? Is this a body snatcher's situation? Have you replaced her with an automaton? Or brainwashed the poor woman? Is there something in the water?*

Gabriel: *No, but there IS something in the air.*

Callie: *No shit?*

Gabriel: *No shit. We talked—or rather I talked. Ad nauseam. I apologized. For everything.*

Callie: *And…?*

Gabriel: *And…we'll see. I'm taking it slow. She knows I'm interested, but I'm just trying to be a decent roommate for now. And I'm still thinking about the idea of a grand gesture like Sylvie suggested.*

Callie: *Any ideas yet?*

Gabriel: *Not any good ones. Not any that would make a difference in the world. Anyway, how about starting our pod tomorrow night? You can meet Lymond and Frederica.*

Callie: *AND ARIA TURNER*

Gabriel: *There MAY be one other person. We're going to invite Lymond's previous owner. She's a retired history prof from Barnard.*

Callie: *Sounds great.*

Gabriel: *So…6:30. Tuesday Pod Potluck.*

Callie: *PODLUCK*

Gabriel: *Bring whatever. If it's warm enough, we can sit outside in the loggia and crank up the gas fireplace.*

Callie: *Can't wait!*

Gabriel set his phone on his desk and looked down at his feet, at the puppy rolling around with his dragon and pouncing on his shoes. "I've got work to do, buddy, so why don't we get you back in your little cave, so I'm not distracted. After my 10:00 meeting, we can go for a walk." He glanced at the window where a gray drizzly day stared back at him. "Gotta go out, little man, even if it's wet. Maybe we can ask Aria and Fred to come too. If there's a break in the rain. Would you like that as much as I would?" He gently scooted Lymond and his dragon into the crate and latched the door. Then he fired up his computer and got to work.

He didn't like interrupting Aria at work—in no small part because he didn't like thinking about her working on that book of hers, the one that would likely feature him in all his asinine glory—but this time, he couldn't help it. The light rain had stopped and his weather app said he had an hour until it started up again. He knocked at the study door and waited until she said, "Come in. It's open."

He pushed the door open and held up Lymond, now dressed in what looked like a stylish puppy version of a faux Burberry-lined trench coat. "We came to ask if you and Frederica would like to accompany us on a walk."

Aria turned toward her window.

"I know it's wet out," Gabriel said, "but the rain's stopped. We've got about an hour-long window before it's supposed to start up again. And this guy's little legs are short, so we won't be going far."

She bit her lip to keep from smiling and purposefully checked her watch, as if her schedule was jampacked with important appointments. "I think I might be able to squeeze in a short walk." She closed her laptop. "Let me get Fred's leash and sweater."

She went into the living room, scooped Fred up, then retreated to her bedroom. Behind closed doors. A few minutes later, she emerged with Fred fitted out in a similar faux Burberry getup complete with coordinated leash.

"Look at that!" Gabriel laughed. "They're matching!"

"I didn't want to say anything before so it would be a surprise. But it looks like Professor Radcliffe's daughter shops at the same Etsy store Heather likes. Caldwell's wife got this for Fred last year for Christmas."

Gabriel looked down at his well-loved leather jacket—a bit shiny at the elbows from years of wear—and his faded jeans and scuffed loafers. "I feel underdressed."

"Let me grab my coat from the closet," Aria said. "It's stylish enough to cover up my poor wardrobe choices."

And that's when he noticed she was wearing knee-high black leather boots over her leggings. Gabriel watched as she shed her oversized sweater—her nipples clearly visible under her worn camisole—and slipped her arms into a fitted, red woolen coat with a diagonal slash of shiny brass buttons lending it an edgy, almost piratical air. She turned to face him, a fashion plate in black boots, black leggings, and a delectable body-hugging swath of blood red up to her neck, and all topped by that mass of thick curls he could not wait to get his hands on again. He stifled a groan as his blood make a headlong dash straight to his groin.

"There," she declared. "All ready."

"Perfect." Gabriel managed to choke out the word as he reached out to open the door for Aria and Fred, who sauntered down the hall at the end of her leash like she owned the place.

"Wait. Got your mask?" Gabriel asked, holding his up.

"I was a Girl Scout," Aria said, pulling hers from where she had it looped around her wrist. "Always prepared."

After that, they occupied themselves with silly small talk about how prepared she would be in case a hitherto unknown volcano erupted in Central Park and left Manhattan covered in lava. Or a tidal wave rose up from the Hudson to engulf the Upper West Side. Or a deluge of actual cats and dogs rained down from the sky covering the whole city in a flood of furry critters.

And while they bantered, Gabriel imagined Aria whispering, I'm always prepared, they're in the top drawer of my bedside table, and then watching as she ripped open a foil package with her teeth and used her slim fingers to roll a condom up over him. And then, thank god, the elevator descended to the lobby and slowly opened on a soft *whoosh*.

"Ah!" Manuel rose from his chair from behind the concierge desk. He was wearing a blue and white polka-dotted mask today. One that looked homemade. Gabriel made a mental note to ask Sylvie for more of those manufactured masks, KN somethings. "Look at you two," Manuel said. "A matched set if I ever saw one."

"Well, Fred and Lymond are certainly matching," Aria said quickly.

"You look like a fashionable couple out for a walk in the park. Let me get the door for you." He hurried to hold the door open as Fred and Aria led the way out to the sidewalk.

Aria gestured toward the park across the street. "Have you taken him over there yet?"

"Not yet, but what the hell, if you're up for it, let's give these short little wheels a spin."

TWENTY-THREE

THEY HEADED TO the crosswalk and into Morningside Park with Fred leading the way and Lymond pulling to keep up. But there were just too many smells and Lymond quickly lost interest in keeping pace with the cat and instead tried to water every shrub and blade of grass and random stick he encountered.

"So," Aria said finally, "what did your sister say about the pod idea?"

"They're in. I'm pretty sure you're the main attraction." They stopped walking as Lymond circled around and around for an appropriate pooping spot and Gabriel dug in his jacket pocket for the roll of doggie bags. "You should know that Sylvie told me the whole mess, the Aria Turner-Gabriel Landon story, was a popular topic in one of her graduate seminars. Seems everyone was #TeamAria."

"How could they not be?" She shrugged. "I mean #TeamGabriel was a bunch of misogynistic incel basement dwellers who posted daily death threats and regularly imagined what it would be like if I were gang raped in the public square."

He flinched like he'd taken a shiv between the ribs. "Oh, god. Aria, that wasn't me."

"I know that now. But no one else does. And no one knew then either."

Gabriel did his scooping duty and walked over to the nearest trash bin. When he walked back, he looked down at her. "Do I need to apologize all over again?"

"Not to me." She cocked her head and studied his face. "But can I ask you a question."

"Anything."

"I looked up your company. Q.BC. In every article I found, the guy at Diamondback Ventures takes center stage. Brian Johannsen. It's all about him and how Diamondback is making a big bet on private blockchain for banks and other financial institutions. But there's no mention of Gabriel Landon."

He sucked in a breath. "My name is still toxic. They're just playing it safe."

"How do you feel about that?"

He laughed and looked off into the distance. "Not great." He felt her eyes on him, watching. But what could he say? He'd fucked up and even if he didn't have anything to do with the giant tsunami of shit that cascaded from his fuckup, he still represented the initial conditions. His actions had set everything in motion. His name was still mired in mud and, probably, deservedly so.

He turned back to find her studying his face. Her expression was so…concerned, brows drawn together, and lips pursed as if she were thinking deep, worrying thoughts.

"Callie thinks I've brainwashed you," he said. "Presumably because I'm still breathing and taking up space in the co-op."

Aria smiled at that. "Committing murder seems unnecessarily messy. Besides I don't know the first thing about disposing of a body."

"Manuel would probably help you."

She smiled and gave him a sideways glance as they started walking again. The chilly damp air, the smell of rain-slicked pavement and wet earth surrounded them. "I suppose there's still time."

Gabriel reached out and let his fingers brush against a row of shrubs lining the walkway, unleashing tiny rain showers as he passed. "She also suggested that maybe I replaced you with an Aria Turner simulacrum. Or that body snatchers did. Or that there's something in the water. Otherwise, why would you have agreed to letting me take in the pup and to starting the pandemic pod?"

She made a humming sound in her throat that made the hair on Gabriel's arms stand at attention. "Well, I was thinking this morning about how"—she shrugged and looked away—"things have sort of, I don't know, shifted between us in the last few days."

"Shifted." His pulse quickened and he slanted her a sideways glance.

I guess proximity will do that," she said with a one-shouldered shrug.

"I thought it was distance that makes the heart grow fonder."

"Ha. Well, that clearly didn't work for us."

"So, let's go back to this concept of 'shifted.' Can you expound on that?"

"I don't have the urge to kick you in the nuts every time I see you, for one thing."

He laughed at that. "On behalf of my nuts, I'm delighted to hear it."

"And I don't feel the need to punch you in the nose or harangue you about all the ways you ruined my life because, in truth, it sucked for a long time, but it wasn't ruined. I mean, I was on Rachel Maddow three times and Ari Melber twice. CNN. NPR. I had an article in *The Atlantic* and one in *The New Yorker*. I was on *Good Morning America*. I have a book deal. I learned a lot about myself through the whole thing. About how resilient I can be. And stubborn and determined. And that maybe my emotional setpoint was a bit, shall we say, aggrieved. And I finally got therapy to deal with my family. And other stuff. Don't get me wrong. There was nothing good about the whole debacle, but I survived and came out the other side stronger. Healthier."

"Aria…."

He honestly didn't know what to say as they meandered down the tree lined path, Lymond still sniffing everything within snout distance and Fred still marching along, tail arched high and swaying back and forth as if she were grand marshal of their little parade. Words were inadequate for what he was feeling—something akin to the flush of abject shame that he was the initial cause of her troubles and the chest-swelling, button-busting pride that she'd had the courage and wherewithal to get through it. Stronger, she'd said. Healthier. All he wanted was to gather her into his arms and hold her close and keep her safe from all the other assholes who might put her through such trauma in the future. And to know all the reasons she'd needed therapy to deal with her family. And what the *other stuff* was.

She shook her head at him and went on. "So, I guess what I wanted to tell you is that I don't think I hate you anymore."

"Aria...."

He repeated her name like just being able to say it aloud it was a gift. Jesus, the muscles in his arms actually ached without her in them. Like there was a physical hole that had been carved out of his center that only she could step into and fill.

"And your apology," she went on. "I've been thinking a lot about that. What you said and then what you wrote in your note..." She stopped and looked up at him. "Did you really mean it?"

He met her gaze, his expression serious. The line of his mouth taut, eyes a dark green. Focused. "Every single word. I may have fallen off the map for three years, but that doesn't mean I wasn't thinking of you." He took a step closer to her. "Every morning I woke up and thought of you, and every day, it was like a grievous wound re-opening. An evisceration. Literally, physically painful. I was filled with shame and embarrassment. Remorse. Regret. Rage. At me, for so royally fucking up something I thought could be...special."

He took another step closer.

"And now? Now I wake up every morning knowing I'll see you before I go to bed. And when I'm in bed?" His lips tipped up in a lopsided smile. "Let's just say I warned you about the fire hazard."

She let out a little huff of laughter and looked down the path toward where they'd entered the park. "Best make sure I know how to use the fire extinguisher."

"Unfortunately, Aria Turner," Gabriel said, his voice low, a crooked smile slowly forming on his lips. "I lied about the fire extinguisher." She looked up at him, questioning, and he bent close to her ear, as if whispering a secret. "There's only one way to quench this kind of conflagration."

TWENTY-FOUR

THEY MADE TACOS for dinner. Fake ground beef sprinkled with chili powder sizzled in the skillet while Gabriel grated the extra-sharp cheddar cheese and Aria sliced lettuce, onions, and tomatoes. They emptied Gabriel's jar of jalapeño slices and opened a new jar of mango salsa. The taco shells were laid out on a cookie sheet ready for a quick broil and when Aria slid them in the oven, Gabriel popped the tops on two beers—an IPA for him and a red ale for her—and poured them into frosted glasses from the freezer. While they cooked, talking was minimal. Touching was accidental. The air was combustible.

After their walk, they'd arrived back home just in time to welcome Professor Olivia Radcliffe for her visit with Lymond. "Please, call me Liv," she'd insisted, dressed in a smart lavender pantsuit as if she were going out to lunch with friends rather than up one floor and down the hall to visit a dog. And when Aria introduced her to

Gabriel, she'd clapped her hands together and very nearly performed a joyous little hop, right there in the foyer.

"Gabriel! What a coincidence. Or maybe it was meant to be," she said cryptically as they made their way to the living room, Gabriel's hand on her elbow guiding her down the hall and kicking a few stray Lymond toys out of the way as they went.

"Why do you say that?" he asked.

"It's a literary reference," she said once she'd taken a seat and bent down to pet Lymond who cavorted about and tumbled over her shoes. "Lymond, the pup, I mean, is named after one of my favorite literary characters, the enigmatic and, for me, endlessly fascinating Francis Crawford of Lymond. A Scot and a true Renaissance man. And his nemesis is an extraordinarily beautiful man"—at this, she tilted her head and let her eyes flick over Gabriel—"named Sir Graham Reid Malett, Knight of the Order of St John, otherwise known as Gabriel."

"And why would it be 'meant to be'?" Aria asked. "If Lymond and Gabriel are enemies, I mean."

"Oh, I strongly suspect this Gabriel is nothing like Lymond's Gabriel—except for the sparkling charm and handsome features," she turned and gave Gabriel a smile and a pat on the leg. "But by stepping in and caring for my little pup, this Gabriel can atone for all his literary namesake's crimes. And there are many to atone for. I suspect you will have to shower this little guy with a tremendous amount of love and devotion to make up for them."

Gabriel laughed as he picked Lymond up and placed him in Professor Radcliffe's lap—in Liv's lap. She ran a hand over his back and the pup put his paws on her chest and proceeded to bathe her face in doggie kisses. "I suspect you'll have an abundance of love here, Lymond," she whispered. "Okay, okay. That's enough kissing."

Gabriel took the hint and put Lymond back on the floor where he immediately bounded across the room and attacked his dragon as Fred watched from her perch.

"Liv," Aria said, "we were wondering how you're doing since your daughter moved out of the city."

"Oh, I keep myself busy. I listen to audio books and music and chat with old friends on Skype or Zoom or whatever it's called these days. I am a bit addicted, I must admit, to online chess and poker, and solitaire, and I always do the Sunday *New York Times* crossword puzzle. And if I can come visit Lymond every now and again, that will be fine too."

"The reason we're asking," Gabriel said, "is that Aria and I are forming a 'pandemic pod' with my sister and her partner. They live in Columbia faculty housing over on Claremont. It's only a matter of time before this city goes into complete lockdown and opportunities to socialize will be few and far between."

Aria went on to explain the concept. "We think it could be an interesting group. We could get together once every other week. Have dinner. Maybe even play a game—Scrabble or poker or something—or have a little book club."

"My goodness," Liv said. "That sounds delightful. I'd clean you all out at poker, though. I may be an old lady, but I'm absolutely ruthless."

"And maybe," Gabriel added, "we could read that book. The one about Lymond and Gabriel."

Liv smiled and patted his leg again. "Ah. But it's not just one book. It's six. And Gabriel doesn't even turn up until book three."

"Who knows how long this pandemic is going to last. We might get through all six."

Liv let out a long sigh and her gaze drifted to the window and the city beyond. "It would certainly be fun to try."

They'd ushered Liv out and Gabriel had offered to walk her back down to her co-op, but she refused, insisting that she knew the inside of the building like the back of her hand. And then, Gabriel and Aria had retreated to their respective workspaces knowing that everything that was said on their walk, everything Gabriel had said during his apology, and everything he'd written in his note was hanging in the air, heating it, scenting it like creosote and petrichor after a desert rain. And it smelled like new beginnings.

Before they started on dinner, she'd switched her black boots and nearly see-through camisole for thick woolen socks and a pink V-neck sweater. Her hair was still damp from her late afternoon shower. He was still in jeans, now wearing a different long-sleeved T-shirt that fit snug across his muscled chest and tight around his arms, this one featuring a bicyclist in midair above a trail in front of a jagged mountain range. It had dates on it, faded now. From some mountain biking competition he'd participated in a long time ago.

"Cheers," he said, holding up his beer. She tilted hers until they clinked and then they both took a long drink, each watching the other over the tops of their frosted glasses.

Aria set her glass down and pulled on an oven mitt. "I'm going to pull out the taco shells. Can you get the plates?"

"Done." Gabriel set out plates, forks, and napkins, arranging them on the kitchen island. "Let's eat in here. Everything will be too messy for sitting in front of the television, and I'm not ready to face the news just yet. And tacos at the dining room table seems a trifle gauche."

Aria nodded, thinking either his grandmother or the school librarian had certainly had an influence on Gabriel's vocabulary. They loaded their plates and soon they were crunching their tacos and shoveling up the debris as the shells fell apart. "I wish we had guacamole," Gabriel said as he opened two more beers.

"I wish we had our very own Mariachi band."

"I wish we were sitting at an outdoor café in Arizona. There's a Mexican place in Scottsdale with a big patio, brick fire pits, and colored string lights. Best guacamole ever."

"The Sonoran Grill?"

"That's the one."

The conversation flowed quick and easy after that and in no time, they had cleaned up the kitchen and moved to the living room, sitting at opposite ends of the couch. They talked about books—about his reliance on the school, and later, the public library and how she'd grown up in a bookstore—and about what made for a good page turner and what made them stop reading and what made them want to throw a book against the wall. They discussed the relative merits of their favorite literary characters— Elizabeth Bennet and Aelin Galathynius for Aria and Edmond Dantès and Robin Hood for Gabriel—which led to a very lively discussion about why these characters above all others, were so compelling, which naturally meant that Aria had to go down the *Throne of Glass* rabbit hole and they had to argue about the best movie version of Robin Hood. And then…nothing. It was as if suddenly all the words in the world were used up and the only means of communication available to them was touch.

Gabriel had already finished his second beer, and he eyed it, his glass sitting empty on the coffee table. Should he offer to get up and get another beer for each of them? Should he reach over for the remote and turn the television on? Should he say something? Do something? He wasn't about to move toward her. No matter what he was feeling, it was her right to take the first step. To say yes or no. Or wait. Or stop.

And so she did.

Aria set her glass on the table and scooted toward him, her eyes locked on his. Wordlessly, she ran a finger down the side of his face, along his jaw, then up to trace the outline of his lips. He watched her face and couldn't help but respond, his tongue darting out to taste her skin. But that was it. Every muscle in his body was poised, ready to take what he wanted, but he remained where he was, one armed draped across the back of the couch, one resting on his thigh.

She scooted closer and his hands clenched into fists. She cupped his face in one hand and, instinctively, he leaned into it, as if resting the burden of his thoughts in her hands. As if willing to share his worries and concerns with her. Their gazes caught and held. Hot and wanting. Questioning and uncertain. Brown eyes turning dark as night. Green eyes flaring gold sparks. And then, she licked her lips and Gabriel thought he was going to lose it right then and there.

"Can I kiss you, Gabriel Landon?"

"Please," he managed to croak. *Oh, god yes! I thought you would never ask. By all that is holy, yes yes yes.*

And their lips met for the second time, and it was sweeter and more painful and more powerful than anything that had happened that explosive night in the middle of a Phoenix public parking lot.

Out of nowhere, Gabriel thought of the Grinch and how his heart had grown three sizes that day and thought, *oh, Grinch, you piker. You lightweight.* He thought his own heart had gone full supernova and he felt tears prick at the corners of his eyes. Grandma Jack always told him it was fine for boys to cry—that his own great grandfather, a rough and tumble Scotsman who'd immigrated from a farm outside the village of Crieff, was always tearing up over something or other—and so he'd cried plenty over the years, but now…Now he struggled to choke back the emotion, the joy, of having this woman's lips on his again— finally. It was heaven. Nirvana. *Salvation.* And if he never touched any more of her, it would be okay. He wouldn't like it, but he could live with it because she'd given him this. This gift of a kiss.

And then she reached up and gently guided his arm from the back of the couch to around her waist and he nearly achieved liftoff. "You can touch me, Gabriel. I want you to."

Then both his arms were around her, one hand splayed on her back, pressing her to him and the other at the nape of her neck, fingers flaring into her hair, holding the back of her head as the kiss deepened. The desire was a living thing. Ravenous. It had its claws in him, but he knew there was plenty of time for more. For the rest of it. That they were in this now. Together. Just like he'd imagined while sitting across from her in that Phoenix restaurant three years earlier. And he felt that same tidal wave of emotion rushing toward him, towering over him, threatening to drown him. Or sweep him out to sea. He was in uncharted territory, but this time, he had control. Because this time, he'd given *her* control. So, this time, he just pulled her close and held her. And kissed her like there would be no more tomorrows.

TWENTY-FIVE

THEY SLEPT IN their own beds that night. In the living room, she'd draped herself over his body as he'd scooted down on the couch—one leg up on the cushions, one leg bracing himself on the floor—and they'd kissed until their lips were bruised and swollen. And then they'd just held each other as if to preserve the enormity of the moment. One hand tucked under his shoulder, her head resting against his chest, feeling the reassuring thump of his heart. His fingers playing with strands of her hair and lightly tracing the curve of her back, up and down, as soothing as a mesmerist.

There was no music playing in the background. No television newscaster reporting the latest Covid-19 case numbers and death tolls. Just the sound of a gentle rain pattering occasionally against the windows, the steady inhale and exhale of their breathing, and the occasional sleepy growly sound emanating from Lymond's crate where he had curled up with his dragon. They'd stayed like that, in a sort of blissful tranquility, until Aria's phone rang.

She ignored it.

And it rang again.

She ignored it.

Another ring.

And then Lymond stumbled sleepily out of his crate, stretched extravagantly, and wobbled over to stand on his hind legs and look at them, his way of announcing, *I need to pee.*

Aria pulled herself off Gabriel and they both sat up, dazed at the intrusion of the outside world into the sanctity of their private space.

"I'll take him out," he said. "You find your phone."

She nodded, brushed the hair back off her face and looked around. She'd left her phone on the kitchen counter, and as she stood to retrieve it, she heard Gabriel telling Lymond to be patient, that he needed to stick his little legs in these little holes to get his raincoat on. Then she shuffled over to the kitchen and picked up the phone. Three missed calls. All from Caldwell.

She heard the door shut as she hit the call back button. "Caldwell?" she said when her father answered, his voice gruff.

"Heather has a fever. 102. And she's coughing."

Aria's stomach plummeted. "Oh, fuck." She climbed onto one of the kitchen stools and dropped her head in hands.

"She thinks the whole thing is just like a cold or flu and that she'll be fine."

Aria rubbed at her temple. "Maybe it is just the flu."

"No. She went to a horse auction outside of Boston last week with a few friends. Two of them are sick too."

"Jesus, Caldwell. Can you get her tested somewhere? Just to know for sure?"

"How the hell am I supposed to do that? From what I see on the news, there aren't enough tests, and, in case you forgot, we live ten miles outside of a barely-there town in fucking Vermont and I don't even have a driver's license."

"Okay, okay. Are you staying away from her?"

"She's sequestered in our bedroom. I practically had to shove her in there and bar the door. I'm in the guest room."

"That's something. You've got an *en suite* bathroom, right? So, there's no reason she should come out and no reason you should go in."

"What about food?"

"Put it on a tray and leave it in the hall. Do not go near her."

"What if it gets worse?"

"She's got the thermometer right? And her phone?"

"Yeah."

"Have her take her temperature every couple of hours and text you the results. No face-to-face contact. And, I don't know, I guess call 911, if it gets up to 103 or if her breathing is labored."

"Jesus."

"And you need to mask up if she so much as opens the door." Agitated, Aria got up and wandered over to the windows, peering out like she could see all the way to Vermont.

"We don't have any masks," she heard her father say.

"My God, Caldwell, are you even watching the news?"

"Aria, we're out in the middle of nowhere so why should we be worried about Covid? I never even see anyone. I'm working on…a new project…and I'm usually holed up in my office."

"But Heather isn't. She goes into town and, apparently, to fucking Boston." Aria took a deep breath. "Okay, do you have a bandanna or something to tie over your nose and mouth?"

"I think I can find something like that."

"How long were you around her before she started showing symptoms?"

"She came home with a fever. I immediately sent her to bed."

"So not long?"

"Thirty minutes?"

"And you weren't masked."

"I did try to stay at arm's length, you know social distancing."

"Social distancing is six feet."

Caldwell had nothing to say to that.

"Listen, I don't know what else to tell you," Aria said finally.

"There's nothing else to say. I just needed to vent. Tell someone. Thanks for answering."

"You call me if anything changes, okay? I don't care what time it is. And tell me if you start feeling bad."

There was a pause on Caldwell's end. "Did I ever tell you that you're a good daughter?"

"God, Caldwell!" Aria pinched the bridge of her nose. Hard. "No, and now's not the time to start. I'll talk to you later."

"One more thing. How's that roommate working out? Lillian Beauchamp said he decided to stay."

How was it working out? After their make-out session on the couch, Aria wasn't entirely sure how to answer that. "It's fine. I guess we're learning how to get along."

"Okay. You take care. I don't want to have to worry about you too."

"Jeez, Caldwell. Call me tomorrow. Or if there's any change with you or Heather."

Aria didn't know how long she stood in the living room staring out the window at nothing, wondering about all the people all over the globe who were sick or had loved ones who were sick or who were quarantined and alone and afraid. She didn't hear the door open or close when Gabriel and Lymond came back in. She didn't hear them when they came into the living room. She gradually became aware that he was standing next to her, his body a hair's breadth from hers, staring out the window with her.

"What happened?" His voice was a whisper.

"Heather, Caldwell's wife, likely has Covid."

He let out a long exhale and she turned and stepped toward him like he was true north and she a compass dial as his arms came up around her and pulled her close. "Tell me."

"She went with her crew to a damned horse auction in Boston and several of them came home with a fever and a cough."

He let out a long sigh and stroked his hand along her spine, up and down, up and down. They stood that way a long while. No words were needed. There'd be time to talk tomorrow. For now, she was glad she wasn't alone. And she was glad the person with her was Gabriel Landon.

Finally, he walked her down the hall, tucked a curl behind her ear, and pressed a tender kiss to her forehead. "I'm here if you want me," he whispered. Not need. Want.

She held on to his hand and studied his face. She did want the comfort of his arms around her all night, but she wasn't prepared to ask him. Wasn't going to invite him into her room, into her bed. Not yet. Not tonight. And then it was clear he wasn't going to be the one to suggest it, so she dropped his hand, turned, went into her darkened room, and pulled the door closed behind her.

TWENTY-SIX

MARCH 21

EATHER'S TEMPERATURE hovered around 102 for three days before it finally started going down. Confined to their bedroom, she texted her complaints regularly to Caldwell: *I'm freezing, my throat hurts, my head aches, I'm exhausted, my body feels like it's been run over by the garbage truck.* The coughing, thankfully, wasn't as bad as Caldwell feared and she didn't seem to have any trouble breathing. He'd managed to wrangle a chair into the hallway by the bedroom door so he could sit and read and listen, but mostly Heather slept. When her temperature dropped to 100, she wanted out of the bedroom. *It's just like a bad flu,* she insisted. But Caldwell told her he didn't want any kind of flu and that he'd push a piece of goddamned furniture in front of the door if she so much as turned the fucking knob.

Aria listened to all this as Caldwell reported in every couple of hours. In three days, it seemed like she'd talked to her father more than she had since she found out she had a father. And more than once during his now-frequent calls, he'd tried to sneak in the subject of their relationship. She didn't exactly shut him down, but she didn't encourage it either. She felt a bit like she was in male apology overload. First Gabriel, now Caldwell. Two data points did not exactly a trend make, but maybe a global pandemic made people stop and take stock. She wondered if she'd hear from her boyfriend from grad school, or the guy she thought she might have a future with from her sophomore year at UChicago. Or from Troy Jordan.

She definitely did not want an apology from Troy Jordan. In fact, she never wanted to hear from him or about him ever again. Whenever a friend from Sedona mentioned his name, she went quiet with a sort of rage-fueled mortification that seemed to live in her skin and make her go numb.

He was the reason she would never go home for a high school reunion. He was the reason for so many things. Therapy had helped, but it hadn't made the issues go away. Especially the issue of trust. And trust, she knew, was standing in the way of her admitting—even to herself, even after kissing him as if the world was ending—how she really felt about Gabriel, his explanation of what happened after he stormed away from her in that parking lot, and his apology. And it was why she was reluctant to hear Caldwell wax poetic about their father-daughter relationship.

Still, she did truly worry about Caldwell, and she didn't want him to think she would reject him like her half-brother Jeremy had done. She worried so much since that first phone call, that she'd told Gabriel she wanted to postpone the first meeting of their pandemic podluck until she could be better company. Thankfully, in his new role as solicitous roommate and tender and attentive man she'd kissed until their lips were practically fused, he'd let Callie and Sylvie know about the postponement and had taken Lymond down to visit Liv Radcliffe to give Aria space in which to pace and worry herself into a funk.

Since then, Gabriel and Lymond and Liv had spent several hours together in the afternoons, drinking tea and playing poker and talking books and travel and Scotland—where, coincidentally, the literary Lymond was from. Aria knew Gabriel was giving her space—not only for her to deal with Caldwell, but also to deal with the seismic shift in their own relationship. The shift that all those kisses represented. And the fact that Gabriel hadn't done anything more than kiss her goodnight—on the forehead!—after the Incident on the Couch in the Nighttime, which is what she'd taken to calling it in her own head.

Was he waiting for her to make another move? Did she want to make another move? Did she want to take it further? The idea of friends, or rather roommates, with benefits had definitely entered the room and declared itself in a demanding voice. In fact, that voice was beginning to make a certain kind of sense. And why not? They were both adults. *Consenting* adults. What would it hurt? It's a fucking global pandemic and no one knew what tomorrow would bring, so might as well enjoy a romp in the hay with the gorgeous guy you're in lockdown with. She wondered what he'd say if he knew what she was thinking. Probably, *Well, what are we waiting for? Let's get to it then.*

Her phone rang again. This time, it wasn't Caldwell, it was her mother. "Hey," she answered immediately.

"Just checking in," Vi said. "I saw that your governor's stay-at-home order goes into effect tomorrow, and I was thinking of you and your new roommate."

Aria quirked a smile at that. Yes, she was sure her mother was indeed checking in, but she was also definitely fishing for info on the roommate situation. "It sucks, that's for sure," Aria said, "but we both can work remotely, so we won't be affected as much as other people."

"Are you two getting along?" Vi asked. "I have to admit, it does make me feel better that you won't be alone. As long as you're compatible."

"We seem to be doing okay so far," Aria said. She knew her mother and she knew exactly how this conversation was going to go. And what her mother's next question would be.

Vi went on, "What does he do that he works remotely? Is he a writer like you? What's his name, by the way? It feels odd thinking of your roommate as 'Aria's roommate.'"

"Why do you need to be thinking of my roommate at all?"

"Well, number one because you're my daughter and you live far away and there's a global pandemic ramping up and I think of and worry about you all the time. And number two, I'm curious. Sue me."

"That's fair," Aria said with a laugh. "Okay, here's the rundown. He works in tech, programming or something, and his name is Gabe." And in case her intrepid mother put 'Gabe' and 'Gabriel Landon' together, she went on. "He has a sister who also lives in the city, and I might meet her soon because we're thinking of putting together a little pandemic pod group. Also, we decided to take in one of our neighbor's dogs—she's older and decided she can't care for him—so, you can rest easy that I'm not going to be alone. I'll have a cat, a dog, a roommate, and maybe a pandemic pod."

"Is that wise what with the governor's order? Aren't social gatherings banned in New York State now?"

"Jeez, I'm not sure," Aria said. "By the way, we think Caldwell's wife has Covid, but she hasn't been tested."

"Is he sick?"

"Not so far. But he's calling me all the time."

Vi let out a caustic laugh. "Sounds about right. That it would take a pandemic to treat you like family."

"He's not that bad and besides—"

"Honey, let's not talk about your father."

Aria drew in a breath. "You're right. That never leads anywhere good. So, tell me how you're weathering the storm out there in sunny Sedona."

As Vi recounted the latest Covid news from Arizona and gossip from Sedona, Aria heard the front door open. What was it with Gabriel walking in on her when she was talking to her mother? At least she wasn't FaceTiming or something like that. She was sure her mother would recognize Gabriel Landon anywhere.

She turned to face the hallway and to show him she was on the phone, and then couldn't repress a laugh and a smile as Lymond came barreling toward her, little legs churning and ears flopping. She held up one finger and Gabriel nodded, understanding.

"Hey, Mom. I'm gonna snap a couple of pics of the dog we took in from our neighbor. As soon as we get off, I'll text them to you." She knew that would likely hurry the end of the call as Vi Turner was a sucker for a cute pet—dogs, cats, turtles, birds, rats, mice, guinea pigs, lizards, snakes, whatever. As long as Vi didn't have to take care of one, she loved them all.

Gabriel watched Aria try to take a couple of photos of Lymond, an often difficult task as the pup, when he was awake, was a textbook example of Brownian motion, darting this way and that, first after a bone and then after his dragon and then after his snake and then after a different bone. Finally, she got a couple she liked, made a few adjustments, and sent them off to her mother.

"I take it you heard about the stay-at-home order," he said, going to the kitchen to open the refrigerator and stand there looking for inspiration.

"I hadn't until my mom told me," Aria said. "What are you looking for in there?"

"I don't know. Liv served me enough tea to float the Sixth Fleet, but her grocery delivery hadn't come in yet today and she was running low on food. So, no goodies. She offered me more tea or a bottle of Ensure. I took the tea."

He'd taken more than tea, actually. He'd taken Liv's advice to heart. After he'd lost a few hands of poker, he gathered his courage and asked Liv what she thought of the concept of a grand gesture. She was a historian, after all, and he was sure she'd know about the value of trying to communicate something through some sort of action.

She'd raised an eyebrow and shot back immediately. "You trying to atone for something?"

He gave her a wry smile. "You could say that."

"It may surprise you, but I do know how to Google, Mr. Landon. When I first met you, I recognized your name. My memory may not be what it once was, but because I taught at a women's college for thirty-five years and was acquainted with Aria when she lived here during journalism school, I paid particular attention to the social media uproar."

Gabriel leaned back in his chair and let out a *whoosh* of breath. Would his name always be associated with the "social media uproar" he'd ignited?

"That said, let me note that having taught at a women's college all those years—right next door to Columbia—I am well aware that bad behavior is not confined to any gender or sexual orientation. However, I have often wondered if the male of the species has a special affinity for it." Liv picked up her teacup and took a sip. "So, I have to ask. Is this grand gesture you mention one designed to assuage your guilt or truly to atone for the past?"

"My guilt is here to stay. I don't deserve—or want— to assuage it because I don't want to forget the wreckage careless comments can cause. What I want is to show that I'm more than my mistake and that..." He shrugged.

"That Aria can trust you? Love you?" Liv guessed.

Gabriel snorted. "You don't miss much do you?"

Liv's mouth curled up in a smug smile. "No. I don't."

"So, got any suggestions?"

"Well, you can't serenade her from below her balcony or anything of that sort. Romance is fine, but that's not what's going to work in this case. It needs to be something that directly addresses the firestorm you loosed upon her three years ago. Something that addresses a need. Something that Aria would be passionate about."

"I did have one idea…"

"Go on."

"I got to thinking about something Sylvie, my sister's partner, said about abused women. My new company specializes in blockchain technology, basically encrypted computer coding for secure financial transactions. I did a little Googling myself and found that one of the problems women in abusive relationships face is communicating with others about getting out of the relationship and getting to a safe place."

Liv nodded thoughtfully. "Abusive partners control access to friends, family, and co-workers. They control access to phones and email, and banking. It's one of the reasons so many women stay in bad situations. They don't know how to escape. And with limited access to money, they often don't have the means to try."

"So what if I created a messaging app with blockchain encryption and then set up a sort of office or center, maybe with help from someone at Barnard or Columbia, to answer incoming texts and to provide assistance connecting with other services to help women get out of bad situations?"

"There are many domestic abuse hotlines around. What would your app do differently?"

"An abusive partner wouldn't even know what it was. We'd disguise it somehow. I don't know. A woman would create an account, but maybe it's about pet care or child care or recipes or music or something. The point is, it appears to be some happy, unobtrusive, banal app that no one would object to. Or we piggyback on an existing app. It's all just an amorphous idea right now, but the point is that there'd be no way anyone could hack the encrypted messages to see what sort of S.O.S. the user is sending. And maybe there'd be some sort of account set up for each person who uses the app so they could save the messages or store other evidence or documents in case they're needed in court. Like virtual safe deposit box for women who need help finding safety."

"I like it," Liv said definitively as she picked up the cards and began to shuffle again. "That's the kind of thinking that goes beyond grand gesture to potentially saving lives."

Gabriel couldn't stop the smile spreading across his face. "I'm going to talk to Callie and Sylvie about it. Get their reaction. And then, I'm going to talk to Diamondback Investments. I'm not sure they'll want to be involved, but it could be a good PR move."

"Do you want PR for something like this?" Liv started to deal the next hand.

Gabriel picked up a card and then looked up. "No." He huffed out a laugh. "I guess that would defeat the purpose. The app has to be nearly invisible to abusers, but the center to which the messages go? I'm thinking that should be called the Aria Turner Center for…something or other. Hell, she can name it whatever she wants."

"What a choice, tea or Ensure." Aria laughed, and Gabriel was yanked back to the present moment. "We should make a grocery list. Despite the governor's stay-at-home order, we can still go to the grocery store, right?"

"That's my understanding. It'd be hard to keep eight million people home and hungry without causing a riot."

He bent to inspect the lower refrigerator shelves in his search for something to snack on.

"I read a piece in *The Guardian* about the order. We can still walk Fred and Lymond and still go out for a walk or a run. Laundromats are open. Grocery stores. Of course, doctors' offices. But everything else is closed." He stood and turned to face her. "The really scary part is that the number of confirmed cases in the city is skyrocketing, and there are over 7,000 statewide."

"And who knows how many more that aren't getting tested. Like Heather. So, what do we do about our podluck in light of the stay-at-home order?"

"Officially? The article said all non-essential gatherings of any size are banned, but I didn't listen to the governor's press conference, so I didn't get the details."

"Shit."

"But maybe if we sit outside? Turn on the gas fire pit on the loggia? It's basically big enough for social distancing if we consider you and me and Liv as a group and Callie and Sylvie as a group. We can sit on opposite sides of the fire pit. Stay six feet apart as much as possible. And mask when they come in the co-op."

Aria shook her head. "I don't want anyone to get sick."

"Of course not. None of us do."

"But maybe it would work." She walked over and shut the refrigerator door. "I really would like to meet your sister, and I don't want to be the one to put the kibosh on this. We shouldn't have postponed just because Heather was sick all the way up in Vermont."

"No." Gabriel turned to her, leaning one shoulder against the fridge. He rubbed a hand lightly down her arm, as if to warm or comfort her. It was the first time he'd touched her since the forehead goodnight kiss after the

Incident on the Couch in the Nighttime. After Caldwell had called with news of Heather's fever. "You were worried. It wouldn't have been any fun for you."

"I don't want to be the one who says no."

"It's fine to say no, Aria. Always. You don't have to do anything you don't want to do. We're in uncharted territory with this virus." And with each other, he wanted to say. "We can still have Liv over since she rarely goes out of the building, but we can wait until the weather gets nicer to see Callie and Sylvie. Maybe we can meet in Morningside Park. Spread out a couple of blankets and have a PodLuck Picnic."

"It's middle of March already," Aria said, thoughtfully. "April will certainly be warmer. Do you mind talking to them about that? It's only a couple of weeks."

"Of course not." His gaze had taken on a soft, almost dreamy quality. Mr. Solicitous. The perfect roommate. "Now, about that grocery list."

TWENTY-SEVEN

T HE GROCERY STORE was a madhouse. Gabriel was glad he'd volunteered to do the shopping because he didn't want Aria near so many people. He'd taken four of her large canvas shopping bags and was wearing two masks—one KN95 that Sylvie had given him topped with a homemade one with baby javelinas that Aria said her mom made and sent to her before she went to London. And he was wearing gloves. He might have looked ridiculous, but when he'd talked to Callie and Sylvie about postponing the PodLuck—which they completely understood—they told him about the recommendations the university was sending out to employees. And what Sylvie's friend, the nurse at Columbia Presbyterian, had told them: double mask and wear gloves when you're in public, wash your hands frequently, use hand sanitizer, wipe down surfaces. And stay six feet away from everyone else. Which was nigh impossible when everyone was trying to get at the toilet paper.

Thankfully, Gabriel and Aria had plenty of toilet paper. But they didn't have plenty of food. Not after a week with both of them in the co-op. So, he loaded his cart with frozen prepared food they could heat up, including several varieties of pizza, every different size and shape of pasta and several jars of sauce, packages of frozen vegetables and frozen fruit for smoothies, two kinds of ice cream plus hot fudge sauce, fake meat in the form of breakfast sausage, Italian meatballs, ground beef, and chicken nuggets, rice and ramen and granola and raisins and boxed milk that would last, frozen orange juice, half a dozen different kinds of cheese and salami and crackers and bread and more beer and by then his cart was full to the brim.

He took his place in line and refused to budge when the woman behind him nudged him with her cart and said loudly, "It's going to get crowded back here if you don't move up."

He turned and looked at her, glaring at her unmasked face. "It's going to get crowded in the emergency rooms too."

After he paid, including having to buy several extra store bags to fit everything, he'd looped Aria's big canvas bags over his shoulders and grabbed the other handles, four to a fist, as he made his way along the several long blocks back to the co-op. Manuel rushed to help as he saw Gabriel struggling with the load.

"Here." He opened the door wide. "Use my little wagon to get all that upstairs. Hold on." And he went into his office and returned with a nylon-sided wagon with big wheels that looked like it belonged at a beach picnic. "You can borrow this next time," Manuel said. "I imagine the store was a madhouse after the governor's order."

"I barely got out with my life," Gabriel said with a laugh, dumping his bags in the wagon. And then he blinked. "That was supposed to be funny, but I suppose in the current circumstances, it could be considered a bit crass."

"Where would we be, Mr. Landon, without crass humor to keep us grounded?"

Gabriel smiled behind his masks. "I knew I liked you. I'll bring this back down when I take Lymond for a walk." And he turned and pulled the wagon toward the elevator.

Something had changed since he'd gone to the grocery store. Gabriel didn't know what Aria had been up to while he was at the store, but she seemed agitated— almost jumpy—as they emptied the bags and put away the groceries. Had she heard from Caldwell? Was he having symptoms? Was Heather worse? Had something gone wrong with her mother? With her book?

She'd been pretty forthcoming about what was going on up in Vermont, so he figured that if the situation had changed, she'd tell him. So, it wasn't about Covid.

Something else was clearly on her mind, but he didn't want to push her to share more than what she was comfortable with. He was trying hard to respect her boundaries even though he was nearly doing himself an injury by not asking why she'd needed therapy for her family and what the hell the "other stuff" was. But if she wasn't going to share, it wasn't his business. Didn't mean he wasn't dying to know. Dying to kiss her again. Dying to do more.

He felt her gaze on him even when his back was turned and he wanted to whip around and say, *What? Did I do something wrong? What are you thinking? Why are you watching me like that?* But he didn't. Instead, they unloaded the groceries with this electric tension in the air, moving around each other as if trying to avoid physical contact at all costs. As if a touch might ignite a conflagration. And they talked about what Gabriel had bought—*two bags of pistachios and zero bags of potato chips?*—and what to have for dinner as if everything between them was normal.

And then Gabriel took the wagon downstairs and the pup outside for a walk. When he got back, Aria was not in the kitchen. Her bedroom door was closed. He knocked softly, just to let her know he was back. Nothing. He pressed his ear to the door and thought he heard the shower running. And then her stereo came on and the blaring music nearly made him jump out of his skin.

That's what you get for being nosy asshole, he chastised himself.

He carefully backed away from her door and went back to the kitchen to crack open a beer. Then thought better of it. He hadn't gone on a good run since he'd banged his head the first night they'd discovered each other in the co-op. His bump was gone, and his black eye had faded to a lovely shade of pale bile green around the edges. Since he'd given Lymond a walk, the pup could go in his crate while he was gone. So, he changed and left a quick note on the kitchen island—*Gone for a run, be back in 45*—and left.

♥♥

An hour later, Gabriel was back, showered, dressed, and finally ready for his beer. In a pair of loose-fitting, drawstring navy cotton pants and a white Henley, he padded barefoot down to the kitchen to find Aria sitting at the island with a glass of wine. And he stopped in his tracks and stared.

"I went down to my stash in the basement and brought up a new bottle." She swirled the wine in her glass. "It's a Barbaresco. Italian. I thought it would pair well with our spaghetti, store-brand sauce from a jar, and fake meatballs."

Gabriel couldn't stop the slow, delighted smile that tipped up one side of his mouth any more than he could stop his gaze from traveling up and down her elegant form. She was just sitting there, on that kitchen stool, her beauty outshining everything else in the room. Her long flowing floral skirt was topped by a low-cut forest green sweater that had already lost its grip on one of her shoulders, revealing a spaghetti-thin red bra strap that made his mouth go dry. And as opposed to the usual thick socks or fuzzy slippers, she was barefoot. Her toenails matched that sliver of red on her shoulder.

She gave an insouciant one-shouldered shrug. "It's a Friday night. Just because we can't go out and just because the world's going to shit, doesn't mean we can't have a nice dinner."

He stepped back, pushed the sleeves of his Henley up to his elbows, and put his hands up as if in surrender. He saw her eyes flick to his forearms and filed that interesting tidbit away for future examination. "I'm not arguing. In fact, I'm surprised I'm able to speak in coherent sentences with you sitting there wearing that."

She smiled. A flirty smile. A sultry smile that rearranged his insides and did something to his capacity to breathe. And he knew with a certainty that something *significant* had changed since he'd gone to the grocery store. *What had she been doing? What was she thinking? What did she want?* Maybe he should go to the grocery store more often. Like every day. Twice a day. If he could come home to this.

"I was going to have a beer after my run, but since you've opened a bottle of wine..."

"I set a glass out for you." Aria nodded at the counter by the fridge. "I didn't start the water to boil for the spaghetti yet. I thought we could, I don't know, maybe talk before dinner." She got up and walked into the living room, her skirt swirling around her ankles.

Gabriel poured his wine and followed, casting a quick glance at the dog's crate and the cat's tree. Both animals were snoozing, oblivious to the antics of the humans of the world. When he took a seat at the opposite end of the couch, Aria turned and faced him.

"So, I've been thinking..." She paused and licked her lips.

He watched her pink tongue dart out and disappear and the muscles in his stomach clenched. "Okay. Thinking about...?"

She glanced toward the windows, toward the view of their little slice of New York City, and he wondered if she was gathering courage from the city itself.

She turned back to him. "About our history. About how I reacted that night in the parking lot. About your apology, and about how I've changed—how we've both changed— over the past three years. And about this situation, the pandemic and sharing the co-op. And given the other night, here on the on the couch…" She gestured between the two of them. "I think there's something between us that never had a chance back then."

She stopped and waited, giving him an opportunity to say something. But because his brain function was inhibited by a sudden lack of blood, he was slow to respond. He swallowed. Shifted on the couch, rearranging himself since the blood intended for his brain had shot straight to his cock. So, she went on.

"I'm proposing that maybe we should give that something a chance."

He reached forward and carefully set his wine glass on the table, then leaned back against the couch cushions slowly, as if any sudden movement might knock him into a parallel universe where Aria Turner was not proposing what he suspected—*what he hoped!*—she was proposing. That they could be together, like they were the other night on the couch only, of course, more. Together like he'd been dreaming of for three years. Like when he'd constructed all those silly scenarios where he saw her walking down the aisle toward him with the red rocks of Sedona in the background. Where they had kids and dogs and grew old. Celebrated successes and mourned losses. Where they lived and laughed and loved. Together. But he had to be sure of her this time. "Aria," he said, "what exactly are you saying?"

She took a deep breath and held his gaze. "I have an IUD, and we're stuck here together, so I think we should have sex."

TWENTY-EIGHT

SHE COULDN'T BELIEVE she'd had the nerve to actually say the words. She'd tried them out when she was in the shower, going over different ways to broach the subject. Considering what she should wear. How she should act. She didn't know what to expect, but it wasn't this. He seemed to be frozen in place. Although clearly his throat worked because he kept swallowing like he was having trouble with his esophagus, like he was having one of those awful acid reflux episodes like Caldwell sometimes had.

"I want to make sure I get the signals right this time, so let me be clear," he said finally, his voice low, body canting forward toward her, gaze inferno bright. "You think we should be lovers."

Her eyes went wide. Panic stricken. "I never said anything about love."

"Oh, pardon me," he said, leaning back with a caustic tone and the quirk of an eyebrow. "You want us to be pandemic fuck buddies."

Wait. This wasn't going how she thought it would go at all. She'd imagined him saying, *Yes. What are we waiting for?* And then sweeping her into his arms, carrying her off into the bedroom and, well, the rest was both too indistinct and too explicit to think about. But she had thought about it. All day. And she was thinking about it at that very moment.

"Well, I don't like that term," she said, even though it had been swirling in her brain all day. "Why can't we just say that we're two people, obviously attracted to each other despite our complicated history, who are stuck together and who want to enjoy each other's company for the duration."

"Enjoy each other's company. I take it that's code for fucking?"

"God! That's such a crass word." This was going from bad to worse.

"I've heard you say it once or twice."

"But as a curse word, not as…"

"Too bad. It's one of my favorite words, for cursing and for describing 'enjoying one another's company.'" His voice was tight as a drum. "Did you know it's been in use since at least the fourteenth century?"

"I don't care if it's enshrined in the first chapter of Genesis! It seems to, I don't know, demean the process."

"The process," Gabriel said, his voice now the definition of tinder-dry irony. "Is that what sex is to you? Is there a specific workflow you'd like us to follow? Kiss on the lips, check. Suck her nipples, check. Suck his cock, check. Flick her clit, check. Spread her legs and ram it home, check. Like that?"

He was angry. Why was he angry? Hadn't she just said she wanted to have sex with him? She slammed her glass on the table and stood, just as Gabriel's arm shot out to grab her wrist, only pulling back at the last moment.

She jerked away from him, and he held his hands up as if in surrender. "I'm sorry, Aria. That was cruel, and I'm an unmitigated ass for saying that shit. Please don't go." He patted the couch cushion beside him. "Don't be mad."

"Don't be mad? What the hell?" She glared at him, then stormed across the room. She stared out the window for a moment, her shoulders rising and falling as if she was taking deep breaths and letting them out slowly. Trying to calm herself. Then she whirled around to face him. "It took every ounce of courage I had to bring the subject up and you're just throwing it back in my face. Like I'm some, I don't know, pathetic sex starved fool or something."

"If there's a pathetic sex starved fool in this room, it's me." Gabriel stood slowly and walked toward her. She stood her ground as he took her hands away from her face, holding them between them.

"I feel like an idiot," she said, tears of embarrassment swimming in her eyes.

"Aria. I'm the idiot, not you. I lashed out like that because my stupid ego was bruised." His voice was all reassurance now, and she wanted to hide in its velvety softness. "How can you not know that I've wanted you since you first walked into that conference room in Phoenix three years ago. Since I first made a fool of myself and hurt you and fucked things up so royally. But that's the point."

"What's the point? I don't understand you."

"The point is that I don't want to just have sex with you. I don't want to just be your pandemic fuck buddy. I want more than that. I thought I'd made that clear."

"I don't know what you want." She sniffed, pulled a hand away from him and wiped at her eyes, reluctant to look up at his face. "You say these things, like with your apology, but I don't know, after everything else, it's just so confusing. It's really hard to trust you. Trust anyone, let alone a man like you. Maybe I'm just really unsure about stuff like this."

"A man like me." He shook his head. "I'm just me, Aria. And stuff like this? Like what? Like relationships? Between a man like me and a woman like you? Because that's what I want, Aria. A relationship. With you. I don't know why that's so hard to understand."

"But why me?"

He leaned closer and she could feel him studying her face. And feel the heat rising in her cheeks.

"Why would you even ask such a question?" he asked. "I know my apology doesn't erase the pain of what happened, but I want to be with you and that's the God's honest truth. I wanted it then and I want it now."

She just shook her head and looked down at his hands holding hers. How could she answer that? How could she describe what sex had meant to her for so many years? How she felt ridiculous when men looked at her. How she felt after Troy Jordan. After being humiliated so many times. With Ryan at UChicago and Patrick at Columbia. How she'd gone out on a limb with Gabriel in Phoenix because she'd been so drawn to him. Because she liked him so much and then he'd betrayed her. So, she didn't say anything. Just shook her head as the words piled up in her throat, stuck.

She felt him take both of her hands in his again. Give them a comforting squeeze, his thumbs rubbing lightly over her skin. "Who made you feel this way, Aria? Someone did something, said something to you."

She drew in a long breath finally and looked back out the window. "It's stupid. And it happened such a long time ago and I should have gotten over it years ago. Besides, I don't want to talk about it."

"You don't have to talk about it if you don't want to, but I'm here and willing to listen if you change your mind."

"It's too humiliating." She didn't know why she was still talking, why she was telling him anything at all.

"You never have to feel ashamed around me. I—" he drew in a long breath, looked away for a moment, and then brushed a thumb across the back of her hand. "I care about you. I care about how you feel and whatever it is you're feeling right now is not great, and that makes me feel...not great." He laughed. "I mean not great in the sense that if someone did something to you, I am feeling this ridiculous macho desire to, I don't know, put my fist in that someone's face or something equally useless and pathetic that would probably only make things worse."

She sniffed again. "Therapy helped, but it never really leaves you. The shame of it. And then it just taints everything that comes after."

She felt his whole body stiffen.

"Aria, listen to me. When I first saw you, it was like being struck by lightning, like every cell in my body came alive at once. I couldn't speak. Almost couldn't breathe. That's how I still feel when I'm with you. Like I'm so fucking alive I'm going to die of it. That's why I was so angry I messed everything up. There are all these emotions rushing at me and instead of trying to jump out of the way,

I want to scoop them up and hold them tight, press them into my very being. But it's not about sex. Or not just about sex. Don't get me wrong, I definitely want to have sex with you. But it's more than that. I can't explain it without saying things you probably don't want to hear. But I want you to know that you can trust me with this, whatever it is. Tell me what happened and then I'll be absofuckinglutely delighted to go fuck the bastard up. And not in a 'we're enjoying each other's company' way."

She laughed at that and shook her head. "I don't want to tell you. I'm afraid you'll look at me differently. And, I've never told anyone. Except my therapist, of course."

"Did telling her help?"

She shrugged. "I don't know. It sticks to you like a bad smell. Have you even been on the receiving end of a skunk?"

"Thankfully, no. But Boomer was. More than once."

"So, you know. It's hell to get rid of the smell. And any flash of black and white fur freaks you out. It's a bit like that with me and men."

"Maybe saying the words out loud will take the smell out of them." Gabriel led her back to the couch, reached for her glass of wine, and handed it to her. "Here. You can fortify yourself with your delicious wine while you tell me your story." He sat and patted the cushion beside him again. "And I'll fortify myself with liquid courage while I listen and formulate my evil genius plan to go hurt someone."

She lowered herself to sit. "It wouldn't be evil. And he would definitely deserve it." She gave him a weak smile, took a long sip, and leaned back against the couch, pulling one leg up under her. "His name was Troy Jordan, and we were in the eighth grade."

TWENTY-NINE

S HE TOOK ANOTHER drink. God, she was one sentence in and would probably polish off the bottle before the story was over. Gabriel noticed her looking at her glass.

"Here, let me get the bottle." He hurried into the kitchen and brought it back, topped off their glasses, and set it on the table. "It's medicinal," he said with a nod for her to continue.

She stared into her glass. "Troy lived two doors down when I was growing up. Our mothers were friends. We played together. Backyard jungle gyms, flashlight tag, Oregon Trail. We spent a lot of time together and I thought he was one of my best friends. When we rode the bus home, I went to Troy's house since my mom was always at the bookstore. I even stayed at their house whenever my mom went to a booksellers conference or to visit her best friend down in Tucson. Later, when we were older, we talked about our crushes and gossiped. And it was all cool.

I loved being at his house because he had a dad. They had a real family.

"When we hit seventh grade, everything changed. I changed. Developed early. Boobs and hips and my period. It was terrible. My sweet best friend, Izzy, Isabelle, was tiny, petite as a little fairy princess." Aria laughed. "I don't think she bought a bra until she graduated from college. Now, she has three kids, wears a C cup, and has a hero of a husband who jumps out of airplanes to put out forest fires.

"Anyway, back then Izzy had a crush on Troy. I didn't go to his house after school anymore because we were both in clubs or sports, and I could be at home by myself or go to the bookstore. So I didn't see him as often, but Izzy was always bugging me about him. She was obsessed. And, she asked me to talk to him, tell him she liked him. She swore he'd been looking at her in the cafeteria and that they would get married and have babies and live happily ever after.

"So, one evening I went to his house and we sat out on the porch and I told him Izzy liked him. He just looked at me weird and said he didn't think Izzy was his type, but that he'd think about it. The whole thing was strange."

She took a drink of her wine and swished it around in her mouth. She didn't want to look at Gabriel while she talked, so she mostly looked into her glass or down at her hands or out the windows at the night sky.

"At least once a month, a group of us went to the movies on Saturday night. We didn't go to watch the films, but more to just hang out for something to do. And of course, there were some kids who'd hook up and make out in the back row of the balcony. The rest of us would just gossip, eat junk food, drink soda, make fun of the movie, and try not to get kicked out."

She felt him take her free hand in his, his thumb stroking gently over her skin. But she couldn't look at him just yet. It was too mortifying.

"That night's feature was some sort of old black and white vampire movie—part of the kind of classic film series the theater liked to run. Troy came by where Izzy and I were sitting with some other friends and told me he wanted to talk to me. Naturally, I thought it was about Izzy. That he wanted to tell me he liked her. So, I went. I followed him down front, to the second row, right in the middle of the theater where nobody was sitting but where everyone could see us.

"You have to understand that Troy had also developed early. He was already tall, maybe 5'11" or so to my 5'3". Broad-shouldered, popular. Cute. Not the smartest tool in the shed, but certainly not stupid. He was already on the JV football team. And he was putting on a performance for his friends that night. I guess to prove how manly he was. Turns out, I was the star of the show." She stopped. Shook her head. Swallowed hard.

"I'm here," Gabriel whispered. "I'm not going anywhere."

She nodded and looked back out the window. "As soon as we sat down, he pushed up the seat's arm so we were closer together. He put his arm around me and pulled me toward him. Strange, but okay. I figured he just wanted to talk quietly so we wouldn't disturb anyone else. Then he slipped his left hand over my shoulder and down into my bra. He squeezed. I froze. Deer in the headlights. He leaned close, started talking.

"He said something to the effect of, 'You walk around school in those short skirts and those tight shirts that show every damn curve, and I can't stop thinking about you. I went to your volleyball game last week and you were wearing those little shorts that ride up in your ass crack and all I could think of was how it would be if I could fuck you.' Of course, I couldn't believe he was saying these things at all, especially to me. We'd known each other since forever. But he kept going, and God, I remember every word of it. He said, "I'm not a virgin, you know. I know how to make it good for you.'"

Aria remembered how he'd squeezed her nipple until she'd wanted to cry out, but nothing happened. Her mouth didn't even open. She'd said nothing.

"I didn't squirm or protest when his other hand slid over my stomach and he unbuttoned my jeans. Slowly unzipping them. Slipping a finger under my underwear. His lips were close to my ear, his breath was hot. He smelled like beer and popcorn. And all I could think of was whether or not the boys would get in trouble if they'd sneaked beer into the theater. Meanwhile, he was saying something about how good I felt and how he knew I'd wanted this, that all the girls wanted him to do this to them, but I was the lucky one he'd chosen. That he'd been watching me. That I was special."

She shuddered at the memory. His words pooled in her head like dirty rainwater in a deep pothole. She'd watched the vampire on screen, clawing his way up out of his grave to grab an unsuspecting victim by the ankle, unable to do anything but sit there.

"Troy said he'd been thinking about how he wanted to touch me since we'd all hung out at the pool that past summer. He pushed a finger into me, hard, and I vaguely wondered what he would have done if I'd had a tampon in. If I was on my period and his fingers came out coated in blood. But I wasn't and he just pushed in harder, finger wiggling and everything in my mind blanking except for the fact that I was so sad that I could never be friends with him again and that his mother baked the best oatmeal and raisin cookies and how his dad made me feel like a member of the family and how I couldn't ever go back to sit with my friends or go to school or be in the world again. But still I said nothing. Did nothing."

She swallowed, took a sip of wine.

"And then he told me to touch him. Said he could imagine me putting my mouth on him. But I still didn't move. I couldn't. My brain had short-circuited and no longer worked."

She shut her eyes and could see the vampire in the movie chasing a woman through the graveyard. She'd wanted to cry out, *Hide! Fight back! Do something!* But the woman in the movie just ran. And Aria just sat there.

"I felt his hand slip out of my underwear and thought maybe it was all over, but then he grabbed my hand and moved it over the hard muscle of his leg and pressed it against his crotch. 'Feel that, Aria?' he said. 'You make me so hard. I'm gonna come. Just for you.'"

She wiped her hands down over her face, and went on.

"He left my hand on the bulge in his pants and shoved his own back under my underwear, two fingers now pressing into me. Fingers moving in and out and deeper and deeper, fingers pinching and twisting my nipple harder and harder until his body jerked once twice three times and he groaned deep in his throat and I felt a tear slip down my cheek and then his hands were gone and he put his fingers to his nose and said, 'Mmm. Smells like fish. Good thing I love seafood.' Then he did something that seemed like he was rearranging himself in his pants and he stood and left me sitting alone in that second row where everyone could see and he walked back up the aisle to where our friends were."

Aria felt Gabriel's thumb, still moving back and forth over the back of her hand and wondered what he was thinking. Why he would want someone who was so stupid to have let something like that happen to her without doing a damn thing about it.

"I realized, gradually, that I couldn't sit there forever. So, I wiped the tears from my face, rearranged my bra and shirt. Fixed my underwear and zipped up my jeans. I remember wondering what would happen if I walked past my friends, out the door, and into the night, but I didn't do that. I went back to my seat where Izzy passed me the popcorn, pinned me with an excited—expectant look—and said, "Well? What did he say? Does he like me?"

She finally looked up at Gabriel to find his eyes brimming with tears. And that put her over the edge. She let out a sob and leaned into him as he gathered her against his warm body where she, for the first time ever, felt truly safe in a man's arms.

THIRTY

GABRIEL HAD NEVER felt such an overwhelming sense of disgust and loathing for another human being. And that was including his erstwhile partners, Cam and Paul. And he followed the news and had strong feelings about political figures, both in the U.S. and abroad, but he'd never hated an individual the way he hated Troy Fucking Jordan. And he'd never hated himself more than he did in that moment, while he held the woman he loved in his arms.

Love. He knew he loved her, wished he could say the words to her. But now was not the time. He realized he'd loved her from the first moment he'd seen her. Certainly, since that night they'd had dinner and he'd been struck like a gong, held breathless by her keen intelligence, her sarcastic wit, her simple, unassuming beauty.

Something about her spoke to something deep inside him and, well, it resonated like a song sung in perfect two-part harmony. Or a damn gong. Maybe it was biochemistry.

Pheromones or something. Whatever. It had made him feel whole. Complete. *Replete*. And he was shattered all over again by how he'd behaved in that parking lot. How she'd pushed him away and opened her car door to put it between their bodies like a warrior maiden wielding a shield. It would have been abhorrent behavior with any woman, but with this particular woman, it had been another betrayal.

"That wasn't the worst of it though," he heard Aria say as she pushed away from him to sit up.

"Hold on," Gabriel set her away from him and bolted down the hall to grab the box of tissues from his bathroom. He sat back down next to her, drew out a handful and handed them to her. Then pulled out a few for himself, remember Grandma Jack's words: *Real men aren't afraid to show human emotion, Gabriel. And if any of your coaches give you that "Man Up!" nonsense, you tell me, and I'll make little poppets for them and stick pins right in their privates.*

"Thank you," Aria said, wiping her nose.

"You're welcome," he said. "Go on, though. You just said that wasn't the worst of it, and I need to know everything so I can plot an effective strategy for Mission Murder Troy Jordan."

She snorted out a little half laugh. "The worst of it was that his two best friends, boys I thought were my friends too, would hold up two fingers to their noses and sniff whenever they passed me in the school hallway. Sometimes they'd say something so very clever like, 'We must be having fish sticks for lunch.'"

Gabriel stared at her, slack jawed. It took him a moment to register exactly how vile that was. And how it could make a young girl—he had a sister, after all—feel about her body.

Growing up was hard enough what with all the fucking pheromones and hormones and body hair and unwanted erections and periods and pimples and…well, all of it… that he could hardly wrap his mind around anyone being so thoughtlessly cruel. But then, he remembered—like a hammer to the head—what thousands of thoughtlessly cruel men had done to Aria after he'd made thoughtlessly cruel comments about her wrapping her legs around him only to reject him. He swallowed and croaked out, "I'll need their names too." He was only half joking.

She reached for his hand and curled her fingers inside his palm, like it was a little shelter. "It didn't last forever. They got tired of it after a while, I guess. By sophomore year, they'd moved on to other prey, and I hardly saw them anymore anyway. They were running with a different crowd, dating girls a couple of years younger. I was in advanced classes, and they were most definitely not. I did learn later that Troy had done it on a dare. One of the boys confessed just before high school graduation. I guess he was feeling bad about it. Wanted to get it off his chest. But for Troy, it was just another notch in his belt to prove he was the big man in our grade."

"God, Aria. I don't even know what to say other than men are bastards. Fucking animals. I would apologize on behalf of all my gender, but those assholes don't deserve your forgiveness."

Aria wiped her nose again and picked up her wine glass to take a long drink. Fortifying herself for what came next.

"It really did mess me up," she said. "I didn't date during high school. It was easy to be the class bookworm since my mom owned a bookstore. But I dragged all that…shit…with me to college too. I thought I could leave it behind, and I did sort of. I mean I had plenty of make out sessions and I wasn't always completely self-conscious, but the problem went beyond that. Troy had been one of my best friends and he betrayed me just to make himself look like some kind of big man. So, how could I trust myself to know who to give myself to? Who to be with. How could I trust myself to know *how* to trust anyone else?"

He couldn't help himself. The words were out of his mouth and floating around the room before his brain caught up. "And did you find someone? To trust?"

She cut him a glance. "Are you asking if I'm a virgin?"

He winced. "No. God, I don't care about that."

"The answer is no and no."

"No and no. You're not a virgin and you never found someone you could trust."

"Oh, I trusted them, all right. At first."

"Shit." He ran both hands down his face and then through his hair. "What happened. Will you tell me?"

"Might as well. In for a penny, in for a pound, as my mother says." She pulled a leg up beneath her again and reached for the crocheted throw she kept draped over the arm of the couch. "I'll make this part short and sweet. I didn't know I had a father until I was fifteen and my mother told me about Caldwell and her brief affair—two nights—with him while he was doing a book event at her store. Caldwell was never a father to me, but once I reached out, he didn't reject me. He treated me as if I were a pet. Paid my way through UChicago, though. Probably helped me get into journalism school. Gave me this co-op. But we've never had much of a relationship. Have you read his work?"

"No," Gabriel answered tersely. "Not sure I want to if he treats you like a pet."

She sighed and looked off into the distance. "The man can write like an angel and a demon both. In the same sentence. His work deserves all the accolades he's received, but in real life, he's actually a first-class narcissist. Unfortunately, I sort of love him anyway." She shrugged and draped the crocheted throw over her legs.

"Anyway, my boyfriend at UChicago was, I thought, a nice, sweet boy, another book nerd like me, who wanted to take it slow. Just a few goodnight kisses and plenty of long conversations. I thought this is nice. Maybe this could work. And then my roommate saw him at a gay bar with his boyfriend. Turns out he just wanted to get close to me so I'd ask Caldwell to read his pathetic little coming-of-age novel and help him get an agent."

Gabriel shook his head in disgust. "Are there any good guys in these stories?"

"Honestly? Not really. The one guy I dated in grad school was worse. After just a couple of weeks, he suggested that since he'd bought me dinner so many times, I could pay him back by arranging an interview with Caldwell. The jerk was doing his dissertation on the impact of the Pulitzer Prize for fiction on American letters."

"What did you say?"

"I told him to fuck off. And then I went out to some party and got drunk and slept with the first guy I met. Some physics postdoc from Egypt or something. I don't even remember his name. Maybe Amir or Abdul. I really have no idea. There were a few others like that. All equally forgettable. All sort of melded together in my head under the rubric of *Why Sex Sucks*." She sighed. "And there you have it. The complete and total fucked up sex life of Aria Turner."

"And that's why everything I said and did and why everything that happened to you because of me was even worse than I could have imagined."

"It felt like the worst betrayal ever, but—" She shook her head. "I'm not special, Gabriel. I've interviewed over fifty women for the book, and their stories prove that what happened to me is not unique. For every woman I talked to, they told their own stories or spoke of friends or family members who had gone through similar trauma. And for women of color—especially ambitious women using their platforms to speak out—it's always worse. Whether online or in real life, it's appalling what men get away with. From juvenile catcalling and mundane immature verbal cruelty to intimidation and physical abuse to downright rape. And that's not even taking into consideration the obstacles women face in the workplace, getting equal pay for equal work or promotions or even being heard and taken seriously in a meeting. God, the stories I've heard…"

Gabriel leaned back on the couch and looked up at the ceiling. "How can the human race continue to procreate when half of it treats the other half like such utter shit and doesn't even think twice about it? When men aren't waging wars on each other, they're waging wars on women. Demeaning them. Controlling them. How do we even survive? How do we change that behavior? Maybe Grandma Jack was on to something with her poppets."

"Poppets?"

Ugh. He wished he hadn't said anything and tried to wave the question away, but she pushed.

"Remember, I'm from Sedona, home of the healing vortexes. I've probably heard it all. Mom has a whole section in her bookstore dedicated to spiritualism and witchcraft and the power of the vortexes. And that included voodoo dolls."

He let out a heavy sigh. "Let's just say Grandma Jack had a sympathy for sympathetic magic. As a potter and a sculptor, she worked in clay and stone, some bronze and marble, you know? Used to say she felt the 'resonating power' of the earth in her hands and could feel it speaking to her when she was shaping it, like it was guiding her toward the final form of the piece she was working on. That all the earth—and especially living, organic things—have inherent power."

"There's nothing unusual about any of that. Get to the poppets part."

He shook his head and gave her an embarrassed half smile. "As you may have already figured out, I, um, tear up and cry easily. Apparently, I inherited this manly trait from my great grandfather. Grandma Jack's father, Callum Landon. And she used to say that if any of my coaches gave me grief about being in touch with my emotions or told me to 'Man up,' she'd make poppets of them and stick pins in their privates." He snorted at the memory. "I'd come home upset about something at school and she'd give me this look and say, 'Do we need a poppet for that?' When I got older, I figured out that it was really about venting your anger on something safe. That if some guy is giving me grief, I shouldn't haul off and lay him flat, but that I could just," he shrugged, "smash a poppet instead. Metaphorically speaking."

She looked at him for a long moment, then said, "With approximately four billion men on this planet, we're gonna need a lot of poppets."

He gave her a crooked smile. "Grandma Jack would've loved you. She was extraordinary, different. Went her own way always." He touched her cheek, ran a finger along her jaw. "And you…you're so brave and resilient. What you went through, what women around the globe go through, it's intolerable, and yet you're doing something about it."

"It *is* intolerable, but it's the world we live in. And it's why my book is so important to me. And to so many others. Why I got a six-figure advance for it. And I know I can thank Caldwell for that too, since he basically convinced his agency to take me on. Even he knows that in the wake of the #metoo movement and the 'grab 'em by the pussy, you can do anything' era, understanding the online world of men bullying women, *threatening* women, is imperative if women are to have any safe spaces in the online world or in the real world. Caldwell may treat me like a pet, but I am his daughter. And he may be a narcissist, but I do think he cares about me. As much as he's able to care about anybody."

Gabriel didn't want to ask, but he had to. He clenched his jaw and scrunched up his face, as if expecting a blow. "How much of your book is about me?"

She huffed out a little laugh and reached out to pat his leg. "As I said, I'm not special. My story is part of it, yes. But you, so far, have only been mentioned in the first chapter. Setting the stage for my own experience. It was what happened the next day and all the days after that were so traumatizing. But most of all it's about all those other women's stories. About all of us."

"Maybe your book is your poppet." Gabriel shifted to sit up. He turned to her, reached out to take her hand. "What can I do to help? To make your poppet powerful? An apology is one thing, but what can I do to atone?"

"Atonement. That's a weighty concept. I don't know the answer to that."

"Can we start with a kiss and then move on to me making you a spectacular dinner of pasta, sauce from a jar, and meatless meatballs?"

She laughed and drew in a long breath. "That's as good a place as any to start."

He leaned toward her and pressed a warm kiss to her lips, then drew her into his arms and rested his chin on the top of her head. "Thank you for trusting me tonight. It means everything to me."

She pulled back and put her hand on the side of his face, rough with a full-day's growth of stubble. "Thank you for not thinking I'm a pathetic sex-starved fool."

"About that. I promise we're going to revisit that topic soon. Not tonight." He pressed a kiss to her palm. "But very soon."

THIRTY-ONE

MARCH 22

VERY SOON TURNED out to be while Gabriel was making coffee the very next morning. Once again, he was up first. It wasn't yet five a.m. when he'd thrown the covers off, needing to move. Get out of bed. He'd pulled on the same clothes he'd worn the night before and had already taken Lymond out for a short morning walk, fed both the dog and the cat, and had skimmed the headlines all by the time Aria came shuffling into the kitchen around six. He'd been just about to turn on the coffee bean grinder when he heard a noise, turned, and saw her bending over to pet Lymond, her breasts hanging down like perfect globes and that pajama top gaping open to provide an unimpeded view of the shadowed valley between them. She was wearing those same pajama shorts, the too-tight top, the long velour robe with the belt trailing behind her like a tail, and her ridiculous fuzzy slippers.

At the sight of her, his lungs temporarily seized up only to start working again with a sudden jerk and a sharp pain. Every cell in his body went on high alert and every hair stood at attention.

He'd replayed the events of the previous evening over and over again until he'd finally fallen asleep around three, still angry and disgusted at himself and every other asshole who'd ever treated Aria with disrespect. Truth was, she was brave as hell. She hadn't turned tail and run when things got ugly. He had. She hadn't disconnected from her life and gone into hiding. He had. She'd been the one to stand tall and speak out while he'd hidden behind his grandmother's metaphorical skirts. What an idiot. He was ashamed of himself.

But that didn't stop him from desiring her. And what kind of asshole did that make him? After everything she'd been through, he still wanted her in his bed. Beneath him. On top of him. Hell, he wanted her more now that he knew what she'd gone through and how strong she'd been to face it all with such dignity.

Jesus. What had he ever done to deserve her trust? Nothing. But still, she'd taken a chance and told him her story even though he didn't deserve it.

He took two steps toward her as she straightened up and brushed the curls back away from her forehead. His gaze rapt, he opened his mouth to speak, but the words were stuck behind the lump in his throat. His heart felt like it was going to go supernovae.

"What? She looked up at him, questioning.

He swallowed. "Is now too soon for that talk?"

Her brows drew together. "What talk?"

"The talk about us having sex."

Her eyes went wide. She put a hand on the island as if to steady herself. "You want to talk about us having sex?"

She turned and looked out the living room windows where the sky was still dark, with a faint tinge of gray on the far horizon. "Now?" She ran a hand over her unruly curls.

"Um, yes?"

She looked up at him. Unsure. "Okay."

He took another step toward her, reached out and traced a finger down the elegant arch of her neck and across her collar bone.

She frowned up at him. "Wait. You were the one who said you didn't want to have sex."

He shook his head. "No. I said I didn't want to *just* have sex. I want to make love to you."

"What's the difference?" Her question came out breathy and nervous, and the timbre of it went straight to his groin. His whole body felt like a struck tuning fork.

"I want to honor the fact that you put your trust in me last night. I want to show you how much that means to me. Not just with words. I want to start this new day with you in my arms."

"Are you sure?" She looked down at herself and gestured as if to say, *You want this?*

"I've never been more sure of anything in my life. In fact, I'm so sure that if we don't move quickly, I may embarrass myself right here in the kitchen over an empty dog food bowl." His heart soared when he saw a smile slowly take shape on her lips.

"Should you put Lymond back in his crate?"

He plucked Lymond off the floor, grabbed his closest toy, and strode into his bedroom, muttering to the dog on the way. Moments later, he was back in the kitchen. But Aria wasn't there. He turned and looked back down toward the end of the hallway where her normally closed bedroom door stood open. He prowled toward it as if it was a magic portal that might vanish at any moment. He reached it, put a single finger up against it, and pushed the door open wider. Peering in, he looked around the room.

It was comfortable with several nice prints on pale blue walls, a few personal photos, and books piled everywhere. There was an armchair and ottoman, similar to the ones in his room, and a queen-sized bed with a thick lavender and cream striped duvet thrown haphazardly over it, like she had just rolled out from under the covers. Which, he guessed, she had. She wasn't a neat freak. The skirt she'd worn last night was slung over the back of a chair with the sweater in a wad on the floor. He'd never been in the room before. And now, Aria wasn't in it either.

And then the bathroom door opened. "I was in the bathroom," as if she had to explain that. "Wanted to brush my teeth again," she said. "Wash my face. You know." She looked away, hesitant, and Gabriel stepped inside and closed the door behind him.

Their gazes locked and held as he stepped toward her, anticipation filling the room like a heavy scent.

"Wait," she said, stepping past him to turn off the light. "I'll keep the bathroom light on, but..."

"You said you have an IUD, but I have condoms. Do you want me to—?"

"I mean, if you're..." She shook her head and looked away, a pink flush on her cheeks.

"I'm clean. I haven't done this in a while, Aria. So, word of warning, it might go rather quickly. Especially if there's nothing between you and me."

"Typical CEO, managing expectations."

He laughed. "Seriously, I'll be more than fine either way, so whatever makes you most comfortable is what I want."

She cast a sly smile up at him. "How about Green Day on blast?"

"Except that." He slipped her robe off one shoulder.

"We could reprise our first night in the co-op together with my Stones playlist."

"No." He slipped the robe off her other shoulder and pushed it down her arms until it pooled at her feet.

"Elgar's *Salut d'Amour*?"

"I don't even know what that is, but no. Absolutely not."

"You don't want any music?"

"The only music I want to hear is you moaning with pleasure when I make you come."

And then his mouth was on hers and his arms were around her and her arms were around him and they were pulling themselves closer and closer, as if they could become one, and the poignancy of their recent night on the couch and the urgency of their long-ago night in the parking lot merged into a cascade of kisses so deep and delicious and demanding and giving that it brought tears to his eyes. And then he was marching her back until her legs hit the bed.

"Sit," he said.

She sat.

"Arms up." He lifted the hem of her shirt. She obliged willingly and he pulled the shirt over her head, tossed it toward the chair, and then just stood and stared down at her until she squirmed under the intensity of his gaze. With a held breath, he reached out and lightly touched one ruched nipple, the color of a delicate coral shell. She flinched as if in pain but let out a little gasp of pleasure and arched toward him.

"Exquisite," he whispered. "Like a work of art." And then his other hand came up and he gently tugged and palmed and toyed with both nipples all the while watching the pleasure play across her face.

"Lay back." She fell back almost lazily, dreamily, on the bed, and he gently tugged at the waistband of her pajama shorts. "Up," he urged, and she lifted her hips so he could slide them off. They ended up somewhere by the chair.

He leaned over her and took one nipple in his mouth, sucking gently, scraping the tip with his teeth. And then he moved to the other breast, but Aria pushed him away. She propped herself up on her elbows and said, "Before this goes too far, I want to see you." She reached one hand down toward the hem of his shirt. "In real life."

"Real life?"

"Before I contacted you for the interview, I did a bit of Instagram stalking. I'm not proud of it, but I've never been able to get the images of you lounging around that pool out of my mind.

"Jesus, Aria," he groaned and closed his eyes at the embarrassment of those memories. "Don't think of that now."

"Then take off your clothes so I can see you. So, I can touch you like you're touching me."

He straightened up, looked down at her and slowly, *slooowly*, reached back between his shoulders and dragged his Henley over his head. He kept his eyes on her face as he ran both hands through his hair, making a grand show of his rippling biceps and the muscles moving beneath the skin of his lightly furred chest. Then, with great deliberation, he tugged at the drawstring of his loose-fitting pants and they drooped over his hips, catching on the muscular curve of his ass. He pushed them down, stepped out of them, and kicked them out of the way. The only thing left was his snug, tight-fitting navy boxers. He arched a brow at Aria as if to ask, *You want these off too?* She nodded and off they went.

Her eyes tracked up and down his body with awe, like she was seeing the stunning beauty of Michelangelo's David for the first time, taking in every muscle and plane and curve. His chest. His arms. His legs. His penis, which was in a very different state than David's.

"Now, Aria Turner," he said, bending over to press a kiss to her belly button and then dropping to his knees. He felt the tension gather in her body and smoothed his hands up and down over her thighs. "Relax. Don't get twisted up inside your brain. Just allow yourself to feel. And know that as much as I want to drive you out of your mind, this," he said, using his palm to cup her mound, "will drive me out of my mind too. I'm going to kiss you until all you can think of is my mouth and my lips and my tongue and my hands on your body. And then I'm going to enter you like a supplicant entering a holy place. And when we're both done, you will know that there is no part of you that is not beautiful and precious and," he choked on the words, "worth worshiping."

Then he gently pushed her legs apart and set out to prove his point.

THIRTY-TWO

WHEN ARIA CAME to, her ears were still ringing, and little streams of tears were rolling down the sides of her face into her hair. Gabriel was still inside her. She could feel his little pulses and twitches and squeezed her inner muscles in response. He groaned against the curve of her neck, and she felt a sated, satisfied smile bloom on her face. His chest was heaving like he'd just run a marathon, but he somehow knew she was smiling.

"Told you," he said on a soft huff of laughter. He lifted his head and looked down at her laying in a splash of sunlight from her window, revealing a bright, clear New York City morning. "I think we're three for three on the orgasmometer. I say we have a couple cups of coffee and a little breakfast and then try for four."

"Oh, God," Aria said with a giggle, "I'm not sure I could survive four."

"Oh, don't worry about that," he said with a wicked grin. "I'll ply you with plenty of fluids and food and make sure you're well-hydrated and well-nourished. When we run out of supplies, I'll go back to the grocery store. It's my new favorite place. Last time, when I came back home, a beautiful woman propositioned me."

She snorted and felt him slip out of her. He lifted himself and plopped down by her side, and immediately she missed the weight of him, the comforting feel of his skin on hers. "Gabriel?" she said, her voice a little quavery.

He tilted his body toward hers and rested his head on one elbow to look down at her.

She touched a fingertip to his lips and pressed lightly. "Thank you."

He grabbed her finger and kissed it. "It was my pleasure." He gave her a half feral grin then. "Seriously. Your first orgasm, when I had my tongue pressed against you and my fingers inside you, nearly killed me. And when you started giggling, literally doubling up from the sheer joy and release of it, I swore fealty to all the gods old and new, as they said on *Game of Thrones*, if only I could make you do it again. I was already on my knees so that sort of supplication was no problem."

She laughed and shook her head at him in wonder. "You are so weird."

"And then, lo and behold, it happened again! One of those gods was listening, at least. Your breasts, your hips, the small of your back, that little place at the nape of your neck and the base of your throat and behind your ears, I couldn't stop touching and stroking and kissing and licking. Tasting. I didn't want to be in you quite yet because then it would be over. I knew I would come too fast, like a rookie first-timer. And then you called out my name—*my name!*—and made that otherworldly sound that hit me right in the solar plexus and then started giggling again. Jesus. It was the best gift anyone had ever given me. Until we came together. Until I slid inside you and you were so perfect and snug and warm, like I belonged there. Until I moved in you, and you arched up to meet me and we found our rhythm and then…Until you cried." He kissed her eyes and rubbed a thumb along the trail of her tears until it disappeared into her hair. And his expression went somber. "And that was the best gift ever."

"Knowing you can make me cry?" Her voice was teasing, but her eyes searched his face for reassurance.

"Damn right." He kissed the tip of her nose. "I'm glad I'm not the only one bawling my eyes out over earth-shattering orgasms."

"You're not the only one," she whispered. "Not any-more."

"So, what do you think?" He pushed himself up and rolled over to sit on the edge of the bed. "Breakfast?"

She smiled. "And coffee and snuggles with Lymond and Frederica." She sat up and stretched luxuriously. "God, I feel like I'm in love with the whole world." She caught herself and went still, casting a quick sideways glance back over her shoulder at Gabriel.

"Don't worry." He moved one finger down her spine, a whisper of a touch. "I won't take it personally. It's probably just a post-orgasm high." He paused and waggled his eyebrows at her. "Although I did notice that you programmed your number into my phone, and in my book that means a serious commitment. Especially with that photo you used as your contact profile."

She laughed. "Yeah, there's nothing sexier than a woman with a hairless cat on her lap and a miniature doxie trying to climb her head."

"Especially when said woman is wearing those barely-there pajamas."

"Hmmm. I'll remember that."

"Don't worry. I'll remind you."

THIRTY-THREE

MARCH 23

"I CAN'T STAY IN BED ALL DAY."

"Why not?" Gabriel asked as they lay together like spoons nestled in a thick chocolate sundae, his arms wrapped around her. He blew a soft stream of warm air over her ear, and smiled when he felt her shiver in response. Again.

"Because, I don't know," she said with a snort of laughter. "Because we basically stayed in bed all day yesterday?"

"You say that like it was a wasted day, but I don't remember it that way." He nipped at her earlobe. "Was it wasted for you, Aria? Was last night a wasted night?"

"No." She shook her head and reached back around to rest her hand on his naked hip. "It might very well have been the best day of my life. That and the day I signed the contract for the book."

He didn't want the book to ruin the moment, but he felt like he had to say something. "I'm glad my part in yesterday's 'best day' is more…desirable…than my part in the other one."

She sighed and, thankfully, let that subject lapse. "I don't think I've spent this much time in bed during the day except when I had the flu or had my tonsils out. I'm hardly ever sick." She reached for her phone on the bedside table and checked the time. "It's three in the afternoon!"

"First," Gabriel said softly, "there's a stay-at-home order that takes effect today. Second, I made you a spectacular brunch of special Gabriel Landon Eggs Benedict and fixed you a delicious Mimosa—"

"With a bottle of *my* champagne."

"With a bottle of *your* very nice champagne and *my* very delicious store-brand frozen orange juice. And, if you recall, we enjoyed those in the kitchen, disproving your assertion that we've been in bed all day and, incidentally, proving that you're not starving or in need of hydration."

Aria sighed. "It was nice…thank you for cooking."

"Third," Gabriel went on as if reciting from a list, "I've already cleaned Fred's litter box and taken Lymond out for two puppy breaks, so they both should be fine. And fourth, it's a Sunday and therefore, officially unofficially, a day of rest. And I'm more than ready for a nap." He pushed his hips forward, nudging her backside with his erection which, after a few hours of rest and relaxation over brunch and a walk, was more than ready to get back to work.

She prodded him in the ribs with her elbow. "I've come to understand that the word 'nap' has a very different connotation for you than it does for me."

"Ah, but all the experts say that strenuous exercise should be accompanied by plenty of rest."

She turned to face him then, her brows drawn down in a frown, her lips turned up in a sly smile. "Your strenuous exercise and your rest appear to be the same thing."

"It's more like our very own closed-loop system. We enjoy our 'strenuous exercise' and then our system feedback gives us the information we need to adjust or improve our behavior in order to enable us to enjoy *more* and *better* 'rest' as we learn each other's bodies. And on and on and on. For instance, I learned yesterday that if I scrape my teeth just slightly over your nipple and then tug on it with my lips, like this"—he bent to show her—"you nearly come out of your skin. Or nearly come, I should say. We could test that data point during our nap."

"Gah…" Aria breathed and arched into his embrace.

"My sentiments exactly."

Two hours later, they were finally up, showered, dressed, and sitting in Liv Radcliffe's living room, while Lymond sat next to her shoes, chewing on his little dragon, still trying his best to tear one of the wings off.

Liv watched him for a moment with a distant, but affectionate smile on her face, then said, "So, the *New York Times* says we've got a Major Disaster Declaration now. From FEMA. Billions in the state's coffers to deal with the pandemic. And, apparently, half the cases nationwide are right here in New York."

"I haven't read the paper today and only had the chance to skim the headlines yesterday before something came up that needed immediate attention." Gabriel shot a crooked smile at Aria who suddenly became fascinated with one of the many paintings adorning Liv's walls. "But I hope like hell that whatever pandemic plans the state had in place are worth the paper they're written on."

"I hope so too, of course," Liv said, nodding. "But my prediction is that this pandemic will make a lot of people very rich. Billions of dollars in a government account makes a fine target for less than fine people. No matter that we've got more than 10,000 cases now, I guarantee you that grifters won't shed a tear for any of them. The rich will get richer and government contracts will flow like water to the friends and relatives of the well connected." Liv shook her head in disgust.

"As a historian, I imagine you've read about plenty of grift and self-dealing from all quarters and across all time periods." Aria said.

"Unfortunately, it seems it's part and parcel of human nature." Liv's otherwise sonorous voice took on an edge. "And did you read about what happened at that nursing home?"

"No?" Gabriel asked and looked to Aria who shook her head and said, "What happened?"

"Out in Washington State. Kirkland. One hundred and twenty-nine people in one nursing home, including 81 residents, tested positive for Covid-19. Thirty-five have died. It's horrific."

"Holy shit," Aria said, silently giving thanks that Heather appeared to be doing better and that, according to his latest texts, Caldwell still hadn't shown any symptoms.

"Apparently," Liv went on, "the first positive tests were on February 28. It's only March 23. In just a few weeks, the virus swept through the nursing home and then, oblivious to the fact that they were infected, staff members spread it to other nursing homes in the same system. Imagine being one of those residents as this is all unfolding. Imagine being closed up in a place like that with all those sick people and with nowhere to go and no recourse if your care is not even adequate. It makes me want to scream."

Lymond, apparently sensing the tension in Liv's voice, dropped his dragon and tried to scramble up into her lap. Gabriel leaned over and gave his little butt a boost and the dog settled in, looking adoringly up at his former owner.

"My kids…" Liv ran a hand over Lymond's back and scratching him behind the ears. "My son's in California and my daughter's in New Jersey. Might as well be the moon. They've signed me up for a swanky place out in Saddle River. It has a chandelier in the lobby." She looked around her co-op at the minimalist elegance of her furnishings and the art and collectibles gathered from travels around the globe. "Do I look like a chandelier kind of woman?"

Liv waited a heartbeat for either Aria or Gabriel to respond and then laughed. "The answer is no. I do not and am not. And they want me to move in on April Fools Day. That's less than two weeks away! I am old and foolish, but not that foolish. Assisted Living with nursing care and hospice for when the time comes." She coughed out a harsh laugh. "I'd rather have assisted suicide."

Aria and Gabriel glanced at each other.

"No, don't give each other that worried look. I'm not about to make a mess by putting a gun to my head." She turned to Gabriel. "Can you pour me some more tea, dear?"

Dear? Aria raised her brows at Gabriel. He really had charmed the old woman.

"They're worried about me, my children. I'm legally blind now and was born with a hole in my heart—atrial septal defect. It's a miracle I've lasted this long. And recently…I've had a few additional medical complications crop up." Liv waved away their concerned looks, shooed Lymond off her lap, and took the cup of tea Gabriel offered. "It's why I wanted Lymond to go to a good home."

Gabriel smiled at that. "I certainly love the little guy."

Liv laughed and reached out to pat Gabriel's leg. "I know. He's easy to love." Then she leaned back and looked off into the distance. "My family had money," she said in a no-nonsense tone, "so I was lucky to have a fine education. I married young, to a man similarly well-endowed." She chuckled. "In the pocketbook, I mean. Mostly." She cut them a sly look. "And then I was widowed young. I had the money to send my children to boarding school and so I did, and then I lived my life, pursued the things I was passionate about. Travel and history. Teaching. I've had a good life. Lots of friends. Lots of lovers. A few were even worth the trouble. One was…special." She stared down into her teacup for a moment, then looked back up. "I've visited beautiful places all over the world, met fascinating people. Had a few adventures my children know nothing of." She nodded as if in affirmation. "All in all, it's been lovely."

Again, Aria and Gabriel shot each other glances, like *Where is she going with this? Why is she telling us these things?*

"It's no wonder my children don't know me," Liv continued. "Or that they want to shunt me off some place where a cheery attendant will undertake to teach me to play pinochle or help me put together 1000-piece puzzles or whatever it is they do in those places." She shook her head. "Don't get me wrong. I don't blame my kids. I love them, but I don't really know them, and they don't really know me. Not every woman is born with a mothering instinct."

She took a sip of her refreshed tea. "Well, I'm sorry that this was not the uplifting visit we usually enjoy, Mr. Landon. No poker today, I'm afraid. I'm in a bit of a sour mood and have much to do to prepare. The politics, the pandemic, the people…I'm tired of all of it." She held her cup up in a mock toast and then put her cup down on its saucer with a little rattle. "Present company excepted, of course."

Then she looked, really looked, at Gabriel and Aria. It was the first time she'd seen them together since they took Lymond in. A big smile transformed her face. "Well, look at you two. So that's how it is."

Aria's face went pink, and Gabriel reached out without thinking to take her hand in his.

"I must say I am delighted," Liv went on, "but not surprised. Now I can rest easy. No matter what happens, Lymond will most definitely be in good hands."

THIRTY-FOUR

MARCH 24

WHEN GABRIEL OPENED the door the following afternoon, he was met by Manuel and a woman he'd never seen before, both wearing masks and both looking incredibly serious. Manuel had texted a few minutes earlier to see if it was okay if he came up with a visitor for both Aria and Gabriel. He invited them in, knocked on the door to the study, where Aria was working, and told her the visitors had arrived.

After leaving Liv's the day before, he and Aria had eaten frozen pizza and made hot fudge sundaes and ignored the news. As they sat on the couch scraping the last of the hot fudge from the bowls and licking their spoons, Gabriel had texted Callie to ask how she and Sylvie were surviving.

Callie: *I can't wait to get back into the lab*

Gabriel: *When will that be?*

Callie: *Next week? You know how small this place is. With Sylvie teaching from here, it's even smaller*

Gabriel: *Yikes. And how are you two surviving without restaurants?*

Callie: *We distract ourselves from the pathetically poor quality of our cooking by playing chess or backgammon after dinner and then alternating watching The Great British Baking Show, The Queen's Gambit, and Schitt's Creek.*

Callie: *But it's hard. Unlike you rich people, us poor professors don't have a fancy gourmet kitchen over here*

Gabriel: *You can come make bad food in ours soon*

Callie: *OURS???*

Gabriel: *:-)* 😀 😀 😀

Then he'd turned off his phone and they'd curled up on the couch and watched an episode of *The Expanse*—at Gabriel's insistence—and then—at Aria's insistence—they settled in to stream the latest re-imagining of Jane Austen's *Emma,* just released and available on streaming because theaters across the country had either closed or people had stopped going for fear of infection. Then they'd gone to bed. Together. In Aria's room. Again.

The next morning, they woke in each other's arms. Gabriel had been the first one to stir as Aria had been lightly snoring into his ear, causing a little tickling curl to flitter about with every inhale and exhale. He slid a hand down over her waist and hips to the juncture of her thighs until she moaned and scooted closer, her own fingertips tracing over the muscles between his shoulder blades and then lower, lower until she spread her fingers to pull him to her.

Now, Aria joined Gabriel as he ushered the two guests down the hall toward the living room.

"This is Mrs. Celia Houghton, Professor Radcliffe's daughter," Manuel said, his voice tight. "And," gesturing to

Aria and Gabriel, he went on, "this is Ms. Aria Turner and Mr. Gabriel Landon."

Celia Houghton nodded to them in greeting. "I would shake your hands, but it's this damn virus." She held up her hands to show she was wearing leather driving gloves. "Best not."

"Please, have a seat?" Gabriel said, cutting a glance at Aria. "Can we get you anything to drink? Is there something wrong? Has something happened to Liv?"

Celia looked around the room and then sat on the edge of the couch. "I'm afraid my mother passed away last night. Or rather early this morning."

"Oh my God," Aria said on an exhale and sank into one of the side chairs. Gabriel laid a hand on her shoulder and let out his own barely audible, "Holy fuck."

"The EMT crew is down there now. We're waiting for the funeral home to come pick up her body. Everything is taking longer than expected because of Covid cases in the city, so we've been letting her favorite neighbors know in the meantime."

Gabriel looked up at Aria, who appeared to be stunned, and then at Celia. "It wasn't Covid-19 was it?"

"No. She…I believe…." Celia cleared her throat. "She'd recently been diagnosed with Stage Four Glioblastoma. She received the diagnosis two weeks ago, but her symptoms started well before that. I think that was why she was sometimes unsteady on her feet, one side of her body would go numb. And she was having terrible headaches. That on top of her macular degeneration and her heart…well, she was on multiple medications and maybe something went wrong. Or maybe it was a stroke."

"I'm so sorry," Aria said.

"We were just with her yesterday," Gabriel added. "I've been spending time in the afternoons with her. Taking Lymond down to visit—you did know she gave us her dog, right? He's in my room right now if you want to see how he's grown."

"I don't know what possessed me to think she should have a puppy." Celia huffed out a soft laugh. "My husband thought I'd gone mad and my brother, well, he wouldn't have anything to do with it. I just didn't want her to be lonely. And then with the diagnosis…well, thank you for taking him in."

Gabriel hurried to his room and let Lymond out. The pup went bounding down the hall and skidded into the living room, across the hardwood floor. Celia patted the side of her leg. Lymond trotted over so Celia could pick him up and hold him. Just for a moment, she pressed the pup to her chest. "She complained about him from the moment I gave him to her, but you should've seen her face. She fell in love at first sight."

Gabriel smiled. "So did I." He cast a glance at Aria. "Seems I'm prone to that."

Aria stiffened, but Celia, oblivious to the subtext, said, "Liv told me you were playing poker in the afternoons. Did you two ever play chess?"

"That was next on the agenda," Gabriel said. "Would I have had a chance?"

"No. I never won a single game against my mother. Not even Chutes and Ladders when I came home from boarding school as a child. She was simply not that kind of person." Celia nodded at the memories. "But I did admire her intellect. She was rather brilliant and I'm sad she's gone."

"She was such an interesting woman. And she was always kind to me." She smiled. "I'm pretty sure she thought my father was a pretentious lout and was rather glad when he moved out and I moved in." Aria looked up at Manuel. "She never said that out loud, mind you, but you know my father didn't always get along with everyone. Especially independent, strong-minded women who were not in awe of his literary magnificence and who didn't share his taste in Cuban cigars, boxing, and betting on the ponies."

Manuel gave her a knowing nod. "Your father is one of a kind and Professor Radcliffe was one of a kind. Oil and water. Although few in the building miss Caldwell, everyone in the building will miss the professor."

Celia nodded, her eyes shining with tears. "Since her latest diagnosis, I insisted she text me every evening when she went to bed and every morning when she woke. If she didn't text, I would call and that always annoyed her. She hated talking on the phone. So, she texted. Until this morning."

"It seems so unreal," Aria said. "We were going to start a little pandemic pod group and have her join us. We will raise a glass in her honor instead."

Celia stood to go. "We should go back downstairs now. I suppose I'll see you in the coming weeks as I do some cleaning and re-arranging. My husband and I will keep the place for when we come to the city, but there are things my brother will want. And things we neither one want. If you'd like, I'll let you know when I come back. I understand you're both avid readers. Perhaps there are books on her shelves you'd like to have. Lord knows her shelves are overflowing. We'll probably want to tidy up a bit."

"What about a memorial service?" Gabriel asked.

"She'll be cremated so there won't be a burial. And with everything going on, we can't do a service in person. I always thought we'd do something in St. Paul's Chapel on campus, but that's not possible now. She was a lapsed Episcopalian. Claimed any historian worth his or her diploma could not possibly be a believer in any benevolent superpower, so maybe a Zoom memorial will be better. Surround ourselves with the marvels of Internet technology rather than the trappings of an ancient religion. I'll let you know when we have something planned."

Celia reached into her purse and pulled out a deck of cards. "Mom told me she'd promised to take care of some of Lymond's medical expenses and she left you a check. And the deck of cards you played with. It's her Cloisters deck."

Gabriel took the deck, turning over the box in his hands and showing it to Aria. "Liv told me the original deck was from the fifteenth century," he said. "It's no wonder she beat me so often. Instead of hearts, spades, clubs, and diamonds, I had to remember game nooses, hound tethers, hunting horns, and dog collars."

"That was my mother for you," Celia said with a sad huff of laughter. "Anyway, I folded the check for the vet and stuck it in the box. And she also left you two a note." She cleared her throat and handed Aria a sealed envelope with the bold script: *For Aria Turner and Gabriel Landon.*

After Celia and Manuel were gone, they retreated to the kitchen and Aria slid a finger under the little sticker seal on the back to open the envelope. "Do you think she…?"

"Hastened her journey toward its ultimate destination?"

"Yeah."

"Seems likely. I mean glioblastoma is awful," Gabriel said. "There was a kid in Flagstaff, didn't go to my high school, but his picture was on jars all over town. You know? Leave your change to help pay for his treatment. He died just before he would've graduated."

"God, that's so sad. And enraging that families have to beg for help."

"I hate cancer," Gabriel ground out. "I don't know if I'd do anything different if I were in Liv's position. I went through it all as a kid with my mom and then as an adult with Grandma Jack and it seriously sucked both times. All the treatments and the meds and the sick room and feeling as if you're helpless to do anything to ease the pain and the fear and the anger. And it's just so fucking exhausting. And knowing the clock is ticking, that the symptoms are going to get worse. Knowing there's a deadly pandemic running rampant in nursing homes. Knowing that you don't want to leave the home you've made for yourself to live somewhere with a chandelier you hate…"

"Everything she said yesterday makes so much more sense now. And leaving a check for Lymond's vet bill?" Aria sighed and shook her head. "There was a summing up about the conversation. She knew what she was going to do." She squeezed Gabriel's arm and unfolded the note, pressed it open, and held it up so they could read it together. "Ready?"

Aria & Gabriel,

There were things I wanted to say this afternoon over tea, but I held my tongue thinking that your lives are none of my business. But on reflection, I thought, why not? I'll be gone and maybe my meddling will do some good. So here goes:

Aria – You are a brilliant and delightful young woman who deserved a better father than Caldwell. You can tell the odious man I told you so. You will succeed despite him. And because you are you. Never let him—or any other person—define who you are or determine what your future holds. Good luck with your book. The world needs your voice.

Gabriel – Regarding our chat over poker the other day, my advice is to be bold and do not not allow mistakes to define you. There's always time to chart a new course. And, if you manage to pull yourself together and put your plan into place, contact my daughter. She will have instructions to help."

Aria looked up. "What plans?"

He shook his head. "It's a big secret. He smiled down at her. "I promise I'll tell you later. Let's keep reading. There's more in the note."

"There is a passage about the discovery of love in The Lymond Chronicles that I've always found particularly beautiful. I'm not going to tell you in which of the six books you'll find it because that would spoil the joy of discovery. (I've left instructions for the series—and its precursor—to go to you when my shelves are cleaned out, as I'm sure they will be.) This is not the whole passage, but it will do for now.

"And I have begun to slake my thirst. But in you
I have found a banquet under the heavens
that will serve me forever."
I hope you both heed the words of a dying woman
and remember that second chances can be the best
chances of all.

Gabriel wrapped an arm around Aria's shoulders. "God…" He choked out the word out and she leaned into him and pressed her face against the cool cotton of his T-shirt, finding solace in the strength and warmth of his body. She heard him sniffle and then laugh softly. "We're going to need to put more tissues on the grocery list."

She spoke into his chest. "And you're going to need to tell me what plans Liv was talking about."

"I will." He tightened his arms around her. "I promise. Soon."

THIRTY-FIVE

MARCH 25

G ABRIEL STOOD at the living room window, looking out over Morningside Park, Columbia's campus, past Callie and Sylvie's street and beyond to the river when Aria found him the next morning. Against the tall windows, his silhouette, broad shoulders, tapered waist, and long legs drew her to him like a lodestone. Behind him, the morning sun shone through here and there as scattered clouds drifted on the horizon. He'd slipped out of bed without her knowing and, significantly, without waking her first. Dressed in a cozy hoodie and a pair of soft leggings, she walked up behind him and wrapped her arms around his waist.

"What are you thinking?"

"I made the mistake of checking my email this morning while you were still asleep."

"It's a Wednesday. I think you're supposed to check email on Wednesdays."

He chuckled and put his hands over hers, clasping them to his abdomen. "I heard from the guys at Seven Wonders."

She stepped around him to look him in the face. "Go on."

"They're all here. In the city. They flew out on Diamondback's private plane. They want me to meet with them face-to-face this afternoon."

"Why in person? Don't they know there's a global pandemic?" Do they not understand Zoom? Or how conference calls work?"

"They've got a buyout offer and are having a board meeting to consider how to counter. They didn't say who the offer's from. Not in the email."

"I don't like the idea of you being around these guys. Who knows what they've been exposed to."

"I'll wear a mask whether they do or not. I don't want to bring anything home." He drew in a deep sigh and let it out. "But I need to be there. I want to hear what the offer is. I don't want to be cut out of this too."

"You said you kept a percentage of the company, but I don't remember how much."

"Two percent." He huffed out a laugh. "As founder, I started at 80 percent, with 20 percent set aside for my first employees. Cam and Paul. They lived and breathed gaming. Then I got my first angel investor—that's when I quit my PhD program to work on Seven Wonders full time. Then Ethan and Noah came on board. They both put skin in the game, so they came on as partners. Then all our shares were diluted when we did a Series A funding round, and my share went down to ten percent. Then, the shit hit the fan and the board wanted me out. I stepped back, but I insisted on holding on to a little piece of it."

"When was the last time you talked to them?"

"As a group? Ten months ago. At the last board of director's meeting. But this isn't a meeting of the whole board. They've apparently already got feedback from the two investors who can't attend, so it'll be Ethan, Noah, Cam, Paul, Brian from Diamondback, and Craig Miller, the Diamondback attorney handling the paperwork."

"Have you ever had a conversation about what happened? They were your friends."

"With friends like that..." A muscle in his jaw twitched and he shook his head. "No, we haven't discussed what happened since the day I was asked step down. I left the meeting, packed up, and went home to Flagstaff. I've talked to both Ethan and Noah a couple of times, but..." He shrugged. "One time they even drove up to Flagstaff. Pulled right up into Grandma Jack's driveway and rang the doorbell like it was a regular afternoon visit."

"What did you do?" She slipped her arms around him, rubbing his back as he talked, feeling the tension in his shoulders ease.

"Considering Grandma Jack was in the process of breathing her last, I told them to get the fuck off the property. That my grandmother was dying, and I had better things to do than to waste my time on so-called friends who'd stood back and said nothing as I lost everything I'd worked for."

"Oh, Gabriel," she murmured and pressed the side of her face against his chest.

"I understand now that they were trying to reach out and, I don't know, maybe make amends or something. I was just so pissed. And hurt. That was the worst part. The betrayal. Ethan and Noah were my best friends. We met at our first grad school orientation event and were like brothers. Or, at least, I thought we were that close. I was so angry they didn't do more to stop me from being pushed out. To stop Paul and Cam from piling on and milking the whole debacle as some sort of brilliant marketing bonanza."

"I remember them, Paul and Cam. From the social media posts. Cam especially."

"He's got an uncanny sense for gaming and can code like crazy, but he's also just plain crazy. I never thought he would be cruel, though. Shallow and juvenile and idiotic, yes. That I could see. That's Paul too. He's a really talented artist, but he'll do anything for a laugh. Get a few beers in him and he's like a Robin Williams character. Can even do all these hilarious voices. Should've been a stand-up comedian, but he never cared if the laughs came at someone else's expense. But Ethan and Noah were different. I thought about reaching out after I got back from Scotland, even thought about how getting Q.BC up and running would have been better with them on the team."

"And how do you feel about Seven Wonders being bought?"

He rested his chin on the top of her head. "I'd be sad to see the brand disappear if that's part of the deal, but if the offer is good…I mean, can't stand in the way of progress, right?"

"Would it be progress?"

"If this pandemic lasts more than a couple of months—and I can't see it winding down anytime soon—there's gonna be a fortune to be made in online gaming. People will be stuck at home trying to figure out how to keep themselves occupied, and with an infusion of cash for marketing and quick turnaround on new game development, the company could really take off."

"What time is your meeting?"

One o'clock. He looked down at his watch and then gave her a sultry smile. "So, I've got plenty of time. Why? Do you have any morning activities in mind?"

She stood on her toes and ran her tongue around the curve of his ear, then blew a whisper of breath over the wet skin. "I'm thinking we could saunter over to the kitchen, *grind* some beans, make some *hot* coffee, *sizzle* up some fake sausage, and have some more of that *delicious* frozen orange juice you made on Sunday."

He laughed. "You had me at *grinding*." He ran his hands down to her backside and pulled her up hard against him, burying his face in the curve of her neck. "But the *sizzle* is making me *hot*."

She spun away from him and darted toward the kitchen. "First one to the fridge wins!"

"Wins what?" He trailed after her.

She slapped a hand to the front of the stainless fridge, leaving a handprint, and looked him up and down slowly. A glint in her eyes. A wicked smile. "Whatever the winner wants."

Three o'clock came and went. Then 3:30. Then 4:00, and Aria had given up waiting patiently and had taken to pacing. Was his meeting *still* going? What was he feeling? Was he upset? What was going through his mind? What was it like to deal with his former partners, the men who had instigated the fucking over of Aria's life?

She'd been doing a lot of grappling with her own feelings lately, especially considering Liv's note. Thinking about living with Gabriel. About having sex with him. About the man himself. How he looked at her, how he touched her, how he made her see herself through his eyes—as someone worthy of being loved. Treasured. Because she'd recently realized that he truly did love her. Aria Turner. He'd practically come out and said it. Repeatedly.

And since that night they'd shared Ethiopian delivery and talked and started breaking down barriers, he'd shown her in a hundred little ways. His easy laugh. That little hum in his throat when she said or did something that made him happy. Coffee in the morning. Roommate notes. All the fake meat he could buy. How she caught him looking at her like she was some miracle even when she was wearing her ratty old sweater or sweats or her hair looked like Medusa was having a bad-snake day. And how he'd kissed his way down her belly last night and nestled his head between her legs then looked up at her and repeated part of that quote in Liv's note: *"In you I have found a banquet under the heavens that will serve me forever."*

That had nearly done her in. And now she knew that all the grappling she'd been doing, all the protesting and justifying and arguing with herself was just because she didn't want to admit she loved him too. That she'd been just as overwhelmed as he was by that tsunami of emotions three years ago and that was why what happened next had hurt so bad.

Now, she realized she wanted them to be together. Live together, not just for the year of his sublease, but for always. She realized that somehow, he'd managed to get under her skin and untie the knot of insecurity that had been coiled inside her since…well, since eighth grade and Troy Jordan. And that she didn't want to have 'just sex' anymore. She didn't want him to be her pandemic fuck buddy, as he so crassly put it. She wanted them to make love like they meant it because now she knew she did mean it. They both meant it.

All those surprising conclusions were revelatory. Like she was just coming to know herself and to understand that she was worthy—not because Gabriel loved her or she was Caldwell's daughter or because she had survived Troy Jordan and the asshole boyfriends and the tsunami of online bullying and had carved out a successful writing career for herself and garnered a book deal, but because she was Aria Turner. Like Liv had said in her note. She knew she would succeed because she was herself and that was everything. And when Gabriel looked at her, he saw *her*. And that was everything too.

She stood in the kitchen and looked out at the living room where Fred was sprawled out on Lymond's dog bed and Lymond was beside it, diligently working to pull the stuffing out of his dragon toy through the tiny nose. And she knew, as if stabbed straight through by Cupid's stupid arrow, that despite everything going on in the world, for the first time in her life she was truly happy.

THIRTY-SIX

T HEY'D BEEN AT IT for hours, gathered around the table in Diamondback's small conference room, and all Gabriel wanted to do was go home, rip off his damn mask, rip off Aria's clothes—or not—and make love to her. Being in the same conference room with Cam and Paul and listening to them "strategize" about the counteroffer was a hundred times worse than the screeching of feral alley cats in heat, a sound he'd heard too often in the middle of the night outside his grungy apartment back in grad school.

Brian Johannsen and Craig Miller, Diamondback's attorney handling the paperwork, along with the rest of the skeleton staff, had done their best to create an all-business environment for the meeting, but everything about it grated on Gabriel's nerves, even though Ethan and Noah seemed genuinely glad to see him.

From the moment he walked in the door, Cam and Paul joked about what a pussy he was for wearing a mask— even though Cam was coughing into his sleeve during half the meeting. At one point, Cam started coughing so hard that Gabriel got up, pulled another mask out of his messenger bag, and put it on over his first mask. The new mask was one that Aria's mother had made, this one with a bright green saguaro cactus, a jackrabbit, and a desert tortoise design stamped on the fabric.

"Anyone else want a mask?" He held up several made from some material with a variety of desert and mountain scenes. Aria told him to keep a stash in his messenger bag in case he lost the one he was wearing.

"It's just a cold," Cam protested, but Brian, Ethan, and Noah all said yes with sidelong glances at Cam and Paul.

"Whether it's a cold or whether it's Covid, I don't want it," Gabriel said. He handed out the masks and the three men laughed at each other as they donned their adorable, hand-sewn face coverings. "Arizona themed with two layers of protection," Gabriel said, not willing to reveal that Aria's mother had made them.

"Let me know where you got them," Brian said, a smile in his voice. "I'd order some with diamondback rattlers."

As Cam continued to cough and to be an all-purpose asshole, tensions remained high. Of course, they were always high when Gabriel was in a room with Cam and Paul. It was probably all him. He was pretty sure he radiated a raw 'fuck you' energy whenever either one said anything about the business end of the buyout. They were gamers and coders, not genius business strategists. Not that a person couldn't be all those things, but Cam and Paul were definitely not. And they'd proven over and over again that their ethical barometers were for shit. The whole situation made his head feel like someone was drilling screws straight into his skull.

Still, they'd agreed upon the terms of the counter-offer and Craig and Diamondback's legal staff was busy preparing the paperwork for everyone to review, sign, and send off. Meanwhile, Gabriel was getting antsy and didn't want to just sit there and wait. Besides, he'd had way too many cups of coffee, his nerves were all jangly, and he needed to pee like crazy. He rolled his chair back and stood suddenly. "I'm gonna take a break. Be right back."

♥♥

When it got to be 4:30, Aria's patience ran out. She picked up her phone and started texting.

Aria: *Are you okay? We're all worried bc the meeting is taking so long.*

To this message she attached a pic of Lymond and Fred looking longingly up at the camera, carefully staged with a handful of liver treats on offer.

She waited a minute or two, then texted again.

Let me know as soon as you're on your way home.

I'm in charge of dinner

Your choice tho

 Homemade pizza with an Italian red?

Veggie burgers and beer around the fire?

Tofu stir-fry?

Me for dessert?

We polished off the ice cream, but we still have hot fudge 

She put the phone down and told herself to get a grip. He'd text her when he could. She just had to be patient.

♥♥

As soon as Gabriel entered the conference room, he knew something was wrong. Something had happened. Across the table, Cam and Paul wore evil smirks and were whispering behind their cupped hands. Gabriel glanced at Brian who gave him a weak smile, shrugged, and shook his head at him. Then he looked to Ethan and Noah who just looked up at him, their faces carefully blank. He stopped mid-stride. "What's going on?"

"Why don't you take a seat," Brian said.

"Your girlfriend's been busy texting," Cam blurted out with a leer, pointing at Gabriel's phone sitting on the table, face up.

Gabriel went still. Everything slowed.

"And you've got your settings so notifications light up your home screen. No need to sign in. Just text alerts for the whole wide world to see."

Fuck came out on an exhale. He felt like his body was on fire.

"Exactly," Paul said with a laugh. "Or at least fucking is on the menu for dessert. That and hot fudge."

Gabriel sunk into his chair, eyes narrowed at the two men across the table. "And you assholes read the texts?"

"We could hardly avoid them," Cam said. "The whole table was practically vibrating."

"Like a sex toy!" Paul smirked, chiming in with an almost euphoric laugh. "I wonder if Aria Turner comes with batteries included."

"Alright. Shut it." Brian said, holding a hand up like a stop sign. "Can you two stop acting like juveniles for one minute? Gabriel is allowed to have a private life and so is Aria Turner."

"Look." Ethan glanced at Noah and leaned forward. "Personally, I think it's cool you and Aria have figured out a way to hook up again. But these two"—he flipped a thumb at Cam and Paul—"are fucking giddy at the prospect of once again turning your sex life into Seven Wonders marketing fodder."

Gabriel wanted to vomit. Or destroy something. Or someone. He stared down at his phone on the table. He'd done this. He'd been careless. He should've never left his phone anywhere near these assholes. And now, he'd exposed Aria to Cam and Paul's sick brand of humor and misogynistic marketing messaging all over again. She would never forgive him. His eyes stung. He wanted to cry.

Noah, sitting next to him, reached out and touched his arm, maybe in reassurance, but Gabriel jerked back like he'd been burned. "For what it's worth," Noah said, pulling his hand back, "I agree with Ethan and Brian. Who you date is your business, but good for you. Good for both of you. You and Aria got royally fucked three years ago, and I feel like shit that I never stood up and said that."

"But think of the attention!" Cam protested. "This situation is tailor-made to get clicks, especially since Aria Turner is such a liberal media star what with all her MSNBC and NPR interviews. We put the Gabriel-Aria redux out there and spin it right and we'll light up Twitter and Reddit. That kind of social media buzz will garner more attention to the Seven Wonders brand, and we can negotiate a higher price. I mean, we're all going to make a mint when the deal closes, but why not goose the share price a bit?"

Brian shook his head in disgust. "Has it ever dawned on you to wonder whether or not a publicly owned company like Microsoft would appreciate being associated with a juvenile, misogynistic social media campaign against two private individuals who are minding their own business and just building a relationship? They're not putting their private lives out on social media so what gives you the right to do that? It wasn't that long ago that multiple restraining orders were in place against both you and Paul as well as several of your most avid gamers. Attacking Aria and Gabriel back then was wrong and attacking them now is wrong."

Cam made a dismissive noise and waved his hand in the air. "You just have no imagination! We all know a little controversy never hurt anyone."

That was it. Gabriel stood so fast, his chair rolled backward, and slammed into the wall. "NEVER HURT ANYONE? WHAT THE FUCK ARE YOU TALKING ABOUT, YOU FUCKING TROLL?"

And then everyone was on their feet. Brian backed up against the credenza on the far wall, his hand on the conference room's landline phone, the one that had a direct line to building security. Noah stood next to Gabriel, and Ethan grabbed Cam's arm even as Paul shot around the end of the table to go toe-to-toe with Gabriel.

"You always thought you were better, smarter, cooler than the rest of us." Paul nearly spat the words and Gabriel was thankful he was wearing two masks. "Well, think again. Seven Wonders has done just fine without you and your fucking ego. *It's my baby, so we're going to do things my way*,'" Paul mimicked Gabriel. "It was you on the magazine covers. You getting the best press. You getting the women panting all over you. You driving the decisions even though Cam and I are the gamers. Even though *we're* the ones who understand our customers. Hell, even though you took all the credit, you hardly even played the games we created!" He waved an arm to take in Ethan and Noah. "The three of you and your grand plans. Fuck all of you. You never listened to us. It was all about the IP, all about your fucking patents, all about what's next, expanding the business, and never about the guys who actually used the product. Who played the games."

Noah tried to pull Paul's arm to hold him back from getting right in Gabriel's face, but Paul shrugged him off as Gabriel just stood there stunned. Shaking. *Processing.* Was this what Paul and Cam always thought? Did they resent him that much? When had this started? From the beginning? When he first asked them to be part of the company? Or after, when they'd all become roommates?

Across the table, Cam tried to break loose from Ethan's hold, but Ethan grunted and jerked his partner's elbow back like wanted to pull it out of its socket.

"Paul's right," Cam ground out. "Bryce the intern saw it. He may have started the whole thing with his first post, but we were the ones who understood how gamers would react. We knew that we could create a social media frenzy because our users would either ridicule you as a loser or take your side as a wounded hero. Either way, Seven Wonders would win."

Noah shook his head and swore, glaring at Paul as he took a step toward Gabriel. "*We* would win," Paul snarled. "And *you'd* be out."

Jesus. Gabriel was speechless. Had they taken advantage of his stupid comments about Aria just to humiliate *him*? To drive *him* out of the company? To ruin him? Was Aria just collateral damage engineered by a couple of jealous jerks who wanted to get laid and have their stupid photos on the covers of magazines? Did her life matter so little?

And then Paul took another step forward. "So, fuck you, Landon," he spit out, literal spittle flying out to spray on Gabriel's incredulous face. Almost right in his eye.

"What the hell's going on in here?" Craig Miller, Diamondback's attorney, appeared in the conference room doorway. "I heard the racket and…*oh*."

Gabriel slowly, deliberately wiped the spittle from his face with a sleeve as Paul leaned forward, put both hands on Gabriel's chest and pushed. Like a schoolyard bully. Gabriel braced himself, and the asshole pushed him again. Jesus. The guy was a fucking idiot. Then the asshole pulled back his arm to throw a punch.

Somewhere in Gabriel's brain, he knew it wasn't a great idea to start a brawl in Diamondback's conference room, that it could put Q.BC's funding at risk, that it could put his whole future at risk, but he also knew it was the only way he could walk out of there and face himself. Face Aria. Face Callie and Sylvie. He wasn't gonna retreat or hide behind Grandma Jack's skirts this time.

So, in an instant, he braced both feet, snapped back his arm, then drove forward and planted a powerful right hook in the middle of Paul's face before the man even had a chance to complete his swing. Paul's head whiplashed to the left and he pitched sideways as Gabriel's body flooded with adrenalin. *This is for you, Aria*, he thought.

Shorter than Gabriel but carrying a good thirty pounds more, Paul reeled back and instinctively put a hand to his nose. "You broke my fucking nose!"

"Good," Gabriel growled. At that moment, Paul was the personification of Troy Jordan and his pathetic little friends and the jerk at UChicago and the idiot at Columbia and every other callous or cruel asshole who had treated Aria like shit because "a little controversy never hurt anyone" or because a woman like her just didn't matter to them.

Gabriel kept his eyes focused on Paul, holding in check the urge to pummel him senseless. He knew it was the adrenalin rush screaming in his lizard brain and that he should rise above the caveman instinct to protect his woman, but he didn't want to. He felt absolutely glorious. Like that punch was for every woman who'd ever been assaulted, harassed, or demeaned. He was a knight in shining armor. A fucking superhero.

Logically, he knew Aria didn't need him to defend her. That she hadn't ever let these assholes defeat her. That she'd turned their attacks into an opportunity to do something good in the world. For herself and for countless other women. Deep down, he suspected this was just as much about his fragile male ego and being thoroughly betrayed by people he thought were friends as it was about standing up for Aria. But it didn't matter. In that moment, all he wanted was to put Paul down. Hard.

And that was when Noah stepped out of the way and said, "Finish him, Gabe."

Gabriel took a quick step forward, leaned in, and plowed his left fist into Paul's gut while the man was still holding his nose. Paul bent over and gave out a furious roar, then butted his head into Gabriel's chest, knocking him back, pushing forward like a bull clashing horns with a rival during rutting season. And then Paul was swinging wildly. He caught Gabriel on the shoulder, on the arm, and then landed a good punch near his left eye.

Enough, Gabriel thought. He spun away and came at Paul from the side, planting a pile driver of a right uppercut then jumping back again to watch Paul stumble sideways and fall flat.

Gabriel glared at Cam across the table. "You next?"

"Fuck you," Cam spit out.

Now leaning casually against the wall near the door, Craig Miller said, "All done, gentlemen? I don't want to have to call security, so you'd better hurry and get it all out before anyone else gets any ideas."

"Go ahead. Call security!" Paul yelled as he struggled to get up. "Let them see what this asshole did to me."

"You swung first, Paul," Brian noted from his spot against the credenza. "Everyone saw it."

"But he didn't even land a punch!" Cam cried out.

Brian shrugged. "Guess he just wasn't fast enough."

"And what's it matter to you, anyway?" Gabriel glowered at Cam. "You were the one who said a little controversy never hurt anyone. I'm assuming this little dustup won't hurt anyone either."

At that, Cam broke free from Ethan's grasp and whirled on him. Eyes like slits, he planted both hands against his chest and shoved. "Get away from me," Cam snarled.

Stumbling back, Ethan's face went dark. "What the fuck?" He regained his footing and lunged forward to grab

Cam's arm and whirl him around just as Cam tried to scurry around the table toward Gabriel. "I should've done this a long time ago," Ethan growled as he drove his fist into Cam's jaw. "And this," he added as he followed with a hard punch to Cam's gut.

Doubling over, Cam took two steps back, coughing and gagging like he was going to vomit. He looked up at Ethan, then sent a death glare across the table at Gabriel. "Fuck you, Landon. You're gonna pay for this." He put a hand to his jaw as he stormed around the table and took Paul by the arm. "I swear to God, you're all gonna pay. You just wait."

Gabriel smoothed a hand over his hair and straightened his shirt. "Fine. Have your attorney contact my attorney. Oh wait." He tipped his head toward Craig Miller. "We have the same attorney, and he saw what happened, so..." He shrugged. "Looks like you two are shit out of luck."

"Come on," Cam said, dragging Paul behind him. "We're outta here."

Gabriel didn't put himself in their way as they stalked toward the conference room door, but Paul and Cam seemed to think he was blocking their path, so they tried to walk straight through him. Cam's shoulder bumped hard into Gabriel's, and that was enough for Gabriel to whirl around and unleash another one-two punch sending Cam ricocheting into the doorframe and collapsing to his knees. And then both men were bleeding from the nose and holding their ribs as they limped out of the room.

Brian clapped slowly. "Jesus, that was long overdue." He looked from Gabriel to Noah and Ethan. "Looks like we'll put off signing the counteroffer papers until later. Craig? Can you send everything out for digital signatures."

"Sure." Craig pushed off the wall and stepped toward the door. "I'd rather not be in a room with those motherfuckers again anyway."

"I wish I could take you all out to dinner to celebrate both what I think is a solid counteroffer and a highly entertaining afternoon, but restaurants…" He shrugged. "Why don't you come to my place, and we can see what the cook has on the menu and celebrate over a bottle of whisky."

Gabriel pocketed his phone, touched the side of his face, and looked down at his bloody knuckles. "Thanks, but no. I'm going home to the woman I love."

Brian looked Gabriel up and down. "Take this thought home with you: although there's no way Diamondback would officially approve investing in your app, I'd like to throw a few dollars your way. From my personal funds. In honor of," he shrugged, "doing the right thing. You know? Probably earn some brownie points from my wife too."

Ethan and Noah exchanged a look. "What app?"

Gabriel held Brian's gaze. "That means a lot."

"What app are you talking about?" Noah said.

"Brian can explain," Gabriel picked up his messenger bag. "I need to get home. Apparently, I'm having hot fudge for dessert."

THIRTY-SEVEN

"OH MY GOD, YOU'RE HURT!"

Anxious to hear about the meeting, Aria met Gabriel in the foyer. "How can you go to a civilized business meeting and come home with a black eye?"

"It wasn't civilized," he growled. "Not with Cam and Paul there."

Barely through the door, Lymond scuttled around his feet begging for attention as Gabriel shook off his jacket and hung it on the peg, all the while staring intently down at Aria, ignoring the dog. That alone, besides the black eye, told Aria that something was seriously wrong.

Aria cupped his chin and turned his face so she could see his eye better. "Tell me what happened."

"Later." His voice was low, determined. "First, I'm going to make love to you."

Oh. Aria's face flushed, her core went molten, and she found it difficult to speak.

"But what about the meeting?"

"It was a shitstorm, and it was glorious, and there's a lot we need to talk about, but first, you need to get naked."

"But—"

Gabriel pressed a fingertip to her lips. "Later. Give me five minutes. Not even. Go into the bedroom and wait for me."

"Wait for you? What are you going to do?"

"Aria." He stared down at her. Then he took her by the hand, led her back to her bedroom and sat her on the edge of the bed. "I need you naked. Now."

Holy hell. This was new. And breathtakingly, startlingly arousing. "Okay." She had no idea what was going on. What had happened at that meeting to put him in this kind of mood? He had texted that he was on his way home, but that was it. And now this.

He turned to leave the room. "When I get back, I'm going to taste you, and I don't want anything in my way."

Well. Pulse pounding, she stripped off her clothes, arranged herself up against the pillows, and waited. When Gabriel appeared moments later, he'd shed his shoes, untucked his shirt, and rolled up his sleeves, but otherwise he was still dressed for the meeting. He walked to the edge of the bed, looked down at her, obviously holding something behind his back.

"Close your eyes."

"Gabriel—"

"Close your eyes, Aria." She did and heard him set something on the side table. "I'm going to put one of those airline sleeping masks on you so you can't peek, and then… well, I promise you're going to like what happens next."

Whoosh. All memories of how to breathe vanished.

She was suddenly overcome with nerves, but she knew she could trust him, so she lifted her head so he could place the mask over her eyes. Then she settled back against the pillow, fingers flexing into the duvet like Fred's paws, wondering, *anticipating*, what was going to come next. And then she felt it. Warm and thick. Sticky. She inhaled. Hot fudge. Drizzled over her nipples. Across her breasts. Down her belly.

From the darkness above her, came Gabriel's voice. "I didn't want to wait for dessert."

Her lips tipped up in a smile, and she made some inarticulate noise in her throat.

But somehow Gabriel knew exactly what that sound meant. "I know," he murmured. "I know." His breath was a whisper against her skin as he pulled one of her nipples into the heat of his mouth. She reached for him, but he pressed her hand back to the bed. "No. My beautiful, brilliant, resilient Aria. You're the one on the menu tonight, not me."

An hour later, after a steamy shower during which they lathered each thoroughly and washed away all remnants of hot fudge, Aria and Gabriel sat at the kitchen island staring down at Gabriel's phone. He'd already told her about the meeting, starting with the juvenile comments about Gabriel's mask and ending with blood, broken noses, black eyes, and bruised knuckles. And he made sure that she understood that the entire social media nightmare was more about pushing Gabriel out of the company than targeting Aria personally.

"Doesn't matter why they did it," Aria countered. "Jealousy or greed or plain old idiocy. Actions have consequences." She pointed to the phone. "They made those decisions then and it looks like they're making them all over again."

They stared down at the text messages Callie had sent while they were busy enjoying early dessert. Messages with screenshots of several juvenile posts and two nicely executed illustrations—probably drawn by Paul, he was the artistic one—featuring Gabriel and Aria. It was the initial volley of what they guessed would be many attempts to turn Aria Turner and Gabriel Landon into social media clickbait once again.

"You'd think the world would have more important things to think about as a deadly pandemic runs rampant, but we need to be prepared. The kinds of bottom-feeding troglodytes who went after you back then won't care about people dying in a pandemic now. They'll care that I betrayed the mancode or whatever and that you're a…you know." He waved a hand at one of the graphics.

"A #metoo harpy."

"Cam's words, not mine. Never mine."

She let out a long sigh and stretched her neck back and forth as if it ached. "God, I don't want to go through this again."

"You're not going through it alone this time. This is not Team Aria or Team Gabriel, this is Team Aria & Gabriel. We're in this together, okay?"

She nodded and stared at the illustration.

"I mean it, Aria." His face went dark, brows drawn together, mouth a determined line. "I'm committed here.

To you, not to them. Not to some perceived image of the kind of man I'm supposed to be. I'm with you. Understand?"

She drew in a long breath and exhaled. "Okay, yes. So, what do we do now? What's the plan?"

"I'm not sure. I can't talk about the deal because although Seven Wonders is still VC-backed, the buyer is one of the largest public companies in the country, and this is the quiet period when negotiations take place and before the deal is announced." He reached out and pushed a few curls away from her face. "Honestly, I don't think the buyer would be too thrilled by the idea of a couple of Seven Wonders founders going on a juvenile crusade to goose the share price in the middle of negotiations. Especially by targeting people on social media."

"There's probably some law against it," Aria said. "Wouldn't that be attempted stock manipulation?"

"I'll talk to Brian and Craig about it tomorrow. Although, they're probably already on it. You should probably talk to your editor, tell your publisher. And I'm sure Brian will help with the new hires for the Q.BC team."

"Should we have a response prepared? A formal statement or something?"

He rubbed his jaw, thinking. "You talk to your people, and I'll talk to mine—God, that sounds so absurdly pretentious—and then we'll make some decisions." He looked down at his knuckles. "I'm going to talk to Callie and Sylvie too," he said. "Get their perspective."

"Ask them to come over," she said suddenly. "Right now. It's only 7:30. See if they've had dinner."

He picked up his phone but looked up at Aria for confirmation. "You sure?"

She felt like she'd been run over by a garbage truck. First Heather and worrying about Caldwell and the virus and the rising death toll, then Liv, and now this. She was itchy to do something. Take some sort of action.

She nodded. "Tell them to bring masks for inside, but we can eat outside. It's time I met them, and I don't want to wait for a picnic in the park."

A response lit up Gabriel's phone. *Because we are so careful about following a healthy diet during these trying times, we were going to have popcorn and pie for dinner. Is this about Paul and Cam and those disgusting posts?*

Gabriel: *Yeah…and Aria wants to meet you* 😊

Callie: *When?*

Gabriel: *Now?*

Callie: *Gotta wait till the pie's out of the oven. We'll leave here in, say, 30 minutes?*

Gabriel: *Perfect. And don't be surprised by my glorious visage when you get here. I had a bit of a dustup with Paul and Cam and came away with a new black eye. I'll tell you all about it when you get here.*

Aria looked up, her eyes welling with tears. "I always thought it'd be cool to have a sister."

"She's gonna love you. Sylvie too." His phone vibrated again with an income text.

Callie: *Men.* 🙄

He laughed, winced, and showed the text to Aria.

"I'd agree, but I've come to realize they're not all bad."

"What did you say?" He looked her up and down. "Does that make the famous Aria Turner a #notallmen advocate?"

"In your dreams." She gave him a swat on the shoulder. "I'm just a #notmyman advocate."

And then they were standing, arms around each other, her face pressed against his chest, his face in her hair. After few long moments, he raised his head and wiped his face on his sleeve. "God, I need a tissue."

THIRTY-EIGHT

"WE'RE HAVING veggie burgers and fries," Gabriel said as he ushered Callie and Sylvie into the co-op. We'll all stay masked when we're inside, but we'll eat outside. It's not that cold and we'll have the gas fire pit and plenty of blankets in case you get chilly."

Callie eyed his bruised face. "You do look lovely, brother."

"They look worse," he said with a grim laugh.

"I should hope so. Where's Aria?" she said, taking off her coat and hanging it on one of the foyer pegs.

"And Lymond and Frederica the cat?" Sylvie added, peeking down the hallway.

"Aria's in the kitchen or out in the loggia turning on the fire pit and piling up blankets. Who knows where Fred is, probably in her roost on her climbing tree. She doesn't seem to mind Lymond, but she's spending less time floor-level these days. And Lymond is in his crate for now. I'll let him out in a sec."

Sylvie held up a canvas grocery bag. "We brought beer, by the way. And fresh-out-of-the-oven deep-dish pumpkin pie. Some frozen brand, but it was good enough for us."

"Any pie is better than no pie," he bent forward to give both women a hug and then pulled back. "I guess we should have a no hugging, no kissing rule."

Sylvie snorted. "From those smiley faces in your text yesterday and the Cam and Paul bullshit posts on Twitter, I'm guessing the no kissing rule does not apply to you and Aria."

That garnered a smile from Gabriel. "No. It most certainly does not."

Out in the loggia, with Aria sitting at his side on the upholstered loveseat opposite Callie and Sylvie, Gabriel surreptitiously fed Lymond French fries—Aria insisted they shouldn't feed him table scraps—and sipped from his beer as the three most important people in his life got to know each other. His veggie burger was long gone, and he wished he'd made two for himself. Being anxious and angry on the one hand and anxious and happy on the other was wreaking havoc on his insides. The adrenalin high from the fight and the sex had dissipated and he was now simultaneously nauseous and ravenous. There was still pie to be had, though. Thank God for Callie and Sylvie.

"So," Callie said. "Tell us what's going on."

Gabriel glanced at Aria and then told Callie and Sylvie the whole story about the meeting and the guys seeing Aria's texts and the fight at the end.

"Good for you," Callie said, holding her beer high in a toast. "Grandma Jack would have been proud."

"Why do you say that? She was a hippie pacifist who was arrested—more than once—protesting the Vietnam War."

"Don't you remember her saying that just because violence isn't *always* the answer, that doesn't mean it's *never* the answer?"

Gabriel snorted a laugh. "No."

"Well, it's likely because you were sobbing too hard from getting your skinny little butt kicked by some kid or the other. And then you had that remarkable growth spurt, and I still remember when you finally took down Jerry Logan when he made fun of you for crying over Mrs. Rhinehold's car wreck. Grandma Jack and I were both proud of you for standing up for yourself. And then she got you that punching bag and we both had fun with that. Was it still hanging in the barn when you sold the place?"

"No," Gabriel said. "I'd basically beaten it to pieces, so I threw it out." He snorted out a laugh. "I made good use of it there at the end, though. I was not in a good mood while Grandma Jack was in hospice. Or after." He finished his beer and set it aside. "And, while today's bout made me feel good in the moment, it's obvious that punching Paul and Cam has not done me or Aria any favors. I have no idea what they'll do next, but if it costs Seven Wonders the deal, they'll be on the losing end of a serious lawsuit filed by the rest of the board members. And if the buyer thinks their posts will damage the brand rather than, as Cam seems to think, enhance it, they might very well stipulate a lower share price or demand that the VP positions heading game development and art & design be taken over by others."

"You mean they could basically fire them as a condition of the deal?" Callie said.

"It's possible. Compared to them, Seven Wonders is tiny. And with a 10,000x-sized bank account, they hold the upper hand."

He shook his head in disgust, thinking about the first graphic showing Gabriel on his hands and knees with a saddle on his back, a bit in his mouth, and the reins in Aria's hands as she rode him. There was a whip too. The second graphic showed Gabriel locked behind bars with Aria dressed in a skin-tight uniform and dangling a set of keys. And a whip, of course. Seemed like Paul was always trying to work his BDSM kink into their Adult Content games.

Sylvie stuck a French fry in her mouth and chewed thoughtfully. "These idiots," she said, "post about Aria as if she is some sort of powerful dominatrix who could subdue even a hyper macho, hyper masculine man. I guess the message is that men have to stick together and double down on the misogyny and control." She dropped her voice an octave. "Keep women in their place, boys, or you'll end up with a bit in your mouth and at a woman's mercy, just like Gabriel Landon."

"It's a sick message," Callie added, "but it obviously resonates with plenty of basement dwellers."

"I'm ready to take on a few basement dwellers about now." Gabriel's jaw clenched and he felt his muscles tighten. He glanced at Aria, "I've got a list of assholes I'd like to put down."

Callie leaned forward and put her hands closer to the dancing orange and blue flame of the fire pit. "I really hope your new company targets a customer base reliant on more than their reptilian brains."

"It's finance, Callie. What do you think?"

She snorted. "That they'll have Ivy League degrees and live in downtown penthouses rather than being high school dropouts living in mom's basement." Callie cocked her head and studied her brother's face. "What happened to Seven Wonders, anyway. Your graphics are amazing, but there's so much violence in the games. I don't remember it starting that way."

"It *didn't* start that way," Gabriel said, remembering how his original goal was to create games he and his sister could play together. Games that would have entertained and kept them company when they'd lost so much as kids. Games that could help them explore and grow and feel better about themselves. Maybe a hike through the forest game where you get points for identifying the most plants and win when you don't get eaten by a bear. Or games about music since Callie loved to play guitar, sang in the school a capella group, and always knew the coolest bands. Not just assassins or war games or stealing cars, but games for girls and boys who wanted to be entertained and challenged and maybe learn something new.

"My IP was all about using AI and machine learning for faster, better, higher-resolution graphics that could learn and evolve as the game was played, getting faster and better along the way," he said.

Aria's brows shot up. "A closed loop."

He couldn't stop himself from turning and giving her a full wattage grin. "Exactly." Then he turned back to Callie, that smile gradually fading. "Seven Wonders, at least how I conceived it, was never about creating the same old games with muscle-bound warriors or scantily clad women with large breasts riding dragons or conquering kingdoms. Although, don't get me wrong, I am all in favor of scantily clad women with large breasts doing whatever the hell they want."

"As are we all," Callie quipped with a helpless shrug and a quick ogle at Sylvie's amply endowed chest.

"The games didn't have to be violent," Gabriel went on, "but they did have to be challenging. Evolving. And yeah, the idea was that they would get better as the gamer got better. Not just in terms of more difficult levels, but the game would *learn* the player and develop ever more challenging scenarios tailored to the player's gaming style. And the player would learn to beat the game and round and round the game would go.

"Anyway, the point is that these guys always pushed for more of the same, thinking that the existing customer base would always want the same type of games. And, to some extent, they were right. The games sold and the business grew. Which led to Cam and Paul thinking that they're the ones who know what's right for the business and that their priority is me not being involved."

He shrugged. "I may have been the founder, but once you bring in partners and investors, your ability to steer your company shrinks accordingly. Now, Cam and Paul think that putting Aria and me back in the social media bullseye will put Seven Wonders back in the limelight and that any sort of publicity that riles up our existing customer base—their customer base, the ones they connect to—will increase the value of the company."

Callie snorted in disgust. "In the vein of no press is bad press."

"In the vein of corrupt stock manipulation, you mean," Sylvie added.

"Exactly," Gabriel said. "Cam and Paul have insider knowledge of the buyout negotiations and are going to try to manipulate the price to benefit themselves."

Aria pulled one foot up under her and brushed a few curls away from her face. "I don't know what's legal, what's merely corrupt*ish*, or what's flat-out illegal, but this is all shady as hell."

"Let's think about this," Sylvie said, leaning forward. "Seven Wonders isn't a small enterprise anymore. You've got, what, at least fifteen games out and several 'coming soon.'"

"How do you know so much about the company?" Aria asked.

"Three obnoxious high-school-aged brothers who love the immersion and excitement of Seven Wonders games. They all got new VR headsets for Christmas so they could play Destination: Alpha Centauri. They're playing with people from all over the globe. It's a whole different world."

Aria glanced at Gabriel, and he shrugged. "Despite Cam and Paul's influence, not all our games are designed for misogynistic bridge trolls. There are a few that are just elaborate versions of capture the flag or adventure challenges. And Ethan and Noah have been pushing for more games for girls and younger players. That's why the buyer is so interested."

"Okay," Aria said, "now you know what we're dealing with. Men who look at Gabriel and me together, as a couple, and see a cash register ringing up dollar bills. We don't know if we need to sit back and see if it will all pass or if we need to get out in front of it...or what. Brian Johannsen and Craig Miller of Diamondback were both in the meeting today, so Gabriel's going to talk more to them tomorrow. I sent an email to my agent and my editor but haven't heard anything back yet. My guess is that they'll want to be proactive. Use this mess to promote the book."

"What's the title of your book, anyway?" Callie asked.

Aria glanced at Gabriel. "*Piling On: How Online Bullying Can Wreck Careers, Destroy Relationships, and Ruin Lives.*"

Sylvie's eyes went wide, she slapped her thigh, and threw her head back on a laugh. "Oh my God, that's perfect!" She took a long swig of her beer and then looked at Gabriel. "How about another round?"

THIRTY-NINE

GABRIEL GAVE SYLVIE a long look. She was up to something, but he might as well let it play out. He stood. "Everyone good with another beer?"

With a yes from Aria and Callie, he disappeared inside. Sylvie leaned forward toward Aria, her expression intent. "Okay, before I tell you what I'm thinking, I want to know how you feel about Gabriel. This may seem like a personal question and none of my business whatsoever and that I'm putting you on the spot, but if you want our help, we need to know. Because if you go public with a relationship—whether it's just roommates or besotted lovers—and then the relationship has a bad ending, shit with Cam and Paul will just hit the fan all over again." She glanced at Callie. "We know Gabriel's in over his head for you. Has been since day one. But what about you?"

Aria looked out over the loggia railing, sighed, and then turned back to Sylvie and Callie. "I love him. I'm *in love* with him." She snorted out a laugh. "I can't believe I said that out loud. I just admitted it to myself this morning and haven't had the guts to say the words to him yet—of course, he hasn't said them to me either—but yeah. I'm all in. I'm not going anywhere. And not just because this is my co-op," she added with a laugh.

Callie reached out and squeezed Aria's hand. "You have no idea how happy that makes me."

"Makes me pretty damn happy too." Aria whispered as Gabriel reappeared with four cold ones.

He stood there for a moment, looking at the three women who had obviously been talking about him. "What'd I miss?"

Aria patted the seat beside her. "We're just getting started on strategy."

"Bottom line," Sylvie said, taking the beer from Gabriel as he handed them around, "is that if 'The Assholes' are going to be strategic about this to try to pump up the Seven Wonders share price, we need to be strategic about countering their narrative."

"I hate to say it, but a higher share price isn't going to hurt my pocketbook," Gabriel said. "So if we can do it without sabotaging the deal—"

"Well, duh," Sylvie said. "But here's the thing. Whatever company is offering the buyout, we know it's public, has buckets of money, and that it cares about shareholder sentiment. Or at least it gives lip service to shareholder sentiment. That's why companies spend millions on branding and public-facing community projects. Sponsoring 10k runs for breast cancer, for instance. And in this case, there are probably millions of shareholders. Seven Wonders trolls may crawl out of their subterranean tunnels to ridicule the Aria and Gabriel story on Twitter and Reddit, but we don't care because our positive narrative is going to trump their negative one and everyday shareholders—the ones who own stock through their 401k's or pension funds and the institutional investors who manage those funds—are going to eat it up."

"And what is our positive narrative?" Aria asked.

Sylvie sat back, propped her feet up on the ledge around the fire pit, and gave them all a big smile. "The oldest story of all. The power of love, forgiveness, and redemption. How in the midst of all the devastating news and dark times of this frightening global pandemic, there exist moments of magic. Possibilities. Lost love and second chances. Three years ago, you met. Fell in love. Made mistakes. And you got swept up in something bigger and dirtier and more destructive than either of you bargained for. That neither of you had control over. Then, lo and behold, the universe stepped in and gave you a second chance. A gift." She waved her hand in the air toward Gabriel and Aria. "And voilà. Here you are."

Gabriel and Aria looked at each other warily as Callie rubbed her hands together and let out a delighted cackle. "No wonder I love you. You're a freaking genius!"

"Yeah, well, I'm just channeling Rashida."

"Who's Rashida?" Aria asked.

"Rashida Dourmaine, my roommate at NYU while we were undergrads. We lived together all four years. She was a public relations and marketing major, and some of that rubbed off on me. We were always a bit like Mutt and Jeff. I'm 5'3 and all curly hair and curves and she's 5'8 and looks like she should be wrapped in a toga and perched on a pedestal in a museum. Plus, she has the most beautiful face ever—people stop her and ask for her autograph all the time. They think she's Ava DuVernay. Anyway, she's at Condé Nast now. You know, *GQ, Vogue, Vanity Fair, The New Yorker*."

"I had a piece published in *The New Yorker!*" Aria said, leaning forward.

"I know," Sylvie said. "Every woman I know in New York City, including Rashida, read it. She knows everyone and is connected to everyone she doesn't know. She will *absolutely* love to help us get out in front of this. And it will end up being good for your book, for Gabriel's profile and his new company, and it won't hurt Seven Wonders either, because if it starts to look like our positive narrative is getting more press and swaying shareholders—i.e., people not breaking bread with the trolls living under the bridge—then Seven Wonders will have no choice but to support it. They won't do anything to counter a story that could bump the share price."

Gabriel watched Aria's reaction. "What do you think about the story line? The lost love and second chances…?"

"You know what?" Sylvie said, jumping to her feet. "I think Callie and I are going to go in and cut the pie. It's time for dessert."

After they disappeared, Gabriel turned to Aria. "What are you thinking?"

She played with the label on her beer bottle a moment and then looked up at him. "I'm thinking that this isn't the way I'd like to go public with a relationship—any relationship. Because it's nobody's business who either one of us lives with or dates or sleeps with, but I approve of the story line, Gabriel." She leaned forward and pressed a soft kiss to his lips. "I love it."

Gabriel went still. His mind racing. "What are you saying? Because if you're saying what I hope like hell you're saying then I need to say it too and not just because we're plotting a strategy, but because it's true and the only reason I haven't said it already is because I didn't want to freak you out any more than this whole serendipitous living situation has already freaked you out."

"I'm beyond freakout," she whispered, placing a hand on his face, cupping his cheek. "I'm past the *I don't want you to move out* stage. Past the *I just want to have sex* stage."

Gabriel couldn't catch a breath, even though the night air was cool and crisp and clean. "Aria…"

"I'm to the *I want you in my bed every night and in my life every day* stage," Aria went on, watching as Gabriel's eyes filled with tears. "I'm to the *I love the fact that you're an emotional wreck who cries more than I do and that you love Lymond and feed Fred and clean out her litter box even though I never asked you to and that you played poker with Liv and make me coffee in the mornings and make me insane at night* stage. I'm to the *I love you* stage, Gabriel Landon, and I'm all in on this strategy."

"Jesus." Gabriel swiped his sleeve across his eyes. "I've fantasized about hearing those words from you, but I never thought it would really happen."

"So you…?"

"Yes," Gabriel said, pulling her to him. "I love you, Aria Turner. Body and soul. Since the moment you stepped into that conference room three years ago, my heart has belonged to you."

The door to the co-op opened and Callie and Sylvie stepped outside to see two people looking at each other as if they'd just awakened from a very, *very* good dream only to discover it was real. They exchanged a glance, each holding two plates with generous slices of pie topped with whipped cream. "We all good out here?"

"Better than good," Gabriel managed to choke out, making another swipe across his face with his sleeve. "And it seems like the perfect time to make my announcement."

Aria looked over, a frown on her face. "What announcement?"

He took a small plate and fork, passed it to Aria, and then took another and stared down at it for a moment. "Well…it's not anywhere near a done deal and I got the inspiration from Sylvie and Liv gave me her two cents and Callie's been one hundred percent supportive, but…"

"Oh, *that* announcement." Both Callie and Sylvie wore big smiles. "You're gonna like it, Aria" Sylvie said. "I promise."

Gabriel cleared his throat and turned to Aria. "This has to do with the plan Liv talked about in her note. You asked about it that day, when we found out Liv had died, but I brushed you off. Here's the thing: Sylvie suggested that if I wanted you to believe I was truly sincere about how I felt about you and about who I am, I needed to prove it. Not just say the words. But do something. She called it a grand gesture. I mentioned it to Liv one afternoon— the day she slaughtered me in hand-after-hand of Texas Hold'em and then told me she'd followed the Gabriel and Aria online debacle and knew who I was as soon as she heard my name. Anyway, I asked her about the concept of a grand gesture, and she told me to do something that would make a difference in the world. Ever since that day,

I've been thinking of what I could do, and I came up with an idea."

He swallowed his nerves and went on. "What do you think about an encrypted messaging app women can use to reach out to a center—The Aria Turner Center for Social Media Accountability—that will basically serve as a front organization for abused and at-risk women seeking help?"

Aria's eyes were huge, but Gabriel kept talking. "So, it'll look like some regular banal app that anyone could have on their phone, but because every message will be encrypted with blockchain technology, no asshole husband or boyfriend can see what messages have been sent. It's essentially unhackable. Totally secure for every user. I'm thinking each user will have some kind of account folder in which they can store messages, photos, documents, whatever they need in case they need to present evidence of abuse in court. And the whole thing can be externally funded and staffed by professionals and students. Women helping women."

Aria's mouth was hanging open in an *oh*. She had no words.

"And, of course, the center could do real work too. Like all those centers and institutes cropping up at universities, it could be a place where researchers come together to study online behavior, or something."

Still Aria said nothing, only now her face was covered in tears. She put her hands over her face and gulped back a sob.

"And we'll have to come up with a name for the app," Gabriel went on nervously. "It needs to be sort of incognito, something so totally innocuous men don't pay attention to it when women download it to their phones. Like 'Recipes R Us' or something. Not that, but you get the idea."

"You did this…for me?" She finally choked out.

Immediately Gabriel scooted to her side, wrapped his arms around her. "For you, yes, of course. But also for all those women you interviewed for your book. For every woman who has been harassed and, especially, for those in real danger and who have no way to get help and get out without risking getting caught. All those women matter. Every one of them. Look at how I grew up. My father died before I was born. My mother was everything to me until she died. Then my whole world was Callie and Grandma Jack. And all the librarians and teachers that helped me along the way. And now Sylvie and you. If a man like me can't take a stand for women—"

Aria didn't let him finish his sentence. She grabbed him by the face and planted a kiss on his lips, then sat back, wiped the tears off her face, and looked at the smug faces of the two women sitting across the fire pit. "And you're helping with this?"

"I like to say it was all my idea," Sylvie said with a flourish. "At least I'm claiming the grand gesture idea."

"In other words, yes," Callie added, leaning forward, and pinning Aria with an intense look. "There are lots of abuse hotlines, but Gabriel's app will add the anonymity and security those lack. It's a good idea. It's not near ready to launch and there's lots of work and organizing to be done, but, of course, we're behind it all the way."

FORTY

MARCH 26

GABRIEL WOKE to the sound of his phone buzzing with incoming text messages. He cracked open one eye and checked the time. After seven. He'd slept late. He *slooowly* extricated his arm out from under Aria's neck and headed into the bathroom, checking the weather outside her bedroom window on the way. Gray skies. Drizzle. It looked like winter.

After taking care of business, he crept past a still-sleeping Aria—clearly not a morning person—and went to get the coffee started. Then, of course, duty called. He headed into his bedroom to get dressed and let an anxious Lymond out of his crate. Pulled a baseball cap on over uncombed hair, slipped on his shoes, and put the little raincoat on the pup. With his own coat on, he grabbed an umbrella from the antique stand under that damned foyer table, quietly unlocked the front door, and headed downstairs, whispering ridiculous endearments to Lymond about what a good boy he was as they went.

Outside, Lymond trotted down the sidewalk visiting tree after tree on their block as Gabriel thumbed through his text messages.

Callie: *Don't look at Twitter before breakfast. It'll ruin your appetite*

Callie: *And don't look at Instagram or FB either*

Callie: *Sylie's talking to Rashida now. They're strategizing… i.e., plotting a PR coup to save the day and send a clear fuck-around-and-find-out message to misogynistic assholes everywhere*

Callie: *btw, I'm listening to them on speaker phone and holy shit. These women are brilliant. And absolutely pissed off*

Callie: *Also, tell Aria that if it wasn't obvious last night, Sylvie and I love her too. We're in your corner, little brother*

His throat thick with emotion, Gabriel pocketed his phone, pulled out a poop bag and took care of Lymond's business. When he got back to the building, he met Manuel coming off the elevator, likely from delivering the morning newspapers. He gave him a hearty hello and hurried onto the elevator, wondering if Aria was already up or if she was still cuddled under that pile of blankets. Naked.

Back upstairs, he unclipped Lymond's leash and peeled off the pup's raincoat.

"In here," Aria called from the kitchen. So, she was up. Likely not naked. Damn.

He rounded the corner and went to plant a good morning kiss on her neck, which she made readily available to him with a tilt of her head and a soft moan.

"I poured you a cup," she said, indicating the cup on the counter, "and picked up the paper."

"Thanks. Dare I ask about the latest headlines?"

She pushed the front section of the paper toward him. "India's on total lockdown."

"Jesus," Gabriel said, skimming the front page. "We're worried about two idiots wielding their social media accounts and India's going to police a billion people on lockdown in the middle of a global pandemic?"

"Correction, 1.3 billion. And the prime minister gave all of them a four-hour notice or something absolutely crazy like that. It's surreal. Meanwhile, our fearless leaders want us to open back up by Easter."

"Unbelievable," Gabriel shook his head in disgust.

"I saw online that the city's up to over 17,800 confirmed cases and at least 200 dead, depending on the source. One site said over 365 dead."

"If we can't even get accurate numbers locally, how the hell do we really know what's happening nationwide?"

"There are a couple of sources tracking the numbers." Aria picked up her phone, opened the browser, then handed it to Gabriel. "I've bookmarked the Johns Hopkins dashboard. It's really detailed."

"I saw this when it first went live but hadn't checked in since. I hate to say it, but this is great." He played with the site for a few minutes. "65,778 cases and 942 deaths so far. That's in the U.S. alone. Globally? We're up to 438,749 cases and 19,641 deaths. And who knows how many aren't reported and recorded. Like Heather." He looked up at Aria. "With community spread, limited testing, and no vaccine, this is just going to get worse and worse."

"Can you imagine facing all this if you lived alone?" Aria said. "Our stupid little Cam and Paul issues seem pretty pathetic compared to all this."

"Did you look at any of your social media accounts this morning? Callie warned me not to look before breakfast, but I don't have any accounts so..."

"I haven't. Let's look together." She put her cup down and moved to stand between Gabriel's legs as he swiveled the stool to welcome her in, planting another kiss on her neck. "But first...you know what?"

"What?" He wrapped his arms around her waist and pulled her closer.

"This.....just this." She pressed her face to his neck and touched her tongue to that place behind his ear that made him shiver. He breathed her in, the fresh, floral scent of her shampoo and the scent of that soft spot at the base of her throat, maybe with a bit of *eau de Gabriel* on her skin. He pulled his own phone from his pocket, thumbed it open, and went to his messaging app. "You'll want to read these texts from Callie. Start the day right."

She read the messages while Gabriel kissed his way across her collar bone. "Wow," she drew in a deep breath and set the phone down. "I'm glad I passed muster, and I'm really glad Callie and Sylvie are warriors. Amazons. Can't wait to meet Rashida too. Riding into battle to save the day. Makes me feel like I'm..." She reached for his hem and pulled his T-shirt up over his chest. "Empowered," she said and tugged the shirt over his head, dipping to run her tongue around one of his nipples, breathing against his chest. "Inspired."

"Christ...Aria."

She danced her fingers down the light fur of his chest to where a copper line seemed to point at the button of his jeans. "Emboldened. Enthused. Stimulated."

"You're also a thesaurus," he whispered into the dark valley between her breasts.

"Hungry." She unzipped his jeans and reached in to wrap her hand around him.

He dug his fingers into her hair and sucked in a breath.

She dropped to her knees. "And oh, so aroused."

FORTY-ONE

ARIA AND GABRIEL listened as the introductions were made. They sat side-by-side, both completely overwhelmed, in front of Gabriel's laptop set up on the kitchen island. They thought the Zoom call arranged by Sylvie and Rashida would only have the five of them, Callie included, but the introductions were still going. Seventeen people were on the call. Gabriel, Adam, a freelance photographer, and Damien, a producer from *Good Morning America*, were the only three men. The rest were women colleagues from various Condé Nast properties and friends of Rashida and Sylvie's from NYU, including two who ran a popular blog and podcast for women trying to balance jobs, family, and creative work—and they were all angry.

They'd followed Aria's story. They'd seen the social media posts—from three years ago and from this morning—and the cartoon meme of Aria, buxom in a black leather bustier, thigh high boots, a whip in her hand, and a heel on Gabriel's shoulder as he knelt before her particularly pissed them off.

What was it with Paul and whips, Gabriel wondered as the conversation gathered steam.

Rashida led the meeting, but her obvious and most enthusiastic sidekick on the Aria & Gabriel PR project was a young editor at *Teen Vogue* who had to be stopped mid-rant on the cultural dangers of toxic masculinity because she was only supposed to be introducing herself.

"Of course, a few people on this call were skeptical of the Gabriel Landon transformation story when I first broached the subject of helping us out," Rashida said once introductions were over. "We had our own Zoom meeting earlier today to brainstorm strategy and to make sure everyone understands that this is not an official work project, but more of a pro bono, volunteer effort we're all willing to spend personal time on and to push internally, where appropriate, within our separate organizations because, frankly, we are still monumentally furious about what happened to Aria and what happens to women online and in real life as they simply try to go about their lives.

"I took a quick "raise-your-hand-if-you've-been-harassed" poll on our earlier Zoom and every woman on this call has experienced some sort of harassment whether at work, at home, online, or just walking down the street living life. It's a fact of life for women all over the world and we're sick of it. We may not be able to change the world, but we believe that together, with our talents and connections, we can make a difference in this situation."

"Hear hear," someone said and others chimed in their agreement.

"Bottom line," Rashida went on, "is that we're in this for Aria. However, we have to also acknowledge the fact that Aria will likely be attacked from the right, from those who want to give men a pass and blame women for the things that happen to them."

Someone on the call hissed out a soft, "Fuck those assholes."

Rashida frowned. "My sentiments exactly, however as public relations professionals we know that you have to be prepared to counter everything the assholes are going to throw at you."

"God, I hate this." Gabriel said, his voice tight.

"Fucking incels," someone else said.

"I'm not saying it's going to happen, I'm just saying we need to be prepared for her professionalism and credentials to be called into question because her career benefited from the initial scandal. Her profile was raised with her appearances on television and radio, her essays in prominent magazines, and now, she's got a book coming out. Now that you two are together, I would bet big money that some conspiracy theorists will say you planned all this from the beginning."

"What the hell?" Gabriel glowered, glancing at Aria. "Neither one of us would have willingly gone through the hell we've gone through the last three years. Especially Aria. What absolute utter bullshit!"

"I'm sure you're right, but it's the way those people think," Rashida said with a shake of her head. "And then there's the question of working with you, Gabriel. Most of us have lived for three years with the impression that you are a misogynistic, self-indulgent, man-child who instigated and then fueled Aria's nightmare. But after a long conversation with Sylvie and Callie, they've managed to change my mind. And I've done my best to convince my colleagues on this call too. The kicker is, of course, that if Aria Turner can forgive you after everything she went through, so can we."

"I'm still working on it," Siobhán, the editor from *Teen Vogue* groused.

Rashida went on without missing a beat. "But it's important to recognize that this sort of skepticism is something we'll have to overcome. There will be a lot of people out there who'll see this as a crass attempt at reputation washing just as you're starting another business. That's why we have to handle this carefully and why we cannot get paid for this. It's not a PR gig. It's a favor. A volunteer commitment."

"Understood," Gabriel said. "And to every one of you in this meeting, I'm more grateful than you can know."

"As you damn well should be," Siobhán snapped back, making both Gabriel and Aria smile. "By the way, what's with the shiner?" Siobhán touched the side of her face to indicate Gabriel's latest black eye.

"Let's just say it's an indication of how determined I am to prevent any harm to come to Aria."

Siobhán gave him an appreciative nod. "Who'd you take down?"

"People who deserved it," Gabriel's voice was terse.

"People as in your ex-partners?" Siobhán said, a hint of a smile on her shiny red lips.

He let out a grim laugh. "You might say that."

"So, here's what we're thinking," Rashida said and started running down the list of ideas.

"First, Adam will meet you tomorrow in Morningside Park for an photoshoot with Lymond and Frederica."

"A mini dachshund and a Sphynx cat? The pets alone will sell this!" Adam chimed in, rolling his hands together as if couldn't wait to get started. "And I can totally hide the black eye. Unless you want it to show. What do you think Rashida? Maybe we can do some with all its vivid purple glory on display, and then we can get the makeup out and hide it."

"I don't care either way," Gabriel said. "Whatever you think will get the message across that Aria Turner is not to be messed with. That no woman should be messed with."

"Right on, man," Adam said. "So, the high is supposed to be around 55 degrees with overcast skies, so we should be able to get all sorts of good shots. And we can totally play this by ear, but it'd be great to get some inside shots in the co-op you share. I'll have a crew with me in the park, but it can be just me if we move inside. Masks and gloves and social distancing. The whole bit. But it's your call on that."

"You three work it out amongst yourselves," Rashida said, "but some good inside shots would—especially of each of you on your own—really help. We're not just selling the Aria & Gabriel second-chance love story, we're selling Aria and Gabriel as individuals who absolutely do not deserve to have their private lives ruined by a bunch of incel trolls."

"Absolutely," and "Damn right!" and "That's what I'm here for," came from various voices on the screen.

Gabriel bit back the emotion welling up in his throat. To prevent him from weeping on Zoom, Aria slid an arm around him and began rubbing soothing circles on his back.

"Just wait," Rashida said in response. "Today, Siobhán and a group of her influencer friends will be posting tantalizing hints about news of a swoon-worthy happy-ever-after story coming soon. These will be on their personal social media accounts."

"Between us," Siobhán said, "we've got over two million followers." She looked down at the phone in her hand. "What do you think about this? *'What badass woman who challenged toxic masculinity and misogyny online has found true love at last? Stay tuned for the juicy—and unexpected—details!'* And here's a follow-up: *'Doxxed, threatened, and abused online and IRL for months, this inspiring journalist is taking charge of her life. With a new book coming soon and a new (and surprising!) love in her life, she is going to rock your world!'*"

"Oh my God!" Aria said, eyes wide. "I need to get my publisher connected with you. They'll want to jump on this ASAP. Amplify it across their platforms."

"Email us both after this call, and we'll get them on board," Rashida said.

"And," Siobhán went on, "after Adam gives us some photos, we'll start posting those too. Adam, how about a few shots where we can't see their faces. Shots of them holding hands. Hugging. Walking the pets, but from the back? So we don't reveal who they are."

Adam gave a big thumbs up. "Love that idea!"

"Of course, it doesn't hurt that both of you are gorgeous," Siobhán continued matter-of-factly. "Even with the shiner. But doing a slow reveal will garner more interest."

"Next," Rashida spoke up, "once we get some buzz going on social media, we'll bring out the big guns. Aria, you were already on *Good Morning America* and in *The New Yorker*, so we're going to pitch follow-up stories. Quick, 'Where is she now?' type interviews, maybe even just short

Q&A's that can be placed in the line-up right away. We can't guarantee that these stories will get picked up, but with your book coming out, I think we have a good chance. From there, I'll pitch *Vanity Fair* on a feature on you and your upcoming book. Sylvie said you'd interviewed over fifty women and so that's the real hook. Siobhán is going to do the same for *Teen Vogue*. As for Gabriel, I'm going to see if I can get someone at *Wired* or *Fast Company* interested in your new company. Callie says it's VC-backed and has something to do with blockchain and secure transactions for financial institutions. That's gotta ring some bells for someone. Again, no guarantees on any of this, of course. And I'll need a contact at—what was it? Diamondback Ventures?"

Gabriel fished his phone out of his pocket and opened a draft email. "I'll get your email from the Zoom invite and shoot that over to you as soon as we're done here."

"Bottom line is this." The fine features on Rashida's face went hard. "We all make mistakes. You fucked up. You paid for it. Aria paid for it. But no one has the right to use your fuckups or relationships for their own financial gain or their own sick circle-jerk jollies. This shit is not okay."

Gabriel knew they were all volunteering their time and expertise on behalf of Aria and women like her, but still, the idea that they'd take a stand for him too nearly broke him. His eyes shone with tears. He bit his lip. Clenched his jaw. Pinched the bridge of his nose. "I don't know what to say except for thank you. I know you don't have to be doing this and—"

Callie rolled her eyes, leaned toward her computer camera, and spoke up for the first time. "Here's the thing about my little brother that you all should know. At over six feet, he's not so little anymore and he can obviously hold his own in a fight, but he used to be a pipsqueak and more than one bully gave him the business when we first changed schools and moved in with our grandmother. It was tough because we'd lost both our father and, several years later, our mother, and our grandmother was…eccentric. I sort of clammed up, but Gabriel was constitutionally unable to do that. He wore his emotions on his sleeve, and if he was sad, he cried. If he was mad, he cried. If he was frustrated, he cried."

Gabriel fished in his jeans pocket and pulled out a wad of tissues. "Thanks for that ringing endorsement, sis. Really boosting my masculine pride over here." He blew his nose.

Aria leaned over, kissed his check, and said, "And I love him for it too."

Amidst the *awws* and *how sweets*, Siobhán groaned, "Oh god," and rolled her eyes extravagantly. "I'm not certain if I'm going to weep or vomit."

Just as Gabriel went to send Rashida's contact info to Brian, a text came in from him. *Paul just called to say Cam spiked a fever overnight. 103. Still coughing like a fiend. 'Just a cold,' my ass. Guess we all need to quarantine now since my money's on covid and I guess we've all been exposed.*

He handed the phone to Aria and watched her face as she read the message. "Shit," she said on a long exhale. "You'll have to let Callie and Sylvie know."

Gabriel to Brian: *Thnx for letting us know. We'll follow protocols and see what happens. Problem is we saw my sister and her partner last night too. Cam's a fucking idiot, btw.*

Brian: *Shit and I know. Ethan and Noah are going to come stay here since 10 days in a hotel room is not fun, we've got plenty of room, and my wife's already been exposed.*

Gabriel to Callie: *Bad news. Asshole Cam has 103 fever & is apparently coughing like he's trying to expel a lung. Looks like I've been exposed and therefore you, Sylvie, and Aria have been exposed. Guess we're gonna hunker down for a 10-day quarantine*

Callie: *Shit. I knew I hated that guy. Well, not much we can do now...*

FORTY-TWO

APRIL 1

I T HAD BEEN GRAY and overcast all day, but Gabriel and Aria didn't care about the weather. They'd been monitoring themselves for symptoms and texting with Callie and Sylvie who were doing the same. And, surprisingly, Gabriel got several texts from Ethan and Noah checking in on them. Maybe they could navigate a way back to their friendship. If they all lived. Fucking Cam.

Although she didn't mention that she'd been exposed and was in quarantine—she didn't want to worry them unless she got symptoms—Aria spent time catching up with Caldwell in Vermont and her mother in Arizona. She filled them both in on the fact Gabriel Landon was her roommate, that they were together, that more social media shit may be stirring, but that they had a plan. And that she loved him, so not to worry. Caldwell, strangely enough, took the news harder than her mother.

"Is he good to you, Aria?" he'd asked. "I don't want you mixed up with anyone who'll treat you like a prize to be won and then tossed aside. I know those men—hell, for most of my life I was one of them—and I don't want my daughter ending up hurt by someone like me."

It appeared that age, vulnerability, and Heather's Covid-19 scare had definitely made an impression on the old man. At one point in the conversation, she could have sworn he actually got choked up. But Aria wouldn't bet money on it.

Vi Turner, on the other hand, was delighted. "I looked him up, you know, back then. I always thought there was something strange about how his partners and all those other gamer-types harassed you, but he never did. He just disappeared."

"That was when he went to take care of his grandmother," Aria explained. "It's not an excuse for not doing more to take a stand against the harassment, but it is a reason that made sense to him at the time. That and the threat of a restraining order to keep him away from me."

"Those were scary times." Vi paused, taking a sip of tea. "Still, I remember that he was certainly a handsome specimen. And those shoulders! Did I ever tell you I have a weakness for shoulders? Back in the day, Caldwell had—"

"Mom! God." Aria dropped her head into her hands.

"Do you love him?" Vi asked. "Because if he loves you and you love him, then that makes me happy. He's an Arizona boy, after all. I'm going to look up his grandmother's art. See if I can get something for the store." She babbled on and on, obviously relieved and thrilled. "One of our favorite customers and her husband are both in the hospital with the virus and frankly, I need a big dose of happy. Send photos. Of you and Gabriel and of Fred and Lymond."

So Aria had sent a few of the photos that Adam had taken of them together, added a few of the dog and cat being silly, and that seemed to be all her mother needed to be reassured that Aria wasn't alone and lonely in the big city.

Later, after they'd taken their temperatures for the hundredth time, they made stir-fry for dinner with frozen vegetables and white rice, opened a bottle of Oregon Pinot Noir, and settled in to watch the news, which they'd been trying to ration so they didn't get overwhelmingly depressed by the state of the world. And for good reason.

The news crew panned a New York City street to show refrigerator trucks parked outside of city hospitals that were being used as makeshift morgues. They listened to politicians and pundits debate the need for vaccines and masking and lockdowns and investigations into where the virus came from in the first place. They learned that as of April Fool's Day, there were 213,372 reported cases and 4,513 deaths nationwide. A stunning 83,948 cases and 1,941 deaths in New York City alone.

On cruise ships and aircraft carriers, in private nursing homes and veterans' homes, the virus was cutting down the elderly, infirm, and those with pre-existing conditions. Hospitals were low on everything from gowns and gloves to ventilators. People were sewing their own masks, as Aria's mother had been doing for weeks, and hand sanitizer and toilet paper were flying off shelves and online retail sites.

Cities and communities around the world were shut down or had restrictions on businesses and social gatherings. The toll on the poorest and the most vulnerable was incalculable, and lockdown meant starvation to many. People were dying alone and un-mourned and unburied. Within friend groups and amongst family members, arguments flared and got ugly as some wanted everyone to either stay home or mask up, practice social distancing, and wash their hands repeatedly and others, like Heather, who even now insisted Covid-19 was no worse than a regular seasonal cold or bout of the flu.

And still, a dedicated—but dwindling—number of incel idiots wasted their time online lamenting the pussywhipping of Gabriel Landon by the harridan Aria Turner.

Finally, the news was too much, and Gabriel reached for the remote. "Backgammon, chess, or curl up and read?" He waggled his eyebrows at her. "Or maybe I could kick your ass at poker. Liv taught me a few tricks."

They'd decided that since both were now exposed, they might as well behave normally—except for the constant temperature-taking and sniffing various items to see if they could smell them—and so kissing and sleeping together was definitely still happening. He shifted on the couch, careful not to wake Lymond who, stretched out on his back between them, slept without a care in the world. Aria stroked the pup's soft belly and glanced over at Fred who had recently claimed Lymond's fuzzy donut bed as her own.

Aria said, "Did you see Rashida's email updates?"

Gabriel looked up. "No. I honestly didn't have time today, and then I forgot. I've been forwarding them to the Q.BC team, though, so I probably should take a look and send it on. What'd it say?"

"There's a lot of news." She opened her email app to refresh her memory. "The first thing is that the Q&A discussion about online bullying for *Teen Vogue's* site had one of the best engagement and click-through rates of any story of the last year. Rashida says that's garnered the attention of other editors." She looked up at him with a smirk. "Speaking on behalf of my profession, there's nothing like a good click-through rate to get an editor's attention."

"Is that why click-through rates are enshrined in the Constitution under the First Amendment?"

"Hey, don't impugn my profession, Mr. Blockchain." Aria gave his arm a soft slap. "And remember, we're betting on the media's ingrained herd mentality to push our second-chance romance story."

"*Moo*." Gabriel intoned and Lymond's ears twitched in his sleep.

Aria rolled her eyes. "Anyway, because everyone wants to jump on the bandwagon—"

"So, it's a bandwagon now, not a herd?"

"God, you're a weirdo."

"Takes one to know one."

"And oh, so mature…"

"Sorry." He blew her a kiss and said, "Go on. I promise to act my age."

"So, it looks like we can get a similar story in *Glamour* sooner rather than later, and Rashida's still pushing for one on the whole book project for *Vanity Fair*. Eventually. *Vanity Fair* wants to talk to some of the women featured in the book, so we've got to navigate that. Rashida says that *if* they bite, they'll probably want their story to come out closer to publication day, so maybe the September or October issue. And both Rashida and my publisher have both contacted the *New York Times* to push for a book review. Probably dropped my father's name a few times in the process, but

Caldwell said if they don't say yes, he'll call them himself."

"He's gone from distant to doting in record time," Gabriel quipped. "But I'm glad he's pulling for you."

"In the meantime, we're both booked for *Good Morning America* on the 15th. It's all remote, of course. Tax day's been postponed, and they want a feel-good story. Next, both *Fast Company* and *Wired* are interested in interviewing you for stories on blockchain, so that's new. It's still a maybe. Nothing written in stone, but they didn't come right out and say no."

"Brian will be thrilled."

Aria went on. "Rashida attached a copy of the pitch email for you to forward to him. 'The Future of Blockchain' featuring Diamondback Investments' newest celebrity CEO. And, last but not least—you'll love this one—*GQ* wants to interview you for a story they're doing on cancel culture and how to 'come back from the dead.' Their words. And it looks like all those photos Adam took in the park and up here in the co-op are really making a difference. They're being shared and tagged all over the place." She shuddered. "It's freaky to be so exposed, but it's also good."

Gabriel's brows went up. "Someone's tracking them?"

"One of Sylvie's students. Turns out she's using us— from the very beginning three years ago through this whole PR rehabilitation project—as part of her senior thesis and is tracking the use of the photos through Google Images. And get this, Rashida said she sent a couple of Adam's photos of you over to *GQ* along with the pitch to include you in the cancel culture story. She already heard back that they want to see what else Adam has. Apparently, since it's nearly impossible to send photographers out on shoots right now, they may want to use an existing photo for the cover."

Gabriel snorted. "God, I would love that if for no other reason than to know that Cam and Paul would go ballistic. Still, it's one thing to be on the cover of a regional business magazine and some gamer publications, but GQ?"

Aria leaned forward and planted a kiss on his mouth. "You're certainly GQ material." She cupped his jaw in her palm. "This beautiful face…these green eyes that make me think of deep forest glens and spring gardens and all lush, vibrant, moist things." He went still as she traced a finger along his jaw and down his neck to his shoulder. "All these muscles. Your shoulders. Your arms. The feel of your skin." She ran a finger from his shoulder down his bicep, and glanced up to see his green eyes go dark with intent. "These pecs I can't get enough of." She ran that same finger across his chest, circling a nipple as he bit his lip and sucked in a breath. "That ass that I want to grab hold of and pull closer…"

"Jesus, Aria. Wait," he said on a sudden inhale as he stood abruptly, gently scooped Lymond up and put him in his crate. Then he disappeared for a few moments, only to return with Liv's deck of cards and the bottle of wine.

"You don't want me to continue to inventory your assets?"

"Oh, I'm happy for you to continue." He set the wine down on the coffee table and took his place at the other end of the couch. "But first, you pick the music. I pick the game."

"I thought I'd already indicated what game I'd like to

play." She gave him a sly smile and played with her phone for a minute.

He cocked his head to listen and then that seductive crooked smile took shape on his lips. "Ah, perfect. This is your 'I'm in the mood' playlist."

She raised her brows at him as if in challenge. "Music is selected. Now, Mr. *GQ*, what is our game for the night?"

He opened the box of cards, pulled out the deck, and held her gaze as he performed a riffle shuffle, a cascade shuffle, and a butterfly cut. "Poker."

"What kind of poker?"

He shook his head. "Strip poker."

Her lips tipped up in a seductive smile. "And the stakes?"

Still holding her gaze, he said, "Till death do us part."

Her eyes went wide. "Wait. What's that supposed to mean?"

"Let's play and find out."

FORTY-THREE

JULY 4

GABRIEL LATCHED the door to Lymond's crate, turned out the light, and closed the door to his former bedroom, now a dedicated home office. Aria had already cranked up the music, and they hoped it would mask the sound of potential fireworks any idiots in the neighborhood might set off. Because the statewide coronavirus case count was up to nearly 396,000 and the death toll for the city stood somewhere around 2,500, the mayor had canceled the traditional July 4 celebration. Instead, the whole thing had been reimagined with short displays in each of the five boroughs starting July 29 and tonight, the grand finale, featuring Macy's signature pyrotechnics, would go off from the Empire State Building. Gabriel was pretty sure the sounds wouldn't travel all the way to their place, but he wanted to make sure Lymond was safe and secure from the noise. The poor little guy, they'd discovered, was afraid of thunder and Gabriel and Aria didn't want him alone and scared by the noise.

With a blocked view from the east-facing loggia, they planned to watch the fireworks in Morningside Park and to meet Callie and Sylvie for a late picnic. Armed with two blankets and a flashlight, Aria had gone down early to stake out what she claimed was the best viewing spot in the park. She had a surprise, she told them all, and didn't want anyone disturbing her while she set the scene. She'd text them, she said, when everything was set up.

God. Sometimes Gabriel couldn't believe how lucky he was. Aria was everything he'd dreamed of in a best friend, a confidant, a lover, and a roommate. Turned out that the trouble with roommates was that he'd just never found a good one before he'd stumbled into sharing the co-op with Aria. Literally stumbled. He laughed to himself as he remembered that first night with his black eye and blacker mood. His mood these days vacillated between euphoria and contentment, and he felt like the luckiest man alive.

Like they often did, his thoughts drifted back to the night Aria had lost at strip poker. April Fool's Day. As he opened the deck of cards Liv had left him, he'd warned Aria that strip poker was serious business, and he wasn't above counting cards or downright cheating. His goal was to get Aria naked and that seemed to be just fine with her. They'd finished one bottle of wine and opened another because why not? And they'd made love on the couch and in the hallway and in her bedroom—*their* bedroom. And then he'd slipped the ring on her finger and whispered, *Until death do us part, Aria Tuner. What do you think? Will you marry me?*

It wasn't a traditional engagement ring, but rather a fine silver band inlaid with turquoise, something Grandma

Jack had made for herself on a whim when she was young and long before she'd had to take in two grieving children even as she grieved the loss of her daughter. Gabriel had asked her about it one time and she'd taken it off and put it on his pinky finger for a moment. *I've never married, you know. It just wasn't for me. But I made this ring as a token for myself. Claiming me for myself.*

And that night he'd claimed Aria for himself. And she'd claimed him. Body and soul.

He went into the kitchen, bending to give Fred a scritch behind the ears before he stepped over her. She'd taken to sprawling in the hallway and they joked that she demanded an ear scritch or a belly rub as a toll before anyone could pass. Silly cat. Aria said Fred had never been bothered by loud noises so he briefly considered taking her along for the picnic. But no, she looked extremely satisfied right where she was.

Flipping open the lid to the picnic basket, he surveyed the contents. Two bottles of wine. Four glasses. Hummus and pita. Four kinds of cheese. Two kinds of crackers. Grapes. Cranberries. Kalamata olives. Cucumber slices and little gherkins. And pickled carrots and onions. Yuck. He hated those things. He closed the basket, secured the lid, and checked his phone. Shouldn't Aria be set up by now?

He checked the time and pulled up his Callie & Sylvie text thread: *You hear from Aria yet?*

Callie & Sylvie: *We were just gonna ask you the same. BTW, what's the big surprise?*

Gabriel: *I don't know. Well, I think I know, but I'm not telling. Shouldn't we have heard from her?*

Callie & Sylvie: *Let's jump over to the other thread.*

Gabriel pulled up the *Coolest Family Ever* thread they'd all been using to text as a group. *Hey, Aria. You set up yet? I'm getting hungry.*

Sylvie: *You're always hungry, G.*

Callie: *A – you sure we can't bring anything? Even another blanket?*

Aria:

Gabriel: *Babe, text me where you are, and I'll come help set up. It's way past cocktail hour.*

Aria:

Gabriel: *Aria, please answer. I'm getting antsy.* What he was really getting was worried. It'd been almost forty-five minutes since she'd left the co-op. Where the hell was she?

A new text came in on the Callie & Sylvie thread. *Don't panic. She may have just lost her phone. It's getting dark.*

Gabriel: *She has a fucking flashlight and it's not full dark yet*

Callie: *Do you know around where we were supposed to meet?*

Gabriel: *Not 100% But I know where we sometimes go to stargaze. I'll head down there now and text you my location. You can meet me there. Give me 10-15 min.*

Callie & Sylvie:

Gabriel grabbed the picnic basket and the other flashlight, stepped over Fred, fumbled his keys as he locked the door, and practically ran down the hall to the elevator. A sick, crawly sensation was taking up residence in his gut and he realized his palms were slick with sweat. *And why was the fucking elevator taking so long?!*

As soon as the door opened, he stepped in and pressed his thumb into the Lobby button. Again and again. Like it'd make the thing move any faster. Once the doors finally opened on the lobby, he saw Manuel packing up for the evening.

"Hey, Gabriel. You heading out for your fireworks picnic?"

"Yeah. Did you see Aria leave?"

Manuel laughed. "Of course. I helped her with the surprise for your sister. Or rather for her partner."

Gabriel didn't want to think about the surprise just yet. "Did she say exactly where she was setting up?"

"Sure. I walked over with her." Manuel paused and studied Gabriel's face. "What's wrong?"

"She's not answering her texts and I haven't heard from her in over forty-five minutes."

"Come on," Manuel said, whipping off his doorman hat and coat and slapping a faded NY Yankees baseball cap on his bald head. "I'll show you."

Less than ten minutes later, they were standing over two blankets, one topped with a pile of cat paraphernalia including a litter box and box of litter, kitty toys, a snug little bed, and a box with a brand-new climbing tree waiting to be assembled. And a cat carrier backpack just like the one he'd tripped over that first night. Only bubble gum pink. With kitty decorations all over it.

Meeeoooow.

Manuel bent to peer into the backpack. "It's a kitten. From the same breeder Frederica came from. Aria got her as a thank you for Callie and Sylvie. For, you know, everything they've done to help you two. And since Sylvie's fallen head-over-heels in love with Fred and doesn't seem to be allergic to her. The breeder drove into the city and dropped the kitten off with me this afternoon."

Gabriel could barely hear Manuel. His head was full of dull throbbing buzzing whining noise like static and sirens and panicked screeching all at once. He pointed back toward the sidewalk path. To under a low row of bushes that you could only see from the blanket side of the path. "That's her flip flop."

"What?" Manuel jerked to his feet so fast he nearly lost his balance. He followed Gabriel's gaze and sucked in a breath. "Okay. Don't panic," he said even as he had his phone out and was dialing 911.

Gabriel went back toward the sidewalk to stand over the flip flop. Like a sentinel. He heard Manuel talking, giving his GPS coordinates to the police, and remembered he needed to text Callie and Sylvie. His hands were shaking as he pulled out his phone and snapped a pic of the solitary flip flop and hit send and followed it with a Google map of his position in the park.

Gabriel: *She's not here. Just this. Manuel's with me. Hurry.*
Callie & Sylvie: *JFC. We're on our way.*

He looked up and realized Manuel was beside him.

"I left everything where it was," Manuel said. "In case of fingerprints. Police'll be here soon."

"I swear to God," Gabriel growled out. "I'm gonna fucking rip them limb from limb."

"You think you know who did this?"

Gabriel turned away from the lonely flip flop and pinned Manuel with a dark look. "Yeah. Two of my erstwhile partners."

"The ones posting all the shit about you two?"

Gabriel laughed. "Yeah. Them. I don't think they're very happy with the press we've been getting, and I bet it's finally sunk in that their stupidity is gonna cost them some real money."

"You threatening to sue them?"

"We were hoping it wouldn't get to that point. Hoping to take the high road and counter everything with all these goddamned feel-good stories. Hoping they'd just decide to shut up and go away."

"Obviously, they've taken a different decision."

"That's an understatement." He ran both hands down his face. "We're selling the gaming company I founded. Their shitposts are probably gonna end up derailing the whole deal or costing them their share of the sale. I don't think they're happy about that."

Manuel swore under his breath. A florid and extravagant description of what he hoped would happen to Gabriel's partners, colorful words befitting a man who'd spent time in a boxing ring and betting on the horses. "We'll find her, Gabriel. This is rank stupidity, and they won't get away it."

As if conjured by the intense focus of Gabriel's thoughts, he turned toward the sound of hoofbeats in the distance.

"Mounted PEP. Parks Enforcement Patrol," Manuel said as two officers on horseback, both wearing dark masks, barreled toward them.

"Thank God," Gabriel said on a long exhale.

The first officer to dismount whipped out a business card with his contact information and held it out. "Which one of you is Manuel Espinosa?"

"That's me, sir, Manuel said. "I'm the one who called."

"I'm Officer Schweiger and that's Officer Mayfield," the man said, stepping forward to hand the card to Manuel, then stepping back, careful to keep a good six feet or so between them.

Manuel glanced at the card and handed it to Gabriel. "And this is Gabriel Landon. He was supposed to meet his fiancée here for a picnic. To watch the fireworks. I helped her carry her stuff over from our building," he glanced at his watch, "probably about an hour ago. And Gabriel found one of her flip flops here."

"When were you supposed to meet?" the officer glanced at the flip flop, looked up at Gabriel, and then down to where he was taking notes on an electronic tablet.

"Whenever she was done setting up," Gabriel said against a rising panic threatening his ability to breathe. "I figure twenty-thirty minutes ago. We were all supposed to meet after Aria texted us. My sister and her partner were coming too. But we never heard from her." He turned around and gestured back to the blanket. "I don't know if she brought her purse to the park, but she usually carries her phone on her. Stuck in a pocket or"—he patted his chest—"stuck in her bra. She hasn't messaged us, but maybe she still has it? Maybe she just couldn't text or didn't want to give away the fact she had her phone with her. Can you find her location?"

"Give me her cell number and full name. And do you know her cell phone carrier?" Schweiger asked as Mayfield dropped his reins and walked toward the blanket, studying the ground and taking photos as he went.

"I think it's AT&T." Gabriel recited her name and looked up her number as he shook his head in disgust at himself. "It's so pathetic. I don't have her number memorized since it's all programmed in my phone."

"Don't beat yourself up. Most of us are that way any-more," Schweiger said. "Now, do you have a photo?"

Gabriel pulled up a photo he'd taken last night. Aria curled on the couch with a book, a cat on her lap, a dog stretched out on her legs, and a cup of tea perched precari-ously on the edge of the coffee table. He held his phone out and the officer snapped a photo and sent it to his partner who nodded when it showed up on his phone.

"That photo along with her name and number is going out on NYPD's Domain Awareness System." Schweiger looked around the area. "If she's not in the park, we'll have people on the lookout for her across the city."

"Thank you," Gabriel managed to croak out even as he felt the sting of tears welling up.

"I'll need your number so we can reach you directly."

Gabriel told him the number and then cleared his throat. "I think I know who's behind this. Cameron Winters and Paul Lansdowne. I don't know if they're in the city, and I have no idea where they'd be staying, but I can find out. Hold on."

Gabriel bit his lip and dialed Brian. As he waited for him to pick up, he told the officers, "I'm calling Brian Johannsen. He's a partner at Diamondback Ventures, and they've got an office in Rockefeller Center. Cam and Paul both live in Phoenix, but they've been back and forth to New York recently. We're all business partners. But the partnership is…not a happy one."

"Is that Landsdowne with an e at the end?"

"Yeah."

Schweiger nodded, still taking notes on the tablet. "Why do you say the partnership is 'not a happy one.'"

"Our company's in the middle of buyout negotiations and the buyer isn't happy with Cam and Paul's behavior. I'm thinking they may be idiotic enough to believe they can use my fiancée's safety as a bribe to not get cut out of the deal—" He held up a finger and then spoke into his phone.

"Aria's missing." His voice caught on the words, and he closed his eyes and breathed through it. "I know. That's exactly what I'm afraid of. Hold on." He put the call on speaker and held up his phone. "I've got you on speaker. I'm in Morningside Park with two police officers. We were gonna have a picnic. Watch the fireworks. She was setting up, but she never texted me."

"I didn't even know they were back in the city," Brian said, "In the past, they've stayed at The Plaza. It's an easy walk down to Rockefeller Center and they're not very imaginative."

Officers Schwieger and Mayfield exchanged a glance. "The Plaza is closed because of the pandemic," Mayfield said.

"Then try—oh, wait!"

"What?"

"Remember when you first came out to look for a place to live? I rented that sweet apartment here in Murray Hill for you?"

"Yeah," Gabriel said, "you told me Cam and Paul wanted to stay in a place like that."

"I gave them the address. Swank doorman building. Eighty floors. Views of the Empire State Building. Just a couple of blocks from my place."

"Jesus," Gabriel groaned out. "With views of the fireworks tonight. I bet they think they'll be celebrating a big windfall."

Officer Schweiger broke in. "Can you send us the building address for the apartment rental?"

"Sure. Hold on. I've got it in my app." The group was silent a moment, waiting. "Okay. You should get it in a sec."

Gabriel's phone vibrated, and he held it out to the officers. Schwieger took it and forwarded the text to himself and Mayfield then handed the phone back. "I bet this is because of yesterday's call from Microsoft," Gabriel said. "Craig told me he'd called all the partners with the news."

"It's nothing we didn't expect," Brian replied.

"Can you elaborate?" Schweiger said.

"We're all partners in Seven Wonders Gaming and we're negotiating a buyout," Brian explained. "And the buyer's board is not happy. Their lead attorney called our attorney last night and told him that if the posts about Gabriel and Aria don't stop, the deal is off and even if they do stop, Cam and Paul may be cut out completely as a condition of the closing. There's a dark history here, but suffice it to say that Cam and Paul have been shitposting all over social media about Gabriel and Aria's personal relationship and the buyer's board doesn't like it."

Schweiger said, "So you think this is some desperate ploy to do…what?"

"To make sure they get their share. Cam and Paul likely panicked. The deal is worth millions, and I'm thinking they chartered a plane out of Phoenix this morning figuring NYPD will be busy with July Fourth, and that they'll fly out here and get away with—"

"Don't say it," Gabriel growled.

"That they'd be able to get away with a harebrained scheme to use Aria Turner's safety to blackmail us because they're afraid they're not going to get a dime out of the deal."

"Wait," Officer Mayfield said as he walked back from taking photos around the blanket. "Is this the Aria Turner who's got a book coming out about online harassment?"

"Yeah." Gabriel looked up. "You've heard of her?"

"I've got three teenage daughters, so I hear a lot of talk about online bullying. If I had my way, none of them would have social media accounts, but the women in my household don't listen to me. Anyway, one of them read a profile about the book in some online magazine, so my wife pre-ordered it for the girls. Your fiancée has become quite the hero at our house."

"Let's hope you find her fast and bring her home safe," Manuel said. "Then you'll be a hero too."

"We'll find her, Mr. Landon," Officer Mayfield said. "If it's a ransom, they're not going to hurt her. At least not right away."

"If they harm one hair on her head, they'll be sorry," Brian said, his voice hard even through the speaker phone.

"I'll make sure of it," Gabriel swore.

"Me too," Manuel echoed.

"Best keep those thoughts to yourselves, gentlemen. Now, it looks like you've got company coming." Mayfield nodded back to where the blankets were laid out and to the open field beyond where two figures were hurrying across the grass toward them.

"My sister and her partner. Aria had a surprise for them. A kitten. It's in that pet carrier on the blanket."

"Why don't you wait a moment over near the blanket. Fill your sister in and take care of that kitten while we look around here," Mayfield said, an arm sweeping the area around the flip flop.

"And we've already got officers headed toward that Airbnb location," Officer Schweiger said, still typing furiously on his phone.

"Let me know as soon as you know anything," Brian said. "And if you need me to do anything, just tell me. I could easily meet the officers at the building if it turns out that's where they are. It's only a few blocks from my place, and I know these bozos and could be a negotiator. Hopefully it won't get to that point, but these guys are desperate—and reckless. And they hate Gabriel and Aria, so…"

"Thank you," Schweiger said. "Give us your number and we'll be in touch."

Brian gave the officers his number and then Gabriel cut the call and hurried over to the blanket where Callie pulled him into a hug as Sylvie dropped to her knees to unzip the cat carrier and extract a very vocal big-eyed kitten with nearly translucent pink ears sticking up from a hairless head. Sylvie got to her feet and held the kitten against her chest. It was wearing a tiny NYU sweater.

FORTY-FOUR

ARIA COULD NOT BELIEVE this imbecilic scheme was so utterly, well, imbecilic. She guessed she should be scared, but these three idiots were so stupid she really wanted to laugh. They acted like they were cosplaying characters in one of the Seven Wonders video games—the game Gabriel had described as too violent and misogynistic and ridiculous to succeed and yet somehow, every new version sold like—what was the saying? Like hotcakes? Or something? In fact, her kidnappers were actually using character names from the game! One was calling himself Thor's Bane, one was Loki's Luck, and one was Ultra Man. Jesus. It was like *The Apple Dumpling Gang* meets *Dumb and Dumber*. She couldn't roll her eyes hard enough.

She'd never met Cam or Paul in person, so she couldn't be sure that none of these three jokers were them, but it was more likely they'd hired a few of their incel gamer guy fan boys to do the dirty work for them.

As far as the dirty work went, it all started when two of them, Thor's Bane and Loki's Luck, had walked straight off the park path and rushed at her. One had held her arms pinned, and the other had slapped a piece of duct tape over her mouth and then put a mask over her nose and mouth and pulled a baseball cap down on her head. Then they'd yanked her wrists together and fitted a zip tie around them. That all made sense, but they hadn't blindfolded her, so she knew exactly what was happening and where they were taking her. Then they'd just left the blankets and the cat right there in the park. She supposed that made sense too in that Gabriel would panic and upsetting him was probably part of the plan. But neither one had noticed when she slipped off a flip flop and left it in the grass, and although they'd groused later about her missing shoe, they hadn't gone back for it.

Ultra Man was waiting behind the wheel in a car idling at the park entrance, and the two men shoved her in the back seat and off they went. Once they'd reached the luxury high-rise in Murray Hill, Loki's Luck and Thor's Bane pulled her out of the car and walked her right past the doorman as if acting like she was drunk would make a difference to all the security cameras the lobby would likely have. Ultra Man, who apparently went to park the car, reappeared soon after they'd taken her up to the apartment. They didn't even think to hide the number on the door. Complete and total idiots.

Then, because she had on a dark blue sweater over her camisole so she wouldn't get chilled in the night air during the picnic, they didn't realize she still had her phone. She'd stuck it in her bra while straightening the blankets and they hadn't even noticed. Of course, she couldn't use it because of the zip tied hands, but she still had it. She was glad she always kept it on silent and that the screen was facing her skin so her boob wouldn't glow with each incoming call or text. And she hoped that as soon as Gabriel contacted the police, they'd be able to contact her carrier and triangulate her location. In the meantime, she just had to keep her wits about her and try to get a message to Gabriel that she was okay.

She cleared her throat. "Um…I have to go to the bathroom."

"You can wait," Ultra Man said.

"Wait for how long?"

"As long as it takes."

"Are you kidding me?" Aria shook her head in amazement. "You think Brian Johannsen and Gabriel Landon are just going to hand over a satchel full of millions of dollars before I have to pee? You do realize bodily functions don't operate on bank hours."

"Shut up," Thor's Bane groused at her. He turned to Ultra Man and nodded toward the man's phone. "Have you heard from them yet?"

Ultra Man nodded. "They sent the email as soon as I confirmed we'd arrived here with the package."

"I suppose the email is a ransom note and I'm the package," Aria said.

"And a pretty package at that." Ultra Man looked her up and down appreciatively. "Even prettier in person."

Okay, that was creepy. But Aria was *absolutely not* going to show these assholes that she was unnerved. She ignored the comment. "Even if you sent a ransom note tonight,

Gabriel won't be able to get a large sum of money together until tomorrow."

Loki's Luck snorted. "Your man has loads of money and Johannsen has even more. A goddamn VC? He probably keeps that much in a safe behind his Monet or something."

"I think you've watched too many heist movies," Aria retorted. "You have to know this is not going to end well. I hope Cam and Paul have already paid you because you'll probably need the money to restart your lives when you get released from prison. Of course with inflation, who knows what your money will be worth by that time."

They all three looked at each other and laughed. "Cam and Paul?" Loki's Luck said. "Never heard of 'em."

Aria huffed out a breath in disgust. "Whatever…"

"Here," Thor's Bane said, pulling back the curtains on the picture window with a flourish. "Enjoy your ringside seat for the fireworks while we wait. Just look at how pretty the Empire State Building is all lit up."

"It's lovely," Aria said, her voice dry as an old matchstick. "Meanwhile, I still have to pee."

"Alright already," Ultra Man said. "Go pee."

Aria glared at him. "Um…I can see the bathroom door from here and while I realize you three probably live in your mom's basements and aren't familiar with the way a woman's body works, I have to ask you to untie me. I need my hands to do my business."

"Okay, okay!" Ultra Man growled at her. "I'm gonna untie you, and then I'm gonna wait right outside the door. And you better be fast."

"I'll be as fast as biology allows." Aria stood and held out her hands as Ultra Man slid a wicked looking hunting knife out of a sheath on his belt and sliced through the plastic tie. Her throat went dry. She hadn't noticed that sheath before. All three were dressed in jeans and nondescript dark T-shirts. Ultra Man, however, also wore a light zippered jacket, presumably to hide his knife.

They'd all kept their masks on and their caps pulled down low over their faces, although she could tell that two of them, Loki's Luck and Thor's Bane, had dark hair—one long and a bit stringy—and that the other was a strawberry blond with hair that curled around the top of his collar. Ultra Man, the fair-haired one with the collar curls, looked like he spent most of his non-basement-dwelling free time in the gym ingesting steroids and drinking smoothies packed full of protein powder. He strutted around like he was quite fond of his physique, and she imagined he also spent his free time in front of his mirror taking dick pics to send to random women online.

Thor's Bane also appeared to be a bit of a gym rat, but he was neither as tall nor as muscular as Ultra Man. And his longish stringy hair was in dire need of a ponytail holder. Loki's Luck, on the other hand, looked like he'd need a god-sized helping of luck to get laid anytime soon. Even though he was the tallest of the three, he was slump-shouldered and thin, and his faded jeans were baggy around the butt as if he didn't have much of a derriere to fill them. For a moment, she pictured all three men lined up on a ratty basement couch with game controllers in their hands. None of them looked to be older than twenty-five or so. And although she couldn't see their faces, she'd probably be able to identify them in a lineup by their body shapes and their voices. She looked forward to it.

"God, you're annoying," Ultra Man said. "No wonder you and Gabriel Landon are a thing." He put his knife back in its sheath. "Go on." He followed her toward the bathroom. "I'm gonna stand right here and you're gonna keep the door open."

She stepped into the bathroom, closed the door, and swiftly turned the lock on the knob.

"Hey! Ultra Man yelled, banging a fist against the door "I told you to keep the door open!"

"I need my privacy," she shot back. "I'll be out in a minute." Then she turned the faucet on full blast and pulled out her phone, unlocked it, opened her messages app, and texted Gabriel. *Beeksom bldg apt 6004. Don't know street addy but I think its murray hill*

A moment later a response from Gabriel came back: *OMG you okay??? I forwarded the info to police. Is it Cam&Paul?*

Aria: *No. So far just 3 men using names from one of your SW game! And texting with someone else…prbly Cam & Paul nearby?*

Gabriel: *Are they armed? Have they hurt you?*

Gabriel: *Police on the way btw*

Aria: *I'm okay. I'm locked in the bathroom. Gotta b quick. One has a knife, but that's all I've seen.*

Gabriel: *Stay in bathroom! That building checks out. Same place I stayed when I came looking for apts. Brian gave Cam&Paul the Airbnb address. If they're not with you, they're probably in another apartment*

Aria: *Did you get a ransom msg?*

Gabriel: *Yes. Brian too. $10mil to split. 1mil In a fucking gym bag left in a Penn Station locker tomorrow noon, to prove our good faith, and the rest wired to some account…probably Panama or Cayman Islands or something*

Aria: *God, so dumb! Add wire fraud to kidnapping.*

Gabriel: *yeah...floored that Cam&Paul think they can get away with this shit. I'm on my way, btw*

Aria: *My guys seem young. Early 20s? Not the smartest knives in the drawer.*

Ultra Man banged on the door again. "What's taking so long in there? And why's it sound like the fucking shower's on?"

"I have a shy bladder!" Aria called out.

Loki's Luck must have joined Ultra Man at the door. "What the fuck's a shy bladder?"

Aria couldn't help rolling her eyes even though no one was in the room to see her. "Means I turned the faucet on because I can't pee around strangers."

"I've never heard such a stupid thing in my whole life," Loki's Luck said, disgust evident in his voice. "And I've got four sisters!"

"Hold on! I'm almost done." Aria called out and started typing on her phone again. Looking down at her hands, she realized they were shaking.

Aria: *They're banging on the door so gotta go*

Gabriel: *No!!! pls stay in there bc cops are at the bldg. They'll be on the way up soon*

Aria: *so fast?*

Gabriel: *Brian guessed they'd be at the place I stayed so cops were already on their way to check it out. Plus shared the ransom msg...turns out cops don't like kidnappers so stay low and out of the way*

Aria: *Got it...*

Gabriel: *Brian lives close and will beat me there so stick with him. Be there soon*

Aria: *What about the kitten?*

Gabriel: *jfc. She's fine. With C&S at our place. Waiting for word so just worry about Aria right now*

"If you don't come out right now," Ultra Man said, "we're gonna break the door down and come in."

"I heard you! Aria stuck her phone back in her bra, snug against her skin, and checked the buttons on her sweater. "Washing my hands now!" She ran her hands under the faucet, turned it off, dried them on a towel, and acted like she was futzing with the door knob. "Shit," she said loudly. "The lock is not cooperating. It's stuck."

"Fuck it," Aria heard Loki's Luck say. "Let her stay in there. Sleep in the goddamned bathtub as far as I care."

"I don't know. I feel like we should keep an eye on her." That was Thor's Bane. It sounded like all three men were standing right by the bathroom door now.

"Why does it matter?" Loki's Luck. "There aren't any windows. She can't go anywhere and there's another bathroom off the bedroom we can use."

"Fine." Ultra Man again. "Our *friends* wouldn't want us to trash the apartment anyway."

"Right. We're supposed to keep a low profile, not go around knocking doors down. So, let's just stay cool, enjoy the fireworks, and wait until we need to do something with her."

"I'll just wait in here then?" Aria said through the door.

"We should just leave her here after," Thor's Bane said on a laugh. "See how long it takes that pussywhipped Landon to find her."

They all laughed then, apparently finding that idea hilarious right up until the moment the front door to the apartment blew open and a swarm of cops swept in yelling instructions.

"Get down! Get down! Hands where we can see them. On the floor! *Now! NOW!*

Aria stood still, listening, her hands gripping the edge of the sink when she heard a voice on the other side of the door. "Ms. Turner? You in there?"

"Yes? Who is this?"

"NYPD. We've got the place secured. Can you open the door for me?"

"Is it safe for me to come out?" She hated that her voice all the sudden sounded all quavery. She hated that her nose was tingling and her eyes were...well, she hated that she was about to burst into tears.

"Your kidnappers in here are cuffed and are being read their rights. And we've got a team on the top floor taking the other two into custody. It's okay for you to come out. We need to make sure you're okay."

"Aria?" A familiar voice. "It's Brian Johannsen. Gabriel should be here soon. The police have everything under control."

She put her hand on the door. She was shaking all over now. "You found Cam & Paul? Are they behind this? Are they here? Have you seen them?"

"Yes, they're behind this comedy of errors. Like the officer said, they're already in custody. And no, I haven't seen them and, frankly, have no desire to set eyes on them again until we're all in a courtroom and they're on trial. For fuck's sake, the idiots rented the penthouse suite on their Seven Wonders business credit card, so it wasn't like it was hard to find them."

My god. How in the world could they be so stupid? Was it a result of desperation? Were they high? High *and* desperate *and* monumentally stupid? It didn't make any sense. What makes someone act so irrationally? As pissed as she was at the two men, she could only imagine how Gabriel felt. They had—at least at one time—been his friends. Or so he thought. At the very least, they had all been roommates.

She grabbed a tissue, wiped her nose, drew in a deep breath, and turned the little lock. Another breath and she opened the door.

"Jesus," Brian said, pulling her into his arms. "Gabriel'd tear this city apart if we couldn't find you. If you were hurt."

She held on to him, tears welling, nose stinging. "I'm sorry." She gulped back a sob. "I didn't realize how upset I was."

"God, don't apologize to me for being emotional. It's not like you weren't kidnapped at knife point and held for ransom or anything."

He smoothed a hand up and down her back until she pulled back and turned to look at her three kidnappers. She shouldn't feel sorry for them, but she did. Or almost did. What was wrong with people like them? She could understand Cam and Paul's desperation. At least it made some logical sense. But these three? Their lives were upended for what they seemed to consider nothing more than a lark. She shook her head and wondered what Loki's Luck's four sisters would say about his short-lived gig as a kidnapper. And she couldn't help but wonder if any of them had ever been harassed. Abused. Teased for being gamers or developing too late or too soon or having acne or stringy hair or whatever. And then she was suddenly filled with an incandescent rage.

She broke away from Brian, pushed past the cop who'd stood at the bathroom door, and marched over to where the three idiots were now sitting on the floor, handcuffed. She waved an arm over them and turned to the cops in the room.

"Officers," she said, "let me introduce these three fine fellows. First, we have the very menacing Thor's Bane. Next is the enigmatic Loki's Luck. And finally, this young man, the one who drove the car in which I was transported down here, is Ultra Man. I, for one, do not think they look a bit like gods or superheroes right now. Just misogynistic rubes who thought kidnapping for hire would be an exciting lark."

She turned back and stared down at the three young men. "Imagine how this is all going to play out. Cam and Paul and their juvenile social media posts just cost themselves a not-insignificant fortune and, I'm guessing, earned themselves a litany of felony charges. As their accomplices, I don't think you'll fare much better. Plus, I'm going to see if there's time before printing to add an extra chapter in my book just for you. You'll be famous! Famous for being ridiculous, ignorant assholes."

"ARIA!"

Gabriel's voice cut through the air. She twisted around and saw him in the doorway. And that's when the dam holding back her emotions crumbled to nothing. She flew toward him. He met her in the middle of the room, arms wrapping around her, pulling her off her feet and up hard against him. He pulled off the hat, tossed it aside, and pressed his face to her hair, a sob escaping as he whispered her name over and over again. She slid her arms around his back, held on tight, and murmured, "I'm okay. I'm okay. I promise. I'm okay."

Amidst the ringing in her ears, she heard Brian ask the officer in charge if she and Gabriel could go home.

"We'll need to take their statements," he said, "but that can wait. We'll get these guys taken care of and hold down the fort here until the detectives arrive. They can contact you all tomorrow to take your statements."

"Thank you," Brian said, and Aria felt him touch Gabriel on the arm. "I'm gonna walk home and get my car. Give me fifteen minutes and meet me out front. I'll drive you both home."

"Thanks, man," Gabriel managed. "For everything."

Keeping his arm around Aria's waist, he ushered her toward the hallway. "Callie and Sylvie are at our place. You want me to send them home?"

Aria shook her head. "No. I want to see them, be surrounded by family. And by Fred, and Lymond and our newest member of the family. Find out what they're going to name the little girl."

"They already named her."

Aria looked up at him. "Already? What's her name."

"They wanted to call her Aria, but I said that'd be too confusing. So they named her Zeni, short for Zenobia, Queen of Claremont Avenue. Named after the queen of Palmyra who was, I've been told, the only woman to defeat a Roman army."

"Oh, that's absolutely perfect," Aria said on a shaky laugh. "Now," she tried to hold back a sob, but failed. "Let's go home."

FORTY-FIVE

OCTOBER 10

TODAY WAS THE DAY. Over the past few months, Aria and Gabriel had worked and planned as the pandemic spiraled around them like a hurricane, sweeping up friends and acquaintances in its whirlwind of destruction. So far, no one in their four-person podluck had been sick. After the Cam exposure and the kidnapping, which they luckily escaped with no symptoms, there'd been an early summer scare when Sylvie's allergies got really bad and they were all afraid she'd caught the virus somehow. She isolated in her bedroom while Callie and Zeni worried and paced and paced and worried throughout the rest of their apartment. But after three days, the allergy medicine seemed to clear up all the symptoms and they figured she was in the clear. Still, they all knew it was only a matter of time.

Izzy, back in Albuquerque was the first of their friends to test positive. Suffering with a low-grade fever, fatigue, and a wracking cough, she quarantined for ten days in their guest bedroom as her husband tried to keep the kids occupied and away from her. And then she went right back to work because, as she told Aria, "It's what nurses do."

Miles's boyfriend in London, who suffered from asthma, ran a temp of almost 104 for four days, had trouble breathing, and was hospitalized for three weeks. He was hours away from needing a ventilator when his symptoms finally began to ease. He was at home, still recovering, and was "weak as a baby," Miles reported. There were a couple of positive tests among people helping in their ongoing Gabriel & Aria PR project too. And even if people weren't sick, the virus still affected everything—including memorial services like the one Aria and Gabriel and over three hundred of Professor Olivia Radcliffe's other friends, colleagues, and former students attended via Zoom.

Case numbers nationwide were up to 7.8 million and there'd been over 214,000 deaths. Globally, the reported cases were at a staggering 36 million and the death toll was estimated at three million. And no one knew how many others had been sick or had died that had never been tested. People were dying alone and afraid and others were recovering alone and lonely. The mood around the country was bad and getting worse as the split between those who believed in science and viruses and vaccines seemed to be pitted against those who, like Heather, were still claiming Covid-19 was no worse than the flu or who advocated treating infections by taking horse deworming medicine.

Gabriel and Aria were having their groceries delivered now, left downstairs for Manuel to load in his little wagon so they could go retrieve them and then return the wagon. They masked up to take Lymond and Fred, when she was in the mood, on walks, but other than their bi-monthly podlucks, they hadn't been in a closed space with other people without masking and social distancing since March. Including when Celia invited them down to pick up the books Liv had left for Gabriel—first edition copies of Dorothy Dunnett's *The Lymond Chronicles* and *The House of Niccolò*—and to see if there were any other volumes they'd like from Liv's collection.

And like billions of others around the world, they had not touched or hugged another human being outside their immediate household in months. At least they had each other.

The public relations "fuck around and find out" mission was ongoing, albeit at a less frenzied pace since news of Aria's kidnapping and Paul and Cam's arrest, but both Aria and Gabriel had done a dozen or more interviews. With Brian Johanssen's support, both Ethan and Noah put out personal statements on Twitter and Instagram in support of Gabriel and Aria, apologizing for their role in what happened three years earlier, and wishing them well. That was all well and good, even though Gabriel and Aria wished they'd had the testicular fortitude to say something publicly three years earlier.

Behind the scenes at Seven Wonders, things got interesting too. Negotiations had concluded and both the Seven Wonders and Microsoft boards approved the buyout at a share price that satisfied everyone. Everyone except Cam and Paul, that is. Because they were considered a flight risk and because kidnapping with a deadly weapon and bank fraud were serious business, bail had been set so high neither one could make it. They were both in Rikers awaiting trial.

And Microsoft had made it clear that neither Cam nor Paul would've had a place in the new venture anyway. The view was, essentially, that their years of locker room behavior had depressed Seven Wonders' potential rate of growth, limited the audience to men, and inhibited their ability to hire the best and the brightest employees because no woman would want to work at or buy products from a company run by men who treated women like shit.

Ultimately, Ethan and Noah left Seven Wonders too, instead spending much of their time working on Gabriel's app and helping Aria and Sylvie set up the Aria Turner Center for Social Media Accountability. The hope was that with the help of Liv's daughter and her contacts, a few of Aria's old professors, and a few friends of Sylvie's, they could convince Columbia's School of Journalism, Barnard, or NYU to house it as an affiliated center.

"It's going to be a place where journalists, sociologists, political scientists—and anyone else—can come together to try to understand how social media affects society and impacts its most vulnerable members," Aria explained to her father. "Of course, its underlying *raison d'être* is to be the call and help center for the app."

With a bark of laughter, Caldwell had called Gabriel a devious bastard, and declared that he couldn't wait to meet him in person.

One of the biggest challenges was coming up with just the right name for the app, and after hours of brainstorming and wrangling over dozens of ridiculous ideas, they still couldn't agree. And then, one evening as Aria was explaining the whole grand gesture idea to her mother over a Zoom call, Vi blurted out: *hat pin!*

"What?" Aria said, befuddled.

"You know me," Vi said, "I love historical fiction and stock—and sell—quite a bit of it. And I love stories set in the Victorian period. I can't remember the name of the book, but I remember there was a brouhaha around hat pins, those long pins women used to keep their fancy hats pinned in place—"

"Okay," Aria interrupted. "But what does that have to do with this app?"

"Wait, you didn't let me finish. Apparently, the 'Hat Pin Peril' of the early twentieth century reshaped gender politics because as more and more women were working outside the home and spending time alone in public spaces, more and more men took advantage of new opportunities to grope and assault them. Hat pins, which were around eight inches long, became the weapon of choice against predatory men. There was even a name for the predators, smashers or mashers, or something. And it got to the point where laws were passed regulating hat pin length and fines levied if a woman was found to have violated the law."

"Oh my god, Mom, that's perfect!" Aria was already Googling 'Hat Pin Peril' and sending texts with links to everyone involved in the project.

Ultimately, they named the app, *Hat Pin!* with the tagline: *Fashion, Beauty, and Homemaking Tips for Modern Women.* It was, hopefully, innocuous enough that an abusive or controlling man would not think twice about it. With the name in place and the coding and secure messaging service almost complete, Aria and Gabriel reached out to Liv's daughter, as Liv suggested in her last note.

Celia responded via email. "I read the *Smithsonian* magazine article you linked to and Oh My God, *Hat Pin?* I can assure you that as a historian, my mother would have adored that name. In fact, she had high hopes for a grand gesture, Gabriel, and set a bit of money aside to help—*if* you were able to pull it off."

Days later, they received a $50,000 gift in memory of Dr. Olivia Radcliffe as seed funding for the center. With similar gifts from Brian Johannsen, Ethan, Noah, and Gabriel—all flush from the Microsoft buyout—they were in good shape to launch and to hire a full-time director and a few student workers. All working remotely, of course.

And just this past Tuesday, *Piling On: How Online Bullying Can Wreck Careers, Destroy Relationships, and Ruin Lives* had hit the bookshelves to rave reviews. Aria and her publisher had just managed to add a final chapter on the kidnapping before the files went to the printer. And of course, Rashida and her crew, along with the media frenzy over the kidnapping, had primed the pump so that the book received maximum exposure. Aria and several of the more outspoken women featured in the book were busy speaking at remote events for bookstores, women's groups, and student groups all over the country.

A couple of times the groups even invited Gabriel to say a few words as he'd written a short but powerful *mea culpa* foreword that several book bloggers swore made them cry. It had made Gabriel cry when he wrote it too. And whenever he was asked to read it. Which, he suspected, was why he'd repeatedly been asked to read it. It's not often that men who'd been featured on the cover of *GQ* wept on a video call with hundreds of women watching.

He was crying now too. And wishing he could reach out and hug every single person who had joined them today in Morningside Park—including Manuel and his wife and Mrs. Feldstein from across the hall, but only after Gabriel had helped find her hearing aids for the millionth time.

Liv's daughter and her husband showed up. And Brian from Diamondback with his wife and Q.BC's growing group of employees, now numbering eleven— were all sitting in pod groups on blankets spread six feet apart and stocked with ice buckets filled with bottles of wine, sparkling water, Champagne and picnic baskets full of cheese, bread, fruit, little sandwiches made with fake meat, and an assortment of wedding cupcakes.

And Gabriel wished he could hug every single person watching via their live video feed as Aria walked toward him, her hair, longer now, pulled back with silver and pearl clips that glinted in the sunshine. In one hand, she held a small bouquet and in the other, she clutched the leashes of Lymond, Frederica, and a frolicking Zeni, all dressed in matching tuxedos and parading down the aisle side by side.

Aria wore an ankle-length, midnight blue velvet dress covered in netting set with tiny rhinestones that sparkled like stars, and Gabriel couldn't take his eyes off her. Her long sleeves kept her arms warm while her wide scooped neck revealed the delicate collarbone that he loved to trace with his tongue. On her feet were the satin slippers that had sat for days in a plastic tub in the guest bathroom shower while Aria tried to get the dye to match the dress. All in all, she was a gift from the night sky amidst the dappled sunshine and fall foliage of the park.

The sight took Gabriel's breath away even though he'd seen Aria in the dress before. Had even helped pin it together. Because Aria had made it herself. Designed it herself. She'd ordered a dress form, sewing machine, and yards of muslin and velvet online, sketched out a pattern, and then watched YouTube videos to re-learn how to sew, a hobby she'd shared with both Izzy and her mother up until she'd gone to college.

Turns out that quarantine and isolation were doing strange things to people—some took up old hobbies like sewing or picked up an instrument, others downloaded apps and studied new languages, still others baked bread, and millions upon millions binge watched streaming shows and played hours and hours of video games.

Aria had studied herself in the mirror before heading across the street to the park and knew that the beauty she saw reflected back at her all came from the inside. From accepting herself as is, from wanting to make herself a better person, for herself and for Gabriel. Because who wouldn't want to try to be the best version of themselves? And for knowing that the gorgeous and kind and honest and *trustworthy* man with tears in his eyes standing at the other end of their little white carpeted runway loved her exactly the way she was. And was willing to fight for her.

Gabriel choked back a sob as Aria approached and took a handkerchief from his pocket to dab at his eyes and nose. Everyone laughed. His tendency to get teary when the emotions got too overwhelming was well-known now and he just waved the hanky at them as if to say, *Oh, well, here I go again.* With every step Aria took toward him, he gave thanks for the gift of second chances, for the grace of forgiveness, and for, well, for the stunning and resilient woman he was about to be able to call his wife.

She would still be Aria Elizabeth Turner. And he wouldn't change that for the world. She didn't want to take his name? Fine by him. As long as she was *by* his side and *on* his side, he would be the happiest man alive. And he was ready to take on anyone who threatened her or their happiness. He would never let the Troy Jordans of the world hurt her again.

That morning, he'd put on the tux he'd had for years, straightened his tie, and studied his face. He'd had a bump on his forehead and the makings of a gruesome shiner when he'd first seen Aria on that March night six months ago. He'd been so stunned at the sight of her—and not a little woozy from the probable concussion—that it had taken a few days to realize exactly what sort of gift the universe had handed him. And then he'd sworn to himself that he wasn't going to fuck up again. He wasn't going to lose this woman a second time. And now, here they were.

She handed Lymond's leash to Callie and Fred and Zeni's leashes to Sylvie and took her place next to Gabriel and in front of Siobhán, that brilliant, sarcastic young woman who never missed an opportunity to voice her opinion and never let Gabriel get away with anything. It was no surprise to anyone that Siobhán, with her take charge and no prisoners attitude, was a registered officiant in New York City and had already performed several weddings for friends. Today she was wearing black, because it always seems official, like the robes of a preacher, she said. Or a judge. Or the devil himself. Black ankle boots, black leggings, a black leather, multi-zippered jacket, and her big brown eyes were covered in dark, nearly black, aviator shades. But that was Siobhán. And Gabriel and Aria were beyond thankful that she—and the rest of the PR crew—was in their lives.

And they were thankful that almost everyone from the PR project was in attendance. They gathered in familiar groups on separate blankets. Rashida was busy art directing while Adam snapped photos and one of his assistants videoed the wedding for the livestream Zoom attendees, including Caldwell and Heather in Vermont, Viola Turner and a few of her long-time employees in Sedona, Izzy and her firefighting husband in Albuquerque, Miles and his boyfriend in London, still recovering from his bout with Covid, and Ethan and Noah, in Phoenix, but working remotely to get *Hat Pin!* up and running and even consulting with Gabriel on Q.BC.

Now Siobhán cleared her throat and started the ceremony. They'd written their own vows and recited them tearfully to each other with someone in the gathering calling out, "Louder or no one in the Southeast blanket quadrant will be able to hear!" And again, everyone laughed. Because despite all the desolation and disease surrounding them, all the safety measures and restrictions preventing loved ones from traveling to be there with them or precluding them from hugging and kissing and dancing together, they'd decided to be fearless. To embrace love when they found it—or it found them. And to celebrate second chances with days like this, days full of joy and friends and family—even if they were gathered far away.

And when the ceremony was over and Gabriel and Aria raised their glasses in a toast, he looked down at his bride, bent to steal a quick kiss, and then declared, loud enough for the people on Zoom, in the Southeast blanket quadrant, and most people in the park to hear, "And now it is time to slake our thirst. Let the banquet begin!"

♥ THE END ♥

When I first came up with the idea for a romance based around consent, online bullying, #metoo vs. #notallmen and set against the backdrop of the pre-vaccine Covid-19 pandemic, several people told me it was a bad idea. And when I added sexual abuse, cancer, and suicide to the mix, the whole concept seemed like a serious downer. But I couldn't let the story go. Once they came to life in my head, I needed to give Aria and Gabriel their Happy Ever After. Lord knows, they deserved it.

Still, I'm well aware that these storylines are triggering. Almost every single woman I know—young and old—has experienced some form of sexual harassment or outright abuse. Whether in the home, at school, at work, online or just living in the world, women are at risk. As Aria says, her story is not unique. And in these fraught political times, America has gone backward when it comes to protecting women's rights as human beings with the right to privacy and bodily autonomy. In Liv's final note, she tells Aria that the world needs her voice. And we need the voices of other women standing up for women. So here's a special shout-out to the editors at *Teen Vogue* for doing journalism right over the past few years.

And the world needs men like Gabriel who take responsibility for their own bad behavior and then to stand up and do something to make a difference. Not everyone can make the kind of grand gesture Gabriel makes, but everyone should want to shape a better world, especially those who lack the agency, the platform, the finances, or wherewithal to stand up for change on their own.

In terms of the pandemic storyline, I contracted Covid-19 in November of 2020 after flying across country to visit my beloved sister who was in hospice dying of ovarian cancer that had taken up residence in her brain. There were tests for the virus, but no vaccines. It was a sad and scary time, but life is full of sad and scary times. Pandemics and brain tumors and growing old and losing control over your own life choices. And falling in love and risking your heart and allowing yourself to be vulnerable are scary things too. Maybe some of the scariest.

It was while visiting my sister in her final weeks that I returned to the romance genre. I hadn't read a straight-up romance in years, and I found it was all I could stomach. A big dose of romance, romantasy, romantic suspense, whatever...it didn't matter as long as it had a happy ever after. Romance helped me weather the sadness of losing a beloved sister after having recently said goodbye to my mother and having lost my father at a very young age. Romance got me through the pandemic. And it still provides comfort with every new story I discover.

THE TROUBLE WITH ROOMMATES is my gift to the universe, a little hug of happy inspired by the stories that sustained me. So, I'll leave you with this thought:

moments of joy, forgiveness,
and second chances exist even
in the darkest of times.

ACKNOWLEDGMENTS

First of all, thank you to Jason, my roommate and husband of 37+ years. It's not always been a bed of roses, but your hand in mine is still one of the finest things I've ever known. Plus, besides our girls, you are my favorite person in the whole wide world. I mean, how can you not love someone who makes you laugh every damn day—and who is also a writer and who reads and edits *multiple versions* of your stories?

Thanks also to Amira and Elena, our creative, fierce, brilliant daughters. You inspire me to be more, to do more, and to try make the world a better place.

Thank you also to my eldest sister Karen, one of the most avid readers on the planet, who always believes in me. And to my mother and sister, who shared our love of reading. I miss you every single day.

And thank you to those who've provided input and support during my ROOMMATES journey, especially to my editor Megan, my colleague Colleen who listens to me go on and on about my stories; my niece Jen and my nephew Nick, and to Eric, a long-lost distant cousin, who was the first non-Makansi to read the manuscript and offer feedback. I'll never forget the text message you sent: *On the plane waiting to disembark. Just finished TTWR. I loved it. For serious, friend. Well done.*

ABOUT THE AUTHOR

Marie K. Savage is Kristina Makansi's pen name. It's her middle name, first initial, and her paternal great-grandmother's maiden name. She grew up a Blank (her maiden name), but always wanted to be a Savage.

She is the author of ORACLES OF DELPHI, as well as a co-author—along with her daughters Amira and Elena—of THE SEEDS TRILOGY, including THE SOWING, THE REAPING, and THE HARVEST, all written under the K. Makansi name.

She is a long-time editor and book interior and cover designer who has worked on 160+ book projects, many of which garnered awards from the Independent Book Publishers Association and the Independent Publisher Book Awards, among others. She is co-founder of Blank Slate Press, now an imprint of Amphorae Publishing Group and has served as editor and designer since 2012.

Get a sneak peek at THE ALCHEMIST OF ALEPPO, due out in 2025, and check out other work from the Makansi Creatives:

www.kristinamakansi.com

 kbmakansi

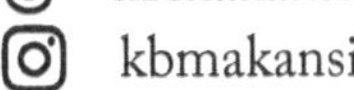 kbmakansi